I0675483

THE CREST OF

THE BEAST

BOOK I ~

THE OATH

C.A. CLARK

Author: C.A. Clark ©
Published in 2014
Copyright, All Rights Reserved

ISBN-13:
978-0692318010 (CA Clark)

ISBN-10:
0692318011

The Crest of The BEAST: Book I, The Oath

Table of Contents

DEDICATION

To my Lord and Savior, Jesus Christ

Thank You for loving me when I was unlovable, unfaithful, and wayward.
Thank You for giving me a Love-Story with You that was worth penning.
And most of all, thank You for giving your life for mine, so that I could spend Eternity With You, the greatest and Truest Lover of my Soul

To my Precious Daughter, Ennaya

And words cannot say enough how infinitely I love you.
You truly are the greatest Gift I have ever received.
…You'll always be my Princess

To my Loving Parents

My Father, a loving, and God-fearing Man of principle,
Who always prayed for, encouraged, and believed in me.
And to my Mother, whose great love of books, learning, and art profoundly impacted me,
Igniting my imagination with pictures and stories of other Times and Worlds.

…You both gave the best you had, now it's my turn to give you
mine
I love you both so very much.

To my adopted Gramma Evie

Whose unwavering belief in me brought greater comfort and
encouragement
Than words could express… You are infinitely valued.
Thank you for bringing so much blessing into my Life.
… I love you, Lady

ACKNOWLEDGEMENTS AND THANKS

Jerry and Betsy Clark—

Mom and Dad, thank you so much from the bottom of my heart for every way in which you both have contributed to my life, my walk with God, and my role as a Christian and a mother. You've provided me with both my roots and my wings… And in particular, my especial thanks to you, Mom, for co-editing this book. Without your help in curbing those run-away sentences, no one would ever have made it beyond the first page—your service has truly been invaluable to this project.

Charles Lloyd Clark—

Thank you for being an Uncle, a second father, mentor, counselor, prayer-warrior, and my very dear friend. The investment you have made in my life goes far beyond measure. Thank you for being such an incredible man of God, and for letting me see Christ through you.

Jane Nordness—

You have been such a special Auntie in my life over the years, always expressing interest in all of my own interests and pursuits. I cherish the countless letters I've collected from you over the years, the way that you share my love of writing and the English language, and all of the experience which your years have offered me. Thank you for investing in my life, and for sharing with me in so many chapters of my life, from childhood until present… You are dearly loved.

Alanna Clark—

Aunt Bebe, I cannot thank you enough for all the love and prayers you have showered on me over the years. Thank you for listening to me, hearing my heart, and always hoping and believing the best of me. Thank you for never giving up on me, and for helping me find my way out of night and back into the light. I love you so very much.

Rhawn Krogh—

You've been an "Uncle", a prayer-warrior, friend and confidante, and (most of all) a Buddy for Life! Thank you for being a stand-in "Dad" to my daughter during those frazzled moments of single parenthood, and for being a part of our family. Thank you for never giving up on me, for always believing the best (even when I could not have been more undeserving of it), and for being such an outstanding example of Christian faithfulness, child-like faith, and shining courage. I can truly say, I want to be more like you. Love ya, Buddy!

Lyna Ramsey—

My favorite Church Secretary! Woman, I love you! Thanks for showing me what practical Christianity looks like in the real world, and for helping give me the courage to be real and show the unvarnished truth. Love your humor and candor! Thanks for showing me that a Christian woman doesn't always have to be "crème brulee", and that sometimes what the world needs is more "raw-hide jerky". You rock!

Pastor Steve and Debbie Hopkins—

Thank you for not only being my spiritual leaders, but for showing heart-felt care and sincere interest in my personal life. Thank you for the invaluable help and support you have been, and for helping me find my footing again. And above all, thank you for faithfully following God's leading in your lives, paving the way for those others who follow after. The world has a great need for Christian leaders like yourselves, who know how to be tender without sugar-coating the truth. Love you both.

Molly Nelson—

Girl, I love you! We've been through the best of times, and the worst of times, together. Thank you for being a godly young woman and peer whom I deeply respect. Thank you for sharing in life with me, the laughter and the tears; for praying for me; for speaking the truth to me in love when I needed it (even when it hurt); and for spurring on me when life had me down, to get back in the saddle and ride again to reclaim my God-given purpose.

Rebecca Duce—

You have been such a precious friend over the years, and your prayers of faith and prophetic gift has encouraged and inspired me more than you will ever know. Thank you so much! I have been so honored and privileged to know you over the years, my beautiful Friend.

Karen Winter-Nein—

You took me and my daughter straight to your heart from the very beginning—what a precious gift your friendship has been! Thank you for being faithful in sharing your prophetic gifting—it has always hit dead-center, and encouraged me far beyond words! Thank you for being such a tremendous blessing in our lives. Love you, Lady!

Deborah Boulanger—

Thank you for making us a part of your family, and for all the good memories, including holidays spent together. Thank you for encouraging me so emphatically in this project, and for never wavering in belief that God would accomplish His purposes through it. I cannot say enough how much your firm faith and belief in me (or rather, God in me) has helped me stay focused and on target. Love you, Girlfriend!

Diane Laursen—

We've shared countless adventures together, laughed until we've choked, and it was your sense of humor that helped me discover mine. You were the first friend to read this book (while still in the rough draft stages), and without your avid enthusiasm and encouragement, I might not have gotten as far as I did. You seemed to love my characters and story as much as I did, and for me, that made all the difference and prompted me to keep on writing… Thank you, my Friend.

Dave and MariAnn Arney—

I so deeply appreciate you both as a Christian couple, not to mention, life-long friends of my family. Thank you both so very much for all of the prayers, encouragement, pep-talks, conversation, and good times. May you be abundantly blessed in Christ Jesus.

Denise Rist—

My precious Friend, thank you for sharing your experiences and your heart with me. You have been such an awe-inspiring example of faith and triumph over tragedy. Your strength has given me strength, and your faith has helped me to see with eyes of faith.

Sally Kelly—

Thank you for practically adopting me as a "daughter", and for loving me (through thick and thin), even in those times when I was unlovable. Thank you for seeing past all the immaturities I struggled with, all the poor choices I made, and for never closing the door. I have deeply cherished your friendship, wisdom, and prayers far more than could ever be expressed. Thank you for every way in which you have contributed to my life over the years; for being a Christian woman, wife and mother whom I could look up to; and for unabashedly sharing with me the stumblings of your youth, so that I could find courage. I love you so much, Sweet Friend.

Cheryl Lang—

Years ago you invested time into an awkward teenager, struggling to find her way through growing up and finding God's will for her life. Today, I would just like to say thank you for those hours you spent with me (away from your own children), and for discipling me. Your testimony and faith are incredible!

Sahar Mofidi—

Thank you for being practically the only friend I had during my time in Charleston, South Carolina, and for sharing in laughter and tears, dreams and heart-ache. I will never forget you, across the miles and years. May God guide you continually.

Rich Bruno—

Thank you for asking me that pivotal question seven years ago, when you said, "What are you doing with your life? You could be writing best sellers! Go write a book!" Thank you for being such a good friend and supporter, and for being my comic-relief—your sense of humor always had my sides splitting from laughter. We've each gone through dark, difficult times, and have come out to sunshine, blessings, and answered prayer on the other side. Thanks for everything. I love your whole family.

Cheryl Knapp—

Thank you for being one of very few friends that I had during my time in New York, and for being a woman, a wife, and a mom whom I could admire and look up to. And thank you also for your kind words regarding my writing capabilities—a little encouragement has the power to go far beyond what is seen on the surface.

Ariana Marie Tosado—

I so admire your pluck and determination (at so young an age!) to reach for the clouds in your goals, and let nothing hold you back! Your enthusiasm and fresh outlook on life has helped light a fire in me too, and for that, I am thankful. May the Lord richly bless you in all your endeavors, as you continue to seek His face.

Berta Phelps Robison—

Thank you so much for your time and interest in helping me through the publication process! Your experience saved me countless hours of research, and I am deeply grateful for that! The Lord richly bless you and yours.

Veronica Ingvaldsen—

I cannot say enough how much it meant to me that you, a busy home-schooling mother of four and a pastor's wife, would take the time to listen to and pray for me. I also cannot thank you enough for helping me finally make the right decision to put my and my daughter's safety first, and for helping us through that transition.

The Lord truly has been faithful. May He richly reward you and your family for helping the least of these.

To all of these, and many more besides, you have my very deep and heart-felt thanks.

Love to All,

"Charlie"

A MESSAGE FROM THE AUTHOR:

At Twenty-five I found myself alone in a New York hotel room, hiding from my baby's father... My life had fallen apart in pieces: I had no home, no family in that part of the country, and few acquaintances. I was trapped... and very, very alone. Fear of the Past haunted me, while personal insecurities and the unknowns of the Future terrified me... How could I ever rise again? **...For anyone who has ever known anguish, fear, regret, and the burdens of guilt and hatred, my prayer is that my books will inspire you with**

Courage and Hope.

...I had grown up with dreams of changing the World. Instead, here I was: lost, confused, and on the run. Deep down, I knew it was all my own fault. I had heedlessly refused to acknowledge the warning signs surrounding this seemingly loving, good-natured Egyptian man who had come into my life, and had plunged head-long into marriage and parenthood. But his laughter quickly turned to brooding shortly after my pregnancy began, as tender gestures disappeared in the face of abuse. Glowing smiles to everyone on the outside hid the fear mounting behind closed doors, as my husband burst into fits of rage and jealousy, threatening to commit acts of violence over perceived acts of insubmission. Shouts and swearing escalated to threats to maim, blind, and disfigure me— or even end my life. Then there was the back-track cover-up, as he would gently console me, chiding me for my foolishness in taking such threats seriously. "Everyone" knew he was a family man who put his wife and child first, and would never bring them to harm—I should stop letting my imagination run wild, because no one would ever believe me. I was simply "depressed and in need of clinical help", and he advised that I surrender myself to the care of a psychiatric facility for mental, psychological assistance. Inwardly, the emotional whip-lash, brain-washing, and warped, twisted mind-games were starting to make me feel as if I truly *was* going insane, descending like Alice down the black rabbit hole and into a frightening world where nothing was as it seemed. I was caught in an elaborate web of deception, so that sometimes I could no longer distinguish truth from lies, friends from enemies. Who could I trust? And however could I get myself—and (more importantly) my fifteen month old child—away to safety? … In dread I had watched the warning signs grow, until the day I knew I didn't dare risk waiting another moment. After my husband left for work, I immediately threw everything into suitcases and, with my toddler in my arms, walked out the door and into the great Unknown. Hours later, isolated and alone in that Long Island hotel room, I was on my knees—pleading for the Lord's strength and help to know what to do next. More than anything, I wanted two things: to know that, 1) despite everything else, a Sovereign God still had me in the center of His hand, and 2) that there was still a purpose and plan for my life… Today I know beyond a shadow of a doubt that He always did, and He always will: **"'For I know the plans I have for you,' declares the Lord, 'Plans to prosper and *not* to harm you: to give you a Future, and a Hope.'" —Jeremiah 29:1**

PREFACE

Many legends have been handed down from one generation to the next since the Dawn of Time, carefully preserved by the Faithful...Such stories passed on from these tales give tell concerning the very first origins of man, and of how the glory of his former immortality—along with Paradise—came to be lost.

This is one of those Legends...

CHAPTER 1—THE WITCH'S MARK

...In the Fourth Age of Man...

The dim light of day was all but hidden behind a tide of ominous, billowing clouds rolling in on blackened skies. Here and there in the distance the boom of thunder echoed against the hush, beginning its chant like the steady beat of a drum. Rain started to descend, pelting the somber high walls of a curtain palisade, behind which the stark spires of castle towers rose up cold and silent against the flinty outcrop of a darkened forest. Below, men-at-arms paced grimly along the stockade, every now and then casting glances up in the direction of the Tower, its edifice rising bleak and forbidding above all the rest.

All at once a fork of lightening zigzagged across the skies, lighting up a partially obscured portion inside the wall, which was overspread with thick vines and half hidden beneath the shadowy boughs of an oak tree. Through this tangle of vines a slight, hooded figure had been carefully climbing with cautious stealth, a satchel slung over one shoulder. Startled now by the crack of lightening overhead, the hooded figure whipped about in the direction of the soldiers on the parapet fortification, revealing the frightened young eyes of a female face, now peaked with fear.

"Over there!" A shout suddenly rang out.

For an instant she froze. But next moment an arrow whizzed through the air, striking the wall near her head as it stuck fast between the rocks. With a gasp the girl instantly fell to clambering over the wall with redoubled speed. Shouts could be heard everywhere, and the great bell was already tolling in alarm as guards could be seen running along the wall towards her. Another arrow whizzed past, grazing her cheek as it did. Panting, she grabbed hold of the sharp stakes mounted upon the wall, hoisting herself up as she hesitated precariously upon the top. It was a long way down to the ground—and there was only a narrow landing, falling away to a steep embankment… *Did she dare?*

A quick glance back at the guards pounding their way towards her indicated that it was now or never… One deep breath… *Jump.* One of the jagged spikes cut her leg as she leapt from wall—and then she was hurtling through the air, arms and legs flailing. She hit the ground faster than she had time to think, and then in the next second was tumbling head over heels down the wooded ravine. The darkened shapes of the forest rushed past she careened down the hill, at last slowing to stop some two hundred feet down. With a gasp she managed to pull herself to her feet, snatched up the fallen satchel, and hurried on with a staggered limp.

Tearing off her right glove, she stared down in desperate fear: the branded outline of a circled tree was seared into her palm, surrounded all around by runes and strange symbols. All at once it lit up, blazing like a fiery torch. The girl let out an excruciated scream, stumbling to her knees as heat like molten metal scorched through the center of her hand. She could hear voices all around her, whispering words she could not understand. All about the forest seemed suddenly to be a frenzy of wild animal noises— calls, shrieks, roars, growls…In terror she spun about blindly in all directions.

"What have you done?" She whimpered aloud.

The voices were growing louder, culminating in threatening hisses.

"*What have you done to me?!*" She shrieked.

Flashes of sporadic images were igniting her mind like wild sparks… She was tugging against chains binding on either side, her wrists slippery with blood as she strained against iron fetters… All about her was a wall of fire… and the chant of incantations was growing louder in her ears… There was the shriek of an eagle, and the flash of a fiery serpent… All at once the image of a black dagger, carved with runes emblazoned over the hilt and blade, blazed in her mind's eyes— simultaneously, the branded mark on her hand again lit up with rekindled fury… Her screams were still echoing in her ears as everything went white. In a daze she slumped to the ground. Everything was reeling as her head collapsed onto the earth, and everywhere the deafening roar of beastly sounds and hissing voices were screaming in her ears.

"I'm not a Witch," she murmured as she slipped into unconsciousness. "I'm not a Witch…"

Everything went dark...

CHAPTER 2—CREATURES OF THE NIGHT

Nearly half a year earlier…

...The rickety creaking of wagon wheels sloshing through icy puddles echoed through the frosty bite of night air clinging to the stilly silence. Ahead, a narrow muddied road wound along through thicketed forests before a lone farm cart and horse. A squalid driver sat hunched in his seat, his chin tucked low as he tightly wound his russet cloak about his paunch; a round gorget collar flopped in the wind about his shoulders, as he tightly drew its coarse brown hood more closely about his jowls. The thinning fibers of his garments were a weak barrier to the biting cold. The wind was to his back from where he sat perched at the front of his jolting load. A gunnysack canvas was thrown over the open top of the wagon to protect the contents from the outer elements. The sky above was barely visible through the thick foray of trees stretching out closely along either side of the twisting road; gnarled branches swept roughly against the blanket of low-lying clouds concealing the heavenly bodies above. The heavy-set driver heaved out a wet, blubbery-sounding cough while he hacked into his fist, choking and sputtering. It was a bad night to be out, that much was sure, and he was eagerly looking forward to warming his hands by the fire of his cottage hearth, his plump wife ready to greet him with a cup of hot tea and supper waiting after his long, wearisome journey away. Sniffling, he wiped his face with the edge of one sleeve as he rubbed his thick hands together, and delivered an impatient slap of the reins to his big grey. Obediently, the Shire horse quickened the stride of his gait and they hurried on.

All at once the cart gave a great lurch forward. The driver's hood was flung back from his head, and he himself nearly thrown from his seat as the vehicle abruptly came to an uncertain halt. The weight of its load swung from one side to another as it rocked dangerously back and forth. Regaining his precarious seating, the driver reached for his whip and cracked it over the back of the animal. The horse strained while the wheels groaned loudly as they ground against the churning mud, yet the weighty cart held fast and refused to stir. Muttering in agitation to himself, the driver stiffly heaved up his girth and hoisted himself over the side of the wheel and alighting with difficulty to the miry clay. Grasping a felled branch lying nearby in the slough, he placed the broad end of it at the wheel's base, and braced himself solidly behind it, urging his horse forward. The sound of their travails echoed through the surrounding wood, horse and master straining together to pry their load from the place where it had firmly lodged. At last the driver reluctantly halted, tossing a helpless glance about him as he wearily scratched his head.

All at once something moved out of the corner of his eye. The driver's blood quickened and he turned about with a start—nothing more stirred from the place, however; the surrounding forest was just as still as it had been a moment before. The man swallowed hard; his pulse quickened and he kept his gaze fixed warily upon the opposite side of the wood, scanning the length of tall pines. Cautiously he moved closer to his horse and his hand crept to the sheathed knife stuck in his belt. Nimbly reaching for the reins, he quickly began to untie its tethers, when a slight rustling in the brush caught his ear. His eye instantly darted in the direction of the sound: yes, there was no mistaking it this time—he was *sure* that he had glimpsed something!

The cart-driver swallowed hard, beads of cold sweat forming on his forehead; with shaking hands he hurried to finish untying his horse. The big grey was already skittishly stamping and pawing the ground in nervous agitation, ears flat and head bobbing. In vain his master fought to calm him, tugging at bit and bridle as he struggled to keep a tight grasp on the halter with sweating fists.

Then of a sudden there it was again, almost undetectable as it glided silently through the trees: a tall, black form sliding noiselessly among the darkened shapes of the forest, and now only a few bounds away. Sweat began dripping into the man's eyes and trickled down through his beard. For a few seconds he fumbled feverishly with trembling fingers, at last managing to slide the harness from the horse's neck; shakily he grasped a thick tuft of mane and stumbled closer to mount. In the blink of an eye a blurred streak of dark shadow flashed past them. With a terrified whinny the big grey reared up on hind hooves, his forelegs pounding the air before him as he broke loose from his master's grip. In an instant the driver was thrown to his backside in the mud, heavy hooves plunging near his head. The next moment the horse had bolted—tail streaming away behind him as he disappeared into the trees, the thud of hoof beats fading away to stark silence in the distance. Gasping and covered in mud, the man hurriedly pulled himself up. Panting and whimpering to himself, he breathlessly looked this way and that, searching for any sign of the phantom devil within the concealing darkness of the wood.

...All was still and silent once again...Then slowly, like an evaporating mist, the fleeting shadows began to melt away to grey...A single black mark began to grow apart from the rest, forming gradually into a shadow of great magnitude as it emerged from the forest depths and loomed upright in the paling gloom. The victim stared open-mouthed, unable to tear his eyes away... Slowly, a pair of bright eyes appeared out of obscurity, flickering for a brief moment as they glinted down upon the harrowed face of the breathless spectator...A low, rumbling growl emanated forth. In a state of terror, the man realized that his dagger was no longer in hand—it had been knocked clean away in his tumble. Desperately he glanced all about him, looking this way and that, his fingers searching franticly in the mud for the fallen knife. The tips of his fingers had only just lit upon the hilt as the rumbling grew louder, culminating ominously into a deep, hissing roar. Feverishly grasping the handle, the man scrambled to his feet and brandished his blade aloft. In the blink of an eye the great shadow bounded away from its place and vanished in a rapid blur. Trembling violently, the driver continued to hold the dagger at arm's length, shakily backing away from the sunken cart as he waved it about threateningly in the air; his eyes were wild with fear as he swung about in blind confusion.

All at once a great gust of wind tore past, and razor-sharp knives sliced through him. The man let out a confounded shriek, staring down in stupefied horror: the knife—and half of his arm—were gone. Stunned, he slowly keeled and fell to his knees, collapsing in the mud as he writhed and screamed in pain: the blood-soaked, shredded end of his sleeve was flapping about a raw, bloodied stump.

Suddenly something wet dripped down across his forehead. He froze: before him was an enormous pair of wolfish paws, hind legs bristling, and claws like iron talons raking the mud only inches from his head. Slowly, his eyes travelled upwards in speechless horror: the shadow was stretching wide in all directions as it loomed high above him, like a massive brass tower against the black sky. For just a moment his eyes widened in wild terror… Then a squealing scream shot through his vocal cords…In an instant ruthless fangs were tearing through his gullet. With a vicious growl the Phantom fell ferociously upon him…All went silent.

CHAPTER 3—A FOOLISH GAMBLE

…The trickle of a water brook could be heard amidst the sound of a light breeze stirring through autumn leaves. A shallow rivulet was streaming its way along a tranquil, narrow bank half hidden in the late afternoon shadows. The black rocks of its stony bed were a deep contrast to the gaiety of vibrant colors calmly waving overhead from outstretched boughs. Far below, a serene pool lay in the cool shadow of a steep embankment stretching high above it, its slated rock arched in a crusted overhang. It was over this precipice and into the pool that the stream overhead now emptied, its thin veins running down over moss-covered rocks into the silver basin at the bottom.

Nearby, a tall, stately black horse waited patiently, the spattered embroidery of his harness dangling along the ground, and his glossy sleek legs besmirched with mud. His head drooped wearily down to munch at a few tufts of wild grass growing in the sandy earth along the water's edge. After a while he slowly raised his regal head, and, still chewing lazily upon the leafy stalks, cast his eye towards the water. For a moment, nothing seemed to stir from the shadowy depths, but then, slowly, a pale white shape began to emerge, growing larger and larger until at last a feminine form became indistinctly visible. A spray of water showered through the air, as a crown of reddish brown hair broke through the surface, enveloping the wet skin of a young girlish face. Blinking, she rubbed the water away from her streaming eyes, and cast a glance back towards the horse waiting patiently upon the bank. She had a simple, yet uncommon prettiness about her, with a frank-looking brow, round nose and ruddy cheeks, and full lips encasing a wide row of white teeth that flashed mischievously when she smiled. Her blue-green eyes seemed to spark as much of impudence as of spirit. Silver ripples spanned in widening arcs around her, as silently she stroked her way back to the shallow end of the lagoon. Stretching out a freckled arm, she deftly snatched a loose white tunic from an over-hanging branch, (which was rather dirtied and wrinkled in spots, particularly a good measure around the bottom edge). Hastily she pulled it over her head, cautiously concealing her body as she emerged from the pool. She was neither very thin, nor overly plump, and of rather medium height. Quickly she tugged on a pair of muddied leather riding boots that had been tossed along the shore. Cinching up the front laces of her kirtle, she reached for an embroidered, pleated gown of blue-green silk.

A twig snapped beneath the cracking of a dry leaf from somewhere high up on the overhead ridge. The horse immediately raised his head, ears at attention…There was a soft rustling…and then silence. The girl glanced quickly at her mount, yet uttered not a sound nor made any sudden movement indicative that she had even heard a noise. Nevertheless, her eyes darted quickly to the reflections dancing on the water's surface. In silence she swiftly pulled the long surcoat over her smock, and slowly straightened. Picking up the reins undisturbedly, she discreetly glanced once more upon the water's reflective face…There was… nothing. …Nothing at all that could be seen or heard…*Wait*…There was the stealthy sound of leaves being pawed lightly underfoot, then the sound of something—an animal—sniffing at the air…*There it was!*...In the water she could now clearly make out the appearance of something with dark brown fur peering down upon her from the top of the rocky overhang…Instantly her gaze jerked upwards: a great hound dog was standing on the ledge high overhead, eyes fixed on her ,with black lips curling against sharp teeth as he bared his chest. Slowly, her hand crept towards the saddle-horn, as cautiously she raised a foot to the stirrup. The great hound made no move, but slowly a low rumble emanated from his chest, followed by a deep bark that echoed harshly through the creviced rocks. For just a moment their eyes locked—and then in a twinkling the girl swung up into the saddle and grabbed hold of the reins.

"H'yah!"

She shouted, digging a hard heel deep into her horse's side. In a flash she took off, streaking through the woods as she pressed hard forward in the saddle. Her hair whipped across her face as she tossed a glance back over her shoulder: the hound was bounding away across the top of the ridge, down the brow of the hill and over the slope, kicking up leaves in his wake and howling after her in pursuit. Just behind him, a figure on horseback could now be seen speeding through the winding shadows of the trees. The girl jerked her focus back, a look of grim determination flooding her countenance. With a cry she gave another strong kick of her heel into the horse's flanks. Together they dove from the thicket and charged out upon an open moor, kicking up mud and sod as they flew away to the west in the direction of the setting sun. Once more she cast an eye back for another glimpse of her pursuer. The horseman and his hound were in full view now and quickly gaining on her. A broad grin broke out across her face, a mischievous look of devilish delight sparking for just a moment in her eye, as she pressed in harder against her horse's neck. Together they flew out across the heather.

The sun was just starting to dip in its descent towards the west. Falling shadows transformed lush hills and forests into deeper shades of amber purple, and the autumn colors of nearby mountains were turned a fierce crimson and gold. Before her, a wide strip of open meadow stretched all the way to the hills and forests on either side, the tall grasses tossed by a lusty wind that whipped about her head. Gradually she slowed her mount to a trot, then wheeled about to face the man pursuing her.

"I believe your tracking skills are somewhat improved, Willan—though it took you near half a day!" She called back to him.

A look of impish merriment showed tellingly in her smile, the color of her eyes shining brighter against the exhilarated flush of excitement in her cheek.

"You ride your horse too hard, girl!" Rejoined the rider who came after, his frame jolting atop his horse. Easing himself gingerly in his saddle, he loosened the cords of the cloak tied at his throat, slinging it away from one shoulder. Leaning forward he patted the neck of his weary horse, its chestnut coat glistening with sweat. He was a young man, not more than four and twenty years, with clear blue eyes, a light-hearted smile, well pleasing face, and golden brown hair that curled down around his ears and over the nape of his neck. He gave a glance down at the hound dog that was now panting with drooping tail, as it quietly padded in behind them.

"Or perhaps I ought to be giving Gharm all the credit for your find?" The girl taunted in a playful, mocking tone. "I should've known you'd never find me without *him*!"

"Aaahh," Willan groaned, as if not hearing her; he lifted a dusty embroidered sleeve to mop the sweat beads gathering on his brow. "It's taken me near three hours to find you!" He exclaimed as he slumped in his seat, running a hand through the tousled hair falling loosely into his eyes.

He squinted back at her with a grin, amused curiosity on his face as he eyed the good measure of soiled shift peeking out from under her wet, disheveled garments hiked up over her knees. The flanks and under-belly of her mount were likewise coated with mud. With a snort the horse wearily lowered his head to the ground, steam evaporating from his muzzle.

"Honestly, Adelheide, you really ought to give the greater care to your horse."

Willan's tone was slightly disapproving (if not reproachful), despite the light-hearted smile he still wore.

"The day may come when your horse will be *all* that stands between you and danger. A wise master therefore gives his horse *just* as great a care as he gives his own bodily self."

He paused to lovingly stroke the chestnut mane of his horse, as he cooed softly to her under his breath.

"There, Flame; you've run hard this day," he spoke in soft tones; "I'll see to it that you get an extra bucket of oats and corn tonight, along with a good rub down when we return."

He finished by giving Flame an affectionate pat on the neck, and Flame responded with an excited little whinny, as if she knew well her master's meaning.

"The way to win your horse's loyalty," he continued on to the girl, "Is by *truly* knowing and understanding him, and giving him every deference possible—not working him to death the way *you* do!" He let out a laugh. "Let us hope *you* shall never truly be in any need of his loyalty—because if *I* were your horse, I know I wouldn't trouble myself to save you, even if your life *did* depend on it!"

The girl rolled her eyes in response to his teasing laughter and gave a proud little toss of her head.

"I think you've heard too many boring lectures from your tutors, Lord Willan; it's beginning to rub off on you!" She retorted with a saucy air. "And besides: I am not *so* convinced that 'twas truly *my* horse you are so concerned with,—or your own self! You could hardly keep up!" The girl laughed aloud. "I do believe I have bested you yet again, Lord Willan!"

A coy smile teased flirtatiously in the corner of her mouth, her eye filled with a look of sporting defiance.

"No, truly, Adlai—" he started in surprised protest: "Look—your mount is practically *drowned* in his own sweat! Have some heart, girl; it would do you good to remember that the horse is the most noble of either creature or beast."

He stroked the mane of his mount a moment longer, before turning to squint back once more in the direction of the sun's descent.

"And besides," he continued with a heavy sigh, "I have ridden near half a day now; and though *you* may care little for the health of your own horse, yet mine is wearied and in need of rest—not to mention that I now ache and am utterly sore in every place imaginable! So I think it best that we turn round now and make back to the Manor."

"Well now, perhaps I've done you some good after all—you're looking more robust already! Honestly, Lord Willan, however do you intend to make a good rider—or even a warrior—if you stay forever cooped up in your study the way you do?...If disappearing—only so that you shall be forced to come and find me—is the *only* way I can lure you out, then I shall make it a daily practice!"

"Adlai," there was again the slight sound of reproof in his tone. "We're not children anymore—and you know very well that I can't...So please: no more fool's errands, alright?"

The girl said nothing, but the impudent smile had vanished from her face and she turned away, a sunken look of disappointment forming into an expression of marked sullenness. She turned to cast her gaze once more across the inviting expanse of moorland before them.

"Hey—" he put a hand gently on her shoulder. "I promise that I will come out with you again as soon as I can—but you really must try to understand: things are different now."

"So you've said before," Adlai answered as she pulled away. "And I'm beginning to believe it always will be that way."

Willan blinked, an awkward, uncertain smile on his face. "What does that mean?"

Adlai slowly shook her head with a small, sarcastic laugh. "Forget it—what does it matter now, anyway?"

She turned back with a forced smile, though she kept her eyes to ground—banishing away the few tears that threatened to reveal themselves, and taking care not look him directly in the face...It wouldn't do to let him see into her heart...especially not the lonely emptiness that seemed to be growing deeper inside her all the time, every moment that she was made to realize that he was growing farther and farther away.

"There's a stream yonder," she said distantly, pointing to a small sliver of silver barely visible over the rippling grass licking at the wind. "We can get water for the horses there."

Without waiting for his reply, she clicked at once to her horse as she gave a prodding tug on the rein, and led the way. Willan slowly fell in behind her, and together both riders and horses, the worn hound lagging at the rear, began to wend their way at a plodding pace across the meadow. Within a short while they reached the shallow river's edge. Adlai slid from her saddle and pulled the reins down over her mount's head, giving him an affectionate pat on his charcoal-grey muzzle.

"Off you go, Storm!" She said, giving him a light slap on the hind quarters as she turned him loose.

Casting an eye back over her shoulder, she caught sight of Willan as he leapt down from the saddle. Stripping off his white tunic and throwing it onto a nearby bank, he uttered a loud cry and charged towards the water's edge. With a sudden leap he dove head-long and disappeared with a great splash beneath the waves. Flame and Gharm followed suit as they plunged in behind their master. Willan at last emerged, laughing and whooping amidst shouts and yells, as he playfully tossed water at his dog, and both lunged and splashed about loudly together.

Adlai glanced back for an instant at this raucous merry frolicking between horse, dog, and master, a distant look showing wistfully in her eye. Right now he seemed so much like the boy she used to know—there was no trace of a stately lord here.

Indeed, at present he appeared utterly oblivious to the ridiculous absurdity of his appearance. Willan carried on in an absent-minded and care-free manner, his broad-shouldered form glistening in the sunlight as he finally waded back towards the bank.

A sudden blush flew over her face, and for an instant she turned away almost in shyness.... He was handsome…in an easy, effortless way that at times seemed almost boyishly innocent, as if he were consciously unaware of his own effect. There was a regal look in his broad brow, as well as in the narrow, stately shaping of his nose and high cheek-bones…Anyone could tell just by looking at him that he had noble blood flowing in his veins…He was completely *perfect*.

A look of longing stole across her face. For a mere moment a telling expression of admiration betrayed itself in the tender warmth of her eyes, while a wistful sigh rose from her breast…Did he—would he—ever see her in the same way?…Hadn't he yet noticed that she wasn't just a young girl anymore, but that she was blossoming into womanhood?…The glimmer in her eye swiftly vanished away, however; all that lingered in its place was again a small, lonely look of sadness. But with another sigh her face suddenly cleared, as she quickly shook her thoughts away. It did no good to dwell on these things now. All she knew was that for now—for now they were both here, together—and that was all she cared about…It did no good to think about the future…especially since her own was so… *dependent*…upon other things. And why spoil a good day with thoughts of things that were not? Right now he seemed utterly carefree and unabsorbed, the way he often used to. With a carefree air he swept up a stalk of grass, clenching it in his teeth with a broad grin as he wandered back towards her. Adlai rolled her eyes, yet couldn't suppress the amused smile spreading across her own face. There was a certain youthful boyishness about him every time he smiled, and that smile had been absent for quite a while… She had missed seeing it.

Turning softly away, with sober steps she returned to where Storm was feeding close beside the river bank, and in silence remounted.

"Ready to head back?" Willan asked, his soaked breeches still dripping water as he began to tug on his riding boots.

Adlai remained silent and answered not a word as he continued to redress. Willan didn't seem to notice as he tugged his tunic over his head. After a moment he paused from dabbing at his face and looked up at her with a questioning smile.

"Adlai?"

Adlai did not even bother looking back. The same coy, mischievous smile was playing on her lips once more, a look of sly intent in her eye. Willan's smile quickly disappeared.

"Adlai—no—" He started quickly, raising his hand as he shook his head in protest; "It's much too late for—"

He did not get to finish. Adlai's face had broken into a sudden grin. With a loud cry she dug her heels into Storm's sides and plunged with a splash into the stream. For a mere moment Willan was left gaping after, as horse and girl forged their way swiftly through the water, then leapt up upon the opposite side. Quick as she might, with another slap of the reins she shot off like an arrow over the moor. Willan was cursing loudly behind her, as he leapt into the stirrup and threw his cloak over the saddle horn.

"*Yah!*" He shouted, as he dug his heels deep into Flame's flanks and took off in hot pursuit after her, Gharm barking loudly as he chased at their heels.

Onwards and towards the edge of the meadow they sped one after the other, then plunged into the surrounding thicket. On through trees and brush both parties charged recklessly at break-neck speed, deftly dodging low over-hanging branches, and startling birds and forest creatures in their wake. Adlai lay low against Storm's body. Throwing an arm up, she shielded her eyes from sharp twigs and branches that reached out like claws and scratched at her face and arms. Something caught suddenly upon her arm; with a loud rip the entire sleeve tore away, and her arm was laid bare. Adlai barely glanced at it though; somehow the excited recklessness of it thrilled her, and instead of slowing the pace she pushed Storm to race even harder than before.

At last they came abruptly to a ravine, where both horse and rider suddenly toppled downwards amidst screams, yells, and startled whinnies. Storm's hooves slid and skidded over loose gravel as they plunged to the gorge's floor. For an instant she caught sight of Willan and Flame hurtling through flying dirt, Gharm tumbling after. Adlai barely missed having her leg crushed between her horse's flanks and the rocky side of the ravine. Storm was visibly trembling; with a frightened whinny he shakily leapt up to his feet amidst clouds of dust.

Adlai gave him little heed— injury had been avoided, which was all that mattered, and once again that same rogue, rascal spirit rose up inside her. Back at the Manor she felt chained and stifled, doomed to a joyless, hapless existence behind its stone walls. But out here—here she could be as undaunted and free as a bird, with no one to stop her!—and she hadn't gone so far in the chase just to give up over a single tumble! No, something, something was calling to her, urging her now: perhaps it was the rare, wild feeling of defying all consequences for a single moment of total, undeprived freedom; perhaps it was nothing more than her own willful, mischievous temperament...Or perhaps it was a secret, curious desire to know how long and hard Willan might push in his efforts to catch and bring her back...And maybe this was the only way to make him aware of the fact that he felt more for her than he was willing to admit...They were never alone back at the Manor House; and whatever his feelings towards her were, he seemed always conscientiously guarded in expressing them. She had been pining for years now, waiting, yearning for him to say or do something—anything—that might tell her what his thoughts and feelings for her truly were. If she let this moment slip by now, it might be forever before another opportunity came again...No, today, she just *had* to push on—she just couldn't return back with him, until she knew *something* about how he felt...This was her day, her moment, and she had to seize what was left of it for all it was worth.

Willan, sputtering, was shakily rising from a pile of dirt and stony rubble, and seemed to be just collecting his wits. Gharm hobbled up with trembling tail behind him, and Flame leapt back up on shaky legs…*Good, he's ready now*, Adlai thought to herself.

"Yah!" She cried, quickly giving a sharp kick to Storm's side. With a harsh slap of the reins he took off again, as she drove him on up the opposite side of the stony gorge. The horse struggled up the embankment, a foamy lather forming at the corners of his mouth where bit and bridle kept him mercilessly bound. His giant black eyes were wide with alarm as he strained to reach the brink.

At last they reached even ground at the ravine's top—then onwards they raced without hesitation through the thinning forest trees. On and on they shoved through ever-widening shadows, till at last the trees completely cleared, and they charged out upon an open grassy hillside. Storm's gallop eased to a cantering trot as they reached the summit of a large hill. Reaching the peak, horse and rider halted breathlessly as they stood upon the edge of an overhanging precipice, and surveyed the entire valley below. Adlai jumped nimbly from his back and scurried eagerly to the edge, pausing as she drew in her breath and stared in wonder at the sight below: from here she could see all the surrounding countryside, along with the tall mountain ranges looming beyond. Far below the view opened up, running on for as far as the eye could see over a grand splendor of lush moors and sprawling orchards, with little farms and villages dotting the countryside. A ways off, and to the south-western edge of a distant mountain border, there rested the broad expanse of the sea, its distant waves crusted in the golden rosy hues of sunset.

Far off to the south-eastern front, purple hills and mountains rose like a sheltering barrier above the form of a little town nestled quietly below, its houses and shops built snugly against its protective back-drop. Set higher upon the hill and overlooking the town, a castle rose steeply within the obscured shade of the southern mountains, its many towers and spires casting long shadows over the village below it. From there Adlai could now see the gleam of a hundred little torches, flickering like the tiny lights of a thousand fireflies in the growing twilight. For a brief moment she felt utterly lost, captivated by the beauty that filled her eye. Dombrey Manor did indeed appear quite lovely from this vantage point, and she realized now that she had oft times forgotten how comely in charm and grandeur it truly was…It was hard to notice and be thankful for such things while she was there. Yet here it hardly seemed to resemble the prison house of confinement to which she so dreaded returning… Everything here seemed so peaceful, so tranquil and quiet…How sad, she mused to herself, that she was only ever able to appreciate its beauty from this distance, and no closer?

The sound of approaching hoof-beats made Adlai stir from her momentary brooding, and she looked up suddenly to see Willan riding up to meet her. Gharm (who was favoring one of his forelegs) followed with apparent difficulty behind him. Without so much as a word, Willan leapt from his saddle, his every step like the thudding boom of thunder as he strode over to where she stood. He was breathing heavily, and the loose fabric of his shirt was torn slightly in places, revealing a few cuts and scrapes over his arms, neck, and chest. His face was covered with scratches and grime, but there was no mistaking the livid expression of his countenance: the stormy look in his eye made her grow deathly still and silent in his presence—she had never before seen him in such an enraged state.

"Are you half *mad*?!"

Willan shouted so loudly and with such force that he practically spat the words out. Adlai flinched; he was so near that she could feel the heat of his breath striking her face. She swallowed hard, closing her mouth in mute submission as she turned her eyes meekly to the ground. He had never before displayed so strong a temper. In fact, now that she thought of it, there had been few occasions in all her lifetime when she had ever seen him appear even *somewhat* upset.

CHAPTER 4—LOST

Willan was known to all as the gentle young Lord of Dombrey Manor, and was respected not only for his title and position, but also for the unmatched grace and kindness he demonstrated towards those beneath him. In addition, he had always treated and looked out for Adlai as if she had been his own sister, even though he was infinitely beyond her in rank, wealth and standing. For not only was Willan a young nobleman, he was Willan Beiholde—Duke and only son and heir of Malen Beihorne WenLaon, King of Rhumendor. As such he would one day ascend to the throne, when his father's spirit would go to rest with his forefathers before him. Yet so unassuming was the Crown Prince in his manner that he appeared almost as much a local as the rest, and for his part he seemed content to have it remain thus. There was no pomp, no ceremony or grand displays attending the young Lord, and even young urchins playing in the streets were not afraid to approach him seeking favors from his purse. Willan was like one of them, and he never seemed to consider it beneath himself to be approached by even the lowliest vagrant. He was the combination of magnanimous nobility and unaffected simplicity, honorable pride tempered with humility. And in many ways it was this quiet humility and gracious way about him (apart from his high standing and handsome appearance) which had awakened in Adlai the growing flame she felt burning bright in her heart. His easy, good-natured spirit and light-hearted smile always seemed to make her forget how distantly beneath him she herself was in rank …It was a bitter-sweet illusion that all-too-often gave way to the stark contrast of cold reality, whenever the stern Lady Ardath appeared. Heart-warming moments of laughter would suddenly turn somber and fade away— like the last fleeting days of summer wilting before the grip of autumn's frosty chill—as the sound of Head-Lady Heromena of Ardath's quick, cold footsteps would come echoing harshly across the stone slab floors in the dark, cheerless halls of the Manor. In such moments Willan would often softly excuse himself and respectfully take his leave, and Adlai would be left to the ever severe, iron-clad grip of the austere Head-Mistress. No sooner would he be gone from sight, when Adlai would pay dearly for her forgetfulness of the unkind truth of her own humble beginnings. There was no mercy to be had from Lady Ardath (especially when one was no more than a penniless orphan of no family standing), whom fortune had strangely chosen to privilege with a wealthy benefactor...

Whenever Willan was absent Adlai would wait through her long days alone, with nothing but the lonely cover of night to look forward to as a shallow reprieve from Lady Ardath's bitter harshness. And there were many times when the night itself seemed no better comfort than the day, especially during those long spells when she would hardly catch more than a glimpse of him, for whole days at a time...During such times it would seem as if he had completely forgotten her. But whenever they did chance to meet, a surge of new-born hope and courage would well up inside her. It was for such moments that she lived and breathed, when all would be well and happy again, and when—even just for a moment—she could feel that she actually held a small amount worth and significance in another's eyes. All moody sadness would immediately vanish away, and in its place would emerge (with rekindled strength) the coy impudence for which she so often found herself in trouble.

Nothing Adlai had ever done had even once provoked any ill-will or disfavor from him. He kindly and patiently bore with all her whims and artful designs, to the point at which she had become guilty of abusing his forbearance. Maybe half of his kindness was due to the brotherly affection he still felt for the play-mate companion of his childhood. Or perhaps part of it arose from some kind of unspoken pity he felt for her...But maybe, just maybe, it had more to do with a deeper personal feeling which Opportunity had not yet deigned he should be permitted to reveal. But whatever it was that motivated him, testing his care and loyalty (by slyly pushing back the limitations of all established boundaries) had, by now, become an open game to Adlai. In her mind's eye,

Willan had evolved to become her champion and protector; his steady defense of her seemed indicative of this point, and the more patiently he bore with her, the more bold and self-assured her behavior became.

Adlai now realized that she had taken it completely for granted as being almost impossible that she could ever, in any way, cause offense with him. It was a mistake which, she now realized with numbed shock, had been very foolish and naïve, indeed. Of a sudden she recalled that there *had* been times of late, when Willan had somehow indicated that he was of less mind for her pranks and games; for even though he still exercised patience, his countenance and behavior had begun to appear more strained in recent times...*Why, oh, why had she so carelessly chosen not to pay attention, and to throw away discretion now? Why had she foolishly revealed the faulty degree to which she had become so blatantly and inappropriately over-confident in herself?...Could it be possible that at last even Willan had reached his threshold for stomaching all of her folly?...And if so, what might it cost their friendship now?*

...Adlai half glanced up at him for a quick second, just to be sure. No, there was no mistaking it this time: he was so greatly heated that he appeared ready to boil over with fury. For the first moment in her young life, she realized that this was *one* time when her willful pleasure-seeking had gone *much* too far—even for her ever-understanding friend. Whatever it was that he had now to say concerning her actions, she knew that it behooved her to hearken soberly to it.

"Must everything always be either a game or a joke to you?!" Willan burst. The usual even-toned complexion of his face was flushed red with anger. "You might have killed us both! My best hound suffers many wounds and requires remedial attention, thanks to you!—while my horse is now limping from our fall in the gorge! And your own you've run half-way to Death's door, by the look of it!"

He threw his hands over his head in an expression of deeply aggravated exasperation.

"When in the name all that is sacred will you at last learn to *cease* from your wild ways and try to be sensible?!"

The sound of Willan's voice had suddenly become strangely strained, as if it might break. Adlai bit her lip hard and kept her eyes fixed unwaveringly to the ground, trying hard to hide the tears fast springing to her eyes. Willan seemed to notice, for he paused reflectively and remained silent for several brief moments. At last he continued in a somewhat softer, more patient tone:

"Adelheide, one day you will learn that not everything is meant to be turned into sport, and that there are some things—and persons—to whom you must listen, and give the greater heed."

Adlai realized with flushed embarrassment that this last rebuke was directed as a gentle, prodding reminder for her not to forget her rank. Her behavior should never have been such that he would have even deemed it *necessary* to remind her that he was her sovereign. Without a word she nodded solemnly, slowly raising her eyes to meet his. For a brief instant she searched his face as she made one last, desperate attempt to wordlessly intimate the depth of her inner feelings for him, and to try draw out some sign of a return. For just a moment a small look of surprise and then confusion flickered across his expression. But then without another word he abruptly turned away, sighing and shaking his head as he went, a look of resignation upon his worn visage as he strode wearily back to his waiting horse. Willan didn't look angry anymore as he silently remounted—only extremely tired. Raising an arm, he rubbed his face with the edge of his long sleeve in a futile attempt to wipe away the stain of ground-in dirt from his sweaty skin.

"Come, we have a long ride ahead of us, and night will fast be falling," he spoke briskly as he situated himself in the saddle. "We are far away from the Manor, and I wish not to risk any more hazards after nightfall."

All at once they were startled by the sound of a shrill whinny. The form of a horse came streaking out from amongst the trees and suddenly flew down the hill in their direction.

In an instant Willan spurred Flame forward, leaping from the saddle and throwing Adlai out of harm's way. The Shire horse belted out a loud whinny as it reared up, hooves pummeling the air dangerously close to Willan's head.

"Easy! Easy!" Willan called out.

Cautiously he approached, hand outstretched, but the Shire horse shied away, a wild look in his eyes. There were cuts and lacerations all over his body, and splotches of mud caked everywhere.

"Whatever do you think happened?" Adlai queried, peering anxiously at the frenzied animal.

"Probably a robbery," he muttered grimly.

"Where do you think his master is?"

"My guess—dead."

He cast a pensive eye back towards the forest, then cautiously reached for the harness. At this the Shire horse reared up with another bellowing whinny, and then in an instant bolted away again, just as fast as he'd come.

Willan heaved a shaken sigh and turned back to Adlai:

"Come, let's be going—and carefully—we know not what we might meet."

He gave one last rueful look at Gharm, then with a sigh whistled for him to follow. The hound reluctantly fell in behind, Willan clicking briskly to his horse as they hurriedly sauntered back up the summit. Adlai silently followed, shame washing through her over how rash and ridiculous her actions had been, and of how spoiled and juvenile she must appear to him now. The thrill and pleasure of the moment was gone; in its absence there was left only the foolish sense of guilt—along with a growing twinge of alarm. For as she looked about now she saw that twilight had fallen, and several stars were already twinkling dimly from their lofty place high up in the heavens. Riding back to Dombrey at night would be very risky, indeed…

At the top of the peak, Willan suddenly pulled in the reigns as he wheeled about and peered towards the far eastern end of hill.

"We're too far from any main roads to find our path back that way," he murmured contemplatively as he stared ahead. "But I believe I know a short-cut through those woods yonder—it should return us back to the Manor in shorter time than by 'whixt we came."

Willan clicked again as he gently redirected his mount down the other side of the hill; Gharm slowly followed with drooping head, his tail hanging stiffly between awkward legs. Adlai remounted and fell in behind, shivering slightly as she went. A stiff wind had come blowing over the hill top, along with the descent of accompanying darkness, and from somewhere afar off in the night silence she could hear the distant hoot of an owl.

The woods were very dark and still now as they entered. They rode on for quite some time upon a poorly-marked and narrow little path, and all the while the forest grew increasingly darker round about them. A partial moon was now risen high above in the night sky, and all around a chilly mist had begun to form, increasing into fog as they continued their quiet passage. Something about it made Adlai shiver, while the deathly stillness of the woods made her hush out all other thoughts as she rode on in silence.

Presently a stench filled her nose, growing more foul and rank with each passing moment.

"*Ugh*! Whatever is that ghastly smell?" She exclaimed, doing her best to hold her breath so as to stifle out the odor.

"Something's dead," Willan murmured, reining in his horse as he spoke and casting a furtive look about.

It was then that they both saw it, lying off in the brush. Willan jumped from the saddle and slowly approached, Adlai following behind him. A break in the overhead trees allowed for some moonlight to filter down, lighting upon the grisly remains of a cadaver, now crawling with flies. Adlai let out a horrified gasp.

"Willan, what is it?!"

"Our missing corpse," he replied, squinting down as he surveyed what little was left of the gory mess.

"You mean it's *human*?!"

He nodded silently.

"Wolves must've gotten him. See those grooves in the dirt? The body was dragged from that direction over there—"

His voice trailed off, as he slowly began tracking the marks in the ground. After about a hundred feet he stopped, turning back with a shake of his head.

"It just keeps going on—wherever it happened, the murder didn't take place here."

Adlai shuddered, cringing wryly as she cast one more look back at the decomposing body.

"Come," Willan said, suddenly grabbing hold of her hand, "We must leave this place at once and get back to the Manor."

Both re-saddled and continued silently on their way. The further they rode, the darker the wood became, so that she could scarcely make out anything. She did her best to keep her eyes trained steadily upon the white patch ahead of her that marked the back of Willan's shirt, reflecting like a pale light against the darkness.

All at once Adlai jerked upright with a start, as she quickly drew in a sharp breath: something had crackled in the dark behind her. Swiftly pulling in the reins, she twisted about in the saddle so as to have a good look. It was so still and silent, she could hear her own heart racing up her throat to start pounding inside her head. Again she tried to brush away the uncomfortable feeling that had been growing steadily inside her for some time now— they were not alone...*Something* was there in the wood with them. More than once now, she thought she had heard the furtive sound of a soft rustling following cautiously behind her in the brush...Something was stealthily tracking them. A small chill went wriggling down her spine—*Could it smell fear?*

Adlai quickly turned about, desperately peering ahead into the mist: the white patch marker that had been riding ahead of her was nowhere to be seen. *Where was Willan*?! A jolting rush of panic ran through her like a lightning bolt, yet she fought against the urge with all her might—he *had* to be here somewhere! She strained her eyes in every direction, her frantic glance darting all over the wood in hopes to catch a glimpse of his white tunic glimmering against the thick blackness. The hoof-beats ahead of her had become dimmer and less distinct...now they were gone. The only sound there with her in the stillness, was the wild beating of her own heart thudding from deep inside her rib-cage. Desperately she tried to shut it out, straining her ears for the sound of Flame's heavy hooves treading the dry leaves covering the ground.   The mist had made her lose all sense of direction....*Was she still on the path?...What direction was she facing now, and which one had he taken?*

CHAPTER 5—JAWS OF THE BEAST

"Willan?" She called out shakily. "Willan, where are you?"

"I'm over here," the muffled sound of his voice came back from somewhere far ahead of her.

"Keep close, Adlai!" she heard him call, "Just follow the sound of my voice."

Adlai turned her face in the direction of his voice, feebly attempting to calm herself and steady her trembling hands. Licking dry lips, she clicked hoarsely to Storm and gave him a light nudge.

All of a sudden there was a loud screeching from above. A large blackbird swooped down over her head, its wings striking harshly across her face as talons grabbed at her thick hair. Adlai shrieked, flailing and swiping madly at the air as she flung her arms over her head in an attempt to shoo the large bird away. It flew off just as suddenly as it had come. For several seconds she was left gasping and trembling violently all over, while she tried once more to calm her failing nerves.

It was then that she noticed it—Storm had barely flinched nor even moved throughout the whole commotion. Under normal circumstances, such a ruckus would have spooked him enough to cause him to rear up or bolt, yet he had hardly so much as stirred. Adlai stopped short to look at him: he was standing stock-still, ears erect and unmoving, as if intently listening to something, and both of his large black eyes were staring unwaveringly into the nearby thicket. Adlai turned her own gaze slowly in the same direction and peered breathlessly into the brush. There it was again…another slow, soft rustling sound stirring from amongst the leaves…

A rippling chill peeled down over her scalp, gripping her in speechless fear so that she froze motionless. Slowly and unwillingly she forced herself to look. It was not even a stone's throw away in the brush… Something… large… and dark…was rising up from its hiding place.

A scream died soundlessly in her throat. She stared, unable to drag her eyes away, as the dark form slowly arose and stood upright high above her, its great shadow looming over them both. A pair of large black eyes were glinting straight back into her own, and her trembling ears were met by the sound of a low-pitched, rumbling growl emanating from some place deep in its belly.

Adlai's heart stopped cold, the hair on the back of her neck bristling with icy sweat. Her quaking lips fell open as she gaped in fixated horror, unable to tear her eyes away, and her hands shook so violently that she inadvertently let the reigns drop. Storm likewise seemed rooted like a tree to the spot where he stood, his unblinking eyes wide with terror, ears pressed flat against his skull, as though the same wild fear had bound him captive as well. She felt a cold tremor pass through his great body, as at last he let out a low, frightened whinny. Frantically, she tried to call Willan's name. Her mouth opened and closed soundlessly, yet nothing but a hoarse whisper escaped her lips.

The menacing growl was growing louder and harsher in its threat, as the glowing eyes narrowed their focus…For a moment its head and shoulders crouched— then in a sudden instant it sprang from the bushes. In a single bound it leapt over Storm, knocking Adlai with such force that she was thrown from her saddle in the blink of an eye. In the next instant she hit the ground so hard that the wind was knocked clean out of her. She could neither breathe nor cry aloud. The taste of grass and dirt was mingled with blood in her mouth. Then without warning a startled squeal of pain escaped her lips: fangs were suddenly piercing through the base of her neck, sinking deep into her flesh as they closed over her shoulder in a paralyzing hold. And then, almost before she knew what was happening she was being swiftly dragged through dirt, grass, and leaves. In a moment she was flung beneath the Creature's body like a small animal of prey, and in the next second the Beast was bounding away with her impaled between its jaws.

With great soaring leaps the Creature effortlessly streaked over felled trees and boulders and scaled massive rocks. Her body shook violently, wind rushing against her quivering frame as she whipped through the air like a rag doll. Violent spasms were shooting through every nerve. She let out a staggered gasp of pain, unable to scream or cry out; all of her senses were crippled by the powerful vise clenched like steel through her shoulder.

The forest was flying past in a rapid blur. Sharp sticks scraped and jabbed her, and rocks cut at her flesh as she was ruthlessly knocked this way and that. Somewhere afar off she thought she caught a few snatches of Willan's voice frantically shouting. But her tongue cleft mutely to the roof of her mouth so that she could make no answer, and soon the sound of his voice was drowned out and utterly lost to her.

The Creature was as fast as he was powerful. Her head was painfully thrown about like a heavy lead weight; she felt that at any instant her neck would surely snap and her head be knocked clean from her shoulders. They were flying with unnatural speed over earth and ground, and all the while the fangs were sinking in deeper and deeper with every bound. Saliva sprayed across her face, running down her neck and saturating her raw, open shoulder with its stinging venom.

Suddenly she thought she could indistinctly make out the form of a second Creature as it came bounding up along beside them. The second appeared to be in hot pursuit of the first. The sound of much snapping and snarling ensued, and the two began to race side by side. Suddenly the second lunged at the first with all his might, the weight of his body slamming into the shoulder of the first Beast. With redoubled terror Adlai now realized that it was only a matter of moments before she would surely be torn to pieces between the two of them. Her captor, though slightly stunned by the blow, immediately quickened his speed and ran even faster than before. Her skull was dashed first upon several rocks, before her temple finally struck against the side of a large boulder, and she fell limp...

Adlai stirred. Black darkness surrounded her now. She was dizzy past all comprehension and barely conscious, and something wet was running down the side of her face from a throbbing pain at the side of her head. But something else wasn't right: they were no longer racing over land as before. Instead it felt as if she were being dragged head-first in a downward direction; her feet now seemed much higher than her head as they skidded over wet ground. She coughed and choked: dirt was showering down into her burning eyes from somewhere above. It was much colder here, and the air was thick and dense with the scent of wet earth. Something else was in the air too—a heavy, putrid stench that stung her nostrils, like the smell of decay. They seemed to be descending steadily downwards in some sort of narrow, cavernous tunnel—she was underground. Her captor seemed more at ease now, for he had slackened his pace, and his hold relaxed.

At length, the Creature halted with a loud snort and dropped her upon the wet soil as it turned to sniff the air. Adlai stifled a cry as her shoulder fell away from his fangs like a piece of flayed, tender meat falling off a spit. With a moan she crumpled to the ground in a breathless heap. Her captor seemed not to be paying much attention to her now; instead he was intently listening for something else, as the glint from his bright eyes flickered in the dark. *What was it this time?* There was dead silence for a moment...Then suddenly from behind, Adlai was seized by the ankles with terrific force! She let out a wild scream of pain and terror; her dislocated shoulder scraped and bounced against the earthen walls, and with a violent jerk she was yanked back up the tunnel. In an instant her first attacker was left behind in the dust, a wild, inhuman howl of rage echoing after her. With a gasp she broke through the surface and to fresh air again. Then she was being swiftly drug across the ground, and next moment was flung onto a patch of grassy earth. *Something* was panting heavily as it hovered over her, its breath blasting hot gusts into her face. Adlai closed her eyes tight and held her breath, trying hard not to let a single muscle twitch…*It was coming—the end must surely be only moments away.*

Suddenly the second Beast started with a snort, as an awful shrieking arose from the opening in the ground behind them. Out of it shot the first Creature, rushing forth like an avenging demon from the Abyss. Adlai barely opened her eyes, but suddenly the Creature above her flew round with a savage snarl, and bounded away. Both Creatures charged with fury upon each other, and a vicious battle began. Left alone now for a few dazed moments, Adlai fell into a fit of gut-wrenching convulsions, vomiting upon the turf. She was shaking violently and trembling all over, icy sweat forming in droplets over her bleeding brow, and she was thirstier than she had ever been in her life. Her swollen eyelids were sticky with blood, and her head was reeling. Yet even so, she could still make out two figures struggling and lunging one against the other. All around the wood was filled with the echoes of unearthly shrieks, snarls, roars, and howling screams, the like of which she had never heard before.

For half a stupefied instant Adlai nearly lost herself. Dark shapes were streaking before her at unbelievable speeds, their forms appearing for but a brief moment before vanishing in a blurred flash of moonlight. The ground beneath was vibrating from the powerful echoes and noises round about. All around the leaves of nearby trees were torn from their boughs and their limbs instantly stripped bare, ripped away as if by the force of a mighty hurricane. A great rushing wind whipping about seemed to pull everything towards the center of its turbulence, as if the Creatures themselves had become the eye of the vortex. The earth beneath was pulling away; like sand shifting in an hour glass, it quickly eroded from its place, sucked away by a power of magnetic force so strong that even the rocks beneath the ground were laid bare. Frantically, Adlai grasped at the exposed roots of a nearby oak tree, and with the free hand of her good arm clung as tightly as she could with what little strength remained.

Again the Creatures collided, spinning wildly about as both rose struggling off the ground and spun higher and higher. For a moment they whirred about suspended in mid-air. There was a sudden clash that sent echoing vibrations in all directions as their bodies locked for just an instant—then plummeted downwards, their shapes falling like fiery coals raining back down to earth.

A great booming noise as of an earthquake echoed all around as they slammed against the earth's surface. The ground shook and rocks split open, a large crater instantly forming in the place where they had struck. The partial light of the moon above spilled down through the trees, lighting upon a great cloud of dust and smoke drifting upwards from the creviced pit. Of a sudden the sound of panting and grunting met Adlai's ears; slowly the darkened form of one emerged to the surface at the crater's edge. With difficulty he hoisted himself over the brink, then turned back to face what lay in the sunken cavity behind him. A gasp of horrified wonder escaped her lips at the sight which met her eyes: even though most of his features remained indistinct and shrouded by shadows, she could still make out his silhouette in the darkness—the like of which she had never seen nor even read of in any tale or legend. He appeared to be neither Beast—nor Man. He did not even closely resemble any creature depicted in any book, and she knew them all. None of them bore any likeness to this Creature. His upper body appeared smooth-skinned like a man's, only very powerfully built. And Adlai could see now what it was which had, only moments before, created so violently fierce a raging wind: massive, featherless wings sprang from the back of the Creature just behind his shoulder-blades. Their pinioned tips barely swept the ground as they unfurled combatively, spreading out like menacing guards that flanked him on either side as he rose upright and stood tall upon the ravine's crest. She could not yet be sure, but he appeared to be at least a head and shoulders' measure greater in height than even the tallest man she had ever seen. A rustling wind stirred from somewhere, blowing furrows through thick, dark fur that sprouted from his lower back and grew down over his hind-quarters upon sleek, wolfish hind legs. A long, slender tail tossed restlessly behind him like the streaking of a whip, yet the rest of his body remained taut and motionless, as if he was intently listening, waiting…

There was no sign of anything stirring from the bottom of the hole…*Where had the other one gone?* Of a sudden the Creature's head snapped in the direction of a darting movement from the other end of the wood. In an instant something again flashed across the wooded expanse—but just as fast the winged Creature sprang up to meet it. Both lurched high into the air, then toppled back to earth in a blurred fury of commotion. Rising upright on hind legs they lunged at one another, each one viciously swiping through the air amidst the frightful sounds of roaring and dreadful shrieks. Long, thick hair bristled upright over their spines in the pale moonlight, their backs arched high with heads lowered as they charged and clashed, knocking each other to the ground to roll over and over. Again and again they rose and fell. Their long tails sliced deftly through the wind like the sharp stroke of a knife's blade. Madly they lashed through the foliage of the surrounding trees and kicked up the leaves from the ground. The pair of great wings was again beating through the air, so that it was again impossible to clearly distinguish much else of either Beast, and there was such a noise of snapping and snarling that she could hardly tell which of the two was either winning or losing.

Adlai quickly came to herself. *What was she waiting for?!* They were fighting over the prize—food—and *she* was the prey! All hope of escape depended on her acting now—and fast! Again she was conscious of the piercing pain that was shooting through her left arm all the way down to her fingertips, as it hung limp and disjointed at her side. She bit down hard on her lip till she could taste the salty flavor of blood—she *had* to push through the pain if she was going to manage any sort of escape. Gritting her teeth, she reached above her head and grasped higher at the base of the naked roots to which she clung, trying hard as she did to regain her footing in the loose, pebbly earth slipping away beneath her feet.

A sudden shriek arose from behind her, followed by whimpering yelps, and her head spun round in the direction of the noise. One of the Creatures was loping away on all fours in defeat, his fleet-footed gait slowed by the awkwardness of a wounded limp, his tail hung stiffly between his legs. With a mournful howl he leapt up upon a great flat rock and disappeared over the ledge.

Adlai froze for an instant as she watched him take flight, and then turned her harrowed gaze back towards the winged Creature remaining. He was once again standing furtive and upright upon hind legs and with his back to her. The dim rays of moonlight shafting down through the mist lit upon his flanks, now glistening bright with sweat, and body heaving as he continued warily to watch the far side of the forest. Silently he raised himself up to full height, shoulders barred apart as he scrutinized the direction his foe had taken. Taut, brawny muscles flexed and contorted in the moonlight, his bared silhouette a terrifying display. Long, pointed ears arose from either side of his head, twitching silently as they stood erect, listening intently for any sound to echo back from the opposite edge of the wood. For several moments he remained sniffing at the wind, till at last he seemed reassured that his enemy would not return. His shoulders loosened and relaxed. With a satisfied grunt his arms fell to his sides, and again he dropped down on all fours.

All at once the root to which she clung broke away. Without warning, she was suddenly tumbling head over heels to the stripped and uprooted ground beneath. Like a streak of light the Creature's head whipped about in her direction, and in less time than it took her to blink an eye he had already bounded to her side. Adlai froze and closed her eyes tight, hardly daring to breathe for fear of waking further notice. He was circling round about her, his large paws padding cautiously over the earth like those of a skilled and practiced hunter. Carefully he began sniffing over her body, his fiery breath striking her skin until at last he reached her shoulder. Adlai stiffened, holding her breath as she clamped her tongue firmly between her teeth so as not to give herself away. Then she felt a warm, wet tongue licking over her flayed flesh and lapping at her gaping wound. Instantly rebounded terror filled her, as everything inside suddenly gave way. A petrified scream gurgled from her throat and broke out in a piercing shriek!

Almost in the same moment the familiar sound of Gharm's excited bark echoed from somewhere not very far off in the distance, followed by shouts from Willan, as through the brush she snatched a glimpse of them streaking through the trees. The Creature's head snapped up, just as Gharm leapt through the overhead bushes with a thunderous bark. With a vicious growl he fell snapping upon the Beast. Flame bellowed out a shrill whinny as she reared up against the night sky, Willan belting out a savage war cry as they charged though the brush and skidded down over the steep embankment. Her assailant flew to the side with Gharm's teeth sunk deep in his shoulder. Adlai hastily rolled to her side just in the nick of time, as hooves came crashing down near her head a half second after. In an instant Willan had leapt from his mount, and with a spring through the air had tackled the Beast. Adlai screamed and clapped a hand tightly over her mouth, as the Creature effortlessly threw both Willan and Gharm from his back and flung them to the ground. But then to her astonishment, the Creature made no attempt to attack or to fight back, but instead took suddenly to his heels like a flash of shadow, vanishing away as quickly as he had appeared. Astounded, she stared after in curious amazement: the Creature had already demonstrated superior strength against an enemy of infinitely greater and more formidable power than any mock display of dread which Willan could have possibly hoped to inspire...*Why then had he so easily given up, with hardly any show of resistance?*

"Adlai!" Willan cried out as he jumped to his feet and rushed to her side. Panting, he dropped down on one knee beside her, and she threw her arms around his neck and burst into convulsive sobs.

"There, there, now!"

Willan seemed as though he was trying hard to sound calm and steady, yet there was no mistaking the shaken tone in his voice. She could feel his heart pounding heavily against her cheek as he quickly pushed her mussed hair from her eyes, briskly lifting her face to examine her.

"Are you hurt anywhere?"

"Yes—my shoulder—" Adlai reached up with trembling fingers to gingerly touch the injured area. "Willan, I don't think I can—"

She stopped short with a surprised gasp: her skin felt completely whole under her touch. Quickly she tugged the neckline of her garment down over her shoulder to have a better look. There was no denying it: even though the garment itself was practically shredded, all the same her wound was suddenly, completely, and inexplicably *gone*...There was not so much as the slightest twinge of pain, neither was there a single visible trace indicating that *any* harm whatsoever had been done her.

"How strange," she murmured in bewilderment, as she stared perplexedly down and continued to explore the area with her free hand, then nimbly reached up to touch her forehead: the place where she had been struck on her temple was also equally sound and unscathed, as if it had never happened. She had no other traumatic markings on her body, save for the scratches she had received earlier from their hard ride through the wood, and their successive tumble in the canyon. Yet otherwise, there was no further sign anywhere on her person indicating that a struggle had taken place. Mystified, Adlai looked up confusedly in disbelief and wonder: *What had happened?*

"Storm is gone?"

The question echoed in her head for a moment before it fully registered—the next moment it fell through her consciousness with a sudden jolt that left her ears ringing. She nodded shakily in reply.

"Poor creature," Willan said sadly with a heavy sigh, "Poor, faithful old friend."

Adlai choked back the hard lump rising in her throat. Storm had belonged to Willan as a foal when they were both still children, and he had given him to her as a gift. And aside from Willan's own company, there was nothing else which meant more to her.

Willan seemed to be temporarily distracted from the sorrow of the moment, however; the guarded expression of his face was again set like flint, as his wary eye silently searched all the surrounding wood.

"Well then, if nothing else is wrong, we must be going at once," he said briskly as he turned back to her.

His face looked pale now, even in the dark, and there was a look in his eye which Adlai could not remember having ever seen there before...*fear*. Without another word he promptly strode back to where she still sat slumped upon the ground, and hurriedly pulled her to her feet. The fur on Gharm's back and tail seemed to stand on end as he stood alert like a sentry watching the edge of the forest, then with a whimpering whine turned his big brown eyes back to his master. Flame herself was already pawing the ground nervously, her large head bobbing anxiously about from side to side as she likewise eyed the distant trees. Willan seized the horn of his saddle and swung up before swiftly hoisting her up behind him.

"I don't know what manner of Creatures those were, but I'll wager they'll soon be back—and they'll have company," he muttered grimly.

He gave Flame a quick spur to the flank, Gharm hurriedly leading the way as they hastily departed from the glen. Far off in the distance they heard a howl go up. Gharm's quick step broke into a run as Flame's hurried trot instantly turned to a gallop, and together the little party sped on beneath the darkened vault of the forest. Overhead, the arched branches of yawning trees spread out like a thickened, black canopy shutting out all light offered by the night sky above.

...Not another word was spoken between them—Adlai hardly even dared breathe—as she hugged her knees tightly together against Flame's sides. Wrapping her arms tightly about Willan's waist, she clung fast, and together they flew on through the chilly night.

The thick clouds were parted a little, revealing that the moon was very high in the sky by the time they reached the stone walls of Dombrey.

"Who goes there?" A gateman called out harshly.

"Crown Prince Willan Beiholde, of Rhumendor, together with Lady Adelheide!" Willan's tone resonated with authority, yet Adlai could still detect a slight tremor in his voice. She peered up the side of his face from where she sat huddled close behind him. Even in the dim moonlight she could see traces of worry behind his proud bearing. His lower jaw was set and firmly clenched, and she could feel a slight tremble pass through his body, though outwardly he appeared unflinching and collected.

"Willan, you're trembling," she whispered.

"It's cold out, and I've lost my cloak," he replied in a short, dismissive tone, shaking it off with a curt shrug.

He continued to look up intently towards the watchtower on the wall, as sentries scurried to unbar the gates. Adlai bit her lower lip and looked away. Willan's response seemed indicative that he was harboring a feeling of foreboding—and perhaps something else…More than likely he was still thinking of her willful thoughtlessness from earlier that evening, and, undoubtedly, of how her actions had opened wide the door to all the harrows from which they had so narrowly escaped …He must surely resent her now, and it could hardly be expected that he should feel otherwise. He had entreated her many times to make an earlier return—indeed, he should never have even ventured out of the castle at all that day, except on her account. And if it hadn't been for her blatant disregard towards his wishes, none of this would have happened. Adlai hung her head, inwardly berating herself for not having acted more sensibly…*Why, oh, why did she always have to go ruining things with her head-strong and impulsive ways?*…Her willfulness had endangered his life too, as well her own…

Her thoughts were interrupted again by a slight scuffling sound overhead, followed by a loud screeching noise, as the heavy bar of the gate was slid from its place and dragged away. The wooden doors creaked on their iron hinges as they were thrown wide open to give entrance.

"Bless ye, Lads!" Willan called as the gatemen stood aside to let them pass. He gave the mare a quick nudge and a light slap of the rein. Adlai leaned in close as they lurched forward, holding fast to him again as pebbles kicked up beneath them, and together they sped under the tall arched gateway with Gharm at their heels.

CHAPTER 6—LADY ARDATH

The sound of hooves clattering over the cobblestones echoed through the courtyard in the chilly night air as they entered the castle grounds. Adlai clung tight, trying hard to shut out the tight knot that was growing at a sickening rate in her gut. Willan was always practical and reliable, and Adlai knew that Lady Ardath was sure to know that it was not at all by *his* doing that they had returned to the manor by so late an hour. Discipline would fall swift and sure now, that much she knew beyond a doubt. But what sort of punishment would the headmistress invent for her this time? Would she be strictly confined to the manor, and have all her precious books confiscated?...Yes, she thought dismally to herself, that was what was most likely to happen—she probably wouldn't be allowed to go out with Storm on their usual rides together for well over a week, if not for an entire month—*oh!*

Her heart sank suddenly. Storm was not with them now. She had last caught sight of him for just a fleeting instant following the attack, right after being knocked from her saddle— and this last memory now began playing itself again and again in her mind. Tears sprang to her eyes now, as she again thought of him— lost and alone out in that dreadful, forsaken place—*what had become of him now? He was sure to be cold, hungry, and wearied half to death—that was, if their deathly night stalkers had not already tracked him down somewhere…* She shuddered, cringing wryly as she tried desperately to shake her thoughts away from this grisly image.

Aside from Willan (who had, of late, grown increasingly busier with managing affairs of the kingdom in his father's absence), Storm was—or had been—the only other friend she'd ever had. She repeatedly chided herself now, her black thoughts clouded over with the weight of helpless remorse, as she realized how much she had taken him for granted. He may have been a dumb animal, but he had faithfully served her, and now she realized that he truly had been her only source of relief and comfort, apart from Willan….The loss of him now was great and heavy indeed to bear.

Her mind wandered dully through the many warm memories of their frequent daily rides together, the wind blowing in his mane as he stood tall, proud, and regal upon some hilltop, with her astride his back. In those moments with him she had felt both wild and free, almost as if there were no other life, nor ever would be again…He had always had such a noble bearing about him, that at times it almost seemed as if he had been born for a greater purpose, than merely to be bound in man's service…Every now and then she thought she had glimpsed it—a calm, quiet look of deep wisdom in his large black eyes, peering silently out at her. Sometimes she used to bring him an apple for a treat on rainy days, when it was too damp and cold to go out for their usual ride. And, leaning against his side, she would rest her head upon his shoulder and quietly talk with him, gently stroking his coat and mane as they stood together alone, looking out in silence upon the wet, muddy courtyard. In such moments when all was still and there was no other sound to be heard, she thought vaguely that she'd caught sight of a distinguishable look of interest and understanding in his eye—as if he well comprehended the meaning of her words, and shared an unspoken empathy for the feelings of her heart. If it had been a particularly hard day, and tears were shed as she cried about her heart-aches, he would sometimes gently lower his great head down over her shoulder, his warm breath blowing softly across her cheek as he nuzzled and tickled her ear with his muzzle…It was almost as if he understood… *What if he really had*? What sort of things might animals think or speak of, if only they could?... If she could have looked through his eyes, would she have seen herself a kind and caring young mistress, a girl who truly loved and valued him?...Or might she have seen instead a very temperamental and heavy-handed task-master, completely insensible to anything other than the pleasure of her own momentary whims?

Her heart sank in dismal sorrow at this thought. She hadn't treated him as best she might, and probably nowhere near half as well as he'd deserved... Yet he had always been there, regardless. He had never seemed to hold it against her, and she, for her part, had never once thought the day might come when she would finally be without him...And now she found herself wishing desperately, more than anything, for a last final moment so that she could—just for once—tell him how truly sorry she was...Would he ever know how much she already missed him?

Adlai had no time to finish with the many lonely, miserable thoughts drifting through her mind. They had just come into the open courtyard, and before them stood the great arched doors of Dombrey Manor. Willan had already alighted, turning back as he offered her his hand and helped her dismount. He looked tired and worn again, as he passed the reins to a few stable hands that had hurriedly come forward to assist him.

"Careful now," Willan called after one of the servants as he led Flame away. "My horse has thrown her shoe and requires special tending. Also, see to it that she gets a good rub down, along with extra food and water for the night. I'll come and examine her myself first thing in the morning."

The groomsman nodded quickly and led her away. Flame's head drooped wearily now, and she seemed to be favoring one of her hind legs (which was shaking to the point of a limp) as she clopped gingerly away across the courtyard. Willan heaved a sigh, reaching up stiffly to rub the back of his neck with one hand, then gave Gharm a gentle scratch behind the ears, as the dog waited in submissive silence beside him. Slowly Willan let out a tired groan, and began with sore and awkward steps to accompany the elderly steward across the courtyard towards the manor steps, the hound following after with lowered head.

Of a sudden Adlai became aware of how embarrassingly disastrous and unruly in appearance she was, for the men servants were already uneasily turning away with discomfort. To her surprise she realized that not only was her entire left sleeve missing, but much of her dress had been torn away as well; only a few shreds of it were left to cover her simple shift underneath, and that too had suffered great damage as it was torn, stained, and muddied all over. With everything that they had been through that night (along with the many unhappy ruminations she'd been turning over in her mind), she hadn't really stopped long enough to notice. But now that she was standing on the hard icy cobblestones of the manor courtyard, she realized that one of her leather boots was also missing—leaving her feet half-shod in the cold, so that she felt suddenly vulnerable and exposed. Her heart sank dismally: there would be *no* escape from being forced to give a *very* detailed explanation to Milady, and Adlai could count on it that her punishment would be very severe, indeed. With a heavy sigh, she turned unwillingly to shuffle behind Willan and the steward.

"Are you alright, Milord?"

The elderly servant inquired anxiously, a note of worry in his aging voice as he walked beside his young master. Willan paused for a brief moment before answering, glancing down as he did to brush the remaining dirt from his shirt and braies. He fingered a few scratches on his upper arm that showed through a tear in his tunic, and slowly ran a hand over the wide sore spot on his dusty buttocks, turning to give a wry smile in reply.

"Oh, nothing that can't be looked after, Remus," he answered with cheery, dismissive matter-a-factness. "Adlai's horse was spooked while we were out riding, and she was thrown from the saddle." He paused to deliver another sigh before continuing: "We spent the greater part of the evening out searching for him, but I'm afraid he's lost to us now—more's the pity, poor creature."

He hesitated for an instant to cast a discreet glance back in Adlai's direction. She shot him a quick half smile in gratitude, taking care to avoid meeting the curious, questioning look from the steward. Willan acknowledged her only by a brief, pursed-lipped smile in return, and she thought she detected an irritated glance in his look. She hung her head again and bit her lip. Never before had she heard him speak a lying or deceitful word, and she knew him well enough to know that this newly acquired skill did not taste at all well to his lips. A part of her wondered why he had not straight-forwardly come out and told the honest truth—but perhaps it was for the same reason she herself now felt inclined to conceal the matter. It was better not to rouse the consternation of those at the Manor by allowing rumors to spring up, and a frenzy of agitated fears to spill out like a plague. It did no good to raise worrisome speculations, especially when they knew not at all exactly *what* it was which they had encountered in the wood; and, even more importantly, they knew even less how they might successfully defeat such a scourge... more particularly, now that they were quite sure that there was *more* than one of their deadly foe with which to contend. To risk having word spread could stir up terror amongst the villagers and town folk...And with the king away, what could Willan do?

Willan was just taking a cloak from the hand of a middle-aged servant woman who had just appeared from the house. Laying it about Adlai's shoulders, he turned to lead the way up the steps without another word. He was very sober minded for a young man of his years. Growing up with the weight of overseeing the kingdom's affairs in his father's absence (with only elderly tutors and advisors for company), had matured him into the serious young Lord he was now, and he rarely made a weighty judgment, nor took any sort of decisive action, without first retreating to his private study. There he would disappear completely for long periods of time (or even entire days on end) to stew and brood, carefully sorting through heavy matters by pouring himself diligently over every related book or parchment on the subject. The sound of contemplative mutterings, along with those of his heavy boots plodding back and forth across the floor, could often be heard from outside the door as he paced about in deep thought. Only the servants who brought him his meals (along with a very select few of his special advisors), would ever see his face during such times, and from Adlai's bedroom window she could oft times see the candlelight from his private sector burning late into the night.

Indeed, it was often that Adlai had begun to feel that the only common link they had between them (other than the attachment of close ties associated with their childhood), was that *neither* of them ever revealed much of their private thoughts to others. Whether in Willan's case this characteristic came borne of natural instincts (or, if it was instead dictated by the compulsion of dignified necessity), she did not know. She was, nevertheless, somewhat irked that Willan's discreet silence came so easily to him, whereas she herself (although she hardly spoke an open word to anyone) felt an uncanny certainty that every peevish emotion she ever held was worn openly upon her sleeve. Willan's nature could not have been further from this. For even of the few of his trusted advisors (of whom he inquired and relied upon in those seasons), Adlai truly doubted that he ever revealed much of his own personal anxieties to any of them…He was a king's son— in every sense of the word—and he was keenly conscious and sensible to the full burden of responsibility which he bore. He seemed instinctively to know that to govern a kingdom was to rule alone, and he dutifully accepted the loneliness of his position with solemn dignity and decorum…But the refrain had taken its toll, and Adlai could see now how much it had aged him…And as much as she respected and admired him for his discretion, she found that she resented him equally much for it. It seemed that he had shut out the rest of the world, and with it her as well.

Whatever he intended now to do, it was apparent that, at least for the time being, he had no intention of revealing the harrowing details of that night to anyone. Adlai felt relieved. She wanted to forget all of it as quickly as she could, and to permanently put it out of her mind once and for all, forever. Storm got spooked and she had fallen; that was the story, and, hopefully, that would be the end of it…And perhaps Willan's story would even serve to somewhat satisfy Milady (if only a little), so that Adlai herself might not be fully blamed for their dreadful and sorry appearance—and particularly, for their late return…Perhaps if

Lady Ardath believed Willan's account, she herself could manage to escape interrogations—and maybe then there wouldn't even be any penalties after all? ...In her heart, Adlai found herself wishing to her core that Willan's frank and simple explanation really was the trite truth of all that had happened—if it had been, there might be hope of Storm's returning back to her...Maybe in time she could find relief for her guilty conscience, by pretending that what Willan had said really *was* true, until at last she could believe it along with the everyone else...Oh, if only...*If only*...

Adlai wrapped the cloak more tightly about herself and trudged after them. Climbing up the wide stone stair, her eye darted upwards: a single, solitary candle could be seen burning from one of the overhead window-panes, its dim light casting pale shadows upon a darkened face staring down in silence upon them. Involuntarily she halted, doing her best to squelch the sickening chill that suddenly ran through her: the light of the flickering flame was, for an instant, reflected in a pair of dark eyes now staring straight back into her own, locking her gaze in their cold, penetrating expression. Then without further ado, the dark figure turned abruptly away, and the light above quickly faded. Adlai gulped, as her stomach dropped like a stone into the hollow of her gut. There was only *one* other person there at the Manor who would have given notice to their long absence, one whom she knew had already long been burning candle-wax down to the wick through the tedious waiting hours of the night...Within moments footsteps could be heard approaching from inside the Manor, echoing briskly across the stone floors. Adlai could feel her stomach slowly tightening in knots as the great wooden doors were flung open upon creaking hinges: Lady Ardath.

A ring of iron keys jingled from where they were fastened to a long, corded girdle that was redoubled and tied low about her hips; the jangling of keys was accompanied by the swift rustling of her full skirts sweeping swiftly across the threshold, as she drew herself up staunchly at the top of the stair. There was no mistaking that she was head-lady of the household: the stately dress of her slate-colored houppelande was embroidered with very fine black brocade—high collared, with a sapphire brooch pinned at her throat. Her ashen-white face made her appear even more ghostly and foreboding in the moonlight. To Adlai she had the look of some sinister harbinger of the UnderWorld, roused from deathly slumbers and ready to wreak her vengeance upon the living. It was much the same look and habit which she wore every day, and had, for as long as the girl could remember. Even so, she had never been able to make herself grow used to the inordinately stern, severe appearance of the head-lady of Dombrey Manor. Her graying hair (usually concealed beneath a silk-veiled wimple), was pulled tightly back in coiled plates at the back of her head, making the sunken features of her colorless visage appear even more austere in the half light of the moon. A flickering candle clutched in her slender, spider-like fingers sent harsh shadows running hither and thither over the many wrinkles etched across her brittle face. Dark hollows formed in semi-circles under keen, quick eyes that took in everything about them at a single glance; these looked out sharply from over a long, narrow nose, beneath which a thin-lipped mouth was drawn up in a tight expression. She appeared to have not yet surpassed her sixtieth year, and though she may (at one time), have been considered quite comely, yet the severity of her manner had greatly diminished any beauty she might once have possessed. It seemed to the girl that she must surely have been born into the world in that withered, hapless state; the mere scorching glance of her eyes seemed to immediately suck up all the joy and life they found, leaving nothing but parched, dry emptiness in their wake. Everything about her cold appearance embodied the very essence of a living death. The only times when the headmistress' cold appearance ever softened into a warm, tender expression was when young Lord Willan was present, and then Lady Ardath fussed over him to no end as if he were her very own son.

"Lord Willan, are you quite alright?!"

Milady exclaimed suddenly in a tone of agitated excitement, the shrill echo of her voice breaking out over the stilly silence like an extinguishing gust of wind upon a flame. The candle burning in her hand was visibly shaking, and Adlai narrowly missed having the hot wax thrown in her face as it was roughly thrust towards her.

"Nothing at'll worth giving worry to— all's well, as you can see for yourself," Willan replied reassuringly in a light and cheerful tone. He was again acting with his usual easy, unperturbed manner, almost as if he had completely failed to notice (not only the late hour of their arrival) but their greatly disheveled appearances as well, as though willfully oblivious to the obvious. He smiled another one of his easy smiles as he spoke, shrugging away with frank disregard all doubts and fears, his unconcerned air more befitting of one who had merely returned late from a country picnic.

"We just got a little lost in the wood; Adlai's horse was affrighted and ran off. I'm afraid she took a little tumble, but otherwise we're quite alright, as you can see, and there's naught to worry about."

Adlai bit her lip, trying in vain to imitate Willan's relaxed posture and unsuspicious mannerisms. Cautiously, she sent a quick glance in Lady Ardath's direction to ascertain whether or not she had accepted the tale. *Too late*…the headmistress' eyes were already narrowing upon her as she met her gaze, her lips pursing together in a hard, firm line as she drew herself up rigidly to full height.

"What I can see, Your Grace, is that it 'tis well late into the night, and that the both of you are quite tattered and bedraggled half beyond recognition!" Milady's shrill voice was becoming even more strained as she continued: "We near sent out a party in search o' the two o' you! And what if something had happened to ye? I—I promised the King your father to look after you, and see to that all is well taken care of in his absence, and I should never dare face him should I be caused to break my word! However should I be able to live with myself, had you come to any harm?!"

Lady Ardath abruptly stopped short as her voice cracked, and she immediately began dabbing at her eyes with a white laced handkerchief. Adlai stifled the compulsive desire to let go the heavy sigh of annoyance welling up in her chest— *that* would be far too telling as to how little she truly cared to trouble herself with

Milady's over-wrought concerns. It was a fact that such emotional displays were a constant ritual whenever Prince Willan was present. The headmistress doted over him as if he were still a little boy, practically worshipping the very ground upon which he tread. Adlai had never been able to figure out for herself if such deep devotion was *truly* inspired out of unpretentious adoration for him; or rather, if she simply wished to firmly establish herself yet further within His Majesty's good graces. Adlai herself liked better to believe that it was for the latter reasons that Lady Ardath behaved thus, rather than admit to the possibility that such affections might be based upon truly genuine grounds. She already knew well that Willan was (without doubt) of an infinitely more agreeable and disarming temperament than she; but it hurt her pride to think that he was favored for the broad magnitude of his character, whereas that she should be slighted merely for having the audacity of being deficient of the same glowing qualities. She could not disown that he complied efficaciously with all the mandates befitting one of his position and pedigree, obeying such dictates in a way that was always dutiful, honorable and above reproach in every possible way. It had been obvious since their childhood that he was in strong possession of a both a pure conscience and a sincere heart—not to mention a readily agreeable disposition, which was something Adlai herself openly lacked. He had always spoken and acted with mild-mannered composure and calm ease around Milady—and as lord and master of his own house, by what reason should he not? In comparison, Adlai herself could never so much as stir in the headmistress' presence without feelings of guilt, nor ever bring herself to look fully into her cold, penetrating gaze without flinching. Willan occupied himself regularly with important matters of state, and had plied himself diligently to his studies in his youth, whereas Adlai herself had found little of her dull education that was to her liking. And many a profitable hour of the day had been frequently wasted in idle day-dreaming about life outside the manor grounds, or else in thinking up grand schemes and pranks that could be discreetly played upon the castle servants. It was a blatant fact that Willan did not in the least own her knack for mischief and trouble-making; indeed, she wasn't certain that he knew how to conceive of doing *anything* that wasn't wholly responsible, or served some sort of greater purpose.

...Yes, it was true—he really *was* perfect, a Prince among men, and everyone had cause to love and esteem him greatly ... And Adlai begrudgingly had to concede that it was possible that Lady Ardath *might* actually care for him, the way in which she appeared. After all, there was nothing about him in which she, personally, could find the slightest fault. Willan was entirely *good*...and that was an invaluable characteristic of which she herself was sorely in want. How different might it have been, she had sometimes wondered, if somehow a gracious whim of fate had intervened at the time of her own conception, favorably turning the tide of circumstances surrounding her own birth—what then? How much of a difference might it have made to her up-bringing and present situation, had she also been granted the prestige, freedom, and privileges accompanying auspicious nobility?

...All the same, something deep inside told her that, even if they *had* been born equals, she still could never have managed to find the same amount of undiminished grace and favor in the eyes of Lady Ardath...not even then. Willan was his own universe, and no amount of fate could have ever changed that. But even if she could never have been *quite* as good as Willan, Adlai now found herself wishing somewhat that she had tried to do a little better in the past. If she had, she might not now have to endure so much mistreatment and open contempt from the headmistress... And all of this was the bitter sub-note of Adlai's whole existence: if only she had been granted the good fortune of being born both good and a nobleman's daughter, Milady *might* have been compelled to treat her impartially, even if she would never have loved her.

For a brief instant Adlai's thoughts were stolen by a subtle feeling of resentment and jealousy towards Willan. It was evident—and was no secret— as to exactly *whose* safety (of either the two of them) Milady was primarily preoccupied. Adlai couldn't help but feel a raw hurt over the firm suspicion that, *had* the Creature of that night actually succeeded in destroying her, no tears at all would have been shed by the headmistress on her account. Ardath might even have secretly mirthed over the fact that at long last she had finally been relieved of her cumbersome responsibilities, and was no longer forced to over-see the upbringing of so "willful and troublesome" a pupil.

A feeling of sudden emptiness and worthlessness sank deep inside her at this thought. She had always known that Ardath cared nothing for her. Yet after her violent encounter, it pained her to think that her young life could have, in an instant, been suddenly cut short and snuffed out, with no one left who cared to mourn her memory. Was there even a single soul there at the castle who might have borne witness to the lonely life through which she had hereto struggled?

Adlai dismissed her brooding contemplations with a sudden surge of defiant anger: why should she care at all for Milady's regard? It was contemptible even to desire her approval for a single moment—and Adlai now gave herself a stern chiding for having ever afore envied Willan of any of Milady's tightly-guarded and grasping affections. Ardath's affections were as easily spent upon others as an avaricious miser in squandering his hoarded wealth of fortunes among the desperately poor and starving. She was a cold, unfeeling shrew of a woman—a smooth-tongued asp seeking hidden favors through pretexts and flattering kisses. She was nothing more than an ardent pursuer for the courtship of the royal purse, and Adlai would not abase herself by mimicking the same simpering flatteries and worshipful attentions. At least *she* had a mind and will of her own—and she would never be made to surrender her own independence on that score! The only comfort to be had was in the knowledge that Willan was now grown and no longer really in need of her, and Adlai herself very soon would no longer be in need of an overseer…Perhaps then Milady's employ would come happily to an end, and Adlai herself be moved from her egregious lot to a more affable situation…possibly with few—if *any*—tethering restrictions left.

Ardath was still sniffling and dabbing at her watery eyes:
"I should never be able to bring myself to face the king, should his only son be brought to harm!"

"There, there, now, Heromena," Willan said with a nervous laugh, as he attempted to console her with a quick kiss on the cheek. "That day's not yet been had, nor ever shall be, if I have naught to say about it!"

Very few persons of the higher household staff ever referred to Lady Ardath by other than her surname, but Willan was an exception. He laid a gentle hand upon her withered cheek, and she grasped it gratefully, clutching him close to herself as she turned over his hand and pressed it to her lips. Willan gave her hair a few brisk strokes and a quick pat as he continued:

"You have faithfully served this house, and shall too, for many more years to come, so let's fret no more o'er this night."

He gave her a light reassuring pat on the arm, and with the other hand he pulled Adlai from where she stiffly stood half hidden behind him.

"And as for worrying about me," he added with another laugh, "Vex not your pretty head with all that, neither worry for what explanation you should be required to give my father, should any ills betide me. My father well knows that I have long been of age, and am thereby responsible for my own actions, so he will never have cause to fault you for any choice of mine.

"And now," Willan added, giving Adlai a prodding nudge forward, "The only charge you have left to guard has been returned back to you, safe and sound right here, as you can see. I offer my humble apologies for any undue consternation which our late return may have caused your Ladyship."

Adlai grimaced inadvertently as she bit her lower lip, stiffening even more at the abrasive touch of Willan's patronizing pat on her shoulder. She cast him a brief look of bitter disappointment, shrinking away distastefully from his hand as she gingerly stepped forward. *How could he speak and act like this? Why was he now treating her as if she were still a child?!* She didn't require tending, as though she were still an infant in need of a wet nurse! Her spirit sank too in misery over Willan's reassuring promise to Ardath that she would always remain in service to his house. Adlai kept her eyes to the ground, doing her best to avoid

Milady's gaze. But the headmistress seemed not yet to notice, as she finished wiping her eyes and replaced her handkerchief.

"Yes, thank you, Your Grace," she replied with a forced smile, as she drew herself up again to full height and regained her composure.

"Well now, I think that I shall leave you to it, and bid you all good-night," Willan finished with a cheery air, giving each a sweeping bow of his head by way of respect, then strode briskly past them both and on through the open doorway. Gharm followed at his heels. The noise of dogs barking could be heard echoing down the corridor after him, as he was greeted by his other hounds in the mess hall. Then all sounds muffled into silence again, as the inner doors closed behind them. Adlai watched him depart in anguished misery; her last hope for salvation had vanished along with his retreating foot-steps.

She could already feel Ardath fixing her steely gaze glaringly upon her. There was not a sound left in the courtyard, except that of a soft howl made by the wind as it picked up every now and then over the chirping of a lonely cricket and the distant bark of a dog. Adlai bared herself, waiting for the attack.

"Uh-hm!"

She winced at the demanding tone of Milady clearing her throat, the harsh sound grating upon the silence, as she turned unwillingly to face Ardath's penetrating stare, and reluctantly made her way up the stone steps to where her Ladyship stood waiting.

"That isn't all you're going to hear about this, Adelheide, do you hear?!"

The headmistress' voice snapped like the sudden crack of a whip, as she snatched Adlai roughly by the arm and pushed her inside. The queasy sensation in her stomach rushed back like a flood as she waited in silence, the great doors slamming shut behind her. Lady Ardath finished barring the doors, then returned with brisk, hurried steps. Whisking past Adlai with a sudden flurry, she once again grabbed her arm with a jerk as she half dragged, half propelled the girl down the hall. Adlai stifled a gasp of pain, trying hard not let any tears show as Milady's hard, bony fingers sank deep into her upper arm with a severe pinch, and she was roughly shoved ahead down the far end of the opposite corridor.

"I am through dealing with you! You—you, and—and your wild, willful ways, and belligerent, obstinate behavior!" Ardath sputtered with rage. "You show blatant disregard for any form of discipline whatsoever, such as would try the patience of the highest saint! The King himself shall hear of all that I am tried with, mark my words!"

Adlai gave up trying to quell her tightening stomach, resignedly yielding herself over to mute silence. The continued assault of unfeeling words pierced her ears, like the barrage of a thousand tiny glass shards raining down in vicious torrents upon her. Milady carried on with agitated excitement, her voice echoing loudly back and forth between the stone floors and the high vaulted ceiling above, so that Adlai's face turned bright cherry-red from embarrassment. She was sure that every word of the headmistress' angry tirade could be plainly heard by the servants in the nearby quarters—all of whom had, undoubtedly, already been roused from sleep by the sounds of commotion in the hall.

Adlai made no answer in reply. To do so would, she well knew, only serve to make matters worse. Instead she did her best to keep a light step ahead of the older woman, as she was rudely thrust through corridors and down halls, at last coming to the foot of a long, wide staircase. Ardath had not ceased nor slowed at all in her vehement prating, the shrill sound of her voice carrying on relentlessly as she impatiently pushed Adlai before her.

"Of what use is it to waste the privilege of a prestigious education upon you, seeing that you care nothing at all for improving yourself in the *least*, nor in showing the slightest consideration to those around you?! No, indeed! And *what* do you demonstrate instead? Only recklessness and utter abandon!"

She paused only long enough to catch her breath, before continuing on in a tone of smug exaltation:

"Well, Lady Adelheide, we shall see what the King has to say to all this, upon his return! And since you care *nothing* for all that has been given you, perhaps the King shall at last find it fitting that you be flung from the house, and back to whatever poor, filthy squalor unto which you were born!" Ardath spat. "Then we shall *see* what will become of all your arrogance and fine airs!"

CHAPTER 7—THREATS

A sudden fear ran quivering through Adlai's core at these words. She was not in the least well-acquainted with her benefactor; he had left for the war while she had been only a child, and she scarce could even recall his face…She had…only *one*…fleeting and final memory of him, if indeed it truly was a memory…Whatever it was, it was all of what she sometimes thought she could remember of him, and it was only a shrouded fragment left in her mind's eye—one which seemed to pertain to a single event ten long years ago…

The King was standing atop the wide, open balcony of a magnificent palace, the ocean breeze blowing through his silvered hair and beard, stirring the fur-trimmed hem of his thick robes as he solemnly raised his right hand. The air all around thundered with loud shouts of acclamation, as throngs of people cheered and applauded their King. There was the hazy image of streets that were flooded by a sea of faces for as far as the eye could see. Garlands and wreaths of flowers mingled among the multitudes of banners and streamers flying gaily from every sector of a bedazzling city: every stone of its buildings and walled ramparts were lime-stone white, from its thick, massive walls facing a wide open sea, to the broad palisade and ivy-covered castle turrets rising high above the rest. The roofs of their graceful towers were a nesting place for the many gulls that flocked round about, driven thither by the gusty winds. Far below robust breezes stirred over the salty sea spray, its filmy waves washing up like soap on a laundering board against the cliffs' base. High above the ocean, the white cliffs of Daven—or so she thought they'd been called— soared upwards to reach the skies. Its precipiced peaks rose up steeply like a forbidding giant, looming high above the rise and fall of the ocean tides. It was upon the ledged cliffs of Daven that the city was peacefully situated—etched against cloudy, bright blue skies, its many brightly-colored flags flapping cheerily in the wind. Adlai vaguely thought she recalled snatches of lush, green gardens from within the palace walls, with flowering blooms of unrivaled beauty, such as she had never seen anywhere else since. And the name by which she'd heard the place called was one that sounded as sweetly to her ears, as the sight of it was lovely to her young eyes…Ruoyn Attilyn, the Citadel and crown jewel of Rhumendor.

…But it had all been so very long ago, that Adlai herself could not now be certain whether she *truly* remembered having actually been there, or if such glimpses from the past had been artificially recreated through things of which she'd heard tell. Perhaps such vivid imagery was nothing more than the dreamy beauty of imaginary things, drawn up during night slumbers while lost in the rare comfort of a contented dream. But whether real or imagined, the vision of that day in her memory was the last and only one she would ever have of the King from that day forth: for it was the same day upon which he'd led forth their masses of soldiers to go to war, far across the north-western seas…She could still vaguely remember seeing colorful bannerettes waving and streamers tossing wildly about on the wind of that bright, sunny day. Tallest and most beautiful of all, however, was the crest which stood flapping in the breeze above the bright fire of the King's golden crown: it was a single white rose emblazed against an azure background, with a gold embroidered border crossed parted per saltire behind it.

Why Adlai so vividly remembered so small a detail over all the rest, she never quite knew. She tried to draw out what details she *thought* she could still remember of the King himself—a hint of silver grey about his beard; a look of solemnity in his tall, proud bearing; a strong forehead, with brows knit together over eyes that (though calm and steady in expression), still belied a silent, brooding look of worry. Raising high his right hand, he accepted the excited acclamation of the crowds. Even if he had not been wearing a crown, Adlai thought that the nobleness of his bearing and stature set him apart and marked him as a true king. He stood tall, staunch, and silent, as if the presence of his person alone embodied the immoveable strength of a mountain fortress for all his people, and his crest a symbol of hope to weaker, more timorous hearts.

…Hushed rumors were already being whispered of the Shadow—for so it had been called—which they were to face across the great waters. Yet as for the King, if he'd felt any fear on that day, it was closely concealed. For many still blinded by the bliss of ignorance, it seemed a day of jubilation and festivities, and a chance for many an eager young man to earn his hire under the king's employ. Many a youthful face was filled with bright optimism at the chance for fame and glory, their giddy young minds swept away by the happy prospect of greater rewards awaiting them upon their return. Pretty young maids decked in bright floral wreaths turned out in twirling skirts and dancing steps to adorn the kingdom's brave warriors with garlands of flowers. For these, it was a moment filled with tears of affectionate pride, as lovers kissed and bade one another ado. Families embraced their fathers, brothers, and sons, and together the entire city gave them a fond and heart-felt fare-well, wishing them a safe journey and God-speed, until such a time as when they should be brought back together again.

…But alas, the coming months showed that a quick end to the war was not to be…Another season—and then two—came and went, as the country waited in earnest silence for any tidings from the front. And then slowly, like the creeping stealth of night, stories began to drift back…Trickling in came dreadful tales, filled with frightful, harrowing details, along with those solitary few survivors who crept back. Ghosts of men they were, some with soul-less expressions, others wild-eyed and muttering strange and deranged words. And through every village that they passed, a tremoring fear followed their departure and spread like a contagion. Yet what it was that they all whispered about, Adlai never knew exactly. But then one day she awoke to find the castle all a flurry of activity, and servants hurriedly bustling about in making preparations...they were leaving. Word had at last been sent concerning Willan and Adlai: they were to be quietly removed from the city for safe-keeping, and taken far away to the northeastern part of the kingdom, to the Manor of a remote little country town called Dombrey; there they were to wait for the war's end and the King's return.

And here they had waited ever since...But all that had been many years ago...And here, in this obscure and untouched, distant corner of world, all thoughts of both the king and the war seemed to have slipped away into the evanescence of faded memory...Here the sleepy little village carried on industriously as it always had for generations; the simple village folk toiled contentedly in the undisturbed surroundings of their little countryside, oblivious and blissfully ignorant to all that was transpiring elsewhere in the world...And so it was that very soon, in time, even Adlai herself had begun to forget what it was which had first brought them here. Even more, she had half forgotten all about the whispered fear that had gripped the hearts of the rest of the Kingdom. They had never known much of trouble here, and it was doubtful that they ever would...And the only troubling fear left to haunt and torment her anymore, was that of Lady Heromena of Ardath.

Now, with Ardath's threats still ringing in her ears, Adlai realized with dismay that she honestly knew little to nothing of the king at all. And when he should return, were that day ever to come, the sad truth of the matter was that at this point he would be little more than a complete and total stranger to her...He knew nothing at all about her. What if he believed Ardath's sharp, condemning accusations? Would he even care to trouble himself with investigating the truth surrounding a penniless orphan—a mere girl, whose existence had somehow (fortunately or not) been thrust upon him? He was monarchy...and she was an undesirable responsibility, with no personal merit whatsoever to offer…Even though his purse had generously afforded her upbringing, and she had supped regularly with the King's son, she knew in her heart that the reality was that they were entire worlds apart, with only a very fragile thread connecting their lives…And simply because Willan had a certain tolerant affinity towards her, did not mean that his *father* would feel the same, much less that he would have any reason to doubt Ardath's stinging description of her.

Adlai herself wasn't even sure anymore what the truth really was. As much as she bitterly resented the headmistress' harsh cruelty as undeserved, no one else seemed concerned over whether it was justified or not… The lonely truth was that the only one in all world (other than Willan, perhaps) who was actually concerned with her own fate, was Adlai herself.

"Well, what have you say to that, then?!"

The loud, echoing demand cracked itself again like a whip over her shoulder, so that Adlai's focus jerked back to the present. She could feel Ardath's eyes leering in the dark behind her, just as she could sense the satisfied smile curling on her lip.

"But Willan told you—we got lost," Adlai pleaded, straining her head around to catch glimpse of the headmistress. In an instant Milady's fingers seized upon her upper arm with such dreadful force that it made the girl gasp. Already she could feel dark bruises forming. With a wrenching twist Ardath spun her about to face her.

"*What* did you say?" Ardath practically hissed.

"I said that Willan already told you—" Adlai started meekly, but was instantly cut off by a sharp, hard slap across the face with the back of Ardath's hand.

"It's *Lord*! *Lord* Willan!" The older woman practically shrieked. "Or do you honestly presume to give yourself such rights of familiarity in addressing his Lordship? Even those who are *infinitely* above you in rank, birth, and position do not even dare to assume such boldness! Such audacious presumption!"

Milady was literally shaking with rage as she spoke.

"You are far too bold for your own good, my girl! He is the son of the *King*! And you dare to address him in so knave and bold a fashion?!"

She grabbed the back of Adlai's shift and shook her violently, knocking her to the floor.

"And who, pray tell, are *you*?"

Ardath's tone was now dripping with mockery and sarcasm as she bent over the girl.

"Some great lady, perhaps, like the ones in all those frivolous fairy-tales you pour yourself into, wasting time away in idle day-dreaming?"

Her words ran off— sharp, cutting, and abrupt, like the quick blade of a knife slicing through a tranquil fall of water.

"You're little better than a *pauper*, living like a leech off of royal favor!"

Ardath screeched out the last of her raging torrent of insulting injuries, her chest heaving and her whole frame shaking uncontrollably with rage. Her eyes were blazing like a wild-fire, burning like hot lead into Adlai's wide-eyed stare. The words stung deeply, like the bitter gall of vinegar. Adlai swallowed hard, trying her best to control the violent trembling that was running all the way down to her toes. Hesitantly she scooped herself up from the floor and straightened herself up, taking in a deep breath as her lips parted to speak:

"Sometimes a fantasy—is better—than a reality," she began haltingly in a low voice. "And even if they are only day-dreams, then at least I still have something to dream about—rather than live my life only to ruin the joy and happiness of others."

Adlai paused just long enough to take in another deep breath, squaring her shoulders back firmly as she stood tall. With determined resolve in her eye she looked evenly into the shocked face of Lady Ardath before continuing:

"I'd rather waste my life in hoping for a better one, than settle for the kind of life *you* lead."

Ardath's whole face was aghast with speechless shock, and her jaw dropped open in mute surprise. But quick as the darting tongue of an asp she recovered herself. In an instant her hand streaked through the air and struck Adlai across the face…*hard*… a ring on her bony finger just grazing the side of Adlai's mouth.

"I have borne with *all* that is within my patience to bear— no one else would have lasted near as long as I!" Ardath was again trembling with anger. "I was entrusted with your up-bringing, and in seeing to it that you were made into a fine lady of court—but you are utterly beyond all help! You have obstinately chosen again and again to remain in the same stupid ignorance and crudeness of manner to which you were born! I see now that trying to turn a wild one such as you into a proper gentle-woman of the king's house is nothing short of a ridiculous joke, and I will be mocked no more!"

Adlai felt a small droplet of warm blood swell into a tiny pool on the cracked edge of her lip, then trickle and run off down the side of her chin from the place where Milady's ring had left its mark. Her tingling mouth already felt numb and slightly swollen, as she discreetly licked over the puffy area with the tip of her tongue. She well knew that she scarce did not dare wipe it away, as long as she remained in Ardath's presence. Adlai lowered her eyes to the floor in feigned submission, all the while fighting hard to hold back the tempest of rage welling up inside her. Bracing herself, she waited for more of Ardath's fury.

"And don't fool yourself for an instant, by believing that I am truly as blind and ignorant as you should like to believe!—I well know that his Lordship meant only to protect *you* with his trite explanation as to your long absence this night! I am not so mindless and stupid a simpleton— I well know what a wicked, head-strong girl you are!"

Her gaze narrowed in a look of deep hatred, bitter disdain smoldering hot like fire in her eyes:

"You were meant to be my torment!"

Ardath hissed through her teeth, nodding her head vehemently as though vigorously affirming her own strong conclusions. The headmistress suddenly lowered her voice, as she crept closer towards the girl. There was a menacing look in her expression—a cold, almost deathly look. Adlai felt a prickling

shiver of fear go tingling down her spine; in silence she held her
breath and waited in dreaded expectation.

"I know that you are sent to be his undoing!" Ardath
hissed again. "What else could be expected from the progeny of
wanton licentiousness?! The sin in which you were conceived
clings to you still—like dry rot in your bones, vice running thick
like a foul poison in your blood!"

Adlai stifled a sudden cry of pain, as the older woman's
steely grasp again pinched her arm so tightly that it made her
wince. Ardath shook her violently, breathing heavily as she
continued:

"I well see what is your intent—how with sultry charms
and vixen ways ye seek to bewitch and take him for your own! I
have seen the dark lust that lurks behind your gaze every time you
look upon him! You daily stalk his steps as if he were prey to you!
Well!"—Milady stopped short as she again nodded vigorously to
herself. "*He* may not yet fully realize what manner of creature you
are, but *I* am not unaware of all your devices!"

Ardath leaned in so close that she practically brushed
Adlai's face, as she lowered her voice even more:

"And of this one thing you may be *well* sure of, Lady
Adelheide: that I shall lie cold and dead in my grave, 'ere I *ever*
allow him to be ensnared by *you*! I won't allow you to be his ruin!"

Adlai stared incredulously at the older woman: could it be
that all her self-imposed austerity and inflexible rigidity had at last
brought her to the breaking point—that she was, in fact, teetering
upon the brink of insanity? It was no secret that she had long kept
a sharp and protective eye over Willan (she had done so for as far
back as Adlai could remember), but her present deep-set jealousy
over Willan's affections (along with the menacing tone of her
ridiculous accusations) bordered upon utter madness. Adlai
blinked but made not a single sound in reply. Her former
embarrassment at Milady's loud and angry outbursts was gone
now; in it's a place a chilling new fear was creeping over her.
Inwardly she now hoped that someone at the manor had already
been awakened by the noise, and would presently appear to
investigate… There was something darkly ominous and evil in the

old woman's eye, almost murderous in its look...*What did she intend to do?...Surely she would never dare...?*

"Your days here are numbered, my fine Lady!" Ardath leaned forward and whispered in her ear. "You are neither his equal, *nor* mine! As such you are still under my jurisdiction, and believe you me—I shall see to that you *never* forget your place here again!"

They had reached the landing at the top of the stair, and the headmistress turned now to throw open the darkened doors to Adlai's bedchamber, and with a hard shove promptly flung the girl inside.

"Best get what sleep is left to be had," Lady Ardath warned as she drew herself up resolutely to full height, "For I shall see you bright and early on the morn. And mark my words, Adelheide: starting tomorrow I intend to put an end to all of this, and to utterly abolish your rebelliousness once and for all!"

The doors slammed shut behind her. For several moments they stood quaking and rattling in their frames. Adlai still stood guardedly, heart pounding in her chest, the sound of the headmistress' threatening words still resounding in her ears. At last the brisk echo of Ardath's retreating footsteps gradually faded down the passageway, and Adlai sank wearily against the wooden doors, a sad sigh heaving up from her chest. She glanced down for a moment, gingerly fingering the new-found bruises on her arm as she squinted in the dark to examine them. At last her arms dropped dejectedly to her sides and she gazed forlornly about her, a hollow ache beginning to grow from some place deep inside her. Ardath's words cut—yet why they hurt so, she did not know. This sort of cringing pain stemmed from more than being merely cast aside and utterly rejected as a person. It was the hurt caused by the slanderous accusation that she was practically no better than a courtesan or whore from the ale-house, seeking to elevate her own position through winsome manipulations. It now seemed as if all of the precious, tender feelings that she had ever cherished in the sacred places of her heart had been viciously stripped bare— defiled and made contemptible through the dirty, perverse nature of the accusation...Did everyone there at the Manor know of her foolish pining for the King's son? She felt suddenly naked and vulnerable, covered over by the muddy shame of ruthless projections...*Why couldn't Ardath just let her be? What so obsessively compelled her to continuously torment her from day to day, as if Adlai herself had no right to feel anything other than total shame and guilt for the crime of her own pathetic existence?...Did she truly have no right to hope for anything better than the paltry pittance of notice which had (reluctantly) been bequeathed to her?*

It hurt deeply to be accused of bringing Willan to ruin for the sole, selfish goal of personal gain...perhaps all the more so because deep down inside, she knew that she already *had*, very nearly, been his destruction. He had risked his life for her—and all because of her childish prank, which had nearly claimed both their lives *twice* in a single night...The blood-guilt for his death, had he not survived, would have been on her head, alone.

Heromena of Ardath had always seemed to possess an unnaturally keen intuition, along with shrewd insight—almost as if she had the ability to see right into Adlai—and detecting her thoughts with startling accuracy...Could it be that Ardath actually saw deeper into Adlai's own nature, than she herself had supposed?

...There was always something strange in the air whenever Ardath was near—a queer, surging sort of energy that always seemed to lurk in the headmistress' shadow when she passed. It had often seemed to Adlai that there was something—almost like a personal presence—that was much more forbidding and mal-intended than the mere visible appearance of Lady Ardath alone. Yet what it was precisely, Adlai herself could never quite put her finger on.

The outer verbal cruelty and physical abuse she suffered was only *half* the gnawing torture her inner psyche was forced to endure. The other half of it was fear. Every passing day was strangling her into silence... She was drowning. And the frightening secrecy surrounding her daily existence was only increased by the mute denial and willful obliviousness of others. Even the servants avoided conversing with her, as though she were a contagion of the plague. The impending threat of the headmistress' dire displeasure was one which none would risk breaching. No one ever seemed easy within the castle Manor; for the most part all moved about briskly, silently, as if afraid to be either heard or seen…Willan was Adlai's very last—her *only*— hope of salvation. If he too ignored her helpless plight, then she would truly be forsaken…

A stifling sense of despair suddenly engulfed her at this thought: what if the only future left to anticipate was one of weary futility, endlessly living out her days alone and forgotten inside these stone walls, with nothing else to look forward to, no loving arms to embrace her?…*Nothing* could be worse than that…Death itself would be a better fate, rather than to have to go on and on like this.

…Even more eerily frightening, it seemed that the farther away everyone else became, and the harder Adlai tried to shake free, the stronger Ardath's presence seemed to grow, like thick cords coiling tighter and tighter about her. It was creeping like a black phantom into her subconscious and sliding itself across her thoughts, drawing her mind deeper and deeper into the dark, twisted labyrinth of the older woman's psyche…Hard as she tried to banish the notion away, there were times when she feared that she would one day be completely swallowed up in the same vengeful madness which had over-taken Ardath… Was it merely coincidence, this uncomfortable sensation she had, that they seemed gradually becoming more and more closely linked, like the binding relationship between an iron-handed task master and a bonded apprentice?…How much longer could she keep holding on while others looked away?

Adlai tried to shake such thoughts from her mind…She felt with a prickling, uncanny certainty that, were she to continue dwelling on such things, she would truly lose herself utterly—and she could not…*she would not*…risk losing her mind, along with everything else…No, the more insane her world became, the more vigilant she must remain in order to stay in control…She would go to a place deep inside herself which Ardath could not touch, a place where there was no past, no present, and no future…Adlai took a deep breath, closing her eyes as she slowly allowed her consciousness to sink to a place far away and deep down inside her...Feelings of fear, of dread, of anything at all slowly gave way to a feeling of numb...nothingness...She might not be able to control anything around her, but she would learn to control her own emotions—even if it meant temporarily having to snuff them out altogether...Someday it would be safe to feel some things again, but not now...the survival of her own sanity depended upon her ability to free herself of all emotional attachments...Pictures, words, all of it began to be slowly erased from her mind, till at last her thoughts were nothing more than a white-washed, blank open space of mindless nothing...There was no sight, no sound here...Adlai's mind cleared, and she slowly reopened her eyes.

Her stomach suddenly rumbled, and with a groan she rubbed it ruefully. Her heart was not the only thing that was now empty. Her mind briefly wandered to what Willan might be doing. He was probably somewhere down in the mess hall below, sure to already be enjoying a side of mutton, salt pork, or one of the cold meat pies from the kitchen, perhaps along with the previous day's baked bread, and a mug of ale from the mead and wine stores. Her mouth began to water at the thought, while her stomach rumbled so loudly that she had to press her fist into the hollow pit of her gut. Miserably she turned away and looked about her room in an effort to distract her mind from her hunger pangs.

The south wing was a very large and spacious room, but very drafty tonight. A great carved bed lay off to the side, hung with heavy tasseled curtains of burgundy and embroidered damask. There was a dressing table, wardrobe, a small fireplace set into the stone wall across from the bed, and a few other choice items about the room; but otherwise it was rather bare. There were tall windows on the north and eastern walls which opened up into a large view of the courtyard below. In the starlight, one might still be able to make out the walls of the terraced gardens off to the north-eastern end of the Manor estate. The dim light of the moon stole through the icy glass window-panes, and slid past limp, partially-drawn curtains to shine briefly upon a single log lying cold upon the hearth. Adlai shivered, rubbing her stiff fingers over her goosy skin, then stopped short: her hands felt raw. Squinting in the dark, she held up her dirtied hands to have a better look: her knuckles were chapped and bloodied. With another sigh she shuffled wearily to the dressing table, lifting a brass pitcher as she tilted it over the nearby wash basin. Something splashed loudly from the pitcher into the bowl. In the dim moonlight she could make out chunks of ice and frozen particles floating in the water. With a grimace she gingerly dipped her hands. The freezing water stung, its bite sinking deep into the raw, open cracks of her skin. Adlai scrubbed as fast as she could, then shook the water from her hands. Wrapping her arms about herself she ran hurriedly to the bed and sprang under the covers, flinging the damp, cold bedclothes over her head as she did so. She could see her breath forming into frosty vapor in the air above her face. For a long while she lay stiff and shaking, till at last the trembling in her limbs subsided. Her eyes grew heavy, and at last she drifted off into sleep…

CHAPTER 8—INSULT

Adlai awakened with a jolt, as she was roughly roused from her slumbers by a strong hand on her shoulder.

"Come now, 'tis way past time to be up and about, and you have a new schedule to keep to!"

Ardath's voice broke out like the sudden shock of a clap of thunder from cloudless skies. Adlai groaned in protest, as her head collapsed back upon the pillow. It had been a night of very poor sleep, owing to the fact that the chill of the room had constantly awakened her, leaving her to toss and turn in her bed. Yet still she was certain that she *had* been asleep, for she remembered dreaming—and what a strange, disturbing dream it had been, too. In it a crow had suddenly swooped before her face—and then she had seen Storm. He was half dead but alive, his proud head bent low, and his body so worn and weary that he barely moved. He was being led slowly back to the Manor by the hand of a strange personage, whose visage had been completely concealed so that she could not make out the face. Then in the middle of the dream she had awakened with a start to find herself suddenly sitting upright in bed. She thought she distinctly remembered having heard a noise which had caused her to wake, yet as she sat there blinking in the darkness it could not be heard anymore. Her head had just begun to sink back onto her pillow, when she thought that she'd caught sight of something—a quick movement, like a long shadow moving across her floor from the direction of the window. With that Adlai had been suddenly wide awake. She did move nor make a sound as she stared warily out the window, yet nothing was to be seen, except the branches of a tall tree striking against the glass as it waved in the wind. Slowly she relaxed. It had been nothing more than the wind and branches beating against the panes. And besides, she thought sleepily to herself, her bedchamber was set much too high for anything more than a stray bird to cast a shadow into. She had drifted slowly back to sleep after that, yet it had seemed that she had been asleep only a short while, when she was suddenly reawakened by Lady Ardath.

"Hurry along and be up with ye, now; we've much to accomplish today," the headmistress said crisply, as she briskly swept across the room to draw back the curtains. Adlai groaned again and covered her head as brilliant sun-light flooded in and blinded her eyes.

"Starting today," Milady continued shrilly, "Your formal education in becoming a proper gentle-woman of refined manners and good breeding is to begin."

The brisk thud of Ardath's shoes pounded heavily across the floor, as she made her way swiftly towards the bed, and in an instant flung the blankets off Adlai's cold body. Groggily, the girl slowly sat up and wearily rubbed the sleep from her aching eyes. It did no good to argue or protest.

"I have tried my best to properly train you, but it would seem that quite *obviously* I have failed. I have chosen therefore to enlist the aid of other tutors to assist me in my task, so that we may yet be successful in changing you from a half-spoiled and unruly child, into a young lady of *some* accomplishment."

Ardath hesitated for a moment as she busily brushed her hands down over the front and sides of her cote-hardie.

"Or at the very *least*, we shall succeed in making your presence less crude and intolerable, so that you might be presented without further embarrassment to the King when he returns."

Other tutors? Adlai sat up quickly at this news. Other tutors for *what*?! She wasn't a man, and she wasn't going to rule the kingdom one day like Willan, she thought to herself irritably. In fact, she wasn't *ever* going to be doing *anything* important. She was never going to be in any position whatsoever which might require her to have any further education. Girls and young women were not expected to know more than the simple duties of overseeing household affairs, and it was clear that Adlai would never be doing much of that either. What, therefore, was the point of an "education"?

"I expect you washed, dressed, and to have eaten breakfast by half past the hour. Be in readiness to meet your new instructors."

Milady flatly rapped out her orders in rapid succession as she headed towards the door, then paused briefly as she turned to the serving woman who had just entered:

"See to it that she's made ready in time."

The servant nodded silently, and Lady Ardath swept from the room. Adlai was suddenly wide awake at these last instructions, and immediately began scrambling from the bed. The severe headmistress of Dombrey was a force to be reckoned with on any given day; much more so now that she had already fallen so far from grace. Hurrying to her closet, she flung open the doors and nimbly reached inside for something to wear, then instantly stopped short. Slowly, she pushed open the doors of her wardrobe and gasped: all of her clothes were gone. In their place were two rows of the same identical frock folded neatly upon each shelf, all plain and uninteresting in appearance, and all of the same coarse, faded grey. There was hardly any difference between these garments and those of a common household servant, except that even the servants' clothes had more color. In silence she thumbed her way through their somber assemblage: there was a total of seven dresses in number, precisely one for each day of the week. Adlai swallowed hard. Was she really to be forced into wearing such drab attire from now on? Was she never to be allowed to wear anything pretty again? She turned to look back at the coifed middle-aged serving woman remaking the bed.

"Please," she asked slowly of the heavy-set woman, "Am I really, *actually* meant to wear these? ...Where are all my other clothes?"

"Don't ask questions, Milady, just do as ye've been told, or we'll *all* pay!" The servant snapped as she puffed back with the steaming breakfast trays. "Ye can see there what ye're to put on; best 'urry, now!"

The woman bustled towards the door with dirty laundry to be taken to the wash room, calling behind her as she went:

"Now 'urry and get dressed, an' eat up yer porridge."

Adlai turned with a dismal face to see a simple breakfast of gruel and a cup of milk awaiting her. Was this poor fair *all* that was meant to tide her over till the noon-day meal, what when she had already gone near an entire day without food already? But the servant's sharp glare quickly roused her. Slowly and unwillingly she turned to obey.

It was already well after half past the hour, when Adlai at last rushed through the long corridors. Racing down halls she made her way in agitation to the solar, the castle's great drawing room and private study. She disdained the flavorless, lumpy gruel, and it had hardly served to satisfy her hunger. What precious little remained of her time she had spent before the looking glass, turning this way and that, attempting in every way possible to try and make herself look pretty from underneath her frumpy frock. Ardath had meant it when she had said that Adlai would never forget her place there again—being made to dress beneath the class of even the lowest ranking servant of the household staff was sure evidence of that. What was more, the bulk of the overly-large garment completely hid her form from sight, so that she almost had more the look of an older child, rather than that of a young woman. Was it truly the headmistress' intention, to try to make her look as homely and unwomanly as possible? With a final, impatient tug at the ill-fitting dress she had at last given up in frustration, and with an irritated grimace at her reflection, hurriedly scurried from the room. Ardath was sure to already be waiting, and no doubt her tardiness would receive much unwanted notice and further punishment, she thought to herself grimly. She was already muttering and cursing under her breath as she sped along.

"*Oh*!" Adlai let out a startled cry. She had been so fully wrapped up in her own thoughts as she sped along, that she had quite failed to notice a rather short personage who had just emerged from the adjacent hall. Without warning she had collided into him with a hard *smack*, knocking him and all he had been carrying with great force to the floor. In the twinkling of an eye papers and books were scattered everywhere, as Adlai looked down with stupefied embarrassment: a surprised, short little figure in long robes lay sprawled upon the stony floor, the hood of a long dark cloak completely flung over his head.

"Oh, I'm ever so dreadfully sorry!" Adlai gasped in apology. "Here, let me help you!"

She hurriedly extended her hand in offering. In a moment the hood was flung back, revealing the balding head and wrinkled, cherry-red face of a panting little man, an expression of surprised confusion on his face.

"Oh, yes! Thank you!"

He exclaimed with a ready smile, as he quickly grasped hold of her hand with gnarled fingers. Adlai hoisted him with difficulty to his feet. He was quite short, barely reaching her shoulder in height, yet at the same time he had turned out to be much stouter and heavier than he had first appeared, being fully swathed in yards upon yards of coarse, dark fabric. He had a very pleasant looking face, with a pair of sharp and brightly inquisitive eyes that peered out harmlessly from behind a pair of silver-rimmed spectacles perched high upon a thin, narrow nose. Beneath this, a broad row of smiling teeth were encompassed round about by a long, thin white beard that reached down to half past his middle. Quite without meaning to, Adlai found herself staring at him with piqued curiosity: the long white hair of his receding hair-line fell down lightly to his shoulders, and just barely hid from sight a long pair of ears with elongated tips that curled upwards against both sides of his head. The little gentleman seemed to notice Adlai's fixed stare, though he made no remark, but hastily recoifed his aging head with a small white cap. Without a word he quickly stooped and began to regather his things. Adlai recovered herself and hurried to help him retrieve his scattered collection of old books, tattered parchments and rolled up scrolls strewn over the floor stones. She quickly assisted in collecting them all into a large bundle, and then placed it—precariously—atop the tall, cumbersome stack of books he had already loaded into his arms.

"I do hope that nothing's damaged or missing at all," Adlai said apologetically.

"Not to worry, not to worry!" The little man replied quickly with a cheery smile; "I know all of these old books like the hind knows the mountains! If anything should happen to be gone, I have committed it all to memory anyway."

Adlai smiled back in relief. She already felt very much at ease with this strange little man, and she was beginning to think that he was one of the most amiable and congenial sort of persons she had ever yet met.

"I'm Adelheide," she began with a quick bow of her head and a short, grateful smile. "Err—Adlai," she interrupted herself with a dismissive wave of her hand, "And you are—?"

"Lucius Hindley—Doctor Lucius Hindley, at your service." He replied with a gracious yet awkward bow, taking great pains not to upset his precious bundle of books.

"I'm very pleased to know you," Adlai rejoined.

"Adelheide! We are waiting!"

The shrill, harsh tone emanating from behind her made the smile vanish away instantly from Adlai's face. With a start, she turned to see the darkened form of Lady Ardath etched inside the shadowy doorway of the solar at the far end of the hall.

"I must be going," she whispered in a hushed tone to Dr. Hindley, who gave her a quick, silent nod of understanding.

Ardath's eyes trailed slowly up and down Adlai's form with practiced deliberation, as the girl hurriedly scurried to where she awaited. Adlai kept her head bowed in submission, barely daring to raise her gaze to meet that of the headmistress. Perhaps if she could satisfy Ardath into believing that she was really, truly penitent, this whole matter might be dismissed the more quickly, and her privileges and personal articles might be returned the more speedily to her. At the very least, she told herself, perhaps if she changed her tactics she might actually get the chance to get ahead in the game…

"I see that you have found your new attire!" Lady Ardath stated briskly in her usual sharp tone.

"Please—am I never to wear anything—but *these*?" Adlai queried softly.

"Full adherence to the mandates laid out for you shall be enforced, as of this hour," Milady drummed out in a loud voice. "I expect from now on that you will arrive punctually, no exceptions! Your daily regimen from breakfast till supper has been carefully planned, so that there shall be *no* lapses of time to waste in idleness, and I shall expect you to give thorough attention to your studies. Any changes or alterations you should make to these guidelines, no matter how small *you* deem them to be, shall result in swift and severe discipline!"

Adlai decided that she would rather not find out exactly what sort of severe discipline Milady meant, so she bowed her head in submissive acknowledgement and hurriedly tip-toed past her.

"Gentlemen!"

The headmistress cleared her throat as she turned away from the girl to address a small gathering of heavy-robed figures (which, hitherto, Adlai had failed to notice were present). She flushed with embarrassment now, to think that she had already been so harshly reprimanded and made a spectacle of before a room full of total strangers, when not so much as an introduction had yet been made.

"I wish to present your pupil: Lady Adelheide, of the House of DuReiyne."

Adlai lifted her eyes and looked about with discomfort at the solemn gathering of elderly tutors waiting opposite her. All bowed gravely in reply. Each wore some variation of the same dull look: uninterested, vacant, and critical. Each looked as if he had spent his whole life locked away in a library, pouring over dusty books and delivering boring lectures to young male scholars. The uncomfortable looks and sideways glances from several indicated that most likely *none* of them had ever before had a young student of the female sex under their tutelage.

"Lady Adelheide, your tutors: Professor Langton, who is to supervise your studies in mathematics and science; Professor Worrell, responsible for geography and politics; Professor Oswald, who shall further lead you in literature, writing and speech; and Professor Ainsley who shall offer instruction in dance, poetry, and music—he shall see to it that you are perfected in all the customary arts of which other young ladies of court are expected to demonstrate knowledgeable capability. I myself shall continue to oversee your progress in needlework, embroidery, and in seeing to it that in every way you look, act, move, speak, and *think* like a young woman of proper breeding."

Adlai glanced about awkwardly and managed a half curtsy. Professor Langton was a very tall, thin, elderly man, with a scholar's hat standing high on his head and pulled down low over his ears. His small eyes appeared withered and dim against the sunken, sallow features and bony protrusions of his face, and he had a thin white beard that trailed down to his collar. His vacant, watery eyes had barely flickered in any direction, nor had his countenance changed in the least throughout the entire introduction. He stood utterly motionless; the only sound made (other than that of nasal breathing through his partially open mouth), was that of the floorboards that creaked beneath the stretch of his yawning frame. Indeed, Adlai thought to herself that he looked more ready to fall into his grave, rather than to be stepping into the active role of a tutor.

Professor Worrell was a balding, middle-aged looking man of corpulent figure and wide girth, with a pair of sharp eyes that looked out piercingly from behind his wire spectacles. His thick lips held a perpetually dour and pursed expression upon his squarely-set jaw, and he had neatly combed side-burns that grew down in wiry profusion over his chops.

Professor Oswald was a slightly built older gentleman with silver hair and clean-shaven face, who smiled in a dignified manner and nodded impressively to everyone present.

The youngest (and seemingly most able-bodied of them all) appeared to be Professor Ainsley, (being of yet still in possession of a full head of ungreyed hair, and noticeably fewer wrinkles than all three of the former). He was a man of medium height who appeared to have not yet reached his fortieth year, and his brown hair and beard were closely trimmed. He handled himself in a somewhat uncomfortable and self-conscious manner, for he tended to carry himself rather rigidly and with vaguely awkward, hesitant movements; also, he seemed inclined to want to avoid (as much as possible) from making eye contact with any of the others.

Milady finished her long introduction, then looked about with furrowed brow as if still searching for someone.

"It seems that there is yet one to our party who is missing—pray, has anyone present seen any sign of Professor Hindley?"

Adlai's eyes lit up for an instant as she looked up with a start: Could it be true? Was the same strange, interesting little man she had previously met in the corridor actually going to be one of her new professors? All eyes turned questioningly to each other now, as heads slowly shook in reply, and a few muttered indistinct answers. Presently there was a muffled knock, and the door was instantaneously propped open. Dr. Hindley was puffing steadily, and he wore a very strained expression from behind his great parcel of books, though he still wore his cheery smile.

"Ah!" He cried as he entered. "I found this room with some difficulty, but am now here at last!"

His cheeks and nose were noticeably ruddier than before, and he was still laboring with painstaking efforts to keep intact all of his precious documents. He waddled with slow, awkward steps across the room, taking great care all the while to maintain with careful balance the handful of loose scrolls atop the tall stack of books. Tiny little beads of perspiration could be plainly seen forming across his forehead, sticking to the wet, curly wisps of silver hair framed around his face. Reaching a nearby table he heaved them atop, resting for half an instant to mop his brow as he turned to face everyone else.

"I trust I have not kept anyone waiting?"

He panted with a smile, nodding to all who were present. He looked even shorter and more peculiar now than he had before, barely reaching past the waist of Professor Langton in height (who was by far the tallest and thinnest figure in the room).

"Ah, Professor Hindley," Lady Ardath greeted him with feigned cordiality, barely attempting to disguise the galled resentment in her voice. She made little effort to conceal the brewing expression of wry displeasure gathering like storm clouds on her face.

"We had just finished with the introductions, but since I see that you share in your pupil's avid enthusiasm for timeliness, I suppose we must make them again."

Adlai cringed at this very rude address towards the Doctor, wincing inwardly to herself as she noticed that the color in his cheeks suddenly paled. It was evident that he was not at all accustomed to being so impolitely and impoliticly treated. He replied not a word in redress, however, but maintained his composure, smiling warmly and bowing his head respectfully to each one in their turn, as Milady once again went through all the introductions.

"Gentlemen and Lady Adelheide, this is Professor Lucius Hindley, instructor in both history and philosophy."

All bowed gravely again, as Ardath let out an impatient sigh and finished with her final address:

"I trust you all have been shown to your quarters and find the accommodations sufficient. Lessons are to begin promptly each morning at nine o'clock, and all meals are observed in the mess hall at the hours of eight o'clock and twelve noon, with supper to be served at the sixth hour." She hesitated, then continued: "And now I shall leave you to your lessons with your pupil."

The headmistress gave a quick, curt nod of her head and turned with rustling skirts to depart from the room.

"Oh, I beg apology, Lady Heromena," Dr. Hindley interrupted quickly, but I inquired of the servants, and there seems to be none yet who knows where my quarters are kept."

He hesitated for a moment under the dark bristling look of the headmistress before venturing further:

"I wonder if you might be so kind as to look into the matter for me, so that I might be able to put my things in order?"

Ardath's mouth tightened into another hard, white line. No one except the young Lord of the House ever dared address her by other than her surname.

"I'll see that the steward sees to it at once," she answered dryly.

She turned once more to leave, then stopped short at the door, as she turned back to look in Adlai's direction:

"Lady Adelheide, I strongly advise that you make good use of the time and knowledge that is being afforded you, for I expect to receive a daily report from your tutors as to your progress in each subject. All of your studies are to be completed precisely within the allotted time. If they are not, your meal-times will be used to make up the uncompleted work, along with all *other* unscheduled time you might have left. Any privileges yet remaining will be suspended, until such a time as I see fit to return them."

Ardath began to leave again, then hesitated once more as she faced the Doctor:

"Oh, and Professor Hindley, I understand that you have come to us under rather high recommendations. I trust I can be sure that you shall be the proper example of punctuality and timeliness to your pupil, and that you shall uphold her full adherence to the same standards?"

Dr. Hindley's face blanched still further than before at this discourteous admonition, yet once again he answered nothing in reply, but cordially gave her an assenting nod of humble acknowledgment.

"I shall ask that the steward see to it that your apartments are kept some place where you shall not be at all disturbed in your studies," Milady continued. Then with another quick nod of dismissal, she turned and swept out the door.

CHAPTER 9—FOREBODING

The hours droned on tediously throughout the morning. Adlai tried to pay attention to her lessons, but her thoughts continued to drift away to other things. It was hardly plausible to think that all of this could have happened so suddenly overnight— no, the headmistress must have been anticipating this change far in advance, and been busily making preparations long before she saw fit to make mention of it. How else could she have summoned tutors so quickly, and already have each one equipped with a precise schedule? Adlai found herself wondering glumly why the headmistress bothered with her education at all, seeing that she had already made it abundantly clear that she viewed all such efforts as a vain and futile waste. The only likely explanation she could think of was (aside from the fact that Ardath seemed more determined than ever to keep her apart from Willan) that this decision must have had something to do with private instructions Milady had received from the King, in regards to her up-bringing. Perhaps Ardath feared that Adlai's independent disposition (and rather less than lady-like behavior) might attract ill notice from the King on his return.

...Adlai shoved her thoughts irritably away. Why bother with trivial details now, and what did it matter how or why these changes had come? This was her present lot; that was all there was to it. And she was sure now, beyond a shadow of a doubt, that this was exactly where she would be forced to stay. Her days of freedom (what little there was to be had) were over now. She was quite certain that Milady intended to keep her so busy with her studies, that she would never again have the opportunity to venture beyond the Manor walls. Yes, she thought grimly to herself; Ardath knew *exactly* what form of punishment was most sure to triumph in breaking her spirit down to a humbled state of submission. Adlai slumped dismally in her chair at this bleak, unhappy thought: she might as well be a prisoner locked high away in dungeon tower—there was *nothing* worse than being deprived of her freedom...At least in a prison one still owned the right of privacy to one's own thoughts. Here she was doomed to have her ears continuously filled by the ceaseless, dull pratings of tutors from morning till night. One series of boring lectures after another, each one delivered in a short variety of flat, monotone voices. None of them carried the slightest note of conviction in their tone, nor indicated the belief that either the subjects they taught—or their pupil—was of very significant importance. The only bright possibility she could foresee, was the afforded opportunity of being able to study history and philosophy with Dr. Hindley. At least *he* seemed an interesting, lively sort of person, and she felt quite reassured that their future hours of study together would be wholly pleasant, perhaps even thoroughly enjoyable.

...But as the morning wore on, she began to wonder when this was to be; she had not seen the good Doctor since his departure earlier that morning. Lessons had begun with Professor Langton, and Adlai herself seemed to be the only one who had *not* been informed as to any of the new tutors' schedules. Thus she surmised that she would simply have to be patient and bide her time, until either he made an appearance or they should chance to cross paths again. She was now well into her second period of study; Professor Worrel was still droning on in tersely-delivered sentences, and seemed momentarily unaware of her distracted day-dreaming. Cautiously she set down her quill pen by its ink pot, as she slowly straightened up in her seat and turned to cast a glance over her shoulder: the world outside the study window was bright and sunny beyond the hostile confines of the Manor walls. A little bluebird had come and landed on the window sill, hopping gaily about as he cheerfully chirped his song. He seemed almost instinctively to know how she felt, for he cocked his head to one side for an instant to study her, before turning to fly off and continue his song elsewhere. Adlai let out a sigh. How she wished she were a bird…Then she could fly away from here and be free of the dreadful Lady Heromena of Ardath, together with all the binding chains of imposed constraints.

Suddenly there was a slight commotion from the courtyard, followed by men's shouts and the sound of servants scurrying about. Adlai jumped from her seat and hurried to the window to see what was going on: down below, she could see Willan hurrying across the yard to meet some stable hands, who were just now leading a bedraggled horse to him… It was Storm.

Adlai let out a sudden cry, then dashed from the study and flew down the halls to the vestibule entrance. Her feet sped swiftly beneath her as she raced down corridors. Her head was so a whirl that she scarcely paused for breath as she darted through the great arched doors and bounded over the threshold steps outside. But her feet quickly slowed and then abruptly stopped short at the shocking sight which met her eyes: Storm was barely recognizable; the gloss of his shiny black coat was now covered with mud, his magnificent mane full of weeds and burrs. His regal head always held high was now bent so low beneath his drooping shoulders, that he looked more like a worn canal horse than the princely steed he been afore. Willan was gently passing him into the hands of the servants to be washed and tended to, as he turned back to speak with someone…It was a heavily cloaked stranger she had altogether failed to notice was present. Adlai could feel her heart beginning to pound harder and harder in her chest, as a little chill ran through her and she shivered in the light breeze. It was all just as she had dreamt. Storm was alive, and had been brought back to them by a peculiar stranger garbed just as this one… What did it all mean?

The stranger stood in a very hunched and stooped position, his body covered by a heavy, ill-fitting garment of very poor quality that was cinched about his waist by use of a wide, rough leather belt. A hooded gorget collar made of animal skin circled round about his shoulders, beneath which a faded grey russet cloak draped coarsely all the way down to his feet, where it trailed upon the ground. His hands were mostly hidden with thick hide wrappings cross-banded about the forearms with leather thongs. In his right hand he clutched a thick cudgel staff fashioned from the slender trunk of a tree; the height of its gnarled, intertwining roots reached just beyond his head as he leaned rather heavily upon it, continuing on in low discussion with Willan. Through the gaps of his cloak fluttering in the light wind, she caught a glimpse of deer-skin breeches, with heavy fur hides from knee to ankle—they were wrapped round about the most twisted, distorted pair of human legs she had ever seen— and held together by use of leather straps cross-gartered about the shins. He had feet which, at a single glance, appeared abnormally and disproportionately large in size, although there was little she could tell of them, since they were entirely concealed from sight by use of some crudely-made leather shoes.…Even though the stranger's face was not turned to her, Adlai got the distinct impression that he was suddenly and instinctively aware of her presence— that he could somehow *feel* her curious gaze scrutinizing him. For of a sudden he softly shifted his feet, discreetly drawing them in so that they were no longer visible, and hid them inside the long folds of his cloak. His hood he kept close over his eyes, concealing the upper half of his face as he continued to keep his head bent low, and leaned in more heavily upon his cudgel. Even with his back bent and hunched over as it was, Adlai could see quite plainly that he was inordinately tall in stature, for even in his stooped position he was equally as tall as Willan. The stranger barely looked up to make eye contact with the young lord throughout their discourse.

Adlai now had the eerie sensation that his focus had swiftly shifted itself from the conversation and was now keenly fixed upon her, though it was impossible for her to have yet passed within his scope of vision. Even as she quietly approached, she noticed that his shoulders grew suddenly stiff and taut; his posture tensed, almost like a wild animal when alerted of a new presence. For a split-second he paused indistinctly in the conversation, as his lowered hood moved ever so slightly in her direction. There was something unmistakably peculiar in what little she had made out of his person. But there was something else about him, something more than just the mere strangeness of his appearance…Something…that was both familiar, and which seemed to incite a frightening fascination…Time seemed, in a surreal sense, to have slowed to a complete stop—as if nothing and no one else but she and the stranger were any longer in existence. She could feel her feet beneath her moving numbly forward, while the only sound she was aware of was the thumping pulse of her own heart-beat echoing inside her ear drums…And much as she wanted to tear her consciousness away, there was an unearthly energy that was *willing* her to come to itself…*It* was calling to her. And something inside her was answering its call, whether she wanted it to or not.

Out of the corner of her eye, she thought she glimpsed Willan look up suddenly in her direction, as if he too had felt the stranger's attention suddenly divert to her. The stranger's head was now turning subtly towards her as the hood cautiously lifted, and for a split-second he looked her fully in the face. Adlai froze: a single streak of light brighter than the sun flashed from a somewhere inside his hood's shadow, filling up both her eyes with its blazing intensity. An eye—the same brilliance and color of a flame of fire—was staring straight back into her startled gaze, blinding her with its power. She could hear voices—strange voices—speaking, whispering to her, in a manner of tongue she had never heard before. All at once the radiant light spanned outwards into a wide arc, then instantly shattered in a hot explosion of brilliant color that penetrated inside her skull.

"Adelheide!"

Adlai blinked and shook herself. She was still staring with eyes locked on the stranger, but his head was again lowered and turned away, so that she could no longer see anything else from under the hood.

"Go on now—inside, and get back to your lessons!"

Willan's tone was so unusually sharp and stern in its command, that she jerked. The deathly look of warning in his eye was surprisingly severe…Yet behind it she thought she detected a slight trace of something else in his eyes…fear?

Of a sudden there was a loud screech. Adlai let out a startled cry, as a large crow dove down over her head, its feather tips barely glancing her face as it passed. Swiftly it sped through the air, then alighted calmly upon the Stranger's hunched shoulder, where it turned back to scrutinize her with black beady eyes. Adlai tried to recover herself and, without hesitation or further question, immediately turned on her heels and retreated hastily back to the house.

No sooner had the heavy arched doors creaked shut behind her, than she slumped in relief against the carved muraled wood, her head sagging breathlessly on her chest. She was trembling all over. What had just happened? For several dazed seconds she ransacked her fragmented thoughts, as she tried hard to recall exactly *what* it was which she'd seen in that instant. She could not distinctly recall much (if anything at all) of his visage, yet somehow she had a convicting sense that *he* had seen something in her. Her eyes had briefly connected with his, and in that second she'd felt as if something were being inexplicably drawn from her—as if her very thoughts had been pulled directly from her mind, delivered over by the sheer force of a will infinitely stronger than her own…What was it which he had seen, she wondered?…She was still greatly unnerved and perplexed, when the door suddenly opened behind her, and Willan himself stepped inside. Seeing her startled, he stopped short, then closed the door slowly behind him before turning to face her. There was worry in his eyes.

"Adlai, what is it? Are you quite all right?"

There was a note of concern in his voice as he anxiously studied her face. She nodded hastily.

"Who was that?"

"A sojourner pilgrim recently returned from abroad. He claims he found your horse caught in a miry bog, and that he recognized the crest and seal on his trappings. He's returned him safe to us now, and in return has requested food and lodging for the night. So I've allowed him to take up a berth in one of the stables."

"A pilgrim—from abroad?" Adlai began questioningly. "Then he must have news of the war—and your father! Perhaps if we invited him to sup with us at even-tide—"

"Adlai, listen to me carefully," Willan interrupted firmly. "I wish to make myself very clear: I do *not* want you to go near this man. In fact, I would like for you to keep entirely out of sight, for the short time that he will be with us."

Adlai nodded solemnly. There was an unmistakably pensive look on his countenance, as he studied her for several moments in silence.

"Willan, what is it?"

"I'm not yet sure that I fully know myself, but there was something very ill-favored about his appearance and manner. A sojourner—or a deserter—he may or may not be. 'Tis best either way that we be on our guard, in any event. These are uncertain times, and I have begun of late to hear more and more strange talk from abroad…Terrible, dark tales. Whatever is happening over there—well, it's enough to change the nature of any man….Please be careful, Adlai."

Adlai felt herself warm over the care in his voice. He seemed once more to be his old self, and their misadventures of the night before seemed (for some reason) to be now gone from his mind.

"Of course," she answered gently, laying a reassuring hand upon his arm. "I'll be certain to stay out of the way."

Willan clutched her hand in his and pressed it to him for an instant, looking deep into her eyes as he did. For a moment they stood in motionless silence together, Adlai lingering breathlessly in his gaze. Then abruptly he dropped her hand and turned away.

"I must speak with the steward in regards to our present guest," he said quickly, then hesitated as he turned to look at her once more. His eyes were lingering searchingly in her own, almost as if seeking to draw out the depth of her feeling. She could scarcely breathe, and all cohesive thoughts seemed to fly far out of reach.

"Thank you for coming to my rescue last night," she at last managed softly.

Willan stared at her for several seconds.

"I could not done otherwise," he whispered.

His fingertips brushed soundlessly over her face, gently caressing her. Laying his hand tenderly against her cheek, he softly traced over her cheek-bone with his thumb. Then suddenly he stopped. His hand dropped to his side, and he straightened up.

"Pray forgive me," he apologized hoarsely as he cleared his throat. "If you'll excuse me, I must tend to this at once."

He gave an abrupt bow, then turned and departed swiftly down the corridor. Adlai watched him go in silent bewilderment, the echo of his boots ringing in her ears even after their sound had already faded down the hall. *What had happened just now?...Could it be possible that it was his own feelings that he was in doubt of?*

"Ah-hem!"

Adlai started, as her bewildered musings instantly fled away. Lady Ardath slowly emerged from the shadows of the palisaded alcove adjacent to the vestibule, her eyes silently studying Adlai's face. *How much had she seen and heard?*

"Your tutors have been left waiting in impatience since you ran off," she said with slow deliberation as she approached. A cool smile played slowly on her lips. Adlai stiffened, swallowing hard as she tried not to tremble. *What would Ardath do to her now?*

"Adelheide, I do believe that I gave very *explicit* instructions, with regards to the propriety and decorum I expect you to demonstrate, along with the diligence you are to show towards your studies. But since your stamina is such that you are incapable of harnessing your attentions, even for a *mere* couple of hours—" she hesitated for finishing effect— "Your afternoon and evening meals for the day are now forfeited."

Adlai's dry mouth dropped open in mute surprise. However could the headmistress think that her concentration would be at all improved upon an empty stomach? Did she actually *intend* for her to fail?

Adlai looked searchingly into Ardath's eyes, trying to find even the slightest shred of human empathy, but all that stared back at her was empty, dark coldness. Without another word Milady turned away. After a few steps she paused and looked back.

"Oh, and one more thing, Adelheide: hereafter I shall see to it that your meals—which ever ones are rightfully earned through achievement— shall be delivered to your own personal apartments. Your company is neither needed nor required in the great hall, and I think it best for all that you have your meals in private. I shall join you when time can be spared."

Adlai stared speechlessly at her, aghast with amazement: meals in the great hall were practically the only times when she got to be in the company of *anyone* other than Lady Ardath. More importantly, it was practically the only time anymore that she got to see Willan, if then. What the headmistress was dictating was quite literally a prison sentence. And to add insult to the injury of being segregated off from all desirable company, she would now be forced to endure the oppression of Ardath's odious presence during the only time she had left to herself...It was unthinkable...Being made to eat all alone was infinitely preferable to that. Adlai's mind was swimming—it was all too much and too sudden.

"But—but I've always eaten in the mess hall before—with the others—" she faltered.

"*I* am not about to be made the laughing-stock of courtiers," Ardath cut in shrilly, "Who may mistake that I am trying to pass off a wild beast for a lady! I'm sorry that I am forced to take such measures," she added dryly, "But you are not the *only* one who will have to suffer through meal-times. I hardly enjoy being entertained by a barbarian, who gulps down her food and gnaws at bones like a ravenous animal." Her tone continued to drip with sarcasm—"So we shall both be forced to endure each other's company as best we can."

Adlai blinked in disbelief: surely Ardath could not possibly expect for her not to see through this; fabrications of such exaggerated proportions were nothing more than a weak excuse to cover other motives. She was enjoying the total control she now exercised in tormenting the younger girl under her authority. And she wanted to be there to watch Adlai's spirit slowly strangle and die.

Milady paused her delivery here for just a moment, as she gave up yet another resigned sigh of feigned tolerance:

"It's a burden which, for the present, I must graciously bear with the utmost patience."

These last words were spoken with a superior air of practiced forbearance, as the headmistress nodded solemnly, then briskly swept away, leaving Adlai staring blankly after her in stunned silence.

CHAPTER 10—DARK MEMORIES

The Manor had long lain in the sleeping quiet of slumber as Adlai turned uncomfortably about in bed, tossing this way and that. Many a futile effort was made to quell the rumbling thunder in her stomach, and dispel all tantalizing thoughts of food far from her mind. She was weak from hunger, and her head ached dreadfully. The rest of the day had gone very poorly indeed. After everyone else had departed for the noon-time meal, Adlai had been left alone to finish additional work in the study, and by the time her tutors had returned from the mess hall her stomach had already started growling. More than once she was embarrassed, as a startled tutor would be interrupted half way through his lecture by the loud complaints of her belly. At one such disruption Professor Worrell had shot her such a sharp, reproachful look, that Adlai had hung her head in shameful silence, while her face flushed purple with humiliation. She had spent the remainder of her distracted afternoon with the ball of one fist shoved deep into the hollow pit of her gut, in an earnest effort to suppress the battery of gurgling noises threatening to issue forth. By the time she had been dismissed for the day she was slightly faint and dizzy with light-headedness. True to her word, Ardath had kept herself well informed as to her progress, and had received none too glowing a report of the day's work. In the presence of all the gathered tutors, the austere headmistress had given Adlai a most severe lecture on the wanton vice of laziness, right before ordering the girl to go directly to her chambers. And after being promptly sent to her private apartments, Adlai was given more study-work to complete as discipline for her "inattentiveness" to her lessons that day, in addition to being forced to make up for the numerous mathematics she had incorrectly completed.

To Adlai's dismay, she saw that most of her tutors already seemed inclined to be persuaded by Lady Ardath's unfavorable view point. She had heard some of them whispering and muttering amongst themselves in the corridor as she'd passed, conferring in hushed tones one with the other. She did not need to wonder what the subject of their discourse was about—she well knew of whom it concerned. To have newcomers to the Manor—individuals who had only barely been introduced into her acquaintance—suddenly passing censured judgment on her, without being offered any chance at vindication, was a harsh and cruel injustice to swallow, indeed. Did her new tutors honestly believe the headmistress' expulsary diagnosis of her "willful, lazy disposition"? Or was it that they were more concerned with pleasing the egregious temperament of the pernicious Head-Lady of Dombrey Manor? For whatever reason they had accepted it, and whatever better impressions she might have hoped to make were now lost for good.

A sudden tear trickled down the side of her cheek, but she whisked it away with a brush of her hand. It was time to get used to the rejection. *But why did Ardath hate her so much?*

Adlai wandered through the farthest regions of her mind, trying to rack up as many memorable clues as she could concerning Heromena of Ardath. To her surprise, she now found that though it seemed she had seen the headmistress nearly every day of all her sixteen years, yet there was very little personal information regarding her of which Adlai herself was actually privy. Ardath had originally hailed from the North Country, but extremely little had ever been said on that subject. And she had been with the King's House for years, likely even before Adlai herself had been born, yet she never spoke of any other house or kin. Because of her elevated position and closer connections with the royal family, Adlai had often assumed that perhaps the older woman was distantly related to the king, thereby obligating the King's generous sense of nobility to sanction her with a provisory position in the royal house.

Adlai searched furtively, all the way back to the only inkling of a memory even resembling a clue… And it had happened so very long ago, that much of it was rather unclear to her now. Try as she might, she could not distinguish if it was in truth an actual memory, or if it was nothing more than the remnants of a child's vivid imagination mixed with a bad dream…She had often tried to bring it back, but a quivering fear always seemed to suppress it, pushing further away so as to bury it. What was it that her subconscious had so desperately sought to erase?

…All she remembered was that there had once been a very wet and stormy day, long, long ago, when she had been playing in the castle library with Willan …Adlai's eyes closed in the midst of her distracted wanderings, and her troubled thoughts trailed away into restless sleep…

Blurry details were fading away, and now the imagery was becoming quite distinct: she was facing the library doorway, an icy rain beating against the window-panes outside…A little girl with fiery red curls was sitting at a table across from a young boy.

"I'm tired of playing chess, Willan! And besides, you always beat me!" The younger child fumed in a petulant tone.

"Oh, come, come now, Adlai; it's just because I've more practice than you, but really—" the older boy tried patiently, "I *could* teach you how to play near as well as I."

"That's what you've said the last two games!" The little girl whined.

"You just have to be patient and learn the stratagem, like this—your problem is that you rely too heavily on the powers of your queen, while underestimating the powers of your knights."

As he spoke, the boy lifted a large ivory knight from a lavishly carved chess board by way of illustration.

"So far you've hardly used them at all, and have allowed them both to suffer easy capture."

"But I don't *like* using the knights; they can't move as quickly across the board!" The child complained sullenly.

"Well then, I should say that your weakness lies *not* in your ability to properly play chess," the boy said with a studious air, "But rather in your haste and impatience. Chess is a game which requires much deliberate attention and focus, Adlai—and *especially* patience."

The boy folded his hands together with a practiced sigh as he once again began a concentrated study of the board, ignoring his opponent's obvious disinterest in the game. The little girl rolled her eyes and folded her arms obstinately, a frowning pout formed stubbornly on her lower lip, and a scowl furrowed across her brow.

"Willan, I *want* to do something else!" The little girl exclaimed at last, flinging her arms exasperatedly to her sides.

"Oh, very well then," he answered with a resigned sigh. "And what would you prefer to do?"

"I don't know," she replied with a simple shrug, "Just something—something different."

The little girl's eyes wandered around the room. For just a brief moment she seemed to look straight through Adlai herself, as though she were no more than a mere shadow in the darkened doorway. Yet the child's eyes travelled on unseeing and circled back around again to the boy.

"Something…like exploring!" She exclaimed all at once. "I'm certain there are other parts of the castle we've never yet seen. We could make believe that we're discovering new worlds!"

"Adlai, I don't much feel like pretending. And anyway, if you've no more mind for our game, then I think I'd rather finish reading my book."

"What sort of book is it?" The little girl asked with mild curiosity.

"It's an epic tale of the battles fought by one of the legendary heroes of Olde."

"Yes, but what's it *about*?"

"It's about a famed warrior who fights to free a captive princess from the cruel powers of a sorceress."

"And does he rescue her at last?" The girl queried.

"Yes, though it's a rather sad ending."

"Why so?"

"He dies after saving her."

Both children were quiet for several moments. At last the girl asked slowly in a soft voice:

"Willan, have you ever *seen* a witch?"

The older boy looked up in surprise.

"No, of course not, silly girl! It's all just make-believe. Why do you ask?"

The child made no reply, but a pensive, almost frightened look was growing in her eye.

"Adlai," the older boy inquired in a more patient voice, "What is it?"

The girl still said nothing, but turned her head slightly in the direction of the library door, as if to see if anyone was listening to their conversation. Adlai slowly inched forward, her ears tingling intently to hear what the child might say next, though somehow she inwardly already knew the answer… If this was a vision of her younger self, then there was only one whom they both feared.

"Adlai…?"

"I think that Ardath is a witch!" The child burst in a breathless whisper.

The older boy laughed incredulously.

"Adlai, that's foolishness!" He reproved gently. "I know that Mistress Heromena does often look *rather* cross, but really, you oughtn't to say such horrible things! Whatever should make you think such dreadful thoughts?"

"Because of how she looks at me," the little girl replied in a stilled tone.

"Oh? And how does she look at you?" The boy asked, trying hard to sound sincere and not to openly laugh at the silly notions of the younger child.

"She sees me—even when she's not *actually* looking at me—it's as if she has eyes in the back of her head, just like witches have. And when she does look me in the face, it's as if she can see right through me—*into* me—as if she knows what I'm actually thinking, or what I've been about."

"Adlai," the boy said with patient sigh, "Adults *often* look as though they know what you've been up to—it's mostly to frighten you into being good, I think. Perhaps if you tried harder to be behave, you shouldn't so easily displease her," he finished dismissively.

With that he flopped down with a leather-bound book onto the cushioned seat of a carved wooden armchair.

"She can *feel* when I'm afraid," the little girl breathed tremulously. "And she relishes in it—she *means* to frighten me. And sometimes when she looks at me, it's as if she's speaking to me through her eyes—" (Adlai felt a shiver run trembling through her at the sound in the child's voice—) "Terrible, evil things—I can hear her thoughts whispering to me inside my head! I think she would kill me, if you were not here to protect me."

The boy laughed softly.

"Protect you from what, you silly girl?! Adlai, really! Why should Mistress Heromena want to do *you* any harm?!"

"Because—" she implored desperately "She's a witch!"

There was something in the strain of the little girl's voice that went straight to Adlai's core with a sickening tug: it was the desperate plea of utter isolation and helplessness, the same one that had been welling up inside of her for years, until now it was screaming.

"Well then, if you're so convinced that she's truly a witch, where's your proof? After all, witches are known to have magical instruments—books on the Dark Arts, and other such articles—what evidence have you?"

"I think that she keeps them secretly hidden away in her bedchamber, where no one else shall ever chance to find them."

"Really?" The older boy hid a dubious smile. "Adelheide, I think your imagination has *quite* run off with you!"

"Well?! Have *you* ever seen the inside of her bedchamber?!" The little girl demanded in agitation.

"No, but still—that doesn't mean anything—"

"If we only found a way to get in there somehow—without her discovering it—I just *know* we'd find something to prove what manner of creature she truly is!"

Adlai felt a cold fear go rippling through her being...This was the part that she could never quite remember, the part which her own memory had shut out and refused to acknowledge anymore. And whatever it was, she didn't want to go back to it again...*ever*.

"No!" She quivered, stumbling forward, "You—you mustn't!"

Neither of the two children seemed either to hear or be aware of her presence, however, and she realized that she was nothing more than a ghost to these visions of her past.

The boy raised his eyebrows quizzically, then shook his head.

"Adlai, enough with this nonsense. This is all total foolishness, and besides, you know we can't—"

"Are you afraid?" The little girl demanded accusingly.

"No, of course not! It's just that—well— we've no business intruding upon Lady Heromena's privacy."

The small child stood rigidly for several seconds, her pensive eyes searching each of his; a vividly stormy expression crept across her face and her eyes darkened with resentment.

"Very well!" She retorted with a bold defiance for her young years. "If *you* are not willing to see for yourself, then *I* shall just have to go in and bring back proof for you!—Then you'll not think I'm making up tales!"

All smiles completely disappeared from the older boy's face now, and he paled substantially.

"Adlai, no—you can't! If you're caught, you'll be severely punished—"

"I'd rather be punished, than have you think me a liar," she replied with stubborn resolve. But after several moments her lower lip began to tremble.

"Willan, please—there's no one else who'll believe me!" She pleaded. Her eyes filled with desperate tears.

The boy sighed sadly and shook his head.

"Adlai, I'm sorry—I just can't—"

He reached out to place a loving hand on her shoulder, but she shook it away angrily. Clearing her eyes, the little girl straightened herself up rigidly, the hurt of bitter disappointment piercing through her tone:

"I should've known you'd never believe me—you always take her side! But if you won't protect me, then I shall have to protect us both!"

With that, the little girl turned away and walked resolutely from the library, leaving the boy gazing after her in concerned reluctance.

…For several moments the older Adlai stared numbed and mystified into his unseeing eyes—she was as much confounded by his response, as she was by the gulf of overwhelming emotions which had so suddenly over-taken her. Yet exactly what it was which she felt she could not tangibly put into words—was it hurt, betrayal, anger, abandonment? She had always looked to him to be her protector… but in the end he had always left her alone to her face her own fate.

The boy heaved a heavy sigh, a remorseful look of guilty shame in his eye. Regretfully, he slowly returned to where his armchair sat in silent gloom by the window and picked up his book.

...The vision of the library faded away from Adlai's eyes, and a new one emerged to take its place. The form of the little girl was moving ahead of her now, her tremulous steps subtle and discreet as a mouse. Hesitantly she slipped past the shadows of arched doorways and carved colonnades, and Adlai did her best to keep her in sight as she quickly followed behind. The halls were already beginning to darken. The wind and rain were starting to howl, beating upon the roof and windowpanes by the time the child neared a tall, silent doorway: the bedchamber of Mistress Heromena of Ardath. It was an isolated wing far away from all other apartments or main rooms in the castle, and there were no servants to be seen anywhere. For a moment the little girl hesitated, as if reconsidering the resolution of her earlier decision. She turned to look cautiously down the hall behind her, and Adlai too followed her gaze: no one. Softly the child crept closer and stealthily laid an ear to the door... nothing. Stepping back, she squared her shoulders. With a deep breath she nimbly gripped the handles, and slowly pushed open the great doors.

The heavy doors creaked loudly on their hinges. Startled, the little girl quickly darted through the narrow opening and shoved them tightly shut behind her. Adlai hurriedly scurried after her, but her form passed straight through the entrance doors, as though she were no more than a ghost. The breathless child was apprehensively pressed against the door on the other side, staring all about her with wide, petrified eyes as though striving to muster what little willpower she had left to venture forward. The only sound that could be heard (other than the howling of the wind outside, and the rain striking the glass panes of the only window in the room) was the wild beating of a smaller heart pulsating inside Adlai's head. A sudden loud clap of thunder rent the air as a forked flash of lightening shattered the darkness, splitting through the partially drawn curtains as it lit up the entire room. For a moment it blinded her eyes, while its bright light lit up the child's peaked, white face and bright red hair. Adlai herself was shaking violently and trembling all over, as the sound of raging thunder continued to echo outside, and she turned back to look. The little girl swallowed hard, then began to make her way softly through the room.

The lightening continued to flash and zigzag throughout the chamber at intervals, but as her eyes gradually adjusted to the darkness, Adlai began to notice more of the apartment itself. Its appearance, like the headmistress', (although very stately) was cold, stark, and severe, as if it, too, meant to frighten away all uninvited guests, and to lock out the world that existed beyond its walls. Though grand in appearance, there were not many magnificent furnishings about it, so that it appeared somewhat dreary and dull. Overall the chamber lacked any sort of luster, and the darkness of it seemed magnified by its bleak, somber colors. As the child wandered through, it was quickly noted that there was hardly a single item in the entire room that was meant purely for decorative purposes; nothing was at all bright, cheerful, or colorful in any way. Everything about the place seemed cold, rigid, and purely functional.

The little girl crept softly across the room to a tall wardrobe she had espied against a wall, opposite a large bed hung with brocaded damask. With a tug the wardrobe doors promptly fell open. Adlai crept forward and peered over the girl's shoulder: there two straight rows of dresses neatly folded upon the shelves at rigid attention. Every single one was some varying shade of black or charcoal-slate, and all lay with exact precision in Milady's closet, like dark sentries silently standing watch at their posts. Adlai had often wondered why a woman in the headmistress' position (with enough monies supplied from the king's coffers) would deliberately *choose* to be attired in the same dark color day after day, month after month, year after year. It was almost as if her black habits were, by their own doleful expression, joining with her in willful mourning over some great loss. The girl carefully laid aside each garment to have a better look, thinking surely to find at least one single garment of more cheerful colors hidden somewhere between them…There was none.

…Then suddenly she spied it: a hidden chest barely visible in the furthest corner of the wardrobe, and almost completely lost from sight. A small iron key was still hanging in the lock. Slowly the girl turned it and opened the lid—a single dress lay in a solitary heap. The young child let out a low, breathless sigh of wonder as she carefully drew it out: it was suddenly as if the sun had crept from its hiding place behind a billowing cloud-cover of doom, and was now radiating in glorious magnificence. It was by far the loveliest and most exquisite gown she had ever seen, and kept almost perfectly preserved. The fabric itself was of very costly materials, the bodice and trailing skirt being garnished with all manner of beadwork, seed-pearls, and brightly colored ribbon, together with embroidered designs of delicate flowers, roses, and pink baby-buds with tiny green leaves, and all of the finest detail and artistry. The ivory material consisted of the most luxurious satin, running on for yards upon yards. An extravagant, starched collar made of a creamy, sheer mesh fabric swept outwards from the plunging, low neck-line; its scalloped edges of fine lace extended in profuse elegance to light delicately upon either shoulder, then fanned out loosely into a wide, arched halo at the back. A pillowy chiffon material capped both the shoulders and elbows like puffy silk clouds, and was gathered together with ribbon ties; beneath these the narrow satin sleeves of the upper arm opened wide into flowing, crenulated wrists, their widening, elongated scallops trailing upon the ground. A jewel-encrusted neck-line framed the pleated bosom of the narrow bodice; beneath the breast, the front and back of it were cinched up tightly with bright, rose-colored ribbons that dangled down over a long, crenulated train. A heavily-jeweled leather girdle completed the ensemble; trailing down the gown's center, a large sapphire surrounded by gold filigree hung from the girdle's oblong end and nearly swept the floor, as the child softly carried it from its resting place.

In hushed awe the girl carefully turned the garment over and continued examining the marvelous handiwork of its design. The mere picture of it seemed like the beauty of a tender spring shoot rising up out of the frozen grounds of winter, coming forth from the hardened earth to blossom and bloom, and there reach out to touch a remote, deadened corner of the world with its life and vivacity…The longer she looked at it, the more likely it seemed to have been made by the faeries in celebration of some great, auspicious occasion, or some festive elvish revelry— such as a grand and illustrious coronation, or perhaps for the midnight magic of an elfin wedding ceremony? ...Mayhap it had been worn by some enchanting princess of immortal descent, for the pledging of sacred vows upon the glorious day of her marriage?...Everything about it was light and cheerful, happy and gay; its very appearance seemed to betide a most joyous event filled with bright, sunny hopes for tomorrow... However had Ardath come by it, Adlai wondered? And why had she allowed so breathtakingly beautiful an article to be discarded and abandoned, banished to dreary darkness amongst a trousseau of cheerless, somber colors—almost like a widowed young bride forced to go into untimely mourning?

The little girl slowly lifted a thick, deadened wreath of flowers from the far corner of the chest. The sprigs of dry leaves and discolored blossoms crunched lightly under her touch upon their withered sprays, and she took pains to lay it back with care. Adlai herself had never seen Milady wear the gown, not even in her younger years for the most festive of occasions...What thief from the past had stolen away all delight, so that the headmistress had chosen to hide it away from all other eyes, and instead to attire herself in her ever unchanging garb of cheerless black?

To be sure, the headmistress' daily dress *did* possess a stiff sophistication and rather cold elegance about it. Nevertheless, the only truly pretty ornament Adlai had ever seen her wear was a tiny sapphire brooch, which she usually wore pinned at the throat on the high black collar of her houppelande. A glance to a nearby dressing table, however, revealed that for some reason Milady had neglected to put it on that day, for there it lay upon the vacant table top...There were only two other objects on the table beside it. One was a large locked box. Adlai knit her brow... *In that box might lie the answers to all her questions... But how to open it?* There was no key to seen anywhere.

The child before her seemed distracted by the other remaining object—a small cameo portrait, half of which was badly ruined and near destroyed. Scratch marks (as of either sharp finger nails or a small knife blade) were swiped across the worn, damaged surface. The little girl wrinkled her forehead perplexedly as she lifted the picture cautiously from its place. Adlai squinted in the dim light from where she peered over the child's shoulder, trying hard to get a better look. The remaining decipherable half of the portrait appeared to be the face of a young man...*Who could it have been? A near relative, maybe? A brother, or even a son, perhaps?* Another thought crept slowly into her mind, but the notion seemed almost too incredible to hold any merit: *Was it plausible to even dare think that it might possibly have been a former lover of hers?!...*The strange curiosity of this new idea made her stop long enough to ponder it: Was it conceivable (even to imagine) that the vindictive, cold-blooded head-lady of Dombrey Manor might *ever* have once lived the life of any normal young woman?—A life involving human warmth, feeling—even love?

A sudden clap of thunder tore through the air. Startled, the little girl let out a piercing shriek and jumped, dropping the portrait to the floor with a clatter. For a moment the bedchamber was lit up by blinding, intermittent flashes of lightening streaking through the tall glass windows. The thunder outside continued to echo on for another minute after the lightening had ceased, but otherwise the room was once again dark and silent as before. The little girl trembled violently, her small face white as death as she darted a glance about for any sign that her presence had been detected. Cautiously she backed away from the dressing table, but a sudden cracking noise beneath her feet stopped her in her tracks: the corner frame of the portrait was peeking out from beneath her foot. Horror filled the child's eyes and she hastily stooped, fingers trembling, as she deftly snatched it up to examine the damage. The thin metal casing was now bent and broken, and the face of it be-smudged from the sole of her slipper. Aghast with alarm, the child hastily reset it in its place.

She seemed suddenly aware that she had already tarried much longer than she had intended, and (though she had yet not succeeded in the purpose of her mission), seemed unwilling to linger further. The risk of discovery was becoming more imminent with every passing moment that she delayed. And it was only a very short matter of time before either her absence would be noticed, or Ardath would make her return. The little girl made a last desperate attempt to readjust the damaged frame, whispering a hushed, breathless prayer that her visit there might remain unnoticed.

...It seemed suddenly deathly still and silent, even more so than before. The air about her had become much colder too, so that her fingers and lips grew instantly numb. The little girl shivered considerably, rubbing her hands over her arms in an effort to keep warm. The stormy clouds in the evening sky had parted, and a dim shaft of moonlight now descended through the partially drawn curtains.

Of a sudden, a strong gust of wind arose out of the stillness and blew with tremendous force throughout the room, whipping back the curtains from the window panes and sending the bed-hangings flapping violently from their place. Then in an instant it died away again, as strangely and quickly as it had begun, like the sudden snuffing out of a candle...The window and door were both tightly shut—where had it come from?

...Adlai was breathing hard, barely daring to stir as she strained her ears in the silence: a chill wriggled down her spine....Then she heard it—the creaking sound of wood swaying ever so softly upon squeaking hinges. She started in the direction of the noise: a large tapestry was rustling softly, its tasseled ends stirring in the stillness from where it was draped over a protruding wall in a half hidden corner of the room. Shivering with fright, the child swallowed hard as she hesitantly drew back the curtained mantle: the outline of a rough wooden door was hidden behind it, a set of skeleton keys hanging from the handle just below the lock. With trembling fingers the girl softly slipped the largest key into place. A loud groan resonated as the door fell open, slamming into the nearby wall. For several seconds it banged about on its hinges, and Adlai drew in a sharp breath. A cold, wet draft emanated from the pitch-black opening of a narrow doorway, as the child cautiously crept towards the threshold.

Suddenly a loud screech tore the silence, and a large crow swooped out from the opening. Gliding through the air it circled round about over her head, then at last dropped down and alighted upon the head of the wardrobe. For several moments it skulked back and forth, stiffly shaking out its coarse black feathers as it scrutinized her warily with beady eyes. Suddenly the glint of the gold framed cameo caught its eye, and in a twinkling—with a quick flap of its wings—the crow dove from its roost, snatching it up in its talons. With another screech he swept past her on widespread wings, and disappeared back into the blackened shadows of the doorway.

The little girl gulped audibly as she stared ahead in wide-eyed fright, timorously inching her way closer with a soft whimper…The headmistress was sure to know now that someone had entered her chambers…*Did she dare to go inside and retrieve it?*

Adlai cast a fearful glance over her shoulder to the rest of the room. It was then that she noticed it: icy droplets of frozen sweat were forming upon her own brow, and the breath of her mouth was rising in a precipitous cloud before her face. The air all around was unnaturally cold…*Something wasn't right.*

She spun back to the whimpering child before her and let out a gasp: a shadowy silhouette now stood in the doorway facing them both, its silent, unmoving form eclipsing the darkness behind. Instantly, a flash of lightening lit up the room, fully illuminating the ghastly apparition—it was a woman with an ashen face, and purple hollows carved in sunken circles around glassy, blackened eyes which now leered down upon the girl. A crooked smile twisting itself across her morbid visage revealed that most of the teeth had already rotted away. The flesh covering her gaunt cheek-bones also appeared half decayed, and what was left was white as death. Wet stringy hair dripped down over her face and shoulders; a loose, partially decomposed winding sheet was hung over the colorless skin of her bony arms, the rotted rags draping upon the floor like a train behind her.

Too late Adlai lurched forward to grab the girl: with a sudden scream of terror the child was instantly yanked away from the desperate reach of her outstretched fingers. Horrified, Adlai watched her disappear inside the darkness, the jolting echo of her last scream resounding loudly behind her. In a state of confused terror she stumbled backwards and fell onto the floor. She could hear voices—strange, unearthly voices, whispering all around her:

"Yes…This is the One!…*She has the Mark*!"

The whispers ended suddenly in a hissing roar of rage. Blindly, Adlai began scrambling backwards on her hands and feet as quickly as she could. Dark, shadowy shapes were circling like black birds above her in the swirling darkness, and her ears were filled with the wrathful hissing of countless whispering voices all about. In a twinkling one of the ghostly phantoms surged through the air—sweeping down from the ceiling, with arms outspread like a hawk it dove upon her with a great swoosh! Adlai felt herself suddenly swathed in endless yards of dank, stinking rags, the stifling profusion of decomposed shreds suffocating her cries for help. In desperation she swiped madly through the air above her head. All at once she could feel cold, clammy fingers grappling at her night dress and clutching at her body, unseen hands half pulling—half dragging—her towards the open doorway. With a shriek of terror, she was sucked inside the black chasm of a chamber.

CHAPTER 11—PASSAGE INTO THE UNDERWORLD

With a gasp Adlai sat bolt upright in bed. She was shaking violently and covered by a filmy cold sweat all over her body, while the soaked bed sheets twisted tightly about indicated she'd been writhing in her sleep. With a groan, she closed her eyes and let out a sigh of relief.

Suddenly the mattress beneath her gave way, and with a startled scream she found herself plunging downwards into endless darkness! The only sound filling her ears was the shrill noise of her own shrieks as she fell through the blackness and into wide open space.

Then all at once everything stopped. Adlai started: she was no longer falling. Instead, she was suddenly staring straight up at the surface of a crude wood ceiling that was only inches away from the end of her nose. With a petrified gasp she realized that she was lying length-wise in some sort of shallow, oblong wooden box, a dim light stealing through the narrow cracks in the boards: she was lying in a coffin.

In an instant she was wildly clawing away at the rough planks with her fingernails. Jagged splinters embedded sharply into her palms, cutting deep under her finger nails as she pushed and banged with all her might against the lid of the container. At last with a loud squeak the loosened nails gave way; the rickety plywood shattered, and she flung the board cover away. Whimpering distractedly with giddy terror, she scrambled shakily to her feet and frantically looked about her. The low, vaulted ceiling of a windowless alcove gave the impression that she was in some remote, underground chamber of the castle. The light she had glimpsed emanated from two lit candelabras that stood erected at either end of the room. And at the very center of the chamber a raised dais of solid granite was fixed, atop which lay a long sarcophagus of black marble. Trembling, Adlai slowly approached and cautiously wiped the dust from the surface.

Strange lettering of very peculiar characters were engraved round about on all sides of the lid, yet she could not decipher their meaning. Slowly she made her way around the full length of the coffin as she soundlessly traced the outline of the symbols with the tremulous tip of one finger. It was to no avail; the foreign characters were completely unknown to her.

The sound of a slow drip broke the stillness. Peering down, she saw a splotch of red bleed out over the top of her bare foot, then trickle down the side of one ankle. A tiny pool of liquid dark crimson was forming at the base of the dais beneath her feet. Her quivering gaze slowly trailed upwards: red droplets were dripping through a crack in the ledge of the overhanging marble, and a thin stream was already running down its side…It was blood.

With a tremendous heave she managed to slightly dislodge the lid from its resting place. The weighty marble grated shrilly as it scraped against the casing. Sweat dripped into her eyes as she strained and pushed with all her might. At last the polished coverture toppled to the stone floor with a horrendous crash. The reverberating echo resounded over and over throughout the crypt for a long time after, before all again subsided into quiet stillness. Adlai stared down into the deep recess of the sarcophagus: the lengthy form of a very tall, decomposed body lay encased in black armor. Concealing the visage of the wearer was a helmet of black iron crowned by an onyx diadem.

Adlai's very skin was crawling. Even though there was neither sound nor movement from the corpse (nor indeed anywhere else in the chamber), she had the uncanny sensation that a new presence was now there accompanying her in the room. All former fears faded away to nothing in its wake. This was a fear unlike any other she had known. A bright red trail ran from the ungauntleted hand of the corpse and flowed into a crack in the granite wall. Dark blood streamed out from beneath the blackened fingernails of shriveled fingers. A glimpse of a slimy, misshapen object came into view, peeking through the clutched grasp of his fist. Gulping hard and shuddering wryly with revulsion, she timidly poked and pried open the decayed fingers. Inside, a muscular organ was steadily dilating and contracting rhythmically, causing a steady pulse to vibrate inside the grisled hand. With a startled cry, Adlai staggered back and recoiled in horror, her blood-stained fingers pressed to her mouth as she stared aghast: it was a beating human heart.

She whirled about to flee but stopped short: she was no longer alone. An entire assembly of black-hooded figures in long flowing cloaks were standing in a half circle around her. The tallest one silently approached, the black blade of a long, slender dagger brandished in one hand as he glided soundlessly across the floor. Scrambling, Adlai pressed hard against the granite wall of the sarcophagus, shrinking away with a whimper. Seizing hold of her wrist, the hooded personage forced the dagger's jeweled hilt into her hand and jerked her arm up over the marble ledge. Adlai let out a cry of pain, struggling to break free from his steely grasp, as the quivering point poised directly above the beating organ. In an instant the blade sliced through the air, the glint of the double-edged point plunging deep through the heart's core.

The dagger fell from her fingers with a clatter upon the floor stones. Adlai sank dizzily to her knees and stared blankly at the front of her nightgown: her left breast was stained bright red. Touching it gingerly with trembling fingers, she found that thick blood was oozing from a depressed cavity which had suddenly appeared in her chest.

Long cloak sleeves swathed her face. She was being suddenly lifted up and hoisted over the brink of the opened casket. The next moment she was tumbling down inside, the hooded figures hovering over the open top, the chant of their hissing whispers screaming in her ears. Suddenly she was falling— plunging—down, down, down…into endless depths...

Sparks of images lit up her mind like the burst of an ignited flame, and pictures like a fiery sea of memories exploded inside her head. Yet these were unfamiliar memories that she did not recognize—and the tale they told was filled with terrible, gruesome scenes of bloodshed and battle. An innumerable host of lifeless bodies lay scattered like an endless ocean over the rolling surface of a sunless battlefield. Ravenous beasts and unearthly creatures roamed the desolate land and ravaged the decaying corpses. The image of a great white tree with wide, outspread branches flashed before her; then all at once a bolt of lightning streaked across grey skies and struck at its center. There was the shrill noise of wood splitting as the smooth trunk was cleft straight down all the way to its roots. The lofty branches instantly drooped and withered, and a river of blood ran from the gory ash of its charcoaled scars. The ground beneath turned wine-red, and blood seeped up through bared roots, until the whole earth was completely saturated; the river of blood itself became a great ocean that stretched out in every direction, for as far as the eye could see. For a mere instant the masculine face of a young warrior in a high-topped helmet of gold blazed suddenly before her. The outline of his features shone with all the intense brilliance of the sun; his eyes were clear and calm like a cloudless blue sky, yet at the same time piercing like a raging flame of fire, and in his right hand flashed the wielded blade of long broad-sword. Stars fell from their places in the heavens, raining down to earth amidst fire and hail, and the sun and moon both turned red as blood. The terrified cry of a thousand screaming voices rent the air, but in the next instant were immediately silenced. And from somewhere afar off in the deafening stillness there echoed back the shrill shriek of an eagle's cry.

...In the next moment Adlai was once more plunged into darkness, her body hurling through the vast expanse of endless time and space. Far beneath her a light at last began to grow; at first it appeared like a smoldering ember, but gradually grew in brightness and magnitude, until the force of it hurt her eyes. She could just make out the wild shapes of flames leaping high to lick the darkness, as a powerful blast of heat struck her face. The cavernous walls of a great abyss were lit up like a torch on all sides as she hurtled past. Jagged ledges jutted out like menacing spears from black cliffs of volcanic rock, against which her form was nothing more than a tiny speck of dust falling through a vast canyon...Far below her, a river of molten lava cascaded like a waterfall from an overhanging precipice, spilling out into a bubbling sea of flame that surged about restively in gushing torrents. Relentless hot waves tossed up angrily against the chasm walls, rushing furiously past as they churned their way through hollowed-out chambers yawning on beneath steep archways of solid rock.

A flame of fiery brimstone streaked past her cheek—and then two—falling ever faster and thicker, until they were as dense as hail raining down, each fiery dart whizzing dangerously close as she fell. The smothering stench of burning sulfur seared her nostrils and eyelids like the branding of an iron, and her lungs filled with fire and smoke. A suffocated scream ripped through her vocals; in a split-second her shift, hair and skin ignited like a leaf of dry parchment, and burst into flame. In the distance the noise of a million cries could be heard ringing up from the depths, the tumult of their screams echoing upwards from the bowels of the earth. Shadowy forms reached up from the molten brine, as she plummeted like an iron weight to the tossing sea below.

Instantly another sound—the powerful shriek of an eagle—split the air. A great gust of wind tore past, and Adlai found herself suddenly snatched up and borne aloft. She caught glimpse of the snowy-white underside of a great fowl stretching high above her, with strong, massive wings beating the air on either side. Great talons circled forcibly round about her body, holding her fast in their sure grip. From behind she caught glimpse of a gigantic pair of lion-like hind paws, each one brightly brandishing a set of sharpened claws that dangled from beneath a powerful, feathered underbelly. A long, thick tail streamed away in the wind far behind them, the glossed end of it fanning out as it sliced deftly through the air and propelled them upwards. With a great lurch they soared up high, until the sea of fire beneath them gradually faded from sight.

They were shoving on towards the vault of the cavernous ceiling, which stretched on and on into pitch-blackness above them. At last she caught glimpse of the broad, jagged overhang of a rocky cliff, and the great winged Creature softly alighted upon the ledge. Adlai hardly even stirred but lay slumped in a motionless heap, her quivering form racked with scalding pain as she let out a moan. All at once a mild wind like a spring zephyr blew down gently on her, and a warm breath stirred over her like the twinkling of sunlight through a delicious summer breeze. Immediately her charred flesh became whole again, and her singed hair healthy and soft, as her cheeks and parched lips again flushed to a lusty color. Adlai drank it in thirstily, breathing in deeply with a contented sigh and slowly reopened her eyes. The great talons gently opened. Blinking in dazed amazement, she arose into glittering light.

It took her eyes several moments to adjust to the dazzling brilliance before her. But slowly fuzzy vision gave way to a clear image. Standing before her was a great white Griffin of *enormous* size, and she suddenly felt incredibly small and vulnerable in its shadow. His eyes blazed bright like fire on ice. A shimmer of colors reflected themselves like dancing lights, as they glanced off of his snowy plumage. They were every shade of the sun in all its radiance—gold and bronze; fiery amber and bright crimson reds, rich burgundies and scarlet; the sun-kissed peach and rosy pink hues of a sunset sky, and the cool purples of twilight. Crystalline lights glittered like a spray of diamond stars beset over his entire body. Overlapping fangs like the teeth of a lion framed his great beak on either side, and she realized now that his mouth was so large in size, that he could have easily devoured her whole without the slightest difficulty. The feathers crusting his ears and beard rustled softly in a light breeze, as he calmly lowered his head and fixed his steady gaze upon her. He was by far the most magnificent and awe-inspiring Creature she had ever dreamt of. He was *much* more than a king of beasts—the appearance of his power and grandeur gave him the look of One who might indeed have been Lord of all the Earth.

"You are frightened, young One."

His voice was like the rumbling of distant thunder, yet at the same time he spoke with the mildness of a hushed whisper.

"Yes," she faltered.

"That is good," the Griffin breathed with quiet nod of his head.

"If you fear Me, then you will have no need to fear anything else, and there are *many* who seek to make you afraid...But the root of Fear is precisely what will deter you from fulfilling your Destiny, should you allow it shelter inside your soul. Fear Me—and *no* other—and I shall be able protect you from all else."

Adlai opened her mouth to speak, but no words came to form an answer; none of what he said seemed to make any sense.

"All shall be revealed in due time, so do not be anxious now," he continued quietly. "Come, I shall lead you back."

He padded softly past her as he spoke, and she now realized that they were standing before a great stone archway that stood towering high above them both. Ancient runes were carved into the arch, and on either side of the doorway stood two giant armored figures of stone. Their wings were unfurled, and each stood with one hand extended defensively towards the abyss, while the other hand brandished a drawn sword high in the air. The grim expression of their dark countenances seemed to portend a dire warning, as if to ward off all who sought to re-enter through the gateway.

"What mean they?" Adlai queried.

"They are the appointed Watchmen of Olde, and they keep watch over the lower regions of the Abyss, and of the Demons of the Deep who are bound there...But the Day shall come when those bound will again be loosed—and great trouble, such as the world has never seen before, will come to mankind."

Adlai shuddered, and cast another frightful glance at the smoking inferno burning in the blackened depths behind them. Then slowly she followed after the Griffin.

They had just reached the threshold of the gateway, when suddenly a tall figure stepped forward from the shadows. The rocky gravel under his steeled boot crunched to powder beneath the heavy boom of his thudding foot step. Black mail glinted in the dim light, as a shrouding cloak fell back to reveal a warrior in full-bodied armor, an unsheathed broad-sword poised and ready in his hand. The noise of raspy breathing emanated from the shadow of his iron helmet, and a familiar diadem crowning his head towered high above her... She had seen it before.

"Will you rob the Lord of the UnderWorld, and deprive him of his due?!" A deep voice rang out with a menacing growl.

"For shame, Lucan!" The Griffin's reproving tone was calm as he spoke. "Is this not a brand snatched from the fire?"

"You know what the Sacred Laws demand—" the Black Warrior replied in a steely tone, "You have already foreseen what will take place!"

The Griffin eyed the Black Warrior coolly for a moment.

"Until it *has* taken place," he answered evenly, lowering his head so that he was at eye-level with his opponent, "She is no legal property of yours!"

"Her fear is strong—the end will not be long in coming!" The Black Warrior hissed.

The Griffin's eyes blazed like a rekindled fire, and the rumble in his steady voice was louder than before:

"And *My* power is all the more perfected *in* weakness! Best to remember that, and not to glory before your time!"

An angry growl emanated from behind the iron visor. In a twinkling the Black Warrior spun his cloak round about his shoulders. The lengthy cape twirled through the air, as the hem of it whipped roughly past Adlai's face. In an instant, great horned wings unfurled amidst a loud screeching. A black cloud of bats swarmed out from under the folds of his cloak, their shrill cries ricocheting against the cavern walls and ceiling, as the torrent of winged creatures whirred past. Adlai cowered as the black coat of mail transformed into iron scales that flashed red in the dusky light. In an instant the Warrior's towering height shot upwards, and with a sudden whoosh he swooped past her. A hail of fire rained from his horny snout and sprayed across the rocky ground just inches from where she stood. With a flying leap he dove over the cliff's edge. The roar of a dragon echoed loudly behind him as he departed.

Adlai shakily dropped to her knees in a frightened daze upon the ledge. In the distance she watched the Dragon sail away into the dark shadows of the canyon. Bursts of flame gushed from his jaws, lighting up the black outline of his silhouette as he disappeared.

"Where did he go?" She asked breathlessly.

"Back to his own kind," the Griffin answered quietly.

Adlai tried to regather her wits.

"What did he mean?! Whatever was he talking about?!"

The Griffin turned back with a serene gaze.

"A task lies before you, one which only *you* have been chosen for."

"*What*?!" Adlai stammered in agitated alarm. "But that's impossible—*I'm* never picked for *anything*!—let alone chosen for something of importance! Please, you have to understand—there's been a dreadful mistake!"

"Be still, Child!" The Griffin's command rang out. His voice was still calm, but there was again the unmistakable presence of authority in it, and at his tone she fell instantly silent.

"Peace."

The Griffin breathed out this last word. Adlai took a deep breath, trying hard to stifle the discomfit of an exasperated sigh (which threatened to disclose exactly how disquieted and little 'at peace' she truly felt).

"You may not have chosen this—or Me," he went on, "But *I* chose you. Even before the foundations of the earth were laid, I ordained and destined you for the task which presently lies before you."

"But I'm so weak and incapable—I don't know anything about how to do any of this—whatever 'this' is! Exactly what is it that I'm intended to do, anyway?! Besides, everyone knows what a rash temperament I have—I blunder through everything! I never say or do the right thing—why ever would you *want* to choose *me*?!"

"Because it is my pleasure to take the weak, the simple, yes—even the foolish—to confound and bring to nothing that which is...*He* relies much in his own wisdom and strength," the Griffin said solemnly, casting his gaze back out across the Abyss, in the direction the Dragon had taken.

"But," he continued, "I am about to show him the power I am able to wield through even the simplest being, whom he perceives as lowly and useless. I shall break the neck of his pride by bringing to nothing all of his plans and devices, and that through the very instrument which he so spuriously scorns—*your spirit*."

"But what about my weaknesses?"

"Child, remember: when you are weakest, that is when I AM the strongest—for the weaker you are, the more you shall depend upon Me; the more My life's force shall be infused *in* you, and the more My own strength can freely flow *through* you...Only believe, and choose to remain vitally connected with Me, and all shall go well."

Adlai could think of nothing more to say in reply to this. And since he was so assured in all he said, there seemed little point in arguing the subject. The Griffin was already turning again towards the Gate.

"Come, this way."

He led the way through the Arched Gate, then turned back to face her once more.

"You will return now to your own world. I shall send others to help you in your mission, so that you will not go alone. Only wait for my instructions. Remember: allow Fear to eclipse your gaze, and you will entirely lose sight of your way. *Keep your eye firmly fixed on Mine, and I will lead you—I will guide you with My Eye.*"

And with that final, mysterious admonition he was gone— soaring away into the darkness, the shriek of an eagle's cry echoing back in her hearing.

CHAPTER 12—THE SOUL HARVESTERS

In the blink of an eye, Adlai found herself once again in her own bed, her mind spinning with perplexed thoughts. Was it possible that all of this could have transpired in the course of a single night? What task was it to which she'd been reluctantly assigned, and who was it that would be sent to aid her?

Suddenly she was thoroughly exhausted. So much had happened that day. Yet her brain was such a distracted muddle, that she could scarce recall much of it. It seemed as if an eternity had already passed since that morning, and the day had seemed even longer on an empty stomach. Ever since that tender moment she had shared with Willan, she had been able to think of little else, except for the lingering look in those crystal blue eyes of his… Then her mind suddenly flashed back to Willan's stern warning—the Stranger! Why, she had nearly forgotten it all! A tremor ran down her spine as she remembered what she had seen and felt when he looked at her—that one ember eye piercing through her like a fire …What secret power did he possess, that had forced her own thoughts to betray her?… Whatever he had learned of her, she was afraid to know… And it unnerved her to think of him being there with inside the castle grounds… At least he was sleeping in the stables, instead of in the Manor… *Storm!*

Suddenly she sat upright in bed. Something was not right in all this, she could feel it. Where was he now? Before she allowed another thought to enter her mind, Adlai was already on her feet, scrambling into her shoes as she hastily threw on her dressing gown and flew out of the room.

All was still and quiet in the courtyard outside, as Adlai quietly crept down the Manor steps and turned towards the stables. The moon was not yet full, and it was half shrouded in cloud. There was not a sound, save that of a rustling wind. Adlai shivered all the way down to her suede slippers, pulling her cloak tightly across her body as she slowly ventured through the open court. With every nearing step, she could feel her heart pounding harder, and she fought with guilt that she was not heeding Willan's stern instructions of earlier. It was wrong for her to disobey him, especially after what her heedlessness had cost them the day before. At the same time, though, Willan wasn't always right about everything—and he certainly was misled in his opinions of his dear Heromena, was he not? And what if there was something very wrong with all this? What if Storm needed her? What if something had happened to him?

Adlai tried to force herself to quicken her pace. At last she came to the stables. With a deep breath she slowly pushed open the creaking doors and peered hesitantly inside: it appeared to be empty. She pushed the door further open and slowly entered. The air was thick and pungent with the smell of warm hay, yet there was no sound, no sign of movement anywhere…*Where was Storm?*

Nervously she licked her dry lips as she clenched and unclenched her sweaty palms.

"Storm?" She managed in a shuddering whisper, "…Storm?"

Softly she tread over the hay-strewn ground, peering cautiously into each stall before passing to the next. Every one was empty. All at once there was a hesitant creaking noise behind her. Adlai jerked around. The door behind her was ajar, swaying ever so slightly on its hinges. She swallowed hard, trying with all her will to dispel her feelings of alarm. It had probably just been the wind, she told herself. Clearing her throat, she was about to move on to the next stall, when something rustled in the straw behind her.

Adlai felt her heart jump in her chest…It was him…The Stranger of earlier that day—he was right here in the stable, lurking somewhere behind her in the dark. The sound had stopped, and all was hushed now—he knew that she was aware of his presence…He was waiting. Adlai made no sound and did not so much as turn her head, but her eyes flew to the place where she had already espied a nearby pitch-fork…It was now or never.

Softly she drew in a deep breath—then seized it. With a spin she made a lunging thrust, but quick as a flash her blow was deftly deflected, and her weapon knocked from her hands with such force that she was thrown to the ground. Adlai leapt to her feet again, whipping round to face her assailant. But then like a streak of lightning the pitch-fork hurtled past her—missing her face by mere inches—as it flew into the last and largest stall at the very end of the stable.

A sudden unearthly shriek pierced the air, and Adlai found herself thrown to the ground as a tall cloaked form stepped between her and the place from whence the sound had issued. At once a dark form rose up into the air, still shrieking as it did so; then with a sudden whir, it flew through the opening of a nearby window. Instantly there was the eery echo of more shrieks, as a stream of dark, ominous shadows flooded past in the cloudy moonlight, their dark shapes etched against the night air like ghostly shrouds. Adlai looked back at the cloaked stranger, who was still standing guardedly with his back to her, watching them disappear into the stilly night.

"What were they?" Adlai gasped when at last she could find the breath and words to speak.

"They are the Guleum—The Soul Harvesters," the Stranger replied quietly. Without looking back to her he continued: "Dark spirits from the Place of the Departed, who come back to feed upon the living and speed the passing of souls into the UnderWorld. Wherever there is fear and violence, there they gather."

Adlai suddenly gasped, and her hand flew to her mouth. "Storm!"

She rushed past him into the end stall from which the Guleum had flown. The stall door banged loudly as she threw it open, then stopped short, her eyes filled with mystified horror. Storm lay upon the floor, but he no longer looked himself at all. His coal-black coat and mane was now turned a slippery, ghostly grey, and his eyes glowed milk-white in the dark as they stared unseeing. He was breathing heavily and sweating feverishly, as if already overtaken in the throes of death. A foaming lather drained from his half-open muzzle, and as Adlai's eyes continued to trail down his form, she let out another gasp. His neck was flayed, completely torn open just above the shoulder, a deep gaping wound oozing out upon the straw beneath him. Trembling, she started to reach out, but the stranger seized her by the wrist.

"Do *not* touch him!"

Adlai looked back at the wound at the base of Storm's neck. The substance running down over his coat and pooling upon the floor appeared darker than blood—it was black. The wound itself was bubbling somewhat as it continued to trickle down with its thick, sticky fluid. Steam arose from the place where it dripped upon the ground, and the straw beneath immediately blackened into ash.

"What's happened to him?!" Adlai cried out.

"The same thing that happened to you."

Adlai looked up in shock. Her mind was suddenly racing with all the vivid images from the wood—and the memory of excruciating pain—all of which she had tried so hard to suppress.

"How—how did you come to know of that?" She stammered.

The Stranger answered not a word in reply, as he silently turned away and bent down on one knee to carefully inspect Storm's wound. Gently stroking him, he began quietly speaking to him in soothing, indistinct tones. At length he turned back to her.

"I know about many things," he continued as he gently stroked Storm's mane, "Such as, that one who cares much for your personal welfare and safety gave you *strict* instructions to stay away from here."

Adlai started with surprise.

"How—how did you know what was spoken to me?"

His hood lifted suddenly, so that Adlai was now able to peer somewhat into his face. She could see a little of the side of his visage, and the one eye that was uncovered glowed again like a burning ember.

"Who—who are you?!" She demanded in a tremoring voice.

The stranger surveyed her in silence for several moments.

"A Wanderer," he said at last, "And that is all you need know for the present time. Don't be afraid. 'Though from now on, I advise you to listen better to the one in whose charge you've been entrusted. Dangers there are aplenty—best not to tempt Death."

Storm gave a low, mournful whinny, and both quickly turned back their attentions to him.

"The poison is fast spreading throughout his entire body," the Stranger said quickly, "Very soon it will claim him, if help is not had soon. He will either become like one of the Creatures of the Night, or his body will die and his spirit go on."

"And what determines which course he shall take?" She quivered.

"That is determined by his own personal will to overcome—if he yields, he will become one of them. If he fights, he may overcome, but the struggle will kill him."

Adlai let out a mournful little cry as she dropped to her knees and reached out a hand to caress him.

"Don't touch him!"

The tone of his voice was so stern and commanding that Adlai half jumped, and quickly dropped her hand.

"One drop of his blood—just one contaminated drop—is all it would take, do you understand?!"

His tone was very severe, in an uncomfortable way that it reminded her much of the same tone Willan had used in reprimanding her

"Whatever are we to do?" She begged desperately. "Can nothing be done to stop it?"

She looked back at him helplessly, pleading for an answer. He surveyed her calmly, but answered no word in reply.

"Oh, this is all my fault!"

She burst as she wrung her hands. Her voice broke, and she stifled a sob.

Suddenly a crow swooped in through the open window, alighting soundlessly on the Stranger's shoulder. Without a word he slowly arose from where he knelt and straightened himself. Adlai looked up at him in sudden wonder: she had not realized how tall he was before whilst leaning hunched upon his staff; but now she was quite sure that he must be at least a head and shoulders breadth taller than even Willan, for her own head barely rose to his chest. The stranger's cloak shifted slightly over his feet. It was then that she noticed it: the hide wrappings covering his feet were gone…and in their place were a pair of large wolfish hind paws, claws slowly stealing over the earth. A spine-tingling thought instantly flashed through her mind, just as memories from the night in the wood speedily pieced themselves together. It was all so familiar—down to the crow now perched on his shoulder.

"It's you!" She uttered hoarsely as she fell back. "You're the one who's done all this!"

Sudden terror filled her. She turned towards the door to flee, but he caught her by the arm and quickly jerked her back, holding her tightly fast.

"Let me go!" She screamed.

"Adelheide, I told you—you've nothing at all to fear from me!"

The pleading tone in his voice sounded earnestly sincere, and Adlai slowly ceased struggling.

"I wish you no harm—" he continued, "See?" He slowly released her. "There's nothing of which to be afraid."

Adlai stopped short to catch her breath. She was crying and breathing so hard that she was practically delirious. So many thoughts and questions were flooding her mind. How could he be one of them, and yet *not*, at the same time? *Why was he not like the others*? What supernatural strength had enabled him to overcome the poison, yet had not been powerful enough to keep him whole, in the form and likeness of a man? ...One thing was sure—there was far more to this strange Wanderer than met the eye. He didn't appear blood-thirsty like the other Creature...Was he the reason why she was still alive? Had he actually saved and rescued her?

At once she remembered the wounds that had been inflicted on her—the wounds that were no more—and her hand flew to her shoulder. Had he been responsible for healing her? And if so, why was it that he could not now do the same for Storm?

"You healed me—I don't know how, but you healed me." Her hoarse voice rose barely above a whisper. "Please—I don't know how you did it or why, but please do the same for him? I know that you have the power to do it—if you really wanted to...Please?"

Her eyes searched his pleadingly, but the expression in them she could not read.

"You don't know what it is that you ask," he replied, turning his face away. "It's not my time."

He stared out the window. Adlai waited impatiently for several seconds, then at last turned to peer out the window as well. What was it that he was looking at? Trailing the direction of his gaze, she looked up into the darkened night sky. The clouds were now parting, revealing a partial moon, but otherwise there was nothing else of note. What was it that had him so preoccupied? At last he turned back to her with a heavy sigh.

"I will do as you ask, if you will follow my conditions. First, you are to say nothing of any of this to anyone. Second, you are to go back to bed immediately without further delay."

"But couldn't I stay? I wanted to be able to—"

She stopped short. The one eye she could see had suddenly begun to burn brightly, so that she could have sworn that it was indeed a blazing fire. And although his expression had not changed and he spoke not a word, yet she sensed for whatever reason that she had aroused and kindled his anger.

"I'm sorry," she blurted hastily with a quick nod, "I'll go at once."

The stable door was barely shut behind her, when she heard a sudden sound that caused her whole body to shudder in dread fear. It was a wild, unearthly sound—yet what it was or why, was more than she could tell. Without so much as looking back she fled to the Manor.

CHAPTER 13—SCARRED

Adlai's eyes flew open with a sudden start. It was still early in the morning; the first streaks of sunrise were already visible upon the horizon, and in the distance a rooster was crowing to the new coming day. She bolted upright in bed. Had Storm made it? She couldn't wait until a break in her studies. She had to find out now—at once—as quickly and as soon as possible, and it would be best if she managed to do so without either Ardath or Willan discovering her. Without wasting another moment she was out of bed and hurrying back to the stables.

Adlai sniffed as she drew her dressing gown more tightly about herself, rubbing her hands over her arms to stave off the chill as she quickened her steps to the stables. The door creaked softly as she gently propped it open and peered cautiously inside. There was no sound. Pushing the door open further she looked about anxiously.

Suddenly the raspy sound of heavy breathing met her ears, followed by an occasional snore. Adlai looked about, searching for any sign of the Stranger, her eye darting towards a nearby mound of hay. Lying in the midst of it, with hay strewn all about, was the most curious sight she had ever seen: a man—or at least, half a man—lay sleeping on the ground. His wraps, cloak, and all outer clothing were cast over the piles of hay next to him. Adlai stared at him in curious wonder: she had only caught snatches of his visage and form before, but now here he was in the open, nothing concealed. For the most part his upper body resembled that of a man's, aside from his inordinately tall and lengthy stature. Upon either side of his head sprouted two of the longest, pointiest ears she had ever seen, and just below his belly, his legs and lower body suddenly gave way to a form akin to that of a wolf or a lion. Thick, dark fur grew from just below his navel, continuing all the down to—not feet, but paws—massive paws, larger than even those of a great wolf. A long, slender tail with a curly tuft of hair at the end (rather like that of a lion or an ox), sprouted from his hind-quarters, and lay curled up at rest in the hay behind him.

For the first time now since they had met, she could at last get a good look at his face. A long, ugly scar ran from some place high upon his scalp down through dark curly hair—across his forehead, darting its way through his right brow (narrowly missing the eye) and across the upper bridge of his nose; it continued on over his cheekbone, until it practically swallowed up all that was visible of the left side of his face with its gruesome mark. The skin all around it was greatly discolored—pasty white and pale as death; and she realized now that this was the part of his face which he had hereto kept concealed beneath the hood of his cloak. From the edge of his jaw the scar ran off and travelled down through his beard over the curvature of his throat, zigzagging its way across his collar bone, and broadening out towards the very center of his left breast. A thick and ghastly scar was carved deep into his skin, as if covering the wound from where a pound of flesh had once been removed directly from the area surrounding his heart. The harsh, outlined design of a tree was emblazoned in charcoal-black over his chest, almost as if seared there by a branding iron; their wide-spread branches fanned out just beneath his collar-bone, with their tangled roots tumbling down over the left side of his breast, descending on until they fastened themselves in tight profusion like a rugged wreath round about the scar.

Then Adlai noticed something else: over the entirety of his left shoulder was a fresh scar, as if a great wound recently received had not yet been fully healed. And instinctively—almost without realizing it—her hand went straight to the place on her shoulder which had been pierced.

A buzzing fly flew by and paused, landing upon the tip of one ear. His ear twitched, as if to flick the pest away, and he stirred. Slowly he rose up with a yawn, and groggily began to stretch. As he did so, all at once a pair of massive wings sprang from behind his back, contorting and flapping shakily as they unfurled, and she realized suddenly that these must be what accounted for the misshapen lump she had earlier detected beneath his cloak. But exactly what kind of wings they were, or had been once (whether like unto birds or reptiles), she could not tell. They were badly scarred and damaged, with no feathers attached, so that they almost had the appearance of a gigantic pair of bat's wings, and were horned like those of dragons she had seen in pictures.

He seemed not yet fully awake, and her presence seemed to still go unnoticed. He continued yawning and stretching himself, turning slightly away from her as he did, so that the scarred side of his face was again hidden. To her surprise, she noticed for the first time, how well-formed the unmarred part of his face appeared. Indeed, were it not for the disfigurement upon the left side, she guessed that he might have been quite handsome once…What had he been and looked like before, and what great evil had befallen him?

All at once he had made a sudden start and uttered a loud cry. The crow let out a startled screech as it flew from its roost on a beam high overhead. It continued to shriek out its cries of consternation while the Stranger's features contorted in pain. Sweat broke out over his face and body, and he rocked himself slowly back and forth on his heels. The scarred half of his face appeared even whiter than before, while the other side was flushed and red-hot, and beads of sweat trickled over his brow. He let out another cry of agony as the eye on the unwithered side of his face became veiled behind a milky glaze, glowing like a swirling mist before the moon. Blood was streaming through the fingers clapped over his throat—running down over his ribs, and streaming across his stomach. For a moment his face went clammy white, teeth gritted together, with protruding fangs curled down over his tightened lips.

At last a drawn-out, heavy gasp escaped his lips, and his face cleared slightly as the color returned to it. Fingers still trembling, his hands dropped shakily to his sides. With that he sank and collapsed wearily upon the straw amidst sighs and groans. Adlai saw now that a raw, oozing opening was slashed across his throat. Gradually, the skin around the area grew discolored with a sickly yellowish-green color framing a purple scar, as the opened flesh slowly closed.

Suddenly Adlai felt that she would vomit, as she dizzily sank to the ground in a faint. For a moment she could see nothing, save a single bright light burning before her like fire, and distantly she could hear someone calling her.

"Adelheide!"

A voice cut through her groggy thoughts. She blinked, trying to get her hazy eyes to focus. The Stranger was bending over her, his ember eye burning bright.

Adlai did her best not to flinch at the hideous ugliness of the marred part of his visage; yet try as she might, she could not seem to pull her gaze away from his horrendous scars, especially when he was so uncomfortably close. The smooth bridge of his nose was somewhat flattened against and flush with his cheekbones, so that (while well-formed) it had something of a look that was not quite human, nor quite animal. It was not quite possible to determine his age due to the heavy distortion of half his features. Yet she felt somewhat certain by what she could see—

along with the apparent agile strength of his body—that he was somewhere in his prime, and no older. Long, dirty, dark brown hair dangled down into the eyes that were fixed upon her. Adlai wasn't certain if he could actually see her with both, so she forced her attention reluctantly on the one upon his unscarred side, which had again returned to its natural color.

"Are you quite alright?"

His voice was calm and gentle.

"Yes," she replied stiffly with a forced smile. Licking her dry lips, she hoarsely cleared her throat, trying desperately to think of something to say.

"Let me help you."

His voice was quiet as he extended a hand to her. Adlai hesitated, staring at it with quelled distaste. Blunt claws grew from the dirty nail-beds of his fingers, so that she wasn't sure that she could even take his hand without scratching or soiling her own. In addition, thick blood stains still covered much of his hand up to the wrist, and even somewhat beyond over his forearm—he was filthy. Gingerly, she reluctantly accepted.

"Thank you," she managed, as he effortlessly pulled her up from the floor.

The Stranger replied with not more than a simple nod in response. Turning away, his wings brushed past her as he bent over to regather his clothes. Adlai took advantage of the moment to hastily wipe the blood and grime from her hands onto her nightdress. If he felt the weight of her stares, he gave no apparent heed to it, but calmly went about re- binding up his legs and paws again as before. Again she noticed that a thin patch of hairy fur grew down the center of his back between his wings, reaching all the way to his tail and furry hindquarters. She almost forgot how rude it was to stare, as she watched him fold his wings behind his back beneath his cloak.

Adlai recovered herself, a little ashamed of her gawking attentions to his awkwardly embarrassing and uncomely characteristics.

"I'm so sorry, I didn't mean to startle you a little while ago," she apologized nervously. "I just—I just came to see if—"

"It's alright—you didn't startle me. I already knew you were here."

"Ah."

Adlai nodded in acknowledgment, though there was little about any of this that she felt she actually understood. So many curious questions were starting to flood in. She groped about desperately in her mind, trying to think of something else to say.

"Are you alright?" She faltered questioningly.

"Yes, quite alright," he replied turning back to her. Adlai glanced at his throat and started in surprise: the ragged wound across his neck had already begun to disappear.

"By this time tomorrow, it should be mostly healed. All that will be left is the scar."

"I see," Adlai lied.

The truth was that in reality she did not actually see or understand *anything* about any of it. How could anyone just suddenly and inexplicably heal in mere minutes from so deadly a wound? However, he spoke with such calm, self-assured, matter-of-factness, that no other reply seemed suitable. And since he was content with his own answer and seem unconcerned with offering any further explanation to satisfy her curiosity, she guessed that his cryptic reply would have to suffice.

"And what might you be called?" She asked, changing the subject.

"Gunar."

"*Gunar?*"

She wrinkled her nose slightly and bit her lip, in an attempt to hide the impertinent smile which threatened to break out in a dubious grin.

"Gunar *what?*" She asked in as sincere a tone as she could muster. "From whence do you hail?"

"From everywhere," He replied shortly, "And 'Gunar' is all the name I own now, at least to any I hold as an acquaintance."

"Ah." Adlai hesitated, wondering if she should go on. "And what does such a name come to mean?"

"Warrior King."

Adlai practically had to pinch herself to keep from laughing. He was powerful and strong enough, to be sure. But everything about his appearance—down to his dirty hands and hair—made him more apt to be King of the flies, or of the dung heap, for that matter.

"Well certainly you must have been left with at least a family name," she rejoined tautly, hoping to hide her amusement beneath false airs. Gunar stared at her in silence for several seconds.

"If you're in need of a further name, then you can call me Cowan."

"And does that *also* come with a meaning?"

"From the Hillside," he replied with a curt nod, and continued to gather his effects.

Who was this Stranger? How had he escaped the fate of becoming a dangerous predator with a morbid blood-lust?...Whatever Gunar was, she was fast gaining the impression that there was much more to him than what he was willing for her to know, and he seemed deliberately intent on restricting all personal details about himself. *If there was only a way to get him to open up...?*

He had the rough appearance and crude mannerisms of a sub-human creature. He wasn't eloquent, yet he spoke with marked authority. There was something about him, something in his manner that seemed to command awe and respect, as much as the powerful spectacle of his person ordered a certain fear. And it seemed that the more answers he gave to her questions, the more her questions seemed to multiply. She was beginning secretly to hope that he would not leave until all the secrets lurking behind his guarded façade lay uncovered.

"Why are you not like the others?" She finally demanded, ignoring the self-imposed rudeness of her interrogations.

"Because I'm not one of them," he answered simply, pulling on his over-sized cloak and cinching it about his waist.

His calm reply was short and brief, just like all of his other answers, so that Adlai was becoming slightly resentful, if not wholly irritated. Though he did not object to her inquiries, yet at the same time he seemed resolutely and stubbornly determined not to pacify her questioning in any way.

"But you look just like—"

Adlai started in flustered impatience, but then stopped short. Gunar was staring quietly at her with a look she could not quite read—what was it? His one good eye had traces of an almost pained look. And he seemed to be not so much looking at her, as past her—as if he were looking off into a place she could not see. It seemed as though he was staring into the clouded regions of a distant memory, some place far away in the misty past.

"I'm sorry," Adlai fumbled in apology. "I really shouldn't be asking you all these questions. I really just came to see if—"

"He's well—he's in there."

He pointed a finger in the direction of Storm's stall. She stared at him in surprise. It was true—he actually could read her thoughts. She was still finding it a little unnerving that he seemed able to answer her questions before she had quite finished asking them. But since he seemed no longer disposed to continue with conversation at present, Adlai could think of nothing else to say. With a meek nod of her head, she stepped awkwardly past him, ignoring his silent gaze as it followed her. But then at once all other thoughts died away, as her ears were greeted by a light, cheerful whinny. Her heart leapt in her chest.

"Storm!"

Storm was already feeding from a nearby trough— just as strong, healthy, and majestic as he had always been. All traces of his grueling battle with death were completely gone, even down to any marks left upon his charcoal coat. He was completely restored to his former self. Already he was impatiently stamping in his stall, head bobbing about excitedly as he shook out his mane, craning his neck about in her direction. Adlai ran to him and flung her arms about his neck.

"I'm so glad you've come back to me!" She cried. "Can you ever forgive me for letting all this happen to you? I promise I shall never be so thoughtless or selfish again!"

She buried her face in his mane, reaching her hand out lovingly to stroke his glossy neck. Storm responded by nuzzling her affectionately with his muzzle. Happy tears streamed down her face as she wrapped both arms round about his neck and held him tight. After a moment she turned back to the Stranger with a grateful smile.

"I don't know by what miracle you've done this, but my thanks and gratitude are owed you, Gunar Cowan…Thank you."

Gunar bowed his head slightly, the touch of a smile showing faintly on his countenance from under his hood.

"You are most welcome, Lady Adelheide," he answered graciously.

"How come you to know my name?"

"I know many things—that, and I know your thoughts."

Adlai smiled at him in mock surprise, a bit of her coy playfulness returning.

"Oh? And what do my thoughts say now?"

"That you have many questions, for which you want answering."

She stopped caressing Storm and turned back curiously at the Stranger.

"But beware of idle interest—it often leads to harm. Answers are not given for the sake of amusing and satiating your curiosity. And the Truth won't come, until you're prepared to act upon it."

As he spoke, he seemed even taller than before. He moved in slightly closer towards her now, lifting his head slightly higher as he spoke, so that she could now again look fully upon all the hideous scars hidden under his hood.

"Are you willing to look the Truth full in the face—the Truth, with all of its ugliness?"

She swallowed hard.

"You speak as though I should be afraid of something."

"You're already afraid."

His words were spoken with the mild hush of a whisper, yet Adlai trembled at them.

"And what have I to fear? Of what should I be afraid?" She retorted airily, straightening her shoulders and drawing herself up to full height so as to appear taller. Try as she might, she couldn't shake her disquieted nerves over this unexpected address. What else might he be able to see? Did he know anything of her troubling night visions?

Gunar surveyed her in silence for several moments, then spoke:

"You fear everything—those who have power to harm—or even kill; those who could cause your heart to break at the slightest rejection…And you fear losing your own soul."

He paused to inch closer.

"Your thoughts are a sea of fear… You should learn to fear me instead."

He paused, and Adlai's face went white.

"Why should I fear you?" She returned with a feigned laugh. "I am ward to King WenLaon himself—no one would dare to harm me!"

"There are those who *would* dare, Lady, and who have the power and capability to do so—but you need not fear this from me."

"*Oh*? Well if I have naught to fear from you, than what need I be in fear of?"

Adlai threw her head back and laughed scornfully, inwardly hoping that he believed her false attempt at bluff confidence. She was fast beginning to think that she had indeed over-stayed her time there—she was no longer enjoying the conversation anymore. The exchange of dialogue had taken an eerily disturbing turn; now she reproached herself for allowing her inquisitive nature to play herself directly into his hands. She was already praying that the conversation would quickly come to an end, before anyone—particularly Ardath—took note of her absence.

"Did you know that if you hold something as small as a coin before your eye, you can fully eclipse something as great in power and magnitude as the sun?" He broke in suddenly.

Adlai stared at him in confused bewilderment. Where was he going with his strange dialogue? Gunar continued:

"It is the same with your fears. Whatever you choose to fear—no matter how trivial—you make into a god. It is of pivotal importance to fear *only* that which is truly worthy of reverence—and which has the power to deliver you from all other fears." He hesitated. "Fear me, and you shall fear no one else—and I can protect you from that which seeks your harm…Just follow my eye."

Adlai's mouth dropped open incredulously in mute surprise. She did not know whether to believe him, or to dismiss all his words as utterly ludicrous. It almost seemed as if he were speaking in riddles; his talk was beginning to sound like the deranged pratings of a madman—or worse, perhaps of a dangerous predator seeking to control his prey. *Fear him? What did it all mean?*

But there was something else about his speech which disturbed her. He was repeating words which the Great White Griffin had spoken to her. *If he could read her thoughts, then was he seeking to deceive her, by mimicking the voice of another in order to gain her trust*?

All at once her eye alighted upon something which she had altogether failed to notice before—an insignia shaped like a seal, and sewn onto the hem of his cloak. It was a white griffin outlined in gold, soaring between a white rose and a white tree…

"I'm sorry, I've quite forgotten the time—" Adlai replied hastily. "I must be going."

She hurriedly pushed past him and then rushed towards the door. Quick as light and faster than she had time to blink, he flashed past and stood before her, barricading her way to the entrance. Adlai gasped, looking confoundedly to the place where he had stood only half a second earlier.

"How—how did you do that?" She stammered. "Please, I've no time for this—now if you'd be good enough to let me pass?"

"Adelheide, remember what I said—take care not to forget. I *can* protect you."

With that last admonition, he discreetly moved aside.

"Adelheide!"

A stern voice was suddenly calling her. Peering past the Stranger, she could now make out Willan's face and form in the doorway beyond, warily surveying the scene before him. She gulped down her quick relief.

"The servants have already been to your quarters, and everyone's been looking for you!"

His tone was that of a severe reprimand. Without further word, Willan snatched her firmly by the arm, ignoring the Stranger as he pulled her past.

"Cook can see that you are given something to eat in the kitchen," Willan called back over his shoulder. Gunar nodded humbly in reply.

"I'm terribly sorry, Willan," Adlai offered an apology as they hurried along. "It's just that Storm was deathly ill—I wasn't sure he'd make it through the night—"

Willan stopped short.

"And now? How is he?" He asked worriedly.

"He's—well." Adlai answered slowly, suddenly realizing how ridiculous and contradictory both those statements seemed, and hoping that he would not suppose her to be merely concocting falsehoods to escape further consequences.

"What?" Willan asked baffled. "How did this happen?"

Adlai looked back towards Gunar.

"The Stranger—I'm not sure how, but Storm was deathly ill last night, and this morning he's in complete health."

Willan slowly released his grip from her arm, turning to look back in the same direction, a mixed look of perplexed confusion and aroused curiosity on his face. Without a word he strode back to where Gunar leaned hunched upon his broad staff, his hood once more pulled down closely over his face. The two discoursed at length for several moments. Finally Willan returned to rejoin her, and together they made their way back towards the Manor House.

"What did you speak of?"

"I've asked him to stay on for a while, to help with the handling of the animals. Also I've been informed that the elderly gardener has recently been taken ill, and the grounds require tending. So I've persuaded our wandering pilgrim to stay on with us for a season or two."

"What do you know of him?" Adlai asked casually, trying her best to sound naively innocent, as though she knew nothing at all.

"Recently returned from the wars—supposedly due to wounds inflicted...Though I suspect," Willan added (half under his breath) in a slightly grim tone of distaste, "T'was more likely he's a deserter."

Adlai looked back over her shoulder. So he *had* been in the wars! Perhaps there was some truth to the fearful tales of which she'd heard only vague, whispered rumors. *Was that how he had been so horribly disfigured?* She turned back to Willan.

"But Willan, think you that it's wise for us to take him into our hire? I mean, what do we truly know of this man?"

"What *I* think would be wise, would be for *you* to better listen to and adhere to my instructions." Willan stopped short to face her. His tone was slightly milder and not as stern as a short while before, but it was a reprimand, none the less.

"Adlai, when I spoke of things not going well on the war front, the truth is that that is a grave understatement...We are losing the war, and our King has already sent word to me that he fears we shall pay dearly before it is over. Should I be required to leave and join him, I need to know that I can trust you not to endanger yourself." His voice softened almost to a whisper: "I need to know that you will be safe, and that you won't come to harm."

Adlai's heart gave a little leap, and her cheeks warmed considerably.

"Willan, I'm so sorry—I didn't mean to cause you any—"

"Here you are! Where on earth have you been?"

Adlai started at this abrupt intrusion. Looking up just in time, she saw Lady Ardath striding with swift, determined steps over the courtyard cobblestones, her long black habit flapping behind her in the stiff autumn breeze. Her lips were drawn up in a stiff, tight line, and her eyes were already boring straight into the girl.

"You've had the entire house in an uproar searching for you! Have you no regard at all for others?!" She demanded shrilly.

Adlai flinched, and prepared herself for punishment.

"I must be on my way," Willan excused himself hurriedly, "I shall be back late tonight, after the hunt."

He bowed considerately, nodding to both women, then strode quickly away. With a sigh Adlai turned back to face the bristling Lady Ardath, and another long, hard day within the imprisoning walls of Dombrey Manor.

CHAPTER 14—NIGHT VISIT IN THE TOWER

Adlai lay awake in the silence, staring up at the overhead hangings of the bed canopy. Today had fared no better than the day before, except for the bowl of broth and a piece of bread she had received for the noon-day meal. After that the afternoon studies had taken a turn for the worse, when she had thrice been caught day-dreaming in the middle of lectures. She had been sent to her personal apartments for the remainder of the evening to catch up on her studies and do additional work—this time without supper. Milady had so far proven true to her word: any meals she received were served within confines of her apartment, so that she was permitted no other company throughout the day…How long could she endure this kind of isolation, she wondered? A hard lump started to grow in her throat, swelling, until she could hardly swallow from the ache. …She must not cry…This was her life now: days and nights that neither began nor ended, but simply ran together, droning on and on without end, without meaning, without purpose…What was the use of hoping for any of it to change?

There was the sound of dogs barking in the distance, and Adlai uncovered her head. The barking was very soon followed by the clatter of horse's hooves, and then the sound of men's voices coming from the courtyard below. Adlai slowly rose from bed and wandered over to the window. Far below she could see Willan with the other huntsmen, returning with their kill. Willan was in a jovial mood—he was laughing heartily and seemed to be in good gaming spirits, the heavy, limp form of a large stag slung over his shoulders as he made for the house. Others followed him, the catch of the day hung on poles which they carried between themselves. Willan turned back for a moment to say something to one of his companions, and for an instant the moonlight lit up upon his golden yellow hair and bright-eyed smile…If only he knew how much his smiles and tender looks meant to her…

All at once Adlai started: the stable hands were already leading the horses away as the men departed for the house, but she could see one person yet remaining: Gunar—and he was staring straight up at her, his flaming ember eye concealed from view by an eye patch strapped around his head from under his hood. Adlai gulped down hard, and quickly drew back from the window. After a moment she cautiously returned and peeked through the glass. He was no longer peering in her direction anymore, but was slowly leading the last of the horses back to the stables. What did he want with her, she wondered? And did he truly mean to frighten her with all of his odd behavior?

All at once something from the direction of her bedchamber door caught her attention. It was a flickering light that lit up through the crack under the door for just an instant… Whoever could possibly be up and about at this late hour? It was just after mid-night, and the last of the servants had turned in a couple hours earlier, so that Adlai had not heard any anything stir for quite some time. Stealing to her chamber door, she softly opened it a crack and peeked out. A familiar stout little figure was some short distance up the darkened hall, the candle clutched in one hand casting its light upon a long, silvery white beard and silver spectacles. His attentions seemed intently fixed upon something on the hallway wall.

"Dr. Hindley!" Adlai exclaimed in excitement as she hurriedly approached. "Oh, I was afraid they'd already sent you away!"

The little man drew up suddenly with a startled look, and as he did so a small object fell from his hand and clattered to the stone floor.

"I'm sorry, I didn't mean to alarm you," Adlai started to apologize.

"No, no, it's quite alright!" He laughed as he recovered himself, then added with a chuckle, "I see that I am not the only one with a tendency towards insomnia!"

Dr. Hindley smiled at her in the same cheery, light-hearted way she had seen before, as he awkwardly stooped to pick up what he had dropped. Curiously, she peered down to see what it was: it was a small iron key.

"I was only trying again to find the door to my personal apartment—I know it must be here somewhere, but it's ever so hard to see in this light."

Adlai looked at him puzzled.

"A door? Here?" She asked in bewildered surprise. "There's no door to *anything* here along this side of the hallway—"

She suddenly stopped short, for right at that moment Dr. Hindley seemed to find something.

"Ah! Here it 'tis, at last!"

He stooped, holding the candle closer to the wall. There, a large painting of a great white tree hung enframed between two affixed candelabras standing cold in their fixtures.

"That tree!" Adlai exclaimed, "I've seen it before!"

Dr. Hindley smiled knowingly, though he answered not a word. His fingers ran over the texture of musty paint on its surface, as if keenly searching for something. At last the tip of one finger hesitated at the base of the tree's roots.

"Here it is!" He said matter-of-factly. Adlai stared. There at the center of the gnarled roots, was a small heart made of iron—

almost indiscernible from the rusty colored backdrop against which it was set. And at its middle was a tiny key-hole.

"I must've walked past this hundreds of times!" Adlai exclaimed in wonder, "Yet I never before noticed its existence!"

Dr. Hindley's face crinkled in a dozen laugh lines, but still he said nothing. Holding his candle up higher, he inserted the key into the tiny opening and gave it two quick turns to the right. There was the sound of something clicking into place. Then he reached up and grasped the part of a statue monument mounted higher upon the wall—it was the carved marble head of a Griffin. A low creaking noise emanated, as of hinges which hadn't been turned for an eternity. A slender crack in the wall appeared, revealing the concealed outline of a small door, as the little man gave a push and it fell back. Dr. Hindley held the candle higher, as the dim light lit upon a narrow stair rising up into the darkness. Adlai held her breath while a small cloud of dust blew out through the opening, and a chilly draft filtered into the hallway where they stood. Stepping through the doorway, Lucius held up the candle in the darkness as he squinted this way and that, peering upwards in the direction of the winding stair.

Adlai winced. It was incredible to think that even Lady Ardath would be so ungracious a hostess as to banish a guest into this desolate, remote, unkempt part of the castle. Dusty cobwebs draped down from the low ceiling and hung all around the base of the crudely made stairs, many of which appeared in great need of repair. Startled moths flew about wildly in their wake, so that Adlai had to bat them from her face, while a few small mice scurried into hiding through cracks in the wall and under the stair... What must he think of such indecent hospitality, she wondered? She cringed at the thought of the elderly little man being forced to take up residence in a place that was so inaccessible and grossly neglected. Was Ardath trying to force him into resigning his newly acquired position? Adlai sickened at the thought of him leaving. For once she felt certain that this was one professor under whom she wouldn't be tempted to fall asleep, nor let her mind idly drift into daydreams. He seemed unfettered by convention, and little concerned with mimicking the mincing, grand gestures of others. Here was someone who at last seemed to have things of infinitely greater significance on his mind. But there seemed to be more to him than a mere passionate affinity for the subjects he held dear—in him, Adlai sensed *conviction*. And whether she consciously realized it or not, *conviction* in a belief was something which her soul earnestly hungered for but had rarely tasted.

"I'm terribly sorry," Adlai apologized in embarrassment. "I expect that the household staff are yet unaware as to the condition of your apartments."

"No matter," Dr. Hindley returned cheerfully with an excusing wave of his hand. "I was merely attempting to estimate what repairs are needed in order to make this place habitable. No worries, though; a little work and some cleaning should get the job done," he continued. "And besides, I have learned throughout the long course of my life to be content with my lot, whatever it may be. And since little was ever accomplished from being *dis*contented, content is what I have chosen to be."

Adlai stared at him incredulously: was it possible for anyone to be so completely amiable, unassuming, and undisturbed in disposition? How was it be possible for him to truly be content with so utterly dismal an abode? ...However his reasoning, Adlai decided at once not to question it; perhaps his being so good-naturedly pre-disposed to find the good in all his circumstances was a blessing to her own good. And no matter how ridiculous she felt his personal philosophies were in practice, at least for now it meant one thing: that Ardath had failed to discourage the doctor into leaving Dombrey Manor.

Adlai's thoughts were suddenly interrupted by a loud groaning from the pit of her belly. Dr. Hindley gave her a look of surprise.

"Good heavens!" He laughed aloud, "Was that the roll of thunder, or the rumbling of an earthquake?"

"Neither," Adlai laughed in return. "I was busy today," she added more soberly, "And I guess I didn't eat much—all that studying I suppose."

The truth was that she was still too embarrassed to admit— even to one as apparently understanding and empathetic as the good doctor—the bitter facts regarding the hardships of her life there. Admission only drove deeper the sense of her over-all lack of control and feelings of worthlessness.

"Well then, we must remedy that at once!" Dr. Hindley rejoined with a laugh. "'Else we shall have the entire household awakened! If you would do me the honor, Lady Adelheide of Dombrey? My sup is a simple fare, yet I should be greatly delighted if you would join me in supping as my guest."

Adlai's face lit up: the thought of at last having something to eat was all the coaxing she needed.

"Thank you," she replied with an eager smile; "I should like that very much."

Dr. Hindley shifted his candle and gave Adlai a small pat on the arm, in an almost grandfatherly sort of way; with a nodding smile he beckoned for her to follow. Adlai cast one more glance behind her down the corridor from whence she'd come; then without another word she stepped quickly through the opening, and pulled the door tightly shut behind her.

It didn't seem so dark and dreadful, now that Dr. Hindley was climbing ahead of her with his light shining back through the darkness. Higher and higher they climbed, till she thought they must surely be climbing one of the tallest towers of the house. Dombrey Manor had a vast number of towers and turrets; yet Adlai now realized that (though she had lived there for almost as long as she could remember), there was much of the castle that she had never even set foot in. How was it that she had never ventured to see more of her own house? ... Probably because every free moment was spent in trying to escape her prison to the freedom of the great outdoors, she reasoned. All the same, however had she failed to notice this before, she wondered? And how many other strange things on the castle grounds had she passed by every day, without ever noticing their existence?

Dr. Hindley seemed in possession of greater vigor and strength than his tiny stature and portly figure portrayed, for he hurried on at such a brisk pace that Adlai was soon winded in her efforts to keep up.

"I wonder that I never knew of this tower," Adlai puffed behind him, hoping that conversation might slow his speed. "Indeed, I never even heard of such a door or stair being mentioned before, by anyone here."

"Quite," laughed the little man as he paused momentarily upon the stair. "Yes, it would seem that Milady thought I should be least likely disturbed in these quarters. Although I must confess," he added with another laugh, "I'm not so certain whether 'twas really so that *I* should not be bothered, as much as that I should not bother anyone *else*!"

"However can you tolerate her ill treatment so well?" Adlai asked in amazement. She felt both surprised and confused over the seeming ease with which he so readily dismissed the rude handling he had received. The little man laughed.

"My dear child," he replied, "By the time you come to be near my age, there are certain things that you find are much easier to let go of, rather than hold onto. And if there is one important lesson which I have come to learn in my life, it is they who are flexible are not easily broken. It is far easier to ride the current, than it is to fight it.

"And besides—" he continued in a slightly more sober tone of voice— "If Milady can so treat one who is both a stranger and a guest in this house, then one must surmise from her conduct that there are those under her who must fair far poorer still. Why then should I complain?"

He turned a knowing eye back to Adlai, and for a moment his elderly face softened with an understanding look of compassion. Adlai averted his gaze as she flushed and looked away. It was suddenly humiliating that Ardath's disdain for her should be so obviously apparent. She cringed at the thought of all that the good Doctor may have already been made privy to…How much had he already heard, she wondered? She glanced up hesitantly to see a warm and tender smile cross his withered features, as he reached out to lay a wrinkled hand gently upon her shoulder.

"There, there, now," he spoke gently, "This too shall pass, never fear. Seasons are oft quick to change...Take courage, and never lose hope."

He turned back to continue climbing the stair, and Adlai somberly followed after.

"You know," he continued over his shoulder, "The best way to keep from being made to feel beneath someone else is to adopt a posture of humility."

Adlai rolled her eyes, her darkening countenance displaying brewing feelings of resentment at the turn the conversation had taken.

"Any more humbling, and I'll be turned into a foot-stool for her to prop her feet upon," she muttered.

"No, please, hear me out," the Doctor answered. "Humility is not the rejection and annihilation of one's self. It is, rather, the freedom to fully accept one's self—both one's virtues, and one's flaws, to the degree that what others say is of little consequence. To be humble is not only to avoid being puffed up with arrogance. To be humble is to accept yourself as *you* are, so that you may in turn have the freedom to accept and love others as *they* are. It is acknowledging that you are *like* others... And in so doing, frees you to forgive them."

Adlai glared in the dim light.

"She doesn't deserve forgiveness," she answered in a low undertone.

"Perhaps not. But you are allowing her bitterness to become your own. Don't you want to be free from that?"

Adlai said nothing.

"The greatest way you can defeat her, is by not allowing her to own your spirit. Treat others with respect and kindness—not because you are forced or because they are deserving. Do so because your own sense of self-respect commands you to rise above their mistreatment of you—and even to show them greater consideration than they deserve."

"Any more respect and consideration, and I'll be her own personal slave!" Adlai grumbled.

Dr. Hindley shrugged.

"Adelheide, though I know little of what your life here has been like, yet I say again: some things are better let go of—otherwise they become harder burdens to bear the longer they are carried…You are young… Do not trouble yourself with carrying the needless weights of a troubled and begrudging old woman. If you do, then you also shall lose your bloom and vitality—and she will have succeeded in making you into a twisted, embittered, shriveled up form of herself. Don't give her the satisfaction of becoming her mirror. Don't allow sardonic morosity to cause you to shut out the life you were meant to live."

"*I* shall *never* become what she is," Adlai retorted bitingly as she climbed another step. "And besides, I'm nothing like her at all."

"Perhaps not," Doctor Hindley replied in a mild tone as he continued ascending the old stair. "But then," he added, "Do you think that when Lady Ardath herself was a girl, that she ever envisioned herself as what she is now?"

"She is what she's chosen to be," Adlai answered in a surly voice.

"*Precisely.*"

Dr. Hindley turned and looked her full in the eye with a penetrating stare:

"She *chose*… And so must you… Character is something which we choose for ourselves one step at a time, one decision at a time, one moment and day at a time… Be careful how you choose… Because whether for good or bad, we never become who we are in a day. And if you do not fight to become the person you were meant to be, then you will fade into that which you were *never* meant to be."

"I'm done talking about this!" Adlai flared.

She was shaking. It surprised her to discover how much raw emotion and anger had been triggered by the conversation. Dr. Hindley peered down at her with a soft look of concern in his troubled old eyes. Adlai hung her head miserably in shame. They had barely begun to be acquainted, and already she had snapped at him…just like Ardath. Would he want to befriend her now?

"I'm—sorry," she faltered out an apology. "If you please, I mean no offense, but I'd—I'd really rather not discuss the subject further."

"Of course! I'm sorry to have vexed you."

Dr. Hindley gave her a sympathetic, understanding smile, as he laid a hand on her shoulder once more and gave her a fatherly pat, then cast an eye back up the staircase.

"Ah, almost there, now!" He said cheerily as he lifted the candle higher and peered up the dark passageway. "Shall we?" He asked with a beckoning nod.

Adlai forced a smile and nodded. The rest of the way though she followed in silence, as she slowly mulled over in her mind Dr. Hindley's very strange ideologies. She'd never heard such thoughts and sentiments expressed before, nor had such notions ever really occurred to her. For a brief moment she amused herself by wondering what Lady Ardath's reaction would have been to his philosophies, could she only have been made privy to his little speech. Adlai could already envision it—her nose shooting up scornfully in the air and her caustic gaze burning spuriously. She could already hear her mordant repudiation of "What absolute rubbish! Such ridiculous nonsense!" *She* would have had no appreciation for the gracious vindication offered by Dr. Hindley's sentiments towards her grave lack of civility and courtesy. For an instant Adlai wondered how the good Doctor might react to having his theories laughed to scorn and flung back in his face by the headmistress. He did not seem the shallow sort to go airing empty sentiments or philosophies from the disengaged comfort of his armchair. There was something about his years and character which seemed to lend credibility to his words, and she got the distinct impression that he would back up all of his principles with the utmost conviction, even if it came at great personal cost. And although his suggestion of humble acceptance seemed far less glorious than the sort of vindication Adlai had in mind, yet something about the quiet strength and effortless freedom he possessed caused her envy. His life seemed almost without care, while hers was daily riddled with dreary complications... Could it be possible that one's outlook actually did have something to do with one's own personal happiness and sense of fulfillment in life?

"Ah, at last!" Dr. Hindley exclaimed suddenly.

They had reached a small landing and now stood facing a little door, while the stair continued on past, winding its way upwards. Dr. Hindley removed the same iron key from his cloak pocket and slid it into the key-hole. The old wooden door creaked as he propped it open with one arm, motioning with his other for her to enter.

Adlai gaped in transfixed wonder: unlike the stair, the room had been carefully cleaned and swept. The warm light of a toasty fire was roaring cozily over glowing embers, and cast all manner of oddly peculiar shadows across the entire room. Every wall was lined with bookcases reaching all the way up to the low ceiling, and there were stacks of books, maps, scrolls and parchments lying everywhere in scattered piles and heaps. Strewn over crudely made table-tops and dangling by strings and wires from the ceiling were all manner of intriguing contraptions and peculiar inventions, while elsewhere were laid out carefully marked drawings for still more curious devices. There was very little furniture: a couple of tables, all of which were completely covered; a small make-shift bed with a well-worn pillow and coverlet; a large armchair, a stool, rug, and several dishes, including a few pots, pans, cooking utensils, a pitcher and a wash bowl. It was hard for Adlai to imagine that anyone could manage to live with so little, although she suspected that Dr. Hindley was the sort of man who knew how to make do with naught, and who came to prefer and prize his books and precious inventions over the convenience of typical amenities.

The Doctor quickly set to work in stoking the fire and setting a kettle on to boil. Adlai slowly roamed through the room in fascination, curiously eyeing all that was to be seen and taking great care not to upset anything. Her host seemed quite at ease as he settled himself into his chair and lit a long pipe. He made no remark or apology for the room's rather disorderly assemblage; and since he seemed quite unbothered by her inquisitive perusal of his possessions, Adlai made free to continue her exploration of all his curiosities.

"I think I failed to mention before that I like to tinker in my spare time," he said at last, wafting out a long puff of smoke that went curling in the air just above his head.

"Oh, I think it's wonderful!" Adlai exclaimed, her eyes shining with enthusiasm. "Pray, what sort of machine is this?" She asked.

"That is my attempt at making a flying device, though some of my calculations and measurements were somewhat faulty. I must go back to the drawing board and re-write my design."

"Do you think you'll succeed?"

"One can only try," the little man replied.

"And what do you do when—if—you fail?"

"Try again! Success is built upon failure—usually an endless line of them! Were I to live in fear of failing, then I should never venture to try anything. And if I am to fail, then I would that it be an *epic* failure!"

"Truly?!" Adlai gasped in delight. "That's incredible! Wherever do you get all of your ideas from?"

The old man laughed.

"Mostly from here," he replied, tapping his balding head with the long mouth of his pipe. "Although 'tis true that I also receive a vast amount of inspiration from my books." He placed the pipe back in his mouth, his arms folded over his portly belly as he murmured thoughtfully, "They have always been my first love."

"You must have books on just about every subject there is to be studied," Adlai offered in comment.

"No, hardly!" Dr. Hindley laughed. "Although, I *do* flatter myself to think that I have in my possession a good many that are well worthy of note."

"What are they all about?"

"Oh, a great number of subjects," Dr. Hindley said, blowing the smoke through his lips once more. "Science, philosophy, history—" he pointed suddenly to a badly worn book with a crumbling binding that she held in her hand. "That which you have there is a great collection of legends written in the old tongue. I've been in the process of translating them into the common language, so that their memory might be preserved for antiquity's sake."

He arose from his chair, set down his pipe, and began pouring tea into two small teacups, then offered one to Adlai.

"I hardly ever get the chance to read such things anymore," Adlai murmured wistfully as she accepted the beverage. She sipped it slowly, then continued: "Milady disdains time spent in reading works of fiction as a frivolous and sinful waste."

The Doctor shook his head reproachfully in answer to this statement, as he continued to slice out thick slabs of mutton onto chipped earthenware plates. Passing along bread and butter he served Adlai her portion, and motioned for her to take a seat. Adlai's mouth was watering before the food even reached her palate. Dr. Hindley, however, seemed to take no notice of how hungrily she devoured the meal. Instead he comfortably resumed his place in his great armchair, slowly exhaling long streams of smoke as he continued staring off in the distance, a look of deep, thoughtful contemplation etched in his brow.

"For how many years have you been employed as a tutor?" Adlai asked finally as she finished the last morsel on her plate. She settled back contentedly, leaning back against a threadbare cushion to let out a contented sigh. It was good to be reminded of what it felt like to be fully satisfied again.

"You could not possibly guess how many years I have stood in the position of tutor," Dr. Hindley chuckled in reply. "Indeed, I believe that you could scarce suppose my age."

"Surely you could not be much past five and sixty years of age?" Adlai inquired, trying her best to appear genuine in her response, though in reality she thought he looked much nearer to being somewhere between seventy and eighty-five years of age. For some reason Dr. Hindley seemed oddly amused at her guess, for he laughed harder than ever.

"In my youth!" He sputtered, as his belly shook like a bowl of pudding from a Yule-tide feast. He thoughtfully took another whiff of his pipe.

"No, I am near two hundred and forty years of age," he said slowly at last.

Adlai gaped in surprise.

"You're jesting!"

"Nay, I do not jest!" Dr. Hindley replied simply.

"That's incredible!"

Adlai sat still for several speechless moments, her mind a whir of busy activity. He surely must have been alive when her great, great, great grandfather was a boy…Adlai's thoughts sobered now, as her mind drifted to other, less desirable subjects…She did not know who her own parents or grandparents were (let alone who her great, great, great grandfather or grandmother might have been). A sudden empty feeling crept over her again: how could she possibly know who she was, or what is was that she was supposed to be, when she did not even know where she had come from?

"Believe it or not," Dr. Hindley's voice cut through her thoughts, "Some of my forebears have lived to see near twice as many years as I—I've aged rather prematurely in comparison!" He let out a long, chuckling laugh at this.

"Where *do* you come from?" Adlai asked with piqued curiosity.

"From the mountain regions to the north, mostly."

"Yes, but what I *meant* was, who are your people?"

Dr. Hindley hesitated for a moment as he gazed at her in silence from the shadow of his seat .

"Why, Dwarves, of course," he replied with an unaffected smile. Dismissively he refilled his tobacco pipe and lit the end.

"Dwarves?" Adlai questioned in disbelief. She had noticed that he did appear shorter and smaller in stature than anyone else she had ever seen, yet for some reason this thought had not fully entered her mind.

"You mean the sort of mountain folk that live in caves and caverns deep in the rock, who mine for gold and jewels?—But I thought that dwarves never liked to come out into the sunlight!"

"Well, contrary to popular opinion (entertained by those simple-minded who like to weave a good tale)," Dr. Hindley stated tritely, "Dwarves are no more opposed to good sunlight than the common folk. And they do much more than merely mine for treasures and live in rocks…Or at least, they did once…"

A somber, troubled look crossed the Doctor's sobered expression, and he put his pipe back to his lips as if to hide his thoughts.

"Well if that's true, then why don't they ever show themselves?" Adlai queried.

"All of that is past history now," Dr. Hindley replied with a pained, yet polite smile, "And is better left in the past. However," he continued more enthusiastically, "If you wish to know more of the Ancient World, I am certain that I can provide you with all the answers you wish to know—only not tonight, since 'tis much too long and lengthy a lesson to get into."

"It must be comforting to know something of the history of your people, and to know who and where it is you've come from," Adlai offered, hoping that the exaggerated enthusiasm in her voice might drown out any envy which she felt. The Doctor beamed at this statement, and his face bore a look of strong pride in his heritage.

"Indeed!" He answered with a broad smile. "I come from a long line of extraordinary goldsmiths, crafters of all manner of fine and costly jewels—even great kings and mighty warriors!"

Adlai smiled impressively, trying hard to conceal her amusement. It was humorous to think of any being of such short stature as having been ever, in any way, perceived as fiercely threatening or intimidating. But to her relief, Dr. Hindley seemed to take no notice of how diverting she found his claims. Instead, he seemed temporarily lost in thought over the glory and splendor of former days; his wrinkled old face almost seemed to grow younger as he continued smoking his pipe, his eyes carrying a far off look as he sat lost in his idyllic day-dream.

"What was your father like?" Adlai inquired at length. The Doctor stirred and looked back at her.

"My father was brother-in-law to the great King of Glorin—ruler of all the Dwarf folk and underlings who dwelt in the mountain regions far to the north…He and my uncle were as close as blood brothers born of the same mother—"

Dr. Hindley stopped speaking abruptly, his mouth opening and closing awkwardly. His eyes filled with a pained expression as they roved this way and that over the flames flickering on the hearth, as if searching hard for something else to say, yet no words came. At last his mouth slowly closed and he lowered his head, slowly putting his pipe back to his lips to puff some more.

"How old were you when he died?" Adlai ventured softly, after several moments of silence had lapsed.

"I was only a young Dwarfling," Dr. Hindley answered with a heavy sigh, "My beard had not yet begun to sprout when he was suddenly cut short in his prime, by forces of ruthlessness and greed."

Dr. Hindley paused, as if trying to decide whether or not he should go on.

"Tell me, what subjects of interest do *you* like to read about?" He inquired suddenly changing the subject.

Adlai's dying curiosity nagged at her to know more about the odd little man before her—what acts of valor had he witnessed, what grandeur had he seen, and what tale of woe was it that he owned now? And how had they all served in making him the enwisened old man he now appeared? An intermingled feeling of sympathy and respect made her bite her tongue, however, so without further questioning she answered him obligingly.

"Oh, everything whatsoever to do with history," she quipped enthusiastically. "Especially legends, and any old tales that have to do with—what was it you called it again? Oh, yes! The 'Ancient World'…I'm hardly ever allowed to read anything of that sort…I don't suppose you could tell me about any of the pieces you've worked on translating?"

"Indeed, I might! Although the one I have in mind right now is not one which I have worked to translate, but rather one which has been handed down to me from my predecessors. I don't suppose you'd be at all interested in hearing it?"

"Oh, would I?!" Adlai burst out in ecstatic rapture.

A beaming smile broke out upon the old man's face again. He pulled himself up in his chair, shifting his weight and making himself comfortable in preparation for the oration of his story.

CHAPTER 15—LEGENDS OF THE FALL

"Long, long ago, before the existence of time and space, when all the realms of the physical and spiritual worlds lived together in harmony—when Old Earth was once young and when animals spoke, and mystical creatures once abided and shared the world of men—there lived upon the earth an ancient race of beings not born of man. They were taller, stronger, and much more beautiful than the children of men, and it was said that they had come from another world altogether outside the realm and time of humans. They were the wisest and the most discerning of all living creatures upon the earth, and it was supposed that they knew and could see all—things past, things present, and things still to come. To this race had been appointed the guardianship of Young Earth; thus they came to be known as the Guardians, for it was their charge to keep watch over her, to judge fairly and to rule wisely over all life and over every living thing. It had further been granted that they should have knowledge of all secrets, mysteries, and all things sacred concerning the Wisdom of the Deep, that they might be armed to protect Earth and her children against the threat of an Ancient Evil. To further aid them in their task, the Guardians were also given gifts of many powers—powers great, awesome, fearful, and dreadful; there was not a blessing or curse in any tongue of man, creature, or beast, that was not fully known to them. Their powers were great, and their deeds and mighty acts of heroism became legendary. Under the protection and watchful eye of the Guardians mankind enjoyed peace and prosperity, living out the length of their days in contentment and peace, while the Shadows of Darkness were kept at bay.

"Seasons, years, and centuries came and went…Millenniums passed…Young Earth slowly grew older, as she watched generation after generation of the sons of man spring up, thrive, grow old, and die, fading like the grass before newer generations of young blood. Yet the race of The Guardians remained constant and unchanging; they continued to hold endless vigil over thousands of generations of the children of men. They never tired nor grew into old age, and none of them ever came to know sickness. None of their number ever crossed over the Waters of Death under the Black Sails of the Departed, nor entered into the realms of the UnderWorld…And thus, over time, the Guardians came also to be known by a new name: The Immortals.

"…Time went slowly on, and a new generation arose from the sons of men: this generation was ignorant and did not remember the days of Olde; they had no desire to recount the great exploits and heroism of the Guardians, nor recall their mighty deeds of valor…As more years were seen by Earth, men became more and more restive. They began to view the Immortals with resentment as strangers and aliens in their lands, and treated them with growing suspicion and hostility…The Guardians continued to endure all this in silence, but all the while the arrogance, greed, and corruption of Man continued steadily to grow. His eye became dark and filled with envy, as he fixed his heart's desire with bitter covetousness upon the one thing he still could not achieve: the secret Key to the powers and eternal life possessed only by the Guardians.

"At last the sons of Earth gathered together to make war against the Immortals, and to drive them out from among the world of men. There, upon the Great Battle Plain of Mundeur, a number of them joined together in a binding covenant—made sacred through the shedding of blood. And they took an oath there, and swore upon the memory of their forefathers and upon the heads of their young children, that they would neither rest nor give up, till at last they had obtained the sacred Keys of Power and Eternal Life.

"On the day of the battle, a great army was assembled upon the fields of Mundeur. A host not only of men, but of talking animals, and also many of the mystical creatures joined them. …And then at last, from far off in the distance they came, and all stood hushed in wonder: Far off to the west there appeared suddenly a great and shining company—brilliant, white, magnificent and dazzling—the Immortals rode out in silence to meet the adversaries which had gathered to fight them. A stilled silence settled over the armies of men, and all sound completely died away as the great white host of the Immortals parted like a wide, shining sea. The great High King—the oldest, wisest, and most powerful of all the Ancient Race—approached. He was far more majestic and powerful in appearance than any of the others. The armies facing him began to tremble at his presence, and a tremor could be felt running throughout the earth and atmosphere, when at last he opened his mouth to speak.

"The sound of his voice was at once soft like a gentle breath of wind, but then broke out suddenly over the throng like the mighty rushing of many waters. Yet the words that rang out that day none could comprehend or interpret. All shook with dread at this, and the eye of man and creature alike was filled with fear. Instantly the sound of his voice ceased, and all was still again…All waited with bated breath, then slowly stirred to look perplexedly at one another: from beneath, a low rumbling emanated up from the ground. The skies became darkened, and fiery clouds flew swiftly overhead, as if nature itself were fleeing in dreaded terror from a dark and terrible scourge. The earth groaned from her depths in great travail, when all about there was a violent shaking as of a mighty earthquake. The ground split suddenly from underneath amidst wild screams and cries, and the opposing armies tumbled down into the fire and darkness of bottomless depths. The rest who survived witnessed in horror, as the great rocks were moved from their foundations, and Earth was laid open and bare to her core. The waters of the Deep gushed from their springs; surging up like a mighty tide from their resting place, they broke forth in raging torrents over the scattering multitudes upon the plain. A great and noisy tumult ensued, as the armies of men and their alliances fled in panic and horror.

"All at once the High King struck the ground beneath his feet. A great fiery light shot up and twisted towards the heavens, its light bending under the dome of the sky as it flew out like an arc to either side; at last it formed into an enormous sphere that completely enveloped the host of the Immortals from view. Within moments the entire valley floor was flooded: Earth covered the nakedness of her shame towards man's infidelity, and all his uncleanness was washed away from her in a great flood.

"Only a few dared look back, as they fled with great speed up into the hills and mountains. It is said that in a moment, the great Sphere suddenly arose into the skies and departed, vanishing away in the direction of the sun, and was seen no more. The place where the Immortals had been was, in an instant, completely covered over by fiery, molten lava and hot brimstone. The earth beneath erupted with loud cracks and thunderings, and everything on the valley floor sank down into the depths as flood-waters crashed over...The Battle of Mundeur was ended—finished before it had even begun.

"Man's hope to find the Key was lost to him that Day, gone with the final departure of the Guardians beneath the avenging waves of judgment. Those few that were not immediately washed away by the flood, nor swallowed up whole by the earth, slowly made their journeys back to their cities and former dwelling places in humbled shame and defeat.

"...Dark days came now upon the world of men: no longer was there any peace to be found on the earth; the old alliances between man, beast, and mystical beings alike crumbled and fell to ruin, and everywhere chaos and confusion took hold. The animals that once talked and communicated like men became suddenly mute and dumb; the magical creatures that once roamed free now hid themselves away in shame and fear, and would not suffer themselves anymore to be seen by men. Instead they went back to their secret places in brook and stream, river and sea; others took to hillock and mountain; to woodland dell, forest glade and glen; into the rocks, caves, caverns, and hollow places of the earth—

each one according to the nature of their kind—and from thence they were never more to be seen. In misery and perplexed consternation the children of men witnessed this sad departure of the Old World; it seemed an ill omen portending desolate tidings of man's future, in a world now emptied of all its former glory…Mankind was truly alone now, utterly abandoned and forsaken by all, there to live as outcasts upon the Earth which had rejected them…All the grand splendor of the Early Age was gone… The Day of the Guardians was over… A New Age—the Age of Man—had begun.

"…Years passed…Men began diligently to rebuild themselves. Cities and governments were reestablished and kingdoms rebuilt, for now they had to learn to survive on their own, and to be their own defender against all outer threats…A shallow peace and fragile tranquility returned again to the world of men; all was stilled once more, as they silently watched and waited… Steadily, fear erased from their minds all the images of glory that once had been…And so, gradually, the memory of the Immortals—and of *other* things—slowly crept into sleep and was scattered like dust into the winds.

"…Then at last, like the quiet stillness before a storm— something began to stir within the Earth once again…Something, which had not been awakened since the Forgotten Days of Olde…Dread and foreboding spread as a great Shadow grew over the Earth…Whispers of the approach of a Deep, Impenetrable Darkness…An Ancient Evil had at last awoke."

The little man stopped abruptly in his narrative to re-light his pipe. Taking in several long draughts, he glanced down through his silver spectacles upon his breathless listener who was sitting rigid at the end of her stool. At last she could stand the silent tension no more.

"And then?" She inquired pensively. "What happened?"

The little man slowly lowered his pipe to look her full in the eye.

"What present age is this?

"The Fourth Age," Adlai answered confusedly, "But I don't understand—what does that have to do with anything?"

"The Fourth Age from *what*?"

The little man asked in a voice so small that it finished in barely more than a whisper, and he was now leaning so far forward in his chair that his face was only inches away from her own.

"Oh, I *see*!" Adlai murmured in a wondering whisper. "The Ages are being counted back from the First Age of Man— from the time of the Guardian's departure from our world!"

"Mmmm."

The doctor gave her a satisfied, yet sober smile as he sat back again in his chair. Quietly he went back to smoking his pipe, a sadly wistful expression in his old eyes. For several moments Adlai sat motionless in her seat, her eyes searching the flames on the hearth as she mused over the story she had just heard. Then gradually a new thought formed.

"And the Evil which has awakened?" She asked slowly at last, "That is what we are fighting—isn't it? It's what our King has gone to war against?"

The Doctor gave her a grave smile.

"But what *is* it, exactly?"

"It is as I said—an Ancient Evil of the Deep, which has been reawakened."

"But whence did it come? How came it to be?"

"It is an Evil greater and more deadly than any other evil you could possibly imagine!"

The Doctor was again speaking in the same hushed whisper as before, almost as if in fear that the mere mention of it might in some way attract the attention of the thing it concerned.

"It is so Ancient, that it goes back far beyond the existence of even our own world."

"How did it get here?" She asked breathlessly.

"Man—or should I say, a *woman*—allowed it."

"*What*?!"

Dr. Hindley looked up again, a small smile again playing on his wrinkled face.

"You sound as if you want to hear another story."

Adlai grinned broadly.

"My latest work has been in translating one of the most ancient tales still in existence upon the earth—it is the story of the love of an Immortal Prince for a mortal maid…I must say, it's been quite a work in translation thus far, and has stretched me full in all my knowledge and understanding of the old tongue in which it was first recorded. There are few yet alive who are familiar with it at all, and none in existence who have ever even heard the language spoken."

"It's a pity that an entire language should be lost and forgotten," Adlai remarked somberly. "Yet at least you're now doing it justice by translating it—hopefully it will be kept and preserved for future posterity."

"And not only so that it might be passed on," Dr. Hindley rejoined, a hint of growing passion rising in his voice, "But so that we might also *learn* from it! It is my very firm belief that those who do not learn from the history of our past, are themselves insensibly doomed to the destruction of repeating it in ignorance. Why should we suffer needlessly to learn life's lessons, when past generations have already paved the road of knowledge to equip us for our journey? We have at our disposal the ability to avoid meeting with the tragedy of the same outcome—if we are only willing to ply ourselves towards *learning* from their errors."

Something about this last comment made Adlai feel uncomfortable, as she remembered their earlier conversation on the stairwell.

"Tell me," She said quickly changing the subject, "What happened to them?"

"To whom?"

The Doctor seemed as if her question had disoriented his thoughts mid-course; he appeared to have already lost track of the direction his discourse had been previously headed.

"The immortal Prince—and the girl he loved—" Adlai stammered impatiently, "What happened to them?"

"Oh, yes!" The little man laughed quickly. "The *inevitable* happened, of course," he added with a sly smile. Adlai drew up breathlessly.

"Oh, do go on!" She begged in mock exasperation. "What is 'the inevitable' supposed to mean?!"

"Well, I must warn you, it's another long story," the Doctor replied, shaking his head with another winking smile. "It's already well past the second hour of the morning, and you've a long day of studying ahead of you tomorrow—think it not best that you hurry back, and get what's left of any little sleep that's to be had?"

"But just a *little* longer won't make any difference," Adlai pleaded, "And besides—I'm already wide awake—and I promise I won't be slack in my studies tomorrow."

"Well, I suppose," Dr. Hindley answered thoughtfully, stroking the length of his long silver beard as it trailed down his bulging girth.

"Very well!" He said at last, slapping his knee.

"...It all began long, long ago, during the Age when both mortals and Immortals lived together upon a Young Earth. At that time, there was once a great Prince of the Immortal people—Orin of the Guardians. He was as fair of countenance and beautiful in stature and appearance as he was also wise, understanding, noble, and just; and it was said that none had ever been his equal. He was loved and adored by all the free peoples of Young Earth, and his magnificence, justice, power, and strength were worshipped and revered by all. But the Prince's prize jewel, which he treasured above all else, was his betrothed bride, the fair daughter of a king of a far away kingdom. Many thought it strange that he should choose for himself a mortal bride from among the daughters of men, but Orin's heart was fully given to her, and he refused to love another. In joyful celebration, the Prince and his betrothed made ready for the great and glorious day of their marriage.

"But then, on the eve before they were to be joined together, it was discovered that his bride had betrayed him—abandoning her love for him, she had turned to another. Moreover it was also discovered that she, along with her lover, had made many enchanting designs against him by use of dark magic arts and witchcraft, and that she had fled away with her new love and hidden herself from her marriage-lord. The Prince was heart-sick, grief-stricken to his core at the discovery of her great betrayal and infidelity; yet even greater was his fear for the danger he now foresaw which would come to her. For little did the foolish Princess know that which she loved was a Shadow, and that she herself had been beguiled and deceived by a trick of her own fancy.

"For back in those days, when Laws of the Deep was at the heart of all life, there was a certain belief held sacred by men and Immortals alike. For it was believed that the human heart—once bound to another—could not be unbound or loosed. This view was especially considered regarding those of the royal line, as there was a superstitious belief that royalty held in its blood-line traces of the divine, unchangeable nature of the Immortals. For this reason, wise Seers who had knowledge of all things sacred, were carefully sought out with the expected birth of each royal heir. For it was also believed in those days, that in the very first moments of life—when a newborn child first opened its eyes—that its first glances upon the world were so pure, untainted, and full of innocence, that a gifted Seer could actually look into the eyes of the child's soul. The Seer would then be able to fore-see the child's future purpose and destiny. But even more, the Seer was able to also see the *other* half of its soul—the one of whom it was predestined by the Divine Will to be joined with for the rest of time. Accordingly, it was in keeping with this belief and custom that marriage alliances were carefully made. And since this was the way that attachments between man and woman had always been formed, and always without discrepancy, this way of life had never before been questioned. For never before had deceit and unfaithfulness come between a man and woman. Great was the shock and incredulous disbelief of all, therefore, over the Princess' selfish choice to depart from her marriage-lord for the sake of another.

"Orin was stricken in his heart—not only with grief for her infidelity—but also for what he understood she had unwittingly done. For in the breaking of her betrothal covenant and the invoking of forbidden enchantments, she had transgressed against the Laws of the Deep which wove all life together in perfect harmony. A strange and deadly curse now lay upon the world of men. And the earth—which had never before known evil—now came to know suffering, pain, and death. The Sun now beat harshly upon the earth in all its furious heat; hail and lightening battered her surface; hurricanes struck the oceans, and flood waters rose from the depths. Fiery rains streamed down from the heavens, and the stars themselves began to die, streaking down from the place where they had hung in the celestial bodies above. All living creatures alike were dumbfounded as they watched their world crumble into ruin, its life-force drained away by an unknown source.

"A great High Counsel of the Guardians was immediately called together in great haste, that it might be decided what should be done to save and restore what was left of Earth. After much searching and inquiry, the oldest and wisest of the Immortals predicted that the Earth was on the verge of annihilation, and that if the course of events (such as they were) remained unaltered, that both Earth and her children would face total destruction and perish amidst a terrible judgment of fire and water. In addition, he foretold that the only possible way for Earth's children to be spared, was for the blood of her betrayer to return to her depths: a life for a life—that through the death of one, new life could be rebirthed. Upon the hearing of this it was thereby directly decreed, that in judgment for the Princess' treasonous crimes against the Laws of the Deep, that she should immediately be extradited for sentencing and execution.

"Grave, indeed, were these tidings when they fell upon the Prince's ears; for, as head of the Guardians and High Keepers of Earth, the responsibility to execute the High Counsel's judgment upon the Princess rested solely upon none other than himself. It was therefore decided that it should be by his very own hand that she should be slain, that through the shedding of guilty blood the sacred balance of life and harmony upon the earth might be restored.

"Great indeed was the Prince's grief. In secret he set out to somehow find a remedy somewhere within the Laws of the Deep itself—a remedy powerful enough not only to redeem the Princess' life, but that could also atone for her crimes and appease the

Divine Justice—thereby saving the world from its sure and imminent destruction. Orin returned again to the oldest and wisest of the Seers for his counsel, and was given a strange and perplexing oracle: it was *indeed* possible for the earth to be saved, *without* the death of her betrayer—but only if the Prince himself was willing to pay a very great price in return. Even so, though it was *possible* for the Princess' life to be saved, still he would have no sure guarantee of her full safety—even after the price was exacted from him in full. The Princess had chosen to be united in an unholy bond to Shadow…in order to be saved, she would have to choose freely of her own will to again become bonded to the Light. Only *if* the Prince were able to woo her back and win her love again, could she be forever saved. If he failed to regain her love, then although the deterioration and destruction of Earth would be belayed, yet his sacrifice for his wayward bride would be in vain: the Princess would be forever locked within the prison of her choice. Her spirit would gradually fade away, disappearing forever into the Shadow which had taken possession of her soul."

Dr. Hindley paused in his narrative, a brewing, contemplative look in his eyes:

"Love is a powerful force… even when given to one for whom it was never intended… Guard your heart above all else, for it is a wellspring of Life… Love is both our greatest source of happiness, and at the same time, our greatest pain; it is our greatest strength, and also our greatest weakness… Love is the greatest gift which we own—it is both free to give and to receive; and yet at the same time it is so costly, that it would cost a man his life. Many have chosen to sacrifice their own freedom and happiness, even their lives—for Love's sake… So before you give the very essence of your soul to another, *know* to whom you give it."

Dr. Hindley's eyes flickered suddenly, as if rousing himself back from the stupor of his inner ruminations. He had a dubiously awkward expression, as if he suddenly realized that he had spoken more than he'd intended. Abruptly he reached for his teacup and took in a lengthy swig, before taking a few more puffs from his long tobacco pipe.

"*Well?*"

Adlai had been sitting in rapt, wide-eyed attention with her chin clutched tightly in her hands, but now she drew herself up in agitated impatience.

"So *what* happened?! Was Orin able to win her back? What sort of payment was he forced to make in order to save them all?!"

Her questions flooded out in a torrent, the severity of her voice demanding that the good Doctor make a short and speedy delivery of the rest of his narrative. Dr. Hindley laughed softly in an amused tone, then slowly opened his mouth to speak again:

"The Prince left the distant lands of the Immortals, departed from his kingdom, and set out at once in search of her. Only he found that he could no longer freely enter the world of men. It was lost and shrouded in Shadow, and since he was a Spirit of and Bearer of the Light, the two could not co-exist together. The Darkness stood as a menacing barrier between him and his Beloved. Were he to enter in all of his glory, Earth and all of her offspring would be consumed by the very sacredness and purity of his essence. Part of his sacrifice included leaving behind his life of glorious immortality—instead to endure the hardships of man's world as a common mortal and a wandering outcast in it, for as long as his journey should endure… So Orin chose to strip himself of his Immortal regality and quietly entered the world of Man: he was no longer the beautiful, lordly Prince of all the known Realms. Heaven's most radiant star had fallen from its heights to Earth. Nothing was left but charred remains littering her now ashen, desolate surface as a token reminder of all that he once was—a perfunctory reflection of glory days gone by. The Darkness—our *own* darkness—left its mark on him, a mark which he would carry for the rest of eternity."

Adlai swallowed hard. Something about the story had awakened something deep inside of her; yet what it was exactly, she did not know. She hastily wiped away the waters welling up in her eyes, and quelled the stony lump rising in her throat. She wasn't used to becoming so visibly moved and disconcerted in the presence of others, much less over a mere story. But something about Orin's undying devotion touched her—along with the depths of his personal sacrifice. Perhaps it was the mutual feeling of understood hurt she shared with his character: Pain had left its mark on her too... Only hers were scars that no one else could see.

"And?" She queried softly, clearing her throat as she blinked away the mist from her eyes. "What happened?"

"He searched and searched far and wide, till at last he had wandered over the entire earth in his travels. Nothing about him any longer resembled the glorious, beautiful Prince of the Immortals, who had once been so highly exalted... At long last Orin found her... But by the time he did, she was already lying upon her deathbed. With tears the Prince fell to his knees by her side, but it was too late—the Darkness had blinded her, and she no longer recognized the sound of his voice. As the Princess was breathing her last, the Prince bent down and kissed her, imparting to her diminishing spirit all that was left of his strength and immortality. And the kiss which he gave—though it was not strong enough on its own to save her entirely—yet it was powerful enough that her spirit was preserved in an eternal sleep, and thus did not depart fully and fade into Shadow. And Earth, though it had already suffered great damages, was likewise preserved in a sleeping state along with the Princess, so that its final doom and destruction was not made complete...To this present day it is said that the Princess sleeps still, her spirit awaiting in slumber for the appointed time when her Prince shall at last return. In that Day, Orin will slay the Black Dragon whose venom poisoned her soul, and shall reveal himself as her truest Lover. She will be awakened when he finally fulfills his promised pledge, and pays the required price in exchanged ransom for her life."

Dr. Hindley stopped again in his story-telling, and took several more long draughts from his pipe, before sitting back in his chair, his hands folded contentedly over his belly. The dancing flames before him lit up the thoughtful look etched in the many wrinkles running hither and thither over his weathered face.

Adlai sat up sharply, her face an expression of flustered exasperation.

"That's *it?*" She burst out incredulously. "*That's* how the story ends? But that *can't* be all that there is! That just *can't* be right! After all, whatever happened to the Prince?" Her eyes darkened for a moment: "And whatever became of that spoiled, self-centered wretch of a Princess?"

"That," Dr. Hindley said with an apologetic shake of his head, "Is all that was left of the fragment I found still intact and recorded in the old language. It's a very ancient piece, and actually rather well-preserved, considering how very aged it is. I actually think that I've come to like this one best of all that I have worked in translating thus far. The ancient tongue in which it was originally written is exquisitely beautiful and poetic, not to mention very rich in depth and feeling…I suppose I also care for it so because I am a sentimental and romantic idealist at heart, and there is something about the care and tender devotion of this story, something which haunts me. The compelling selflessness of Love's sacrifice touches and moves me. It touches and moves me with its raw, courageous beauty—like a glittering diamond set against the black back-drop of betrayal. One thing is always true: the blacker the darkness, the more brilliantly the light shines out from it."

Adlai rolled her eyes.

"It seems a pathetic waste to me," she retorted bluntly. "The stupid Princess might have saved herself and everyone else a whole lot of trouble, if she hadn't acted so selfishly and made such a muddle of everything. If I were Orin," she added sulkily, "I don't think I should have troubled myself one wit to save her."

The Doctor laughed.

"I take it then, that you did not much enjoy my story-telling."

"No, not as much as I had expected," Adlai answered glumly. "And besides: however is one to appreciate a tale of True Love, when only *one* of the characters does all the loving, and the other couldn't give a snit about all he was forced to sacrifice for her?"

"*Forced* is one way of putting it," Dr. Hindley answered in a corrective tone. "I, however, think that one of the greater morals of the tale is simply this: that love is not so much a *feeling*, as it is a *choice*. And if there be any truth or merit to this story, for what it is worth, I believe that the Prince *chose* to love her—undeserving as she was. His sacrifices, great as they were, were made by a heart that was *willing* to lay itself down, for the greater good of others. For of all the greatest stories that have ever been told, there is none greater or purer, than that of the one who would willingly lay down his own life, for the life of another."

"Yes, yes," Adlai waved this comment impatiently away. "It's all very well in faery-tales. But in real life—with real people—that would be completely impossible. No one in his rightful mind would ever love anyone so utterly undeserving and beneath himself!"

"Beauty is often said to be in the eye of the beholder: the true value of an object is not decided in and of itself on its own merit; rather, it is determined and priced according to the one who values it—the greater the value he places in it, the more costly it becomes, and the greater a price he is willing to pay to obtain it."

"Tales such as those don't make good stories, for the simple reason that they just aren't believable," Adlai said dismissively. "What woman in her rightful mind would spurn the love of one she ought to have worshipped, for another not even comparable to him in any way?!"

"…Well, 'tis a sad truth that human nature is so greatly flawed, that it often has little appreciation for that which it already possesses. The fickle nature of humanity is that it is ever ready to give up that which it already has, in exchange for the luring enticement of that which lies just beyond its grasp…Often it is the tragic case that people will gamble away their entire lives, only to find their so-called treasure is nothing more than a mirage—a fleeting shadow; a lush, beautiful garden meant to disguise the ugly morosity of a tomb…There is nothing in all the world that a man can gain, which can ever compensate for the eternal loss of his immortal soul…"

Dr. Hindley seemed again suddenly lost in thought, so that Adlai was beginning to think that this must be a constant habit of his. Perhaps the inevitable disease accompanying philosophers, was that they were cursed to think a vast deal beyond what was healthy for those in possession of a sane and stable mind. She had never before met anyone whose mind seemed to wander so frequently, or who seemed to find some deep, hidden truth in every single subject that was mentioned. Was he intent on turning every conversation into some sort of philosophical discussion concerning his own intellectual views?... Adlai had heard of such men before—how their restless, roving search for truth and meaning often dragged them down into madness and insanity... Perhaps she was looking at such a one now. So lost was he now in his thoughts, that he seemed to have completely forgotten all about her presence... Upon what high plateau of spiritual truth was he now?

Adlai rolled her eyes again, as she let out a low, disgruntled sigh.

"Well, I, for one, have little appreciation for stories whose heroines turn out to be nothing more than spoiled girls—let alone spoiled *Princesses*," Adlai muttered half under her breath. "It's absurdly ridiculous that so much should be wasted upon those who have no appreciation for what they've been given...especially when so many others are left in want. The Prince should have left her to the just punishment of hell-fire!"

Dr. Hindley stirred as he smiled thoughtfully to himself.

"Yes, there is no sight near so keen as *hind*-sight. But I think that if the Princess herself could have foreseen all the grief and sorrow which she was about to bring upon herself and others through her choice—well, I think she would not have been so easily tempted...No, life is never so black and white as we should like it to be, and oft times mistakenly believe that it is."

The Doctor's eyes suddenly appeared veiled in deep introspection—an almost ominous look of foreboding, as they glinted sharply in the firelight. He no longer seemed to be paying note to anything else in the room; instead he continued to stare fixedly into the fire, as if preoccupied with secret deliberations within himself.

"Beware the grey areas of life," he murmured aloud.

Adlai looked up in surprise: his voice had adapted an almost eery intonation, and something about his strange change of mood and behavior made her feel at once strangely uncomfortable—and even somewhat frightened.

"Yes, beware of that which is neither black nor white," Dr. Hindley said in a brooding voice, "For it is often then that choices made are of the most dire import, with lasting consequences… Never decide hastily upon anything in which you are yet in doubt…Choose your steps carefully…choose them wisely…He who runs does not see the trap laid at his feet."

Adlai could feel a twinge of fear go trickling down her spine, and she hastily arose from her place.

"I quite forgot what time it is," she said with a feigned yawn. "I think I should be going, before it's too late."

Dr. Hindley seemed to wake with a sudden start from his stupor.

"Oh, yes, of course!" He answered with a startled laugh. "I'm so sorry! Yes, yes; you must hurry back at once, before you are missed!"

Adlai cast a glance towards the window shutters; dim cracks of light were already peaking though, so that to her chagrin she realized that it was already morn—they had talked the whole night away. She groaned inwardly at the thought of having to face another long, tedious day of study with no rest beforehand, and her stomach, though previously full, was already starting to gurgle again with hunger.

"Oh!" She cried out with surprise, "It's already dawn! Yes, I must be going at once, before—"

She could not bring herself to finish her thought, for she well knew what sort of consequences she would meet with, were her absence to be discovered. The doctor nodded quickly in response, as if to excuse the necessity for any further explanations. Adlai gave a quick bow of her head in thanks, and hurriedly departed from the little room in the tower.

CHAPTER 16—DEPTHS OF A WATERY TOMB

She had just made it back to her bedchamber and barely closed the door behind her, when presently there was a knock.

"Oh! I see you're up already, Milady!" The maid said with surprise upon entering. "Best hurry with your breakfast now; you're wanted right away by his Lordship, just as soon as you've finished."

Adlai's ears pricked up. It wasn't usual for him to request her presence.

"Did he say what matter it regarded?"

"No, Milady. He only requested that you meet him by the fountain in the garden."

Willan? What could he possibly want to speak with her about?

Adlai barely even bothered to look at the breakfast trays, there were so many questions pouring through her mind. *Was it good news? Was it bad?* There wasn't time for anything else— she had to find out at once! Without delay she speedily dressed and scurried from the room.

Out the back door and over the castle lawn she flew towards the terraced gardens of Dombrey Manor. As she entered the alcove she paused to brush out her dress and sweep her hair from her face, making a futile attempt to disguise both her haste and excitement. Clearing her throat, she made her way with more dignified airs across the stone-paved path leading to the garden's center.

It was a little warmer today than it had been of late. A slight breeze rustled the few remaining leaves of the nearby trees and bushes along either side of the walkway, and a dim sun shone vaguely from an overcast sky. There was hardly any sound, not even the chirping of a bird as she tread softly through pillared archways. At last she came to the edge of a great pool at the garden's center. From here, other terraced pathways and alcoves continued in divergent directions; all met together at the heart of the garden, however, where the arched roof overhead opened up directly above the pool.

There was no sign of Willan anywhere. Adlai let out a flustered sigh, then turned to check her reflection in the murky waters of the pool. A gentle wind sent ripples spreading out in ever widening circles upon its hushed surface, as her bobbing reflection stared back at her with a hesitant, uncertain expression. How did she truly appear to others, she wondered—and particularly, to him? She wrinkled her brow, grimacing fretfully as she tried hard to picture herself through his eyes. But try as she might, she couldn't decide whether the girl staring back at her was pretty, or only ordinary in appearance. Did he consider her looks at all striking or remarkable? Ruefully she noted that the sad grey color of her ill-fitting dress did little to lend assistance. However he perceived her, though, she was certain of one thing: there existed no other maid who had yet caught his eye, and she was the only lady of even *slightest* rank (even if only as the King's ward) for miles around…Surely he could not help but notice her, or at least to be conscious of her ever-growing regard for him?

Adlai's eye wandered slowly from her own reflection, drifting upwards to that of a stone figure reflected in the water just beyond her own image. A tall woman loomed high overhead, her eyes staring unwaveringly out over the water. The face of the statue had been expertly sculpted with the greatest care and precision, down to the last flawless detail; her expression was so life-like that she almost appeared real. And she would have been exquisitely beautiful, Adlai thought, were it not for a rather cold, disquieted look to her which made Adlai herself feel a little uneasy. In her molded hands she carried two objects: one was a double-edged sword which she brandished aloft. The other hand was somewhat extended, as though she were half offering, half guarding the other object she held. It was a set of three sun-dials, each ring overlapping the other, so that all together they formed a sort of odd ring. Beneath the foot of the statue was a carved open scroll with an inscription on it. Adlai strained her eyes, peering closely so as to make out the writing from where she stood, yet found that she could not make it out. Her eyes traveled slowly back up the statue's form, till once again she found herself staring directly into its eyes…They seemed so life-like, that for half an instant she was not so certain but that the statue was not staring back. A little shiver ran through her, and she jerked her focus away with a snap…It was only carved stone…nothing more.

"There you are!"

Willan's warm, cheerful voice broke through her disturbed contemplations, so that she immediately spun round.

"Willan!" She cried with a relieved smile. "I was beginning to fear that you weren't coming."

"My apologies, Adlai; I just had a few last things to finish, before meeting you here. The wife of one of the tenant farmers came to see me—her husband Hamish delivered payment here near four days ago, and hasn't been seen since… She fears the worst."

"Willan," Adlai asked hesitantly, "Do you think that was the body we found?"

Willan swallowed hard.

"There's no way of knowing for certain, though the same thoughts stirred in my own mind as well."

"Did you tell her of our findings?" She queried.

"No."

"Why didn't you? For Heaven's sake, Willan! Why ever would you keep that back from her?!"

He stared at her in silence. Suddenly she felt a surge of anger. When was he going to stop pretending that none of it had happened?

"The townsfolk ought to be warned, Willan! There are ravenous fiends stalking the countryside, and you just go about life as if nothing had happened!"

"What would you have me to do?!" He shot back, seizing hold of her arm. He was breathing hard, the strain etched across his face. "Adlai," he said in a lowered voice, "Why do you suppose I've been hunting of late?"

"I—I had supposed that it was to take your mind from weightier matters," she faltered.

"I go in search of the Beast. Only a few of my most trusted men knew the true reason behind my last hunting expedition. It is best for everyone else to believe us to be simply in hunt of wild game, rather than know the darker nature of our business. If word gets out beforehand—it will spread terror among our people... I will *not* risk that."

"And Hamish's family?"

"She has half a dozen mouths to feed, and no means to run the land," he sighed. "The loss of her husband spells ruin for their whole livelihood. I've assured her that I will lend her whatever assistance we can spare, but I'm afraid it won't be enough to help them survive."

"Any success in your search? Have you found any clues as to the Creatures' where-abouts?"

He shook his head ruefully.

"The trail went cold. Whatever it was, let us hope that it has departed from these lands."

Adlai suddenly noticed that Willan was heavily cloaked, as if in readiness for some sort of journey, and that he had a rolled, sealed parchment in one hand. Hesitantly she looked up at him in a questioning look of disbelief.

"Willan, where are you going?" Her voice wavered.

"Oh, yes, that!"

Willan laughed in a way that was suddenly strained, as if trying to make light of something difficult. Yet there were unmistakable traces of worry and concern in his eyes, and he almost seemed want to avoid meeting her gaze. For a moment he fumbled awkwardly, as if attempting to delay the delivery of unwanted news. His smile vanished away as he cleared his throat:

"That's actually why I've asked you to meet me here," he answered soberly, "for I've something of import to tell you."

He paused briefly, his eyes studying her face as if searching for some indication as to how best to relay his news.

"You see," he added slowly, "I've just received word from our King that he has need for me to leave Dombrey promptly upon an urgent errand. That is why I must away on my journey—

practically this very moment—and to embark by ship for the neighboring kingdom of the south. There I seek to persuade King Menasis of Sundor to join us against the black scourge threatening our free lands." Willan paused, his eye lingering once more in hers. "And though it is not my wish to leave you here alone—" his voice trailed softly, and Adlai detected the unmistakable traces of mist in his eyes, "I must depart at once."

Adlai remained in shocked silence, her ears still ringing with what he was saying…There was a question growing in her mind—a question which she desperately did not want to ask, because deep down she already knew its answer.

"Willan," she began tremulously, "Are we being invaded?"

He swallowed hard, taking in a deep breath as he did so.

"Our borders have not yet been breached—but I fear—" his voice broke off, so that he did not finish.

Adlai's thoughts were reeling. The war was nothing new to her. She had grown up with it always existing somewhere in the background shadows of everyday life, to the point that she had become almost numb and complacent to its existence… But now… now it was *here*… And she realized that she hadn't really before given it much thought that there might be open war in their own lands. Her mind flashed back to the first day that the King had been summoned by his Liege-Lord, the Emperor of the Western Isles. Though no one knew much of their strange new foe, all had been confident that the end of the war would come very quickly… None had foreseen what was coming.

She searched Willan's face, and was now surprised to see that he had tears in his eyes.

"Adlai, I don't wish to frighten you with what I've heard…But this Darkness… It's the greatest Evil that we may ever face. Much of the free lands to the west have already been hazed to the ground, with naught remaining of its earth or people but stubble and ash. They say that the Shadow—or the Black King, as some call him—is the incarnated Demon Erebus, somehow loosed from the UnderWorld. He leads an army not of men, but of monstrous, ravenous beasts—a hoard of blood-thirsty, barbarous creatures that swarm the earth like locusts, devouring all in their wake. Their powers—*his* powers—are such as we have never seen before." Willan hesitated. "If I don't hurry aid to our King soon, all our hope will be lost."

Willan barely whispered these last words, yet they fell on her ears with a resounding boom. She felt as if she couldn't breathe. A chilling fear was creeping over her. This army of beasts…were they the same phantom Creatures Willan had been hunting?… Was the first on-slot of the enemy just beginning to trickle in?

Her thoughts jolted back to Willan—what of him? He was everything to her …If something were to happen—if she lost him—then her whole reason for existence would be suddenly gone…However could she carry on?

"For how long will you be away?" She quivered.

"I do not yet know. If all goes well and I am successful in my mission, I hope to return soon with a gathering of armies, and then I must join our King."

Adlai turned away, still trying to grasp the full meaning of his words. In a daze she looked out past the castle walls to the moors and forested mountains far beyond. Was it possible that this beautiful country, with its tranquil forests, majestic mountains, and peacefully flowing rivers might come to destruction, and that all she loved might cease to exist?

"Adelheide?"

Adlai blinked and turned back numbly towards Willan.

"What is it?" His voice was almost tender.

"I'm afraid," She whispered hoarsely. "You're all the friend and family I've ever known, and I'm just afraid to lose that."

"There, there, now!" He whispered comfortingly, affectionately stroking her hair. "We must hope for the best. There is still much that lies between us and our adversaries. We still have the advantage of the mountain regions of Roiem along our northwestern front. And we have the barrier of the oceans off our coast, and our sister countries to our south…All is not lost yet."

He hesitated, and his hand rested gently on her cheek. Adlai looked away, fighting hard against the tears stinging her eyes, as she bit her lip in an effort to keep them from spilling over. Willan said nothing but remained silent. After a moment he softly grasped her chin in his fingers and pressed his lips to her forehead. She winced. This moment would have been everything she'd ever longed for, were it not for the circumstances on which it had arrived.

After a moment he pulled himself away, brushing away tears of his own. Slowly he removed a sapphire ring from his left hand. Taking her hand in his, he softly slid the ring upon her finger, then pressed her hand to his breast. Adlai suppressed a startled gasp, and looked up quickly in surprise.

"This was my mother's. I would have you keep it with you, until my safe return…Keep it as a token of my… regard… and of my promise to come back safe again, when all is over. Would you honor me with this?"

He was again searching her eyes. She blinked back her tears and forced a smile in reply. Willan's heavy countenance lifted a little and he beamed in satisfaction, quickly pressing her hand to his lips.

"And take this too," he added, pressing into her hand a long dagger in a jeweled sheath. "This is my favorite dagger—it's always brought me good fortune. If I know you have it with you, I'll feel better about leaving."

Adlai stared at it in breathless awe, uncertain of what to say.

"Adelheide," his voice was suddenly firm and authoritative. "Do *not* go out past the walls of Dombrey. It isn't safe anymore."

… And then, without another word, he was suddenly gone, striding down the little stone path to the courtyard outside. Adlai thought her heart had stopped. Dizzy, she sank down upon the stone ledge of the pool and tried to catch her breath, as she watched him disappear. It felt as if the wind had suddenly been knocked from her body. Her life—and her freedom—was walking away through those archways. Her head was spinning, her fingers fumbled feverishly along the stone as she sought to steady herself. Suddenly she felt the ring slip from her finger, and heard a splash in the water next to her. Her heart gave a panicked leap: she had only owned it a few moments, and now her most treasured possession was already gone—she had to find it! But where was it? Blindly she plunged her hand in the direction of the splash, her fingers grasping about in the water as she teetered precariously over the brink.... Then before she knew what was happening, she was falling head-long.

Cold, dark waters enveloped her on all sides now as she struggled to see where she was. Dimly she caught sight of something shiny as it slipped silently past her... Willan's ring. Adlai lunged and quickly caught it, then turned back to look up again towards the sunlight. To her shock she realized that she could not detect any light at all; instead, everything about her seemed to be growing darker, as if she were falling deeper still into the recesses of the pool. Frantically she turned this way and that for any sign of the surface. Her hand touched upon something floating in the waters next to her, and instinctively her fingers closed over it. She blinked in surprise at what she was clutching: it was seaweed. Fields upon fields of seaweed were waving about her in the stilly silence. Astounded, she peered down for some sign of the pool's bottom...There was nothing. Both the seaweed and the dark waters disappeared into a sea of black beneath her, so that she could make out nothing else. A sudden panic filled her...*What was this place?!*

Wildly she began kicking and flailing, fighting to swim up towards the surface. The water was frigidly cold now—so sharply, that it almost seemed to burn the skin off her flesh with its bite. Suddenly her hand struck against something over her head...It was...ice. Adlai pushed hard against it...Nothing. She pushed and heaved, but not so much as a tiny budge or crack appeared. In a second she was pounding and clawing at it—to no avail: the icy barrier was immoveable. It seemed to be steadily growing, expanding out and spreading downwards, as if pushing her back into its black, endless depths. In terror she strained against it; her strength was failing, and it already seemed that her heart was ready to explode in her chest. Her lungs were screaming for air. For how much longer would she be able to hold on?

Of a sudden she could make out the hazy shape of something frozen in the ice just above her hand…It was the shape of a human hand, and then an arm…Her eyes widened as she now saw the form of a face just above hers, unseeing eyes staring blankly back into her own…It was…Willan.

A scream bubbled soundlessly from Adlai's lips. She was fighting, shoving, pounding against the wall of ice with all her might now, when of a sudden she caught sight of something else. There were more shapes—everywhere she turned, she could see them now: a countless sea of cold, dead, lifeless bodies trapped in the black ice above her. In profound horror, she turned from one face to another, till at last she espied one more whom she recognized… Mistress Ardath. Gradually she ceased struggling, and looked about helplessly in despair. They were dead, and she was about to meet her own death as well. There was no way out…This was the end.

The last of the air left in her lungs finally bubbled through her lips, as sea water trickled through her nostrils and seeped into her mouth. Suddenly the stinging salt water was pouring down her throat, flooding into her excruciated lungs as she went into choked convulsions. In silence her struggling form drifted downwards into a watery tomb devoid of light or sound… It would not be much longer…

CHAPTER 17—ADVENT OF THE ELVES

Adlai's body went limp, her arms drooping in the water above her head. Then dimly, she became aware of a faint light glimmering in the distance far beneath her…Were these the final throes of death, before passing from this life into the next?...The orb was steadily growing, shafts of pale green light growing brighter and brighter as they spread upwards through blackened depths. Other smaller lights now began to emerge from the great light; as they drew nearer, she saw that each was accompanied by a strange dark form. The shadowy shapes began to approach, slowly circling round about her at a distance, yet what they were she could not distinguish. Out of the corner of her eye she saw one of them dart very near her head, but then with a quick swoosh it streaked away and disappeared. Their numbers were quickly growing; they seemed to be closing in around her now, and she could presently make out pairs of eyes glowing in the darkness. All at once, one of the shadows emerged from amongst the other forms. Adlai blinked in astonishment, as for the first time she saw what it was. A lovely feminine face with a serene, tranquil smile met her wondering gaze. Her brow was crusted with all manner of exquisite seashells, moonstone, raw agate crystal and other precious gems, with hair the color of sea foam streaming out behind her. Long ears fanned out into fins that graced either side of her head. There was an ethereal beauty about her visage; her delicate nose was molded more closely to her face than that of a mortal woman, with gills along her cheekbones, so that she more resembled the water fowl of the ocean. Her upper body was feminine in shape, with skin that shone with the opalesque brilliance of a glistering pearl. Over her breast was a glossy hard cover, of the same smooth pink glazed finish as the inside of a sea shell. And as Adlai looked more closely, she realized that it was *indeed* the formation of a shell—a series of shells—both large and small, and fitted perfectly together into armored plates upon the upper torso. Just below the belly bright, shimmering scales appeared; for instead of legs and feet, the body ended in a graceful fish's tail, a large pair of dorsal fins gracefully fanning the water current beneath in quiet, sweeping motions...It was a mermaid. And there about her neck hung an ornament that was the same glowing light Adlai had already seen. As the other shapes quietly drew closer, she could see that all of them were indeed Merfolk—

both mermen and mermaidens—and about the throat of each was a tiny shining light.

The first one quietly approached, gently taking Adlai's face in her hands she pressed her lips firmly to the girl's mouth and slowly exhaled. A breath of air gushed through Adlai's parted lips as warm oxygen flooded through her, filling her lungs and spreading out into every fiber of her being. Taut muscles slowly relaxed again, as she freely exhaled and drew in another breath. She could breathe under water! In mesmerized amazement she looked back to the mermaid, who responded with a gracious smile, silently folding her hands over her breast with a low, respectful bow of her head. Taking Adlai gently by the hand, she began softly to speak in a voice and language Adlai had never heard before. It was hypnotic, like the rhythmic beating of ocean waves; the sound of her voice and words actually seemed to paint colorful pictures, like that of early morning sunlight upon a peaceful sea. Slowly, Adlai began to realize that she could comprehend the Mermaid's words:

"Welcome, Honored One, to our World. I am Jhonreia, daughter of the Sea King Anteaon, Lord of the High Seas. We come now in Earth's time of need to offer our help and lend our aid…Come."

Jhonreia gently took Adlai by the hand, pulling her close as she turned deftly on her side and began to swim in the direction of the giant orb. Next moment Adlai was surging smoothly through the current alongside her. As she turned to look back over her shoulder, she saw that other Merfolk were silently following after, and that they were being flanked on either side by an escort of armored Mermen. Each was, like the Princess, breathtakingly beautiful in appearance and assemblage. The mermaids had, like the Princess, the same flawless skin that glowed like abalone or mother of pearl; the men folk, however, were completely covered in iridescent scales—from head to fin—and were of as many different colors, stripes, and markings as there were fish in the sea. The Sea Princess' guards wore armor similar to that of their Lady, only much weightier and more solid; instead of shell breastplates, their suits of armor were of jasper, onyx, carnelian and hematite, with heavily plated helmets upon their heads, and warriors' cuffs over their forearms. Each held in hand long silvery spears that split the current with a flash of light, dividing the waters before them as they swam on either side without a sound.

"Have no fear, Young One, of the shadows you have seen," Jhonreia was speaking in calm, reassuring tones. "The end of all things is not yet to come, and there is still a part which only *you* can play...Only take heed, and listen carefully to the instructions you are about to receive. We cannot go with you all the way; but I shall take you to Ones who have the power and wisdom to aid you in the mission you are about to undertake—give careful ear to all that they tell you...We are almost there."

The light had become so bright that Adlai could barely see anything anymore. All other color vanished away into white light. She could still feel Jhonreia's fingers grasping her hand; together they shot through the current. Of a sudden Jhonreia's grip on her wrist tightened, and with a plunge they dove head-long into the giant sphere of light. Then all at once the Princess let go. And the girl realized that she was no longer swimming through water any more, but instead was falling head-long through a great chasmic void of swirling colors, and on into a wide open space of white nothingness...

...Adlai gave a sudden jolt: had it been only seconds, minutes, a day? Or had an entire eternity passed? The Mermaid's words were still echoing dimly in her mind as she blinked in dazed confusion and tried to make out her whereabouts. Colors and shapes were returning again; she was no longer under water in the realms of the Sea Kingdom. Gingerly her fingers moved over a dry, crispy texture, just as she heard a crackling crunch beneath her hand: she was lying in a pile of dry leaves. The familiar smell of the forest hung in the air about her, together with the scents of birch and pine. Before she knew it, she was staring up into the pale colors of early sunset, peaking through the branches of overhead maple and oak trees, their arms heavy-laden with autumn leaves. Slowly she stirred and sat up to look about her: she was sitting in the middle of a forest glen. Pale, warm sunlight was streaming through the trees at the edge of the glade, and from there she caught glimpses of rosy pink clouds drifting quietly over forested hills and wide, open meadows. Rising to her feet she brushed the leaves from her skirt. Her clothes were completely dry, without the slightest indication that she had so much as fallen into a rain puddle. There was no sign of a single body of water anywhere close by… Where was the Sea Kingdom? …Where were the Merfolk?

Adlai was distracted by a sudden movement amongst the trees before her. Something was moving slowly through aspens along the forest's edge, making its approach in silent procession to the place where she stood. In the fading sunlight she could make out a glowing company of beings wending their way quietly in majestic formation. The shining hems of their garments barely seemed to brush the ground beneath their feet. Their complexions were pale, their skin almost seeming to shimmer in the twilight, and the well-chiseled features of each face were strikingly beautiful, with long, graceful ears that curled up the sides of their heads. All were exceptionally tall in stature, and all were richly appareled—their light and airy garments embroidered with colors brighter and deeper than any she had seen before, and decorated with exquisite ornaments that glittered over their dress and trailing robes. Many carried in hand long, silvery staffs, with a bright light set like a lamp atop of each. Adlai held her breath in speechless amazement: their regal appearance, colorful array, and elfin features indicated that these were indeed the woodland Elves who inhabited the hidden dells of the forests and mountains.

The procession continued their silent advent till they at last reached the very place where she stood. Then like a gentle wave they parted and drew up abreast on either side before her, as a smaller procession of woodland animals and other curious creatures filed solemnly through their midst. Curiously she saw that they were unwinding a shimmering sheet like gossamer fabric over the grassy path; yet when she looked more closely, she saw to her amazement that the coverlet was actually a silk being spun out quickly by thousands of tiny spiders, and that the sparkle and shine was created by countless little dew drops carefully woven into their fragile design. Behind them followed a little procession of animals, scattering flower petals over the silken carpet. Little lights like fireflies flew and bobbed overhead, darting here and there, till at last one came and lit upon her hand. With a gasp she saw—not an insect—but the lovely form of a tiny being with delicate, iridescent wings—it was a faery-sprite.

All drew up suddenly to attention, as two heralds stepped forward and lifted the tendril shafts of silver trumpets to their lips. The notes that proceeded forth did not remotely sound anything such as what Adlai was accustomed to hearing from such an instrument. Instead, it was more like the music of a thousand little bells, their soft, tender notes peeling forth with the resonance of joyful gaiety. Then suddenly it ceased, as the heralds solemnly bowed and drew back. One and all slowly turned about to face the far rear of their company, and ceremoniously bowed their heads in obeisance. Adlai stretched on her toes as discreetly as she could, straining to see what sort of illustrious being it was whose splendor commanded the homage and respect of so magnificent a retinue of attendants. At once she noticed that there was one light which shone out more brightly from among the rest; indeed, it seemed to be growing greater and more brilliant with each passing second, as for a moment it hung suspended in space. Gently it floated above the entire entourage, till at last it formed a shining sphere of gigantic proportions, which at last came down to rest upon the far end of the carpet.

Once again there was a sound like that of music playing, only this time it was not created by any kind of instrument fashioned by hands. It was like the music of the wind as it plays upon the leaves; of when raindrops beat softly over the waves of grassy green meadows; and of when rays of sunlight spill down upon lush fields. It was like the song of a happy brook as it gurgles merrily on its way to greater streams and rivers, and of birds singing gaily on a spring-time morn. All were joining together in joyful symphony, as nature's choir continued singing in harmonious chorus.

As the melody continued, the luminous form of a lovely young woman suddenly emerged from the orb and alighted upon the ground. She appeared quite young; indeed, Adlai guessed that she could not be any older in age than she herself. There was a certain trusting simplicity in the violet eyes that looked out sublimely upon the world around her; the features of her innocent face were almost child-like in appearance, and from her head soft waves of hair fair as light fell gently past her shoulders. She seemed to have the sober-minded, curious wonder of a young girl who had only just begun to learn about the world around her, and there was a self-consciousness that blushed in the rosy apple of her cheek and was carried in the slight shyness of her step. She was clothed like a bride; her garb was of such a light, fluffy substance that it almost had the appearance of blossoms clothing the boughs of cherry trees in the springtime. To her surprise, when Adlai looked more closely, she saw that the fabric actually *was* made of layers upon layers of flower petals and blossoms, and that here and there were also sown daisies and little flowering sprays and buds of various kinds. Over the young woman's tresses was wrapped a twisted, stemmed wreath of tulips, irises, daffodils and lilies, and all around the air was filled with the floral fragrance of springtime. Everywhere she passed wild flowers sprang up quickly and blossomed in wake of the footprints left from her unshod foot. From her shoulders grew a pair of wings that were as light, colorful, and delicate as those of a butterfly. In one arm she carried an abundant bouquet profuse with freshly cut blooms, and in the other hand she carried a small rainbow. Padding sleekly along side with the prowess of bold, confident steps was a mighty lion, shaking out the glory of his great golden mane as he sauntered undisturbedly through the throng. A low, rumbling roar resonated softly from somewhere deep in his chest, as the king of beasts made his silent, triumphal entry accompanied by his quiet lady. On the other side of her, a little white lamb walked cautiously beside; he had the shaky first steps of a newborn, yet with each step his legs grew stronger and more accustomed to use, till at last with a happy bleat he broke into a frisky trot. The young woman gave Adlai a sweet, serene smile as she drew near and gave a gracious bow of her head. Then without a word she moved silently aside, and turned quietly to look behind her as if in waiting.

Adlai followed the direction of her gaze back up the pathway, and saw that another being had also alighted from the glowing sphere of light. The second young woman was beautiful in face and form like the first, although her features appeared somewhat more matured. There was a vivacity which she exuded—from her bright, excited eyes of deep sky blue, to her rosy red cheeks, and joyful, buoyant smile. She moved with the beauty of self-assured confidence and easy grace. All throughout the wood there was a warm fragrance, accompanied by the chirping of crickets as on a midsummer's eve. Her golden hair was like a radiant splash of summer sunshine, and entwined about her head were primroses and leafy green laurels wrapped around thick cuts of harvest grain. The iridescent, fast beating wings on her back were the colorful design of a dragonfly's, their bright turquoise and emerald hues bathing the light around them in vibrant color. Her flowing tunic was light and airy, and appeared to be made of sheer muslin and silks. Woven into the fabric were images of the sun shining in all of its magnificence amidst clouds of pink and purple; rays of sunlight streamed down over green, flowering hills; trickling streams and cool blue rivers flowed on through yellow fields of wheat and barley. She was accompanied on one side by a tall, milk-white unicorn with a long beard and golden horn; on the other, a nightingale of colorful plumage sang gaily on her shoulder. In one hand she held an olive branch, and in the other a small turtle-dove sat perched upon her forefinger. The girl did not seem much older than Adlai herself, and she found the young woman's carefree energy and exuberance to be deliciously infectious. There was something about the air of her unaffected simplicity that was openly inviting. She seemed not so much to walk as she did to dance, as if she were blissfully twirling upon some celestial cloud far away. To Adlai she seemed much like a young girl just venturing out into a wide, open world filled with infinite possibilities, and armed with the bold hopefulness of limitless aspirations; there was nothing at all sober or timid in her appearance, and neither was there a single hint of self-doubt. In fact, for a moment Adlai almost expected for the maid to seize her suddenly by the hand and carry her away to that wonderful world she seemed to inhabit—a world free from pain, harm, and disappointment of any kind; a world in which anything—even the impossible—was obtainable…Was it truly possible to live a life of such carefree joy, to be forever free and unfettered?

As the radiant young maiden drew near, she also bowed with the same courteous greeting of the first, then also took her place beside the other. The air around became cool and crisp with a light breeze as a third woman now advanced towards them. She appeared older than either of the first, with fiery curls of the deepest red framing a lovely, ivory-complected face. Her smooth skin was as luminescent as a freshwater pearl, with quick, green eyes that glistened above a dainty, crimson mouth. Her thick hair was partially braided in long sections down her back with brightly colored ribbons, and throughout her lavish tresses were laid an abundance of jewels—diamonds, sapphires, and amethysts. From her hands, wrists, and throat dripped still more exquisite gems of the finest cut—rubies, garnets, and pearls. Her clothes, all of the richest silks, satins, and costliest velvets, were a profusion of deep, exotic hues—burgundy, scarlet, purple, and violet—while her robes were a rusty splash of crimson, gold, and copper tones. She was accompanied by two little red foxes and a great grey wolf, all of which loped beside her down the path. As she swept over the earth the leaves of the trees overhead suddenly turned to gold and amber and fell softly from their boughs. The ground beneath was quickly laden with a thick, profuse covering of fall leaves that stirred and rustled in the wind. She had ridged wings resembling those of a dragon; feathery scales with colorful markings like a peacock swept away from her shoulders, their scalloped edges brushing over the gay swirl of leaves falling at her feet. There was a noble grace about her, and something that was magnetic—almost bewitching—in her personality, that seemed to draw the younger woman in under her spell. She had the seasoned look of a woman in her prime, with an air that was at once both pure, yet effortlessly sensual. Her advancing step was more deliberate and audacious than either of the first two, yet still she had an unassuming personal warmth. It was as though she were subtly aware of the lure of her own charms, and yet consciously maintained a purposeful sense of virtue which over-ruled any temptation to entice. She had a look of experience which made her appear somewhat worldly-wise, but untainted. She possessed the vibrancy of strong passion, but had also the look of one who was wisely temperate and discerning in all matters. She seemed as if she had acquired the ability to carefully sift through each lesson which experience had afforded her, and over all to have gained keener foresight and discretion from it. It appeared as if she had attained a vast, satisfying wealth of knowledge, and yet at the same time was still in pursuit of more. She was in every way the image of perfection, so that if Adlai had not been so overcome with awe, she might have been tempted to be deeply envious. The satisfied demeanor of the older woman was indeed the picture of total fulfillment, which Adlai inwardly hoped might someday become hers to own as well.

She delivered a nod of assent along with a gracious and bestowing smile, then like the others moved aside. It suddenly occurred to the girl that the nature of all these personages bore strong resemblance to the changing tide of the earthly seasons— could it be that these higher beings might indeed be the Keepers and Mistresses of such? ...If so, then there was only one still remaining who had not yet made her appearance.

All seemed to hush now in silent anticipation. Adlai waited breathlessly, as the air all around grew steadily colder. Suddenly there was the merry jingling of sleigh bells. Snowflakes began to fall lightly down to earth, covering it in a smooth, thick coat of new fallen snow. All around the air was suddenly filled with the distinctly delicious scents of pine, cinnamon, huckleberry, mistletoe, and fresh, clean earth. All the creatures and attendants standing at attention suddenly bowed low with seeming greater reverence than had been shown to all of the former three. A magnificent silver sleigh drawn by six prancing white horses made their way through the archway of trees amidst the music of bells. The driver was a stout, cherry-nosed dwarf with a white beard and bundled in thick furs; with a merry smile he doffed his cap congenially to Adlai as he drew the horses up before the exact place where she stood. A tall, veiled woman slowly arose from her enthroned seat at the back of the sleigh, and ceremoniously descended before the astonished girl.

Lady Winter indeed had the marked bearing of royalty, and there was a regal stateliness about her which commanded awe and respect, as though she were superior to all. As she drew back her frosty veil, Adlai gave a short gasp. Everything about her had a startling beauty, from her snowy complexion and midnight eyes, to the crown of twinkling stars set over the luster of her brow, and her jet-black hair falling almost to her waist in smooth, curling tresses. The high lace collar of her gown was formed from hundreds of snowflakes and ice crystals, and long, puffy sleeves of the same fell gracefully away from her bare shoulders. The sparkling sheen of her dress was pale ice-blue. The dim lamplight round about glistened brightly upon a myriad of diamond crystals set over her entire person, so that her whole form was alight with dazzling brilliance. From her back sprang the snowy-white feathers of a swan, their graceful tips barely touching together as they arched in queenly regalia. The long train of her robes was of much lengthier profusion than any of the others had been, with a white fur draping off one shoulder to hang over her arm.

A sudden panorama of brilliant color broke out across the starry sky above, spanning out as it shimmered and swayed in the chilly night air. The light of it lit up the Lady's face, indicating that she was beyond doubt the eldest of all four. She had a look both of ageless beauty and timeless wisdom, as if she had lived to see all of a thousand lifetimes or more. Her countenance was calm and peaceful, with a serene but sober smile which just barely touched the corners of her mouth. Her tranquil dark eyes had a penetrating stare, as if they could see straight into the very depths of Adlai's heart and soul. The girl flinched somewhat at this, lowering her head in respect as she shrank back from the unshirking gaze of the one who stood before her.

CHAPTER 18—THE ORACLES' PROPHECY

After a few moments she dared to look up, and was surprised to find that the woman was smiling down warmly at her, a look of tender compassion in her eyes. For an instant Adlai thought that she had the nurturing look of a mother, coupled with loving wisdom. And something inside her suddenly ached with longing for the mother she herself had never known. Would she, whoever she was, have been anything like this?

"Ieuna, daughter of favor and promise, we salute you!"

Adlai started at this strange greeting, looking up confusedly at the tall woman addressing her.

"There—there must be some mistake! My name's not—"

"No, there is no mistake," the woman interrupted. "I am Yuel, Muse of the Winter Season, and these are my sisters—the fellow Mistresses of Nature's yearly change. We come at the bidding of our father, Melchizedek, to bear gifts to she who is soon to be a royal bride—for you shall presently rule beside your marriage-lord with a golden scepter of righteousness. We come also to give you our prophecies of things which have been foreseen, and to lend our aid in preparing you for the way which lies before you—including, also, its dangers."

With that, Lady Winter gave a regal bow of her jeweled head and stepped back, turning slightly and motioning towards the youngest, as Spring nimbly stepped forward.

"Ieuna, daughter of Life and Promise, listen to these words that I say, and let them take root in your young heart. I am Sirene, Muse of the Springtime Season, and youngest daughter of Mother Earth and Father Time. In the days that lie ahead, difficulties—even sorrow—will come to you, but you must not despair. Remember, unless a seed first shrivels up, dies, and falls unto the earth, it cannot bear fruit. Life is born out of death. Take comfort in this thought, therefore. And also, take comfort from the simple consolations and pleasures of life—even one as simple as a single flower." She paused, and gently laid her bouquet of precious blooms into Adlai's arms, then continued: "In times of hardship, one is often tempted to overlook such simple blessings. But these are Heaven's smiling gifts, sent to ease Earth's children in times of trial; they are meant to remind us that goodness yet remains, and one day shall return again to stay. Do not borrow trouble from Tomorrow, for Tomorrow has enough trouble of its own. Sufficient to the day is its own toil and trouble therein. So learn, therefore, to breathe deeply of the life you have today, and of this moment... Yesterday is history past, and Tomorrow is a mystery— but Today is a *gift*—that's why it is called the Present."

Adlai smiled gratefully, not quite sure what to make of these strange sayings, but feeling strangely comforted none the less. The warm fragrance of the flowers was intoxicating to her senses; and for reasons she did not quite understand, she felt almost happy for the first time in a long while. As she drank in their scent, the bouquet suddenly burst into a colorful cloud of swirling butterflies that flitted away on the evening breeze. Adlai gaped in wondering awe, as Sirene gave a low, graceful bow of her head and stepped back, and the second Muse moved forward. Her face shone with a radiant joyfulness as if she were ready to burst from joyful excitement:

"Welcome, Ieuna, child of Prosperity and Rejoicing! I am Sunefaere, Lady of the Summer Season. You have found favor and grace with the Powers of the Deep, so that you have been chosen to partake of richness and blessing beyond all you could fathom! Do not be afraid, for a Guardian shall be revealed to you, to watch over and to protect you from harm, and from the Deadly Dragon which seeks your demise."

Adlai's skin prickled at the mention of a dragon. Why was it that this particular creature seemed to play a continual theme— not only in legends, but in her own life as well? This was the third time it had come up... And she wanted to blot out from her mind the night she had passed in the UnderWorld.

"But fear not," Sunefaere continued, "For the one who comes to you is greater than he who seeks your hurt, and it is in his power to utterly subdue all who rise up against him. And remember: for every snare that is laid, no matter how many, a way of escape shall always be provided for you…You are never forgotten, no matter how alone you may feel, or how desperate your times may become…Only trust, believe, and obey."

With that, the dove perched upon Sunefaere's finger suddenly lifted wing and fluttered to the girl's shoulder; alighting gently, she cocked her head to one side and cooed sweetly. Adlai's mouth dropped open in delighted amazement, as the bird strutted back and forth on her shoulder without the least disturbance.

"This is Hope; let Hope lead you in your path."

Without warning, Hope instantly took wing and flew off into the skies. Adlai gazed on in disappointment.

"What did I do? Where did she go?"

"Do not fear; she has gone on to that domain in which you dwell—there she will meet you, when she is needed. Feed Hope, and Hope shall sustain your soul. Never allow Hope to die, for where Hope dies, Despair comes in and makes a soul its permanent residence." The Muse seemed to sober slightly with these words, but then her face again brightened: "Take heart; there is no darkness so great that the light of Truth cannot penetrate through! Rise up, therefore, and seize your Destiny!"

Adlai almost laughed aloud in delight at the way in which the young Muse so joyously relayed her message. In her presence, it was almost inconceivable even to think of trouble. Sunefaere flew back to her former place, and the third Muse approached. Once again Adlai held her breath in mesmerized wonder, as the Lady of Autumn's cool green eyes met her own. The air around suddenly smelled fresh of fall rain, and Adlai thought she could hear the distinct sound of raindrops falling softly, like gentle chimes in the wind.

"Greetings to you, Ieuna, one who is soon to be crowned Queen! I am Astrial, Muse of the Autumn months, Mistress of the Four Winds."

Adlai very nearly gasped, as the great Lady acknowledged her with an illustrious bow. Rising slowly, the Muse again parted her crimson red lips to speak:

"My dear child, your heart is already yearning—not only for greater things, but also to be joined together with the one who, from the beginning, was pre-ordained to share with you in your journey…Resist the temptation to accomplish all these things on your own, or to force the hand of Destiny, for in so doing you may pierce yourself through with many sorrows. All that which has been foretold shall presently come to you, though its arrival may *not* be in your own time. It shall come to you, nonetheless— its arrival shall be sooner than you imagine, but longer than you would wish. Do not despise the journey you must travel in order to get there, for the journey is equally as important as the end, and the lessons that you shall learn on your way are of equally great import. Every journey must begin with a single step, so despise not the day of small beginnings. Let nothing be wasted; even the most adverse of circumstances may serve as your tutor and guide—ignoring such valuable lessons will be to your detriment. And remember this truth: weeping may endure for a night, but joy comes in the morning; beauty will arise from the ashes. A stick of incense never smells so sweet, as when it is set afire and consumed... Your life is to be a torch shining bright in the darkness: set yourself ablaze, and the whole world will come to watch you burn."

Lady Astrial pressed a hard object into the girl's open palm. Adlai looked down into her hand: it was a small gold key, of delicate and intricate design.

"This is the Key of Faith," the Muse continued, "And despite its delicate size and appearance, it is much stronger and sturdier than it looks; it can open any door that must be opened, no matter the shape or size of the lock. Only take care: use it often, but use it carefully and with wisdom, for there are some doors which are *not* meant to be opened. Faith placed recklessly in the wrong person or idea can prove a dangerous step, one which may end in entrapment and demise. Take care, therefore, that your faith is firmly placed and established upon the solid foundation of proven Truth, that misleading doors be not opened, and you yourself be led astray upon an erring path."

She paused, looking with a keenly contemplative expression into Adlai's eyes:

"You bear the blush of a young girl whose heart has already opened to love, but I would caution you: do not awaken or arouse Love, until it is fully time...My eyes do not yet see as clearly as our elder sister's, so is not known to me whether the course upon which your heart is presently set is the correct one, or not. I sense that he is of a noble heart and soul—but whether or not he is intended to share with you in your own destiny is something which has not been disclosed to me. The only word of advice I can give you is this: Guard your heart; guard it well, for it as a wellspring of life to you. Only pour its waters upon soil which has been already prepared to receive it. Otherwise your precious life-spring may be thrown into the gutter... Wait, I tell you, and do not seek to arouse love until the proper time...It will come to you."

Adlai trembled a little at these words, swallowing hard as she did and quickly pocketing the little key in her dress. Her mind was racing in confusion, and for an instant she felt almost sickened. It wasn't possible that she could be with or love anyone else, except Willan...He was *perfect* in every way. He was everything she could ever possibly wish for and more, she was sure...Could it be possible that they were not destined for each other? Adlai calmed by reminding herself that the Muse had not said of a surety that Willan was *not* the one; no, she had acknowledged that she had not the ability to see that far. Adlai relaxed. There was nothing yet to fear or be agitated over; it had been merely a word of precaution to be patient and wait.

"Ieuna," she continued, "A good name is more to be desired than gold. Yours is befitting of a Princess, and means "Beautiful Lamb". Have a care: you are being sent out now as a Lamb among wolves. You must be wise and perceptive as a serpent, but harmless and faultless as a dove."

With that, she bowed her head. A crisp breeze now stirred the air, as the Mistress of Winter moved forward with the exquisite poise of formal grace. A starry glitter glistened in the Muse's dark eyes, like a celestial host set against the black velvet of winter's night. Tiny snowflakes drifted down upon her head, melting into her hair as they alighted. As the fragile form of their pristine designs dissolved, strands of silvery white suddenly appeared, streaking down through the contrasting wealth of ebony. Gradually it grew thicker and thicker, till at last all of her black curls had completely disappeared, and her twisted locks formed a frosty halo draped like icicles over her shoulders.

"Beloved Child, Welcome," Lady Winter breathed with tender smile, taking Adlai's hand gently in her own. "I come to offer my gift of foresight to aid you in what you are about to undertake."

The color of her eyes suddenly swirled milk-white like a foggy mist. Immediately a frosty wind began to howl round about them both, tugging and pulling at Adlai until her hair was whipping about her face. Then slowly they began rising up together into the air. A surge of energy was flowing from the Muse into her own body, and a similar energy seemed to be transferring back—*what was happening?* They were suspended in midair, encapsulated within a thin shield of wind, sleet, snow, and ice, while all of time seemed suddenly to stand still. The electrical current continued to flow back and forth between them, but Lady Yuel remained utterly motionless. She was no longer looking at Adlai; rather, her transfixed stare seemed to penetrate straight *through* her, as if she were seeing afar off into the deepest recesses of the girl's heart—depths which even Adlai herself could not fully fathom…The Muse seemed also to be looking afar off into the distance somewhere. And something in her eyes made Adlai tremble… What was she was seeing?

"I see…two paths before you," Yuel mused in a low voice, as if she were half conversing with herself. "Both paths are marked with pain and suffering… one is winding and filled with toil, but its outcome is a happy and satisfied end, marked by a joyous event…Of the other…it appears straight at first, but its course quickly becomes twisted and gnarled—the dangers of it are far greater than the first…"

The Muse's eyes widened for an instant, and a tremor shook suddenly through her body. Adlai almost winced from pain, as Yuel clenched her hand more tightly in her own. Suddenly the Muse's eyes flew open, and she let out a gasp:

"The path is suddenly ending…I—I see where it ends!…It ends in…death!"

Without warning, the current surging between them instantly broke. The whirling gale round about immediately ceased, as Yuel suddenly let go of the girl's wrist. Adlai fell to the ground, hitting it hard. Shakily she picked herself up, and tremblingly looked about. All still remained standing in quiet waiting, as if nothing at all had occurred. Even Lady Winter herself seemed in her original, unaltered state, as she stood calmly over the trembling girl. Confused, Adlai looked about her, searching one silent face after the other, as she turned back pleadingly to Yuel:

"Please," she begged in quivering voice, "You must have been able to see which I will choose—tell me, please! Which path shall be my fate?"

Yuel shook her head.

"Fate is simply a word used by those who choose to ignore the responsibility of their own choices. There is *no* such thing, as Fate. There is only Destiny, that unto which you were made to aspire. If you wish to keep your course steady, then it is not enough for you merely to seek to avoid the path leading into the Darkness—you must *aim* towards your Destiny. If you do not, then your lack of vision will be your own undoing, and you will not be able to tell the paths apart when you come to them. Instead, *know* your purpose and your destiny—know for what you were meant, and fulfill it."

"But surely you must at least be able to tell me what signs surround each path?" Adlai pleaded. "Please tell me—what should I look for?"

The Muse again shook her head slowly.

"It is not for us to know all that the future holds, nor all the choices which mortals shall make. If we had knowledge of such things and were able to foretell all, then man might lose his courage. Our task is not to dictate to man what his actions will be, as though he were nothing more than a mere pawn. Our purpose instead is to inspire him with hope and gird him with strength, that he would have the courage to reach for what would otherwise seem impossible. …The Great Eye of The Deep is looking for such as are willing to avail themselves to his purpose—no matter how weak or insignificant—that he might prove himself strong on their behalf. He does not call those who are equipped. Rather, he equips those who are the Called. Dark Days are soon to come upon the earth, but man has foolishly become confident in his own power and strength…The Deep knows what is in the heart of man; he knows better than to trust himself to men. For that reason, he seeks such as are merely willing to place themselves at his disposal. A willing vessel—and not strength—is all that is required. Man's strength wrestles against his, because it has a different mind and will of its own. That is why he chooses instead the humble, the unassuming, even the seemingly weak and insignificant. One of his greatest gifts to humanity is to redeem that which was worthless, and to allow his own strength to be perfected in the weakness of his creation. Once a willing soul chooses to surrender and yield itself to *his* purpose, a greater force—such as the world has never seen before—shall be wielded, a power stronger than either death or life… You, Ieuna, have been chosen. Fear not, therefore; only surrender yourself—he will guide you with his Eye. And the Guardian—he too shall guide you and help you better know it, till at last you recognize where it is leading you…Take heart… Just believe."

"I give you my most heart-felt thanks for your kind encouragement, but please—" Adlai begged once more, "Can you give me no other advice? What should I guard against?"

The Muse studied her for a moment, then spoke:

"If you would be better prepared, then you must know and guard against the hidden weaknesses of your own heart…Know your heart; know it well. Know all of it motives, fears, affections, desires, and ambitions…Go deep down into the hidden places where even *you* are afraid to go—go all the way. Your greatest and most deadly enemy is not from without—it is from within—in the places of your character which you choose to ignore. Remember: even a great chain of steel is only as strong as its weakest link. If your weaknesses are not surrendered to *his* strength, then your adversary will seek to use this to his own advantage. Do not allow your heart to betray you, nor be deceived by any of its good intentions, for the road to Destruction is paved with such... Know your heart... Know it well!"

These last words by the Muse were spoken in such a dire tone of warning, that a shivering chill ran down the length of Adlai's spine. So many perplexing things had been said to her already, and not much of it seemed to make much sense at all. Was it all a riddle that she was meant to solve? Her mind was such a confused muddle that she could hardly think clearly. And though she felt that all these words were intended to comfort her, it now felt as if they had had the reverse affect... Oh, if only something— even just a tiny bit of it—made some sense to her! At least then she might stand a chance of figuring it out.

"The hour grows late," Lady Winter lifted her voice as she turned back towards the others. "My sisters and I must leave you now."

Adlai started, a sudden feeling of fear filling her at the thought of being left alone in an unfamiliar place.

"Do not be alarmed," Astrial said comfortingly, as she stepped forward and laid a reassuring hand on the girl's arm. "My servants the Winds shall attend to your safe return."

"Ieuna, I have one last gift that is meant for you," Yuel spoke. She lifted up a tiny crystal vial containing an amber liquid that was hung upon a delicate gold chain, and placed it over Adlai's head. Fastening it about her neck, she continued:

"What you now possess is a cordial tonic of very strong healing powers; it is made from the precious sap of the Tree of Life. A drop or two placed between the lips of a dying man has the power to restore him back to full health. But have a care: this is a very precious gift, and one which others shall covet, should they come to know of it. It is not to be revealed to anyone, nor is it to be used carelessly or in waste, but only in the direst of circumstances."

With these last words, the Muse rose to ascend back into her silver sleigh, and the others too made ready to depart.

"But wait!" Adlai cried out suddenly. "You have not yet told me where my name came from! Please, there is one thing in all the world which I very dearly desire to know—where have I come from?"

She felt ready to burst into tears. This was the closest she had ever come to knowing anything of her original identity or her parentage, and she felt as if her last link to the past was disappearing along with the departure of the Four Muses. Lady Yuel's eyes softened with compassion. Cupping the girl's face tenderly in her hands, she leaned forward and gently kissed her forehead. A warm, tingling sensation pulsated through Adlai's skin where Lady Winter's lips had touched. There had been so few times in her life when she had been physically touched in any way tokening of affection, that she felt nearly starved for it—to know that she was precious and loved. Yuel reached out her hand and caught up several falling snowflakes, then breathed softly into her open hand. In an instant the snowflakes melted and hardened into a thin sheet of ice as clear and transparent as crystal glass, as the Muse held up in her hand a tiny mirror before Adlai's face.

Adlai gasped: reflected back to her was her own self, yet it had none of the plainness of appearance or dress which she expected. Instead, the shining face of a lovely young woman stared back at her. She had all the regal bearing and sophisticated dress of a royal Princess, with a tiny jeweled crown set over her brow. Upon her forehead appeared suddenly a strange inscription in runes of glittering gold.

"What is that?!" Adlai asked in breathless amazement.

"*That* is how we see you, and how we know who you are. And the inscription written upon your forehead is your very own name, the name which we have called you. It is how *he* sees and knows you. Others shall try to erase your identity, by writing their own in its place—do not allow them to steal your soul… *Remember who you are.*"

"Please," Adlai begged, "You see so much—do you not know anything of my mother and father? Who were they?"

The Muse studied her for a moment.

"All shall reveal itself in due time, Child; be patient, and wait for it. The knowledge you seek has not been revealed to me, but I perceive that the blood which flows through your veins has traces of royalty...The other details of your past remain clouded, so that I cannot see clearly now...But one thing I am able to sense: and that is that you were—you *are*—greatly loved. I do not know fully the reason behind all that has happened to you, but I sense keenly that they sought to protect you—that is why so much has been hidden from you, and the reason why you are no longer called by that name."

"Protect me from *what*? What did they fear?"

"That has not been revealed to me," Yuel replied gravely, "Although my spirit tells me that the past is not so distantly connected from the present. Sixteen years ago, a strange new planet was birthed in the heavens. Its surface was blood red, and it was followed by a single lone star circling in orbit round about it. Our Ancient Father consulted with the Powers of the Deep, and it was revealed that this strange new sign marked the beginning of great trouble and birth pangs to be suffered by Mother Earth, and that a Dark Evil would soon come to the world of men. The single star, however, pointed out a strangely different sign: an Oracle foretold that the star indicated that a young woman of royal lineage would play a significant role in all of these events—either for good or for evil. She was to be sought and made ready, that she might guard against he who would seek to use her for his own devices. To her it would be granted the heart of a Warrior, and so that she might fulfill her destiny and fight against the impending Shadow. That is why I and my sisters have been sent to you. And that star which you see far off to the right—"

The Muse pointed up towards the night sky, and Adlai followed the direction of her finger. At last she espied a tiny, single star not much bigger than a speck shining dimly by itself in the darkness.

"That is the star which has brought us to you," Lady Winter said, turning back to Adlai with a smile.

The tall woman looked lovingly upon the young girl for several moments, then at last turned and climbed back into her sleigh. The frosty white horses were already pawing the ground with their hooves, as the dwarf gave a light tap with his whip and shook the reins. As they whisked away, the Muse turned suddenly back towards Adlai, a dangerous look of dark warning flashing through her wide, black eyes.

"Tell no one your name!" Her voice rang out. "Never speak of it to anyone! Remember, tell no one who you are!"

The words kept echoing back in the falling snow. Terrified, Adlai remained frozen and rooted to the spot, a shivery chill racing like lightening through her core.

…Everything which happened next, happened in such a whirring flurry of activity, that she could scarce so much as catch her breath. Everything about her was suddenly swirling; wind was blowing in all directions, sweeping round about her like a great hurricane, and everything was flashing past in a rush of blurred color. The great company of Elvin Nymphs slowly faded and disappeared into the dark back-drop of the forest behind them. For an instant she caught sight of Sirene's rosy lips and violet eyes before they faded away amidst a spray of showering, gently falling petals; Sunefaere's sunny countenance evaporated like dew drops into a brilliant ray of sunlight; and Astrial's deep green eyes suddenly disappeared in a colorful gale of swirling red leaves. The very last glimpse Adlai caught was of Yuel in her horse-drawn sleigh, her frosty veil streaming behind her in the wind. With a loud crack of the handler's whip and a sudden head-long plunge, Lady Winter along with her sleigh, driver, and fleet-footed team all sprang with a giant leap into the night-time sky, disappearing in a great flurry of snow.

…Everything was spinning wildly now, faster and faster and faster—till at last even color was blended together, and all that was left was colorless light. The same blinding light as before now penetrated through her skull; then suddenly it exploded, and Adlai was forcefully thrown forward…

All went suddenly dark, and became still and quiet. Adlai felt herself crumple in a dizzy heap, then slowly staggered to her feet in delirium. The bright light had faded away, and she squinted in the pale new light which now greeted her. Her ears were still ringing, as gradually she became aware of the new sounds around her…it was the sound of trickling water. To her surprise, she found that she was once again standing beside the great pool in the alcove garden of the Manor, looking up towards the great stone statue. For several blinking moments she stared about in bewilderment. All at once she caught sight of Willan disappearing out the garden gate. *Could it be possible? Had no time passed at all since she had left?!* Her eye flew down to her hand: the sapphire ring was still there, right where Willan had left it… She had never lost it. For an instant she was tempted to run after him, to overtake him and beg him to take her with him. It was all too overwhelming—she just couldn't face the Dark Shadow alone.

Adlai started to follow after, but of a sudden stopped short…Though a moment earlier she had herself been all alone, yet now she was certain that once again she could feel another presence. A slight noise grated in the air, like the slow grinding together of rock or granite… Out of the corner of her eye, she saw a quick movement behind her as it suddenly moved away. A silent chill began to tingle down her spine once again, as she turned cautiously in its direction. Almost instinctively, her eyes traveled unwillingly to the platformed pedestal at the pond's center…The stone statue was no longer standing in its place.

CHAPTER 19—BITTER DISAPPOINTMENT

Adlai was already trembling violently even before she felt something steal up very close behind her. With a spin she found herself staring straight into the cold expression of the statue's face. Her sculpted eyes suddenly flickered, closing and then opening again. No longer were they unseeing rock—instead, lipid black eyes stared back into Adlai's harrowed gaze. The rest of the statue's facial features suddenly began to wriggle and stretch, till at last her stone lips parted and her mouth fell open.

"Doom, Doom, Doom!" Her voice rang out loudly. "Earth's end draws nigh; her children and inhabitants go down unto her depths!"

The statue drew very near as she cried out, her tall grey form towering high over that of the terrified girl.

"Beware of he who comes clothed as a Spirit of the Light! For he is come that he might reawaken the One who must not to be disturbed! When once he has succeeded, he shall receive powers greater than any the earth has seen before—power to utterly destroy and annihilate all living!"

Adlai was so overcome by fright that she thought she would presently faint, when the statue pressed her face close into her own, her black eyes filling up the girl's wide-eyed stare.

"He will seek to use you, that you might lead him to what he seeks! You must *not* let him find it! Do *not* allow him near the Chamber of—"

The stone statue did not get to finish, for of a sudden there was a small rustling in the bushes behind them, just as the squawk of a crow met Adlai's ears. Without warning the carved image instantly turned with a springing leap towards the nearest wall, her form dissolving into the rock as she vanished away from sight. Adlai caught in her breath with a short gasp and jerked about—she already knew whose tall, dark silhouette it was which stood silently waiting from the shrouds of the surrounding foliage. Sure enough Gunar's familiar form slowly emerged from the shadows. He wasn't wearing the cloak and wraps he typically wore to hide away his strange, beastly appearance. *What was he doing here?* And what was it that the stone Lady was about to warn her of? Was it more than mere coincidence that Gunar should chance to be there at the very moment she was about to receive a dire warning? ... Adlai flinched as she avoided his stare. There was something markedly strange in the timing of his presence there at the Manor. Was it possible that he had something to do with the Stone Statue's warning?…There was a reason he had come to them—and she was more convinced than ever that it had little to do with merely returning a missing horse. He had a secret mission of his own—a hidden agenda—in coming. Once again Willan's warning flew back into her memory. Slowly she cleared her throat and licked her dry lips.

"What are you doing here?" She mustered her demand in a flat tone, inwardly praying to some higher power that her voice might convey some of Willan's unquestionable authority, and conceal her trepidation. Too late she remembered that it did no good: he was already reading her thoughts.

"I've been assigned to tend to the garden, along with the rest of the Manor grounds," Gunar responded quietly.

At this, she noticed that his calloused hands were indeed covered with dirt stains, and that his naked upper body also had traces of mud mingled with rain and sweat. Adlai promptly wrapped her arms about herself in an attempt to quell the shivering chill shaking through her. Everything about him unnerved her— from his monstrous appearance, to his ability to see right into her deepest thoughts. Gunar remained calmly before her, his arms and torso bare in the autumn breeze, yet without so much as a visible tremor.

"I see." Adlai's voice was almost hoarse. "If you'll excuse me, I must be getting back to the house."

Adlai hastily pushed past him and nearly broke into a run as she fled in the direction of the gate. Willan—and safety—were just outside. She couldn't take one more moment at Dombrey Manor. Her heart was pounding in her chest as she dashed down the stone path towards the little arched gateway. Her hand had just touched upon the door handle, when a great wind suddenly tore past her and practically knocked her off her feet. With a startled cry she looked up to see Gunar barring her way to the door.

"Let me pass!" She practically screamed, flinging the full force of her weight against him.

"Let him go." Gunar's voice was authorative and commanding, yet at the same time calmly quiet. "He can't help you now. Let him go."

Adlai was suddenly wildly kicking, punching, slapping—all in a futile effort to force him out of her path. Gunar deftly caught up both her wrists and held her fast as she continued to struggle against him. At last her outbursts gave way to tearful sobs, as she drooped helplessly. Slowly he released her, and she collapsed in a defeated heap to the ground. Without another word he silently strode away and was gone.

Scrambling to her feet she nimbly jerked on the door handle. It fell open as she tumbled through and bolted for the courtyard…Was it too late? Might she still be able to catch Willan in time? Frantically she looked this way and that: he was nowhere to be seen. With a dash she made for the stables. There were only a few servants about, and a lean grey cat wandering lazily through the open yard, as hens pecked about between the cobblestones. *He must have already left*, Adlai thought breathlessly.

Adlai barreled through the stable door, scattering a group of stray chickens in her wake. Quickly she harnessed Storm with bit and bridle, cinching tight his saddle as the stirrups fell jangling at his sides. In an instant she leapt nimbly onto his back, reins firmly clenched in hand. With a sudden cry she drove a hard, determined heel into his side.

Like the sudden break of thunder, they burst through the open doorway and took off towards the castle gate. A hay wagon was just making its way through the gate of the courtyard as they flew past, very nearly knocking the poor farmer tending it into the ditch. Startled cries and angry shouts followed after them as they sped on through the dirt and cobblestone streets of the small village of Dombrey. Adlai did not look back. Soon the entire village was left behind them, as they passed beneath the arch of the last town gate and flew out upon the wide open road, its course winding out before them through fields, moors, farms, and the forests that lay beyond. At last she espied a small party moving at a slower pace ahead of them along the red dirt road. Her heart gave a sudden leap in her chest—it was Willan. Giving Storm another slap, she hurried to catch up.

"Willan! Willan, wait!"

Adlai screamed wildly as they neared the horsemen travelling in the dust ahead of them. The party slowly halted, as one of the riders at the center turned to look back over his shoulder, then slowly wheeled around and rode out to meet her. A relieved smile broke across her face and grateful tears sprang to her eyes. All the rest of the world was falling apart around her, and he was the only sanity she had left… She didn't care what the future held; all that she knew was that no matter what, she and Willan must never be parted, and that she never again wanted to leave his side.

Willan slowly approached, an awkward look of startled surprise and confusion in his uncertain smile as he drew up. Adlai flung down the reins and tumbled to the ground, then broke into a run. A look of alarmed concern crossed his expression, as he likewise jumped from his mount and turned to greet her. Without warning she flung herself into his arms and burst into an uncontrollable torrent of gut-wrenching sobs.

"There, there, now!" He tried in vain, attempting to cover over his surprise as he consoled her. "What's all this? What is it?"

He gently stroked her hair, then pulled her back so as to look into her face.

"I can't stay in Dombrey without you!" Adlai broke out haltingly. "I'm so afraid—I can't be left there alone—couldn't you take me with you? ...Please, Willan?"

She searched his face imploringly, desperately clasping his hands tightly in hers as she turned her tear-stained eyes hopefully up to his. Willan was suddenly speechless, his expression lost in a look of stupefied shock. Then gradually, it wore away to an uncomfortable look of recognition. His mouth closed resignedly and he pulled back, uttering a deep sigh as he shook his head and slowly turned away. The hopeful plea in Adlai's eyes vanished. In numb disbelief she stared after him—*was he actually leaving her?!*

"Willan, no!" She started to plead with him—"*No!*"

She was crying hard again, clinging tightly to his arms with the desperation of a small child in a futile effort to prevent him from leaving…*How could he do this?! He couldn't be leaving her…He just couldn't!*

Willan was almost rough as he shook her off now, unprying her fingers and catching her hands in his own. Firmly he gripped her shoulders and held her out at arms' length, a safe distance away from himself.

"Adlai, please!"

His firm tone was half a plea, half an authorative rebuke. Adlai didn't pay any heed.

"Willan, don't! *Please don't!* …Willan?"

Through her sobs she looked up at him, her large, tearful eyes searching deep within both of his. Willan averted her gaze as he let out another long sigh and turned to look up at the grey, overcast sky far above.

"Adlai, I'm sorry—I just can't," he started reluctantly. "Please, let's not forget ourselves—"

He turned to cast a worried glance over his shoulder to the armed horsemen waiting in silent attendance behind him; some of them already wore telling grins on their faces as they sought to hide the smirk behind their smiles, a look of keen amusement playing visibly in their expressions. Adlai refused to pay them any attention, but kept her focus trained on Willan's face instead…She didn't care now…She *couldn't* care… She'd gone too far to care about what others thought. He couldn't abandon her like this, not when she had nowhere else to turn…Why did he suddenly seem so distant, and why was he not showing any sign that he cared about her now?

"Adlai, we're not children anymore," he managed at last with difficulty. "I know my place—" he paused, a pained look of discomfort in his face, as if trying to decide whether or not he should continue—"It is time that you learned yours."

His words rang out like a death sentence. She blinked numbly, as if not fully comprehending what was being said. Slowly she let go of him and fell back in stunned silence… He *did* know and understand the depth of her feelings for him…and for some strange and inexplicable reason… he had chosen to reject them.

"So that's it," She choked hoarsely as she cleared her throat and stepped back. "You won't have me because I'm not your equal."

A look of mixed alarm and embarrassment flew over Willan's blanched features, and he reached out to catch her by the arm.

"No, that's not it at all," he pleaded, vigorously shaking his head. Adlai pulled away.

"Please—," he continued quickly, "You've not understood my meaning: now's not the time for any of this, and I must hurry without further delay—for all our sakes. Please, don't do this— I've enough that requires my full attention already, and I need to know that I can trust you to stay out of harm's way. Please, do be a good girl, and show yourself the responsible young lady of good breeding I know you to be. Hurry back now to the Manor before all is turned into an uproar at your absence. Try to focus on your studies and responsibilities while I'm away; that way the time shall pass more quickly till my return—I want to have every cause to be proud of you."

He gave her a nervous pat and quick kiss on the forehead as he spoke, as if he were consoling the fragile emotions of a desolate child. Adlai drew back in disgust, suddenly realizing how he perceived her. She was nothing more than a teenage girl to him after all; undoubtedly he perceived her feelings as nothing more than a trivial, adolescent infatuation…He was merely patronizing her now.

"Adlai, please," Willan begged, casting a glance back over his shoulder once more, "I really must be going now. But I promise that I shall return as quickly as I can…Please, don't think so much on these things now—grant me some relief in not being forced to worry about you as well, when I am already so hard pressed by other urgent affairs."

Adlai gave a start. *Was she really nothing more than a troublesome burden to him?!* A sudden look of fiery contempt and indignation flashed fiercely in her eye, and a surge of smoldering anger began to burn inside her.

"No," She retorted coolly, "I should not wish to trouble you for the world."

With that she shook his hand off and strode back to where Storm stood waiting. Willan remained uncertainly for several moments, his face the picture of regret as he watched her retreat. Then with a resigned sigh he remounted his horse, turning back to rejoin the other horsemen awaiting him. The faint sound of laughter drifted back to her over the wind as she hauled herself back into the saddle. The heat rose suddenly to her face, and her cheeks flushed bright cherry red with humiliation. She looked back to see Willan making his way uncomfortably back inside their parted circle. Without offering explanation to his men at arms, he immediately broke into a gallop as he once again resumed the lead, and all his men quickly fell in after.

For an instant her anger dissolved, melting away into a feeling of sudden despair she watched them depart. An aching, lonely emptiness engulfed her. She felt suddenly buried beneath the mound of open shame she had incurred upon herself. Whatever had possessed her to go revealing her heart so openly to him, let alone publicly and in the presence of his nobles? She had previously thought that nothing could possibly be worse than being forced to remain alone under the harsh cruelty of the headmistress... But now... being spurned and ridiculed for her hopeful trust was so much worse. It would have been better if Willan had never known anything at all; at least then she might have still have had some of her own pride and dignity left... The degradation of it was almost more than she could bear.

Numbly she turned Storm back by the way they had come, her stomach sickening with every step over her disgrace. Adlai let out a dismayed groan, wincing to herself at the thought. However could she have been so stupid and simple, as to have expected him to willingly bring her along, without so much as a second thought? Especially when it involved the intrusion of a young, unskilled female into the rough perils and rigors of a man's world. She was naïve and inexperienced—they were all seasoned, trained warriors. She must have appeared half mad to them all.

Her mind flew back suddenly to the next unwelcome thought: what might she expect to meet upon her return? No doubt the servants had already apprised Lady Ardath of her hasty departure; it was already well past the time when lessons were to have been begun, and it was certain that her tutors had already long been kept in waiting. Of one thing she could rely on: that her truant behavior would not be allowed to go unpunished— especially when it had *everything* to do with Willan. No doubt the headmistress would surely use his abandonment of her to her own advantage...How severely would she be punished *this* time, now that the young Lord's restraining presence was no longer there?

Adlai slowly drew in the reins as she brought Storm to a halt. She had come to a crossroads, and before her a sign pointed the way to the little ferry town of Camden, not more than two days journey away; in the other direction was the way back to Dombrey. Turning about in the saddle, she peered hard down the road: she had never been that far away before. Indeed, the surrounding countryside of Dombrey was all she had seen of the world in years... Did she dare to venture out alone into the great unknown which lay beyond? She looked back for another moment, wondering what she ought to do. The shameful fact that she was being forced to return against her own will and all desire was bad enough... And then there was the painful thought of what the future held when Willan should at last make his return: their reunion would be strained by the awkward embarrassment of their last meeting; there would be none of the simple ease of their former friendship. The thought of being the object of Willan's condescending pity made Adlai feel suddenly nauseated to her core. Oh, why could she not have been satisfied with their farewell in the garden? The gentle tenderness of their final good-bye had been perfect. And if she had left it that way, then she could have ignorantly gone on wishing and pretending that someday he would love her...Why did she have to go compulsively ruining things, like she always did? Willan had become her opium. And she was addicted to his very presence in order to soothe her pain, make her life bearable, and somehow in some way give her life some sort of tangible meaning. And just like that, it—he—was gone.

Gunar's words came echoing back in her mind, and she found herself suddenly wishing regrettably with all her heart that she had listened, wishing that somehow she could undo all that had just recently transpired. Why ever had she allowed herself to become such a simpleton, believing in the giddy, happy endings promised by idle faery-tales? For the first time in her life, she found herself in bitter agreement with Mistress Ardath on one fact: she *had* read far too much fiction, and her naïve, trusting faith in them had at last been rewarded in the cruelest form of irony possible. She had so savored their deliciously tantalizing visions of victory and glory, had been so caught up in creating elaborate images of her own triumphant, happy ending, that she had not once bothered to question whether or not her dreams were grounded in sound fact. And now the horribly painful truth came down like the lash of a whip: bastard children did *not* marry royalty, anymore than common girls of no family could ever hope to be transformed into princesses... And her naïve stupidity had been justly punished…How could she have believed that her own story ever once stood the chance of ending like one of those?

Adlai numbly shook herself back to the present. She was here, now—and no one was present to stop her. She could become the master of her own destiny: leave Dombrey forever, never again to return. She could ride to Camden, take the ferry to the next town, and from there to the next, until she reached the wide open sea. She could disguise herself as a boy and work aboard one of the ships, and from there sail on to lands' end. Hang them all! None of them wanted or needed her, and she did not need any of them. She would grow strong; she would rise above all her heartaches and adversities… And in time, all the burning memories might finally fade from her mind.

With that final thought, she turned with somber resolution down the red dirt road towards Camden.

CHAPTER 20—SNOWY RESCUE

Within a few hours the sky overhead became darkly overcast; and by mid-afternoon the sun was completely hidden from sight. The former light drizzle was now reaching icy temperatures, as a stiff, strong wind began to whip about. The red road became sludge under the beating rains, and Storm's cantering trot was forced to a slow plod as he labored onward. Gradually, the mud turned to icy slush as snowy sleet descended; at last nothing was left but snow blowing over the hilly countryside.

Adlai shivered as she looked worriedly about her: she could no longer distinctly make out the way. She turned to look behind them, but discovered that she could no longer see by which way they had come. All around them was swirling white; she could barely distinguish Storm's head just inches before her, and the only sound left to be heard was the shrieking of the wind.

All her empty, aching feelings of earlier were gone now; in their place was more foolish guilt, along with a steadily growing fear. Her journey had only just begun, and now it dawned on her how miserably underprepared she had been. In her haste she had not so much as taken a cloak for the outdoors, neither had she any saddle bags packed with money or provisions for the way. And now she was starting to realize that, even if weather conditions had been favorable, the chances of her making it far were very slim, indeed. No young woman ever travelled alone and unaccompanied by an escort; her lack of preparations had all the look of desperate haste, and would be a dead give-away that she was on the run.

Even worse, what if she was mistaken for a thief? Storm's royal trappings did not in the least match her appearance and humble dress. And even if her hair was shorn and she had clothes for the part, could she really successfully convince all other eyes that she was nothing more than a young boy? The thought of being alone at sea and surrounded by scores of coarse, harsh seamen made her very uneasy…What would her fate be, she wondered, were it discovered that she was a girl?

Adlai swept all these thoughts hastily away from her mind and turned now to look anxiously about her with a shiver, her hunched form bowed before the driving winds. Were they still on the highway, or had they left it? …Where was anything? …With a sudden rush of tingling fright she realized what she had already begun to suspect: they were lost. Would they be able to last the night and make it until morning?

Adlai shook herself. Her numb fingers were frozen to the reins, so that now she could hardly move them. Stiffly she rubbed her frost-bitten arms, now burning from the cold. Ice had already collected upon her lashes and frozen upon her wet hair and clothes, and the breath in her lungs was like the wrench of a steely vise.

Storm was standing motionless in the growing snow bank, his head bent low against the vicious winds beating against his trembling body.

"Storm, C'mon!"

She called through chattering teeth. Painfully she drew one frozen leg up over his neck and slid down his icy flanks. Her trembling fingers slid along his side till at last she grasped hold of his mane.

"Storm, c'mon Boy!"

She pled, taking hold of his muzzle as she shakily patted his nose in an effort to rouse him. But the horse didn't stir.

"Storm!" She cried. But her voice was lost against the howl of the wind. "Storm?"

Slowly she reached up and wrapped both arms around his neck, as a hard lump grew in her throat. A tear slid silently down and froze upon her cheek. For several moments she clung to him, shaking with silent sobs against his still body. Then at last she pulled back. She had to find shelter, and quickly, or else she would soon die out here. But where?

Adlai cast her eye this way and that, shielding her eyes against the harsh winds. She could see nothing. Hesitantly, unwillingly she staggered forward and began moving. It didn't really matter what direction she went, as long as she kept going.

She just had to keep forcing herself to put one foot in front of the other. After several steps, she paused to look back in the gale…Storm had disappeared from sight. Miserably she looked ahead: she would be dead within the hour if she didn't find shelter fast.

For an instant she stood quaking in the cold, then sank down hopelessly to her knees in the snow drift. Snow wafted over and covered her body in its cold, suffocating blanket. Her eyes slowly closed…It wouldn't be long now…All she had to do was just give in, just go to sleep …Her eyelids fluttered for a few seconds, then slowly closed, and everything grew dark.

Adlai stirred. Was she still in her own body, lying there upon the frozen earth? If so, why did she feel suddenly warm? And where had the light come from? Blinking, she looked up: a bright light was hovering over her. A handsome young man with a beautiful face was bending over her. His smooth features were completely flawless, radiating with a luminescent brilliance. His hair was fairer and brighter than light, almost as white as snow. Powerful, majestic wings like an eagle spread out from strong shoulders, but the rest of his form was hidden away within the bright light. He was smiling warmly down upon her, as, dazzled, Adlai gaped up at him. If this was what happened after death, then Adlai felt that she would gladly forfeit a thousand lives.

Taking her by the hand he drew her gently to her feet, his height towering over her in massive strength. All at once she realized that she was no longer cold and wet. Her hair was falling in loose, shimmering waves down over her bosom, and a long, seamless tunic of the softest and lightest fabric streamed out beneath her and covered her bare feet. Laying a hand softly on her hair, his fingers swept down to caress her cheek. Suddenly he lifted something that was fastened at her throat, and Adlai gave a start: it was the gold chain necklace Lady Winter had bestowed upon her, its crystal vial dangling down over her breast. Carefully he removed the stopper, and a tiny droplet of the amber fluid spilled over. With that he touched her parted lips, and it dissolved onto her tongue. A sudden burst of flavor splashed over her pallet. To her surprise, she found that she could see even more clearly than before—and his gaze was lingering unwaveringly upon her. There was something almost familiar about his eyes…What was it?…There was a look of the deepest, most gratified pleasure in his countenance, as if he could see straight into her very heart of hearts…But there was something more…it was…acceptance. Acceptance of all that she was, of all which her character and personality encompassed, even its flaws… It was the intimation of tender, almost reverent devotion. The light of his eyes conveyed an expression of the highest esteem and regard. Adlai felt tears rush to her eyes for a moment that seemed completely timeless. The expression in his eyes needed no words, they said everything.

Her body was rushing with all kinds of strange new sensations—warmth, light, strength, vitality, and exuberant energy were all shooting through her, down into her very fingers and toes… He was speaking to her now—in a strange but familiar sounding tongue. The sound of his voice reminded her somewhat of the sounds and voices she had heard when the Muses had spoken to her…But what was it that he was saying to her?…A sudden painful longing filled her, so that she felt she would not be able to bear it if she could not comprehend their meaning. Her eyes begin to glisten with tears, as she suppressed them with a warm smile.

"I wish I could understand and know your language," She whispered hoarsely, "Then I might be able to speak with you."

"But you can."

Adlai started in shocked surprise. He was still speaking in the same strange ethereal language as before, but now there was a second voice speaking to her—and it seemed to be coming from within her own mind.

"Listen carefully—follow my eye, and you will learn it. You can learn both to understand and speak with me, as you can also learn to know and read my thoughts, just as I know and understand yours."

Adlai's face lit up with a delighted smile that beamed all across her face.

"What's your name?" She breathed.

"I have many names, Ieuna," he replied, smiling down at her. His eyes seemed to emanate flashes of light as he spoke. "But for now you may know me as Christofini. All that is Light belongs to me; I am spirit and flesh; the First and the Last."

He reached out suddenly overhead, as if to catch something, then slowly brought his hand down before her. Perched on his finger was the little dove the Muse had given her. Adlai let out a cry of delight.

"Never let Hope die," Christofini said softly, as he placed something else in her hand. It was the little gold key.

"Some doors are not meant to be opened," he continued, "But you can be sure that where one door closes to you, another shall be opened."

"So I must go back," Adlai sighed in disappointment.

"Yes."

"But when shall I see you again?"

"When you need me, I shall come to you. Only do not look for me. ...Remember—I shall come to *you*."

He drew back slowly.

"It is time."

"But so soon?" She pleaded. "I've only just met you!"

"It is enough. Don't be afraid—just believe."

Christofini's face began slowly to fade away into the halo of light which surrounded him. With bitter-sweet longing she watched him depart—the colorful fire of his eyes was the last to disappear.

...Adlai coughed, and groaned. Snow was packed inside her ears, and she had no feeling in her face. Slowly she stirred... Something seemed to be moving above her in the snow. She could feel it pawing through the snow heap... Something was trying to dig her out. Adlai froze: no human would be about on a night like this. There was the muffled sound of it sniffing, accompanied by grunts somewhere near her head... And in the distance, the sound of a wolf's cry went up... It was a wild animal. In terror she lay deathly still, not daring utter a sound, and desperately praying for it to leave…. Then suddenly without warning she found herself hoisted up from the snow bank. Adlai let out a horrified scream.

"It's alright!" A firm voice reassured her.

Immediately she stopped struggling, blinking through hazy vision into the darkened face before her…It was Gunar. Adlai let out a groan, and slumped into his arms. And with that she was being lifted up into the air, as windy gusts tore past her face. Craning her neck slightly, she saw that they were now soaring high over the earth, Gunar's massive wings steadily beating the air in great swooping motions. His one good eye glinted bright like fire as they continued their ascent into the beclouded night sky. Adlai clung tightly to him and did not dare to let go. And then with a sudden swooping drop that sent a sickening lurch through her stomach, they were descending. Peering down in surprise, she saw that they were already descending onto the snow-covered courtyard of Dombrey Manor. Wearily she sank back, and her eyes slowly closed…

CHAPTER 21—THE BEAST AND THE ROSE

Adlai groaned and slowly turned. Her head was throbbing, her nose swollen, and all over her skin felt puffy and sore from frost-bite. She was shivering with cold one moment, burning up with heat the next. Her shift and bedding all around were soaked with sweat. Coughing and sputtering weakly, she opened her watery eyes. The dim light of a few candles burning was the only light flickering in the darkened room. The household physician was bending concernedly over her, and to the far end of the room she caught sight of another familiar silhouette watching from the shadows—Lady Ardath. Adlai moaned again and shut her eyes. She was back. Back to life at the Manor, just as she had left it. And it had all been for nothing.

"Well, I do believe we've made our way through the worst of it!"

The apothecary announced with relief, as he rose from his stooped hover over the bed.

"Indeed, so I should hope!" Ardath's voice cut in shrilly. "I've yet to hear of anyone dying over anything as petty as a mere trifling cold."

"All the same," the physician added somewhat hesitantly, "I would still advise several days of bed-rest, along with plenty of nourishment—and no exertion of any kind, including study. We don't wish to have a return of anything worse, as long as Lady Adelheide's strength is not yet fully regained."

Adlai cracked one eye partially open and peered cringingly in the direction of the headmistress. Even in the dark she could already feel the headmistress begin to bristle in the waiting silence.

"Very well, then, as you wish!" Lady Ardath returned at last in a sharp tone. "Though I still believe you to be overly cautious, and that all of this is foolish waste."

The physician surveyed the headmistress gravely but made no reply.

"If she's well enough to eat, then I advise that she be fed at once," he said finally.

Ardath stepped forward into the flickering light, her lips tightening in a hard white line.

"I shall have one of the servants send up a bowl of broth—and if she's well enough to eat, then she can feed herself. My servants are made busy enough tending to more important household affairs, than to be bothered with being made to wait hand and foot upon Lady Adelheide," she replied crisply, "*Especially* when she has brought all of this entirely upon herself!"

The physician drew himself up stiffly.

"Never the less," he replied with a note of authority, "I am sure that the King will want to be made aware that all has been done to aid in the care and speedy recovery of his ward."

Adlai could scarce believe her ears. No one before had ever dared answer back to the Headmistress. She peeked discreetly over the blankets to catch sight of Ardath's face turn red with anger, her eyes smoldering with bridled rage.

"Yes," she answered at length, the strain of her voice unusually high, as if it would crack: "I am certain that he will. And so he shall. Nevertheless, once all this nonsense is passed, my usual discipline shall be fully enforced—I will *not* reward rebelliousness with liberality."

With that, the headmistress swept out in a flurry from the room. The physician soberly followed, and Adlai was left alone to drift back to sleep…It was a wearisome and troubled sleep, filled with thoughts and images—first of Willan, and then of Storm…In a dreamy haze she found herself standing out in a wide, open meadow, the last shafts of summer sunlight catching upon the gallant black figure of a regal horse, loping away in the distance ahead of her.

"Storm!"

She started to run.

"*Storm!*" She called out desperately again.

But Storm seemed not to hear her. With a toss of his majestic head, his sleek black coat shining in the setting sun, he cantered away, his supple body moving at a graceful, hypnotic gait… Then he was gone.

Adlai awoke with a start. It seemed as if only a few hours had passed. Rising up on her elbows against the propped cushions, she cast an eye in the direction of the window: twilight had already fallen, and it was now late into the evening. Had she actually slept through the previous night and on through the entire day? The servants had apparently been by, for a small candelabrum was lit upon a tray of cold broth, sitting upon the bedside table. What was it that had awakened her so suddenly, she wondered? Something had startled her awake, of that she was almost sure… Something—a sound—had roused her from the silence of her deep slumbers.

Adlai sat up straight in her bed—the shutters to her windows were creaking slowly in the wind outside. The glass paned doors were slightly ajar, so that a slight breeze was stirring the curtains from their place. The hair on the back of her neck started to prickle as she slowly rose from the bed. Removing the candelabrum from the bedside table, she gingerly crossed over the cold floor stones towards the open window. Leaning out she tried to pull in the open shutters and fasten them, when a sudden gust of wind burst through. The long curtains flapped wildly as it tore past; the shutter in her grasp broke away and flew clattering against the outside wall. Instantly the silver candle holder was knocked from her hand. For several seconds it rolled over, echoing across the floor as wax spilled all over the stones. Immediately the flame went out, and the room became dark.

The air felt suddenly cold, and Adlai could see her breath freezing in the stilly moonlit air before her, as her heart began to pound inside her chest. The shutters were still banging about outside, as she fearfully turned to look back across the room. She was certain that she could feel a presence there in the darkness... There was a soft rustling noise, and out of the corner of one eye, she caught glimpse of a slight movement in the shadows of the hanging curtains around her bed. Softly she bent and retrieved the branched candle holder, cautiously inching her way closer. With a deep breath she brandished the heavy end of the silver high over her head and flung back the curtain. But faster than she could blink an eye, it was dashed from her hand and fell clattering to the floor. Adlai turned back breathlessly to see two eyes—one bright as fire—staring straight back at her.

"Whatever are you doing here?" She demanded in angered exasperation. "You nearly frightened me half to death!"

Gunar answered nothing, but his eyes slowly lowered and his ears drooped like a dog's at the sound of her scolding. Something dropped from his hand and fell lightly onto the crimson hangings draped down over his large paws. Adlai peered down to see what it was. A single white rose lay upon the floor, a few of its crumpled petals strewn over the stones. She looked up in surprise. Gunar averted his eyes, and awkwardly stooped to retrieve it. In silence he rose up again and held it out to her. For a moment she hesitated, unsure what to make of it all. He seemed so different tonight—so strangely vulnerable and exposed, that for an instant she almost felt a regretful pity for him. He was so strangely different from everyone else—so alone. He didn't fit in with man's world, any more than he fit in with that of wild beasts. He was, and always would be, a misfit, doomed to wander aimlessly, and to be rejected in every place where humanity dwelt. How lonely must it be to him, she wondered? He seemed so painfully conscious of the disfigurement of his ghastly scars, trying ever so hard to conceal the hideous ferocity of his beastly form from all other eyes. And yet for whatever reason, he had chosen to reveal himself and be open to *her*. Slowly, she reached out and accepted the rose from his hand. Whatever did he want from her, she wondered?

Immediately the dire warning of the stone statue streaked through her thoughts. With a shudder she pulled back and turned coldly away. Whoever he was—whatever he was—she had a growing suspicion that it was more than coincidence that he had happened upon them when he did... Was he the dark one who was to bring so much danger and destruction?

"You are thinking of what the Dryad spoke with you," Gunar's voice cut through her perturbed contemplations.

"Yes—how did you?" Her jaw dropped, but she hastily recovered herself: "Oh, yes, I forgot—you read minds." She hesitated perplexedly. "What did you call it?"

"The Stone Statue—the Dryad inhabiting the rock formation down by the garden pool—you are thinking of the things she said to you."

"Yes," Adlai answered somewhat distractedly, the creased furrow in her brow deepening a bit as she looked curiously at him.

"How did you know what it was? Are there many more creatures like that?"

"Yes. But most of their kind do not show themselves to man anymore."

"Why ever not?"

"Because they, for all their wisdom and powers, were in the end found to be as short-sighted and foolish as man, and they have never forgotten their shame."

There was a certain solemness—almost sadness—in Gunar's voice as he spoke. He was silent for a moment, then continued:

"You are afraid that I am he of whom she spoke."

He said this last part with an unaffected calm, as if he were little concerned with trying to persuade her one way or another. Adlai let out a long breath as she shook her head confusedly.

"I scarce know what to think anymore. And so much has happened in the course of the last few days that I hardly even know myself. After all that the Muses told me, I—"

She stopped short, abruptly darting a glance up at him, a twinge of fear in her eye. She couldn't be too careful—she knew far too little of him to take him into her confidence already, no matter how disarming in manner he might presently seem. Lady Winter had strictly warned her against relaying her new name to anyone…Was it too late? Had he already read her thoughts, and did he already know about it?

Gunar said nothing, but slowly picked up the branched silver candelabrum from where it had fallen on the floor. Blowing softly on the cold wicks, the candles immediately lit up with a gently burning flame, as he quietly handed it back to her. Adlai took it back and looked up at him in stunned amazement.

"How did you come by so many powers?" She asked incredulously. "Who *are* you? Where have you come from, and why are you *here*?"

The uncensored questioning broke forth without ceremony. Gunar continued to view her with his usual undisturbed manner, his placid features unmoving. What was it that made him that way, she wondered? Was he dispassionately phlegmatic and lacking all emotional attachment, or was it something else? Was it the higher power of a governing inner peace which kept him always so composed and unfazed? …Or was it something darker and more sinister which kept him stolidly impassive—like the unhurried behavior of a predator toying with its helpless prey?

"I am here because I am needed," Gunar replied, "And I come from many places. And as for who I am, perhaps you ought best to answer that question for yourself."

"How could *I* possibly know who or what you are?!" Adlai retorted in indignant surprise. "Is it always your intent to obscure your meaning with strange sayings? Or do you mock me with all of your riddles?!"

"*If* it will make you search harder for the truth," Gunar replied simply. "It is my experience that men are the sort of creatures who do not readily receive any truth which is easily handed to them. *If*, however, they must work at unearthing the truth for themselves in order to obtain it, then that Truth—when found—often stands a greater chance of taking root and of thriving."

"Enough!" Adlai snapped. "It's late, and I've no time for this nonsense. Tell me plainly who you are, and what you want: Are you for us, or for our enemies?"

"Neither," Gunar replied with plain straight-forwardness.

Adlai stared at him in mute bewilderment, unsure what to make of all these blunt answers to her inquisition, and even less sure how what to make of him personally. She was starting to be deeply frustrated, but at the same time her curiosity was piqued now, more than ever. She felt an insatiable, driven need to know every last detail and secret about him. *What was he was hiding, and why?* His peculiar statements and odd behavior made her feel uneasy and fearful, just as they also compelled her growing trust of him. However did he manage to be both unpretentiously frank, and yet elusively hidden all at once? His flat directness did not give him the air of one seeking to lure her into deception, and he seemed to care little of her opinion to bother in creating falsehoods... At the same time, however, what if his seeming sincerity really *was* a bait meant to entice her into the clutches of a greater evil?

"How can I know whether or not I should trust you?" She demanded at last.

"You can't."

Adlai let out a frustrated sigh as she scrutinized him warily. But Gunar merely stared back at her with his usual relaxed, unflustered demeanor.

"Then *you* tell me," she demanded tritely, "Are you *safe*?"

"No."

Adlai stared at him for several moments, unsure whether to stay or run. Why did she feel so drawn to him? His answers were all frighteningly direct. In fact, she was almost beginning to think he was rubbing it in her face. He had the power and ability to wreak havoc and annihilate them all—yet for some reason against all natural instincts associated with his kind, he was completely self-possessed and contained. It was like the terrifying power and might of a lion, confined in the simple harmlessness of a lamb. Of all the hazards and evils she had faced, he was probably the most dangerous of them all—why then did she feel the absurd inclination to trust him by taking him into her confidence? She shook herself. *What was wrong with her?!* Gunar's mind powers might be significantly more powerful than she had before thought. She must not yield to its persuasion, no matter how strongly she felt compelled… She could not—must not—give in…Not, at least, until she could be *sure* of what he was.

Adlai glanced down at the leafy stemmed bloom still in her hand.

"Why did you do this?" She asked at last.

"I thought it might help to cheer you," he answered clearing his throat. "And," he added with a knowing smile, "Someone wise once said that flowers are heaven-sent blessings, sent to bring comfort in the midst of suffering." He sobered again. "Remember to take your troubles one day at a time, rather than heaping all your trials altogether. Leave tomorrow to worry about itself—each day has enough sorrow of its own. If you don't, you will miss the gifts sent to ease you through the burdens of Today."

Adlai started. She wasn't certain whether to take comfort in this reminder, or to be annoyed at his rhetorical counters.

"If you're so concerned with easing my discomfort, then perhaps you oughtn't to have delayed so long in your rescue upon the moor! Honestly, you seem to always wait 'til I'm near half dead before you arrive!"

"I *never* arrive either early or late—but always, *exactly* on time."

"Oh, and why is that?" She retorted dryly with a sarcastic laugh. "So I can savor the suspense of wondering how short or prolonged my death may be in coming?"

"No, but so that you remember your need for me. Had I come earlier, you would have not known your need for me, and my efforts would have met with resistance."

Adlai's smile quickly disappeared. He *had* tried to stop her from leaving, just before she had fled from him there in the garden. *Had he foreseen all that would happen, before it had actually come to pass?*

"Besides," Gunar added with a short smile, "The blessing of being found near half-dead, is that you have now managed to escape the severity of her ladyship's pre-meditated punishments. She cannot so openly mistreat you, when held accountable to the King for your life."

His smile broke into a broad grin at this last statement, but Adlai chose to ignore it.

"Did you know what would happen to me?" She questioned.

"Not all. I only see into the future that which I am permitted to see, and that, for the purpose of a higher cause. Even with all my powers, I must yield to the authority of One who is higher than I. My abilities are therefore subject to his power and authority; without him I do nothing on my own."

"*Oh?*" She asked quizzically with raised brow, a new curiosity forming in her mind. "And who is the Master of yours?"

"One who is more powerful than any other created being—either in this world, or any other. One who has the power of life and death by his very thoughts alone, who possesses the powers of all the known realms combined. He sits altogether outside of Time, and is the First and the Last of his kind."

"Did you say 'the First and the Last'?" Adlai cut in suddenly.

"Yes," Gunar replied.

Her thoughts began to race. It couldn't be—was it possible? Christofini had used the same words. She had almost convinced herself that it was nothing more than a beautiful dream…but now? The image of Christofini's face was already swiftly fading away from her memory; she could remember little other than that she had found him strikingly beautiful, and that everywhere there had been light…*Light!* In a flash her thoughts flew back to the Spirit's grim warning: "Beware of the one who comes clothed as a Spirit of Light!" What if her exotic vision actually was all just as the Stone Statue had foretold? If so, then he had already successfully sought her out and found her! A tremor of fear slid down her spine. He truly was very crafty and powerful indeed, to have known precisely which one of her weaknesses was the strongest… And he had played on them, targeting her through the deepest of her inner-most desires: her need to be valued and loved… If his powers were all that Gunar claimed they were, then he must have foreseen her. He must have known that she was heart-sick, aching for love to be returned to her…And he had then disguised himself in the most effective way possible, creating a believable mirage from all the shattered pieces of her heart's longings…And she had so foolishly fallen for it. The Muses' warnings came back now, echoing solemnly in her ears: "Guard your heart!"

Adlai backed away with a start.

"You're a spy!" She accused loudly. "You've been sent here to learn about me, and to trick me into betraying myself to you!"

Gunar made no reply, but there was a sudden change in the look in his eye…Once again, he looked painfully vulnerable, as if carrying some inner secret hurt. Why did her accusations sometimes seem to awaken some deeper feeling inside him?

"Ieuna, I have longed both to carry and to protect you—but as of yet, you have been unwilling."

Adlai blanched pasty white. It was plain that he now knew more of her identity than she herself did. The Muse's warning was already coming true—and she was in the gravest of danger.

"I don't know what you're talking about!" She sputtered. "That's not my name—I've never even heard it before!"

"You have," Gunar replied with calm frankness, "But hereafter to avoid raising your alarm, I shall refer to you simply as Heidi."

"*Heidi?*—But that isn't my name either!"

"It could be your name."

"And what's wrong with Adlai, or even Adelheide to, for that matter?"

"Nothing, only I think it has something of a sweetly innocent ring to it—and I like to call you by a name which no one else ever shall."

"That's because it's so *plain*!" Adlai snorted. "I'm a lady of the House of DuReiyne—not a simple serving woman living in some village hovel!"

"And so—" Gunar started slowly, "To *you*—a simple serving woman is beneath your notice, except for when it comes to debasing her lowly position?"

Adlai stopped short, as pictures of Headmistress Ardath flew into her mind. She had always thought of herself as completely unlike the proud, disdainful old woman in any way… Was it possible that she had somehow acquired Ardath's unapproachable haughtiness and contempt?... Perhaps she was more like her than she'd supposed.

"No—I didn't mean that—" Adlai started. "It's just that—"

"And I suppose, then," Gunar interrupted quietly, "That I am little more than a mere Beast to you?"

His question hung in the air for several long moments, as Adlai's mouth soundlessly opened and closed like a fish. At last she lowered her eyes in misery to the floor. Her fingers twisted awkwardly about the leafy, thorned stem of the rose still in her hand. Swallowing painfully, she searched desperately for something to say in response… It was suddenly as if she could see herself through his eyes: she had never asked him to save her, but from that first night until now he had not stopped saving her. And she had barely offered him the slightest ounce of gratitude or acknowledgement in return. She had heaped demands on him with the petulant whim of a disgruntled child. Perhaps he didn't owe her an explanation after all, for *anything* he did. For some unfathomable reason, he had loyally protected her from harm—and she had rewarded him by openly despising him. And whether she wanted to see it or not, the truth was that she was transitioning into the very thing she hated: a superficial young woman, whose shallow mindset was thinly disguised by the contempt she demonstrated for others she considered insignificant. But it was more than this revelation of herself which pained her. She had the acute sense that she had hurt him, and for that she now felt an aching remorse.

Gunar did not seem inclined to wait for her answer. With a burdened sigh he rose, shaking his head soberly as he did, a somber look in his expression.

"Those who distain others live in fear of being despised themselves," he said, looking her directly in the eye. "Insecurity and the need to prove one's self is sure evidence of inner contempt and lack of value." He hesitated for a moment. "Unless you learn to believe and see again through the untainted eyes of a simple child, you will never be free—you shall never truly *live*."

Gunar went to leave, but paused at the window.

"I took longer to come to you, because I thought you would wish for me first to save your horse."

Adlai started.

"Storm?! He—he's really—"

"Safe and sound, back in his stable. While with him, I sent another to watch over and keep you safe until my arrival."

Speechless with baffled surprise, Adlai searched for something to say, but no words came. Here she had been, cynically accusing him—and all the while he had been carefully overseeing every last detail regarding her, even bringing Storm back from death's door, and sending a guardian angel to be with her in his place. Gunar didn't wait for an answer, but there was a brief glimpse of sympathy in his eye as he looked back at her one last time. Then with a sudden great rush he spread his wings and was gone.

Feelings of shame and remorse washed over her. Numbly she gazed down at the white rose still in her hand. She wasn't worthy of his simple gift. With a choked sigh she let it drop onto the bedside table.

CHAPTER 22—FACT AND FICTION

The days that followed were a short respite from the usual vigor of Adlai's daily routine. True to her word, Milady made certain that she returned to her new regimen within three days of bed rest. Adlai deplored the idea of being forced to return to her studies, yet there was one particular tutor whom she was most anxious to see. She chided herself for having been suspicious of him before—there was nothing in the little old man of which to be wary, and he might yet prove a good friend and mentor.

A week passed, and then two; yet to her surprise there was no sign or mention of him. By the beginning of the third week, Adlai could stand the suspense no longer. Braving up all her courage, she decided at last to approach Lady Ardath on the matter.

The headmistress was overseeing several servants. Adlai swallowed, clearing her throat to speak:

"Milady?"

Ardath turned sharply in her direction. Her brow was already sternly raised, her lips tightly pursed together in an agitated line at the unwarranted intrusion.

"I trust that your studies are all in order for the morning?" She questioned coldly.

"Yes," the girl answered in a low voice. "If you please, I was wondering when Dr. Hindley might be expected to resume his duties in guiding my lessons?"

For an instant the older woman blinked, as if the question didn't register.

"Doctor *who?*" She demanded impatiently.

"Hindley—Dr. Lucius Hindley—Tutor of history, literature and philosophy?"

The headmistress stared at her for an instant, a flicker of vague confusion and uncertainty in her eyes.

"There is no one by that name of which I am familiar," she answered at last in a blunt tone. "Our funds at present are greatly spent. And with the state of the war, certain amenities must be foregone, so that provision can be made for other necessities. A vast deal has already been spent in securing the tutors already present in our employ—" (she paused to motion impatiently to a servant), "And what with these incurred expenses, I have found it necessary to keep our staff such as it is, without the trouble of any further additions."

Adlai stared in stunned silence, searching the headmistress' immoveable features. Could she surely mean that…?

"But what of my studies—" she faltered, "What of history, literature, and philosophy?"

"Those are not deemed expedient to your present education, nor do I feel that their merit is so great as to be required. You have already had enough on such subjects in your up-bringing, such as it is—a very little should suffice."

The headmistress quickly rapt out her reply in terse tones, then promptly turned on her heel and strode past the bewildered girl. Adlai scarcely moved. No more history or reading? What did she have left to look forward to now?

Even more perplexing was Ardath's denial of having any knowledge of the Doctor at all—how could he have simply vanished, almost as if he had never existed to start with? What was going on at the Manor, and why were so many strange, inexplicable occurrences coming her way?

Adlai went straight at once to the wall across the hall from her bedchamber. For a moment she stood staring unbelievingly before it: here was the white marbled breast of a Griffin; and beneath the molding under it, the candelabras with the painting of the white tree fixed between them. Her eyes trailed the details—it was almost identical to the tree emblazoned on Gunar's chest. And just like the roots twisting around his heart, there was a keyhole disguised as an iron heart hidden somewhere among the roots… But *where*? Try as she might, she could find it nowhere, though her fingers pressed and scoured all over… It *had* to be here, somewhere! It couldn't have just vanished, could it? With a frustrated sigh she took a step back. If there was a door, the outline of it must be concealed by the molding along the wall. Dazed, she turned to leave. *What was happening?!* A person simply couldn't be there one moment, and then just disappear the next, without leaving even the vaguest, apparent sign that he had ever been?

A new thought suddenly came to her, and it was one which sent a trepid fear through her mind…It had been such a long, lonely life here; she had felt so alone and needy for some kind of love or friendship—could it be possible that her starved imagination, desperate for an outlet of some sort, had at last succeeded in fashioning a world of its own? Was this new friend nothing more than a mere figment of her own imagination, the created invention of a starved and isolated mind?...Had she finally crossed that thin expanse which lay between the outer brink of sanity and utter madness?

That night she lay awake, her mind lost in troubled thoughts… Was she living in a dream world of her own making, a world in which some trick of her mind had at last turned fiction and fantasy into fact? …She pushed herself deeper into the pillows, as if to shove away the awfulness of this thought…What if *all* of this wasn't real?...What if *everyone* whom she had met in recent times—Gunar, the Nymphs, Christofini—were all nothing more than beings she had concocted in her deluded mind?

Here she checked herself—no, that was giving herself *far* too much credit! Even if she had possessed the creativity to conjure up such creatures, their personalities were infinitely beyond anything of which she herself could have imagined, and nothing at all like the sort of characters which she would have chosen. The perplexing enigma of Gunar was sure evidence to that point—not even she could have invented such a puzzling paradox.

A sudden noise outside her chamber interrupted her thoughts, and she sat up with a start. All of the other servants had long been to bed...*Could it be possible...?* She did not wait to rationalize this one. In an instant she was on her feet, scurrying across the room to cautiously open the bedchamber door...There was nothing. With a sigh, she turned back to bed. It was hopeless. She might as well accept the fact that it had never happened. Sinking back into the covers, she found herself suddenly wearied. Her eyes slowly closed, and she drifted off into a discomfited sleep.

Strange, troubled dreams drifted through her subconscious. She thought she had caught sight of Dr. Hindley, his hunched figure turned away as he opened the little door in the hall. All at once he turned to look back at her with his usual, friendly smile:

"Come, follow me!"

"But you're not even *real*!" Adlai protested.

"Everything will be explained in due time," the Doctor called after, "Just follow me—use the Key."

With that he disappeared, and the door closed after him.

Adlai sat bolt upright in bed. None of it made any sense, but somehow and for some reason she did not know, she felt compelled to go back and look once more. Within moments she was again standing in her dressing gown before the same place she remembered the door having been. Taking in a deep breath, she carefully moved over the painting inch by inch...Nothing. Her hands dropped to her sides as she let out a sigh. She was losing contact with reality, and she needed to stop before she went insane altogether.

She was just turning away, when at once something hard turned under her foot: it was a little gold key on a necklace chain. Adlai let out an ecstatic gasp of excitement as she snatched it up and examined it...Yes, there could be no doubt—it was indeed the very same key which the Nymph had given to her, although it seemed to have lost a little of its shine and brilliance, and now seemed slightly dull in color. Instantly she remembered what she had been told, and now she felt guilty that she had not thought to use it before now…She couldn't let it tarnish and rust, or it would become useless. For an instant she stared at the key, then back at the wall. *She* couldn't find the door, nor even the keyhole, but maybe—could it be possible that the key could find these things on its own? Taking another deep breath, she held the key directly before and pressed it against the portrait on the wall.

"Please," she prayed, "Please be able to find it."

The key suddenly stuck. Quickly she opened her eyes: the key was growing hot and shone bright as it sank into place; within seconds a shining metal keyhole had materialized before her very eyes. Adlai let out a gasp of wonder. With trembling fingers she gave the key a slow turn…*click*. Nimbly she reached up and grasped the Griffin's head. A thin, bright light blazed across the wall, carving the outline of a small door; all at once a door handle materialized beneath her hand. She was already shaking with giddy excitement as she gave it a determined yank. With a creaking the door fell open. A gust of cool air blew upon her face, as she stepped over the threshold and closed the door firmly behind her.

Adlai strained in the darkness, peering ahead into the dark void before her. Feeling along the stones of the wall she searched for the bottom of the stair. The little gold key was still clutched tightly in her hand when suddenly she felt it move. To her surprise, the key was glowing like a bright ember in the darkness, and it was speedily changing form—growing larger, its shape contorting and stretching outwards so that it no longer resembled a key at all; the head was becoming wider, thicker, and the pronged teeth of it were reaching outwards, twisting back and around until it had transformed into a torch. A flame instantly lit upon the top as Adlai, still in shocked surprise, gazed all about her.

It didn't seem as dark, dusty and dirty as before, and the steps of the stone stairway actually appeared in much better condition than they had formerly been. Very soon she found herself running on light step up the staircase; and in what seemed very little time at all, she found herself standing directly before the little door leading to the Doctor's private apartments. She was nearly breathless with excitement, as she reached out to tap lightly upon the door. Her hand had not even quite touched upon the wood, however, when a cheerful voice from within immediately called out:

"Come in, dear Child! Do come in at once!"

Adlai started, then suppressed a quick smile. She wasn't certain why anything should surprise her anymore. So many strange things had happened of late, that perhaps the faster she learnt to adapt to it all, the better—and also the sooner she might come to uncovering the answers to all the questions pounding inside her head. So without hesitating another instant, she pushed open the little door and stepped inside.

CHAPTER 23—THE OATH

It was quite as she had remembered seeing it last—Dr. Hindley's inventions and contraptions (along with miscellaneous books, scrolls, and parchments) lay strewn everywhere. There was a roaring fire upon the hearth, and the little man stood hovering over something heating in the fireplace, with his back turned towards her. Straightening up with some difficulty, he turned round now to face her with a merry grin.

"Ah, yes! Here you are, at last!" He exclaimed with a great, beaming smile.

"You—you've been expecting me?" She asked incredulously.

"Oh, yes! Of course!"

"But how? How did you know that I would come?"

"I knew you would come, because I was sent on a mission by another—and my purpose here, as of yet, is far from complete," he answered with his usual brisk, undisturbed frankness.

Adlai gave a puzzled expression:

"I don't understand."

"No, indeed; I hardly expect that you should," the little man answered again with a ready smile.

"How is that no one here remembers you at all? How is that *possible*?"

"Well, I can only suppose that has something to do with the one who sent me."

At this she peered more intently at him.

"But to be able to make everyone here to forget you *entirely*—what sort of power is that?"

Lucius returned her gaze with a serious look:

"The *greatest*. Power infinitely beyond all which you or I could even possibly begin to imagine."

Adlai felt a slight twinge of fear at his words. *What was his purpose here? Who had sent him, and why?*

"But do not trouble yourself with these details now," he continued. "There are much more important things to discuss, and I know that you have come with questions for me—what is it that you would like to know?"

Dr. Hindley had been dishing out a meaty stew from a black iron cauldron as he spoke, and now he passed her a dish. The tantalizing aroma made her mouth water, so that for an instant she half forgot any questions she might have had, as she quickly fell to consuming it.

"Yes, um—quite—" she started with her mouth full. *There were so many things she wanted to know—however was she to start?... Yet there was one particular subject which was now more pressing than any other—that of Gunar. But how much did she dare tell, without the risk of revealing too much?...Perhaps if she started with topics more benign, he might not suspect anything...*

"It really wasn't much, I probably shouldn't have bothered you—" she started apologetically. "It's just that you're such a viable source of knowledge—quite invaluable, really."

Dr. Hindley smiled deeply, a look of pleased satisfaction on his demeanor.

"Well I'm quite happy to be of service, particularly when it affords me the pleasure of another's company, such as yourself."

Adlai smiled awkwardly, still desperately fumbling for a more innocent and less obvious way to make her approach.

"About the Immortals—the Guardians—whence did they come from?"

"They—or at least *he*—has always been. Days without beginning, or end."

"The Great High King," she breathed.

"Aye."

"And have the Immortals no other names?"

"Men have called them many things—the Ancients and Ascended Beings; Faeries, Heroes, Angels—even Gods."

"I see," Adlai fumbled, "And what do you think they are?"

"Faeries, *no*—that word cannot possibly come *near* to describing what they are! ...Besides, 'Faery' is simply another exalted title for a winged Nymph—or more precisely, a Muse— those of higher rank among the Nymphai, possessing of stronger blood."

"Then Muses are Faeries of the Nymphs, and only they have wings?" Adlai interrupted.

"That is correct—those of the Ancient Fae, at least by all accounts I have ever read. The Nymphs themselves were made, as man, mere reflections of differing aspects of the Immortals."

"And what then might be the difference between the Fae and the Immortals? Are they Gods, then?"

"The Guardians themselves..." Dr. Hindley paused and stroked his beard. "I believe that, whatever they might be, it is utterly beyond our understanding... That, and that only *One* can lay claim to the title of a God."

"The High King of the Guardians," she nodded. "You speak of him as though he were utterly set apart in a cast unto himself."

"He is. All that is or ever has been in existence, has its existence through him. There is no comparison."

"I see… And speaking of comparisons, pray, what might be the difference between 'Faeries', and other mystical creatures—Elves, for example?"

"Supposedly the Elvin Race came to be when the Faery Nymphs intermarried with Mortal beings, though no one knows for sure."

"Then the Elves are half-breeds?"

Dr. Hindley's countenance darkened.

"Child," he replied in an earnest and sober voice, "Things belonging to the Mystic World demand our reverence. Never speak lightly nor disrespect things of which you do not understand—to do so is to draw the attention of the Eye of Evil."

Adlai nodded and lowered her eyes.

"The only thing that can be known," he continued, "Is that the Elves more closely resemble humans' appearance (though perhaps taller), and are without wings, like the lesser Nymphai. Yet they still maintain some of the characteristics, wisdom and strength of their unhuman origins—magic flows in their veins," he added with a smile, "Though not as pure and powerful as their esteemed relations—their blood, of course, being diluted. As such, they cannot change form or disappear at will, as their relations the Nymph folk."

"Ah." Adlai hesitated. "And what of Muses?"

"Muses are the Faery hierarchy and mistresses of the Nymphai. They are the Original Faeries—the very first and oldest of that Ancient Race, and there are few of them left in existence. It is said that they have wings because they were the first image reflections created of the Guardians, and were born together with the sunrise on the first day Earth drew breath. They have been since the Dawn of Time. In fact, some believe that when the Guardians left, that the Muses of the Faeries were given the choice to join them in Paradise. But instead, they selflessly chose to stay behind and care for Earth and her children, whilst concealed in disguised anonymity. Though whether this be fact or fiction, it has always been a subject of great debate amongst scholars. But what *is* known, is that they have been reputed throughout literature as being sources of great wisdom and inspiration—Oracles even, whose eyes are able to see far into the misty realms of the future, since they are so closely connected with the Eye of the Deep... One belief that is commonly held, is that they are the natural daughters of Mother Earth and Father Time."

Adlai hid a knowing smile, averting her eyes lest she reveal too much of what she already knew.

"And the rest of the Nymphs? Why are they different from the Faeries?"

"Some say that they were made lesser beings in order to serve the Fae; others, that they are the mixed descendants of inter-marriage between the Faeries and Elves, who adapted to their selected environments. As they grew further away from their origins, their magic and power weakened—hence the reason why they, like the Elves, have no wings. They have become short-sighted and have forgotten what they are—or rather, *why* they are."

Dr. Hindley paused thoughtfully:

"Faith and belief are powerful things: they are the wings of the spirit; they make the soul what it is. And without them, the soul dies."

"How sad!" Adlai murmured. "To think that an entire race should be lost!"

"Legend says that as the imprint of the Old World fades from their beings, they lose all magic and finally become mortal. And a soul that loses touch with its own purpose is a soul at war...with everything. And so we see it continue today: Man toils, struggles against, and fights with everything—his Maker, his brother, and finally the Earth in which he dwells. He forgets in whose image both he and his brother were made, and that everything around him was made as mere reflections of his Creator. In so doing, he destroys both his identity and his own soul."

For some reason she knew not, his words made her want to cry.

"And what will happen once they fade away entirely?" She murmured in a hushed whisper. "Can they not be brought back?"

"It is said that someday—when faith and belief are revived, and when the Guardians return again—that the lost Nymphai will emerge; they will shed the skin of mortal flesh, and their wings will grow back…in the day when their blood answers the Call."

Adlai's heart quickened at this. Dr. Hindley pressed his face more eagerly towards her:

"You see, Child, Faith can do the impossible—it can move mountains, even bring what is dead back to life. *Faith* is what causes our spirits to soar upon heights, when all of Hell is determined to drag us down into its depths."

"How does one have such a faith?"

"It's not simply *having* 'faith', but rather, it is in *whom* you have your faith—*that* is where you find your true strength!"

"Faith in— *him*?"

"Yes. Faith is simply the key that unlocks the door."

"The key that unlocks the door to his power?"

"No. *His* power is a wielded force which cannot be locked up or contained! Rather, faith is the key that unlocks *you*. It is the key that unlocks and frees your spirit from the prison of your own fears, doubts, and inabilities, and opens you up to become a vessel—a vessel through which he can exercise his boundless power… The Eye of the Deep is ever searching, looking for those who are of faith that he may prove himself strong…"

For an instant Adlai felt she comprehended what he was saying, but then its meaning became lost again. She felt frustrated. He seemed at once so wise and discerning, so knowledgeable and experienced—and so foolishly deluded all at the same time. Perhaps it was prudent to change the subject, before the murky waters of his wandering mind proved too deep to fathom.

"And what of the MerPeople?" She queried.

"Descendants of the Nymphai, who adapted to the water sources—the Naiads of the brooks, streams, and rivers; the Nereids of the oceans and high seas. Other nymphs include Oreads of the mountains, Dryads of the forest, and the Hamadryads—Dryad nymphs whose life-span is bound to that of the tree with which they are connected. They are born with it, and they die with it. "

Adlai tried to feign interest, but all his former talk of the Eye and of 'his' power was bringing back to memory things Gunar had said to her—things which both frightened and made her uneasy. Lucius seemed to notice, for he paused to look at her.

"Something tells me that the chronicles and origins of Earth's other children is not the *real* reason why you have come... Is something distressing you, Child?"

Adlai bit her lip.

"Actually, the question I had was...well, actually, I don't quite know how to put it," she fumbled again. "I guess I was wondering—do you have any books about magical sorts of creatures, or beasts possessing strange powers?"

"Oh, indeed!" Dr. Hindley replied pleasantly. "I have quite a vast majority—but is there something in particular which you wish to research?"

"I was wondering if you might have anything regarding creatures that are not fully human, but not fully beast as well—and also, who possess incredible strength and speed?"

The Doctor slowly lowered the cup of tea from his lips, a wary look both of startled surprise and fear showing in his old eyes.

"You ask about something which has long lain forgotten and shrouded by the mist of Ancient time," he spoke in a grave and troubled voice. "There are few alive who yet remember such things. But tell me—how came *you* to know of it?"

"It doesn't really matter—" she responded with a casual shrug. Averting her eyes, she lowered her head closer to her bowl so as to avoid meeting his keen stare. She wasn't yet certain if it was wise to tell the good doctor all about the strange goings-on of late—especially Gunar.

"What do you know of it, then?" She continued, gulping down another spoonful of stew.

The Doctor rose up slowly to stoke the fire. The light from the hearth flickered across the weathered lines of his worried face, as he slowly turned back to her.

"You ask about a certain race known as the Neiphile," he said at last. "The ancestry of the Neiphile goes back countless centuries—millenniums, even... All the way back to the days of Olde...to that cursed day when Earth lost all that was once truly pure, wonderful, and valiant in her. You may recall from our last conversation, the tale of the Battle that was fought by man against the Ancients?"

"I remember, though one thing confuses me—if it truly happened, how is it that none ever speak of it?"

"They do not speak of that which they wish to hide from memory and to *forget*," the Doctor said emphatically. "The sad truth of it is, that they've mostly succeeded in their willful forgetfulness."

His eyes grew dark with foreboding as he began to smoke his long pipe, staring off into the distance.

"…They had no idea what sort of curse they would bring upon themselves!" The Doctor murmured grimly.

"*Who?*" Adlai pleaded earnestly. "*Who* brought a curse?"

The Doctor turned his gaze solemnly back towards her.

"On the day on which the great battle was to take place, the armies of men swore an oath, and made it sacred by the shedding of blood. There, they vowed never to rest nor stop searching, till at last they had found and taken that which was guarded and kept secret by the Immortals."

"And what was that?"

"Sacred mysteries kept secret long ago—those having to do with Immortality, and also, of Great Power."

"So what happened?"

"The inevitable—they lost the battle… But the oath which they swore—*the Oath* remained…Slowly, gradually, it overtook them like a strange disease—binding them, body and soul, with its greed and lust for power. Those countless few who survived that day when Earth swallowed up her disloyal, began to witness a strange evolution: gradually their forms became altered, till at last they were transformed altogether. No longer were they men, but great, monstrous, inhuman beasts! Outcasts and vagabonds—like ravenous wolves prowling the earth—so they roam about in the desolate regions of the wild, looking for any whom they might devour…They cannot truly live, nor can they die, but are more like phantoms from the Underworld—shadows, in whose souls there no longer dwells any light. They are condemned to wander forever over the earth, roving bands of murderous fiends, forever consumed by blood-lust; their hunger does not wane, nor can their insatiable greed be abated…All who fall prey to them are slain, or else come under the Curse."

Adlai squelched a shudder that tingled all the way down her spine. But for Gunar's rescue, she would have been killed and devoured… And had he not miraculously healed her afterward, she most surely would have become one of them. Where might she be now, were it not for him? And what of Gunar *himself*? How was it that he had the power to save her, yet not himself? He obviously had fallen under the Curse—and yet for some inexplicable reason, he was completely unlike the rest—self-controlled, conscientious, even caring… And unlike the other Beast, Gunar had wings… None of it made any sense.

"It is said that they are being preserved for the Dark Day when the Shadow returns to claim their allegiance, and shall require that they fulfill their Oath of long ago."

Adlai shuddered again.

"They are damned, then?" She faltered.

"Aye, they are." The doctor answered soberly.

"And nothing can be done about it? I mean, there is no way at all for *any* of them to redeem themselves?"

The doctor looked up at her again, a puzzled, perplexed look in his eye.

"No, they are what they are—and once a man becomes one of them, there is no going back."

"But what if one of them was good?" Adlai insisted. "What if one was somehow able to overcome the venom—"

She halted abruptly, because at the mention of "venom" Dr. Hindley looked up quickly, a questioning look of subtle suspicion in his eye.

"To overcome his instincts," she corrected herself slowly, "If he—somehow—learned to control his hunger, or even if he started doing good? Wouldn't that somehow liberate him from the Curse?"

"Such a thing has never happened," the Doctor shook his head slowly, "And no, it would not be possible. Their Greed is not something that can be controlled: it is a consuming wild fire burning in their veins at all times; they have no choice but to yield to it—they are powerless to do otherwise. Once infected, it overcomes the mind, strength and willpower of the victim…None are powerful enough to withstand it…*and* live."

Adlai tried to steady her trembling, hiding behind her cup of tea as she turned to look away. Vivid images of Storm fighting for his life were flooding through her mind. How was it that Gunar had managed to save him? How was it that he, himself, although altered in form, seemed to have overcome its power to dominate and control him?

"You seem troubled with deep thoughts," the Doctor noted. "What brooding meditations have stirred your contemplation?"

"Oh—it's nothing," Adlai answered quickly with a casual smile. Inwardly she hoped she looked convincing enough. But the Doctor only shook his head.

"My dear Child," he began as he relit his pipe, "You might well be able to fool another, but this old fox—well, let's just say that when you've lived to be as old as I am now, there are some things that you just *know*… And you can sense when others know far more than they are willing to admit. And though I think you sensible in being thus guarded, I would caution you—stay far away from such things."

Adlai's shoulders sank, and she gave up with a sigh. Before she knew it, she was telling the Doctor everything about the night in the wood when she and Storm had been attacked, and also of Gunar—how he had rescued her, and of how he had brought Storm back to the Manor and was now employed as a hired hand there…Yet for some reason she did not fully know, she chose not to relay the other times when she and Gunar had interacted. Something about their conversations felt strangely intimate, so that she felt shy and embarrassed to speak of them. She also did not know what to make of all of his strange sayings—which, in many ways, still seemed like riddles taunting her with some sort of obvious secret she had not yet been able to decipher. No, it was best not to relay such details to Dr. Hindley until she knew more.

The Doctor seemed satisfied with her story, however, for he did not probe further. Instead he sat thoughtfully smoking his pipe, staring past her with a sober and contemplative expression in his old eyes.

"What you have just told are strange things indeed, and I hardly know what to make of it." He paused, his withered brow furrowed together, his mouth still opening and closing as if searching for something further to add—

"I can only say this: be careful—be extremely careful. The Power that motivates these fiends is far darker and more sinister than any of us can fathom. 'Tis possible that it has chosen this time to cloak its true intents under guised pretexts… Spirits of the Darkness may indeed clothe themselves as ministering agents of Light, simply that they might conceal their true purpose."

Adlai started at this last remark. Her thoughts jolted back to the words spoken by the Nymph of the Stone Statue—and her vision of Christofini, along with Gunar's confession that he was under the control and guidance of another…

But of course! It was all too obvious! How could she have been such a fool?! How could she have been so blind and stupid, as to have not clearly seen through it all? And especially when Gunar had done so very little to hide it—his trite, blunt answers to her questions almost seemed to mock her, taunting her with his true intents…She was almost sickened. What dangerous game had she been playing, by very nearly entrusting herself to him?...And what was it that he could possibly want from her?

"Are you sure that you have told me *everything?*" The Doctor questioned.

Adlai started at the direct probing of his question.

"As much as I can remember," She lied. "Why?"

"Well, because there is something very strange to all of this account you have given me: it would even seem as if this creature—Gunar, I believe you called him—was seeking you out for a particular reason and purpose. But *why*, I ask myself, should he interest himself with *you?*"

Adlai's thoughts were already spinning. There was something about her—perhaps what the Muses had told her, and maybe even more—which she was now certain that Gunar knew about. But why should any of that make her of significance to him?...Suddenly she remembered the Muses' prophecy—that she had a significant part yet to play in all the events about to unfold in the future—'for good, or for evil'—that was what they had said. Of a sudden the food in her stomach settled like a cold rock in the pit of her belly...Of course! Even the Stone Nymph had spoken of it! He *needed* her to lead him to something! Something that had to do with a chamber of some sort, somewhere...

Adlai felt that she was suddenly turning hot and then cold all over, her strength sapped away as of by a burning fever... The Muses had foreseen it, and it had come true all too soon. He had, like a predatory beast, sniffed her out and found her...But what exactly was it that he wanted? And for what evil purpose was she so intrinsically needed?

"Adlai?"

The Doctor was now leaning towards her, a look of worry and concern on his face. Adlai suddenly realized that she was now breathing heavily, and that her whole body was trembling; sweat had already broken out over her skin, and her hands in her lap were nervously twisting and untwisting her loose night shift.

"Are you quite alright, Child?"

"Yes—quite," she answered with a forced smile, licking her dry lips as she spoke. "If you please, I think I'm just suddenly tired. If you have no objection, I think perhaps I ought to retire."

"Oh, yes, of course!" The Doctor replied with a nervous laugh. "Yes, you must take care to get your rest—do come back and visit me, though, when you can."

She nodded with another forced smile, and rose to leave, as the Doctor followed her.

"And Adlai—"

She turned back quickly at the door as the Doctor called after her.

"Yes?"

"Be careful."

The sound in his voice sent a cold tremor peeling down her back.

"We do not yet know who nor what it is which we now face. And for some reason unknown to us, he has singled you out. Be on your guard. I'm here for you, limited as I am, anytime that you should need me."

Adlai smiled gratefully and gave a quick nod. The Doctor tarried another brief moment, an unmistakable look of fear and worry in his countenance, as he reluctantly closed the door behind her. She lingered only an instant, her heart thudding in her chest and a growing sense of nausea churning in her gut. Then she turned quickly and fled down the stair.

CHAPTER 24—SHOCKING SURPRISE

The following day went tediously by, but Adlai was so distracted, that she could hardly bring herself to focus on her lessons. Her nerves felt raw and on edge, and every sound seemed to make her jump with a start. She felt like a tiny mouse, waiting for the cat to spring, or else to be lured and baited into some kind of trap…

She waited breathlessly…But nothing happened. Another day and night came and went without event. A week went by, and then several more, till at last a month crawled by…Still, there was nothing. Nothing changed or altered its course out of the usual, and the only sight Adlai ever had of Gunar was on a handful of occasions when she caught glimpse of him through a window, either minding the grounds or heading towards the stables. After the first two weeks had gone by without event, Adlai made up her mind to give it up. As long as she kept clear of him and made every effort to avoid drawing attention to herself, she would be safe. As for herself (though she had never before found her studies to be of any interest), she now found that she preferred them to anything else. At least here, surrounded by the business of tutors and lectures, followed by numerous studies—here she was not alone, and Gunar seemed disinclined to make any approach while others were present. Her studies almost seemed to bring her relief; as long as she was busy, she wouldn't think so much about all the questions hanging in the shadows of her mind like haunting apparitions. Now she paid very dutiful attention to every lecture and lesson given, plying her tutors with as many questions as she could think to ask. And though a few at first responded with surprise, her change in behavior seemed generally welcomed by all, so that even Mistress Ardath seemed to note it. And although her countenance maintained its usual severity, yet there was little with which she now seemed able to find fault.

The night hours were the only times left which Adlai now dreaded. Long after the last of the servants had departed to their quarters, she would lay awake in awful silence, listening …waiting. But very soon she had solved this problem as well, by asking each of her tutors in succession if they might have further books for her to study. In this way she kept her mind busy, burning candle wax long into the night, until at last she would fall into an exhausted sleep…For the very first time, she found herself grateful that life could be so dull. At least if it were boring, then nothing truly dreadful was happening. Here, within the confines of the Manor and the rigors of her daily studies, here she was safe—at least for a while.

…And during the rare moments when her mind was not occupied with her lessons, Adlai turned her thoughts elsewhere: Willan should be returning home soon; he'd promised that he would—and then all would once again return to normal. And surely by then enough time would have lapsed that he would no longer think of the awkward parting of their last moment together. Adlai could feel her face suddenly flush red with embarrassment every instant the memory of it came back; but each time she shoved it back as hard and as forcefully as she could into a vacant space in her mind, hoping there that memory would begin to fade. That was all in the past, she reasoned; since then she had turned over a new leaf, and the new Adlai would soon prove to him that she had *much* more on her mind than romantic notions of intimate interludes. She was determined that when he should see her next, that there would not be a single trace of the teenage girl he had left behind. She would show him that she was strong, completely untouched and unmoved by their last encounter, as if he had no more than disappeared from sight than she had dismissed the whole matter from her mind. He would soon see that she had not given his slight of her a second thought, and that she had had sent his memory into exile, along with that last fleeting glimpse of him disappearing into dust upon the open road. She would prove that there was not the slightest measure of close feeling left for him in her heart anymore; she would remain aloof and busy with her studies, ignoring him just as he had done to her.

...But deep down, she knew all of her striving was in vain. And she was more afraid than ever that she would always love him...no matter how much she scolded and begged herself to forget. Even worse, was the feeling that she was now forced to lie to her own self, suppress all natural feelings, and instead to conjure up stilted, artificial emotions to take their place. Was she doomed to live in this mechanical way? It was all so exhausting....For no sooner would she nearly convince herself that she had banished away all feelings, when she would suddenly catch herself idly in the midst of some pleasant day-dream of him. There were several nights now when she cried herself into a wearied, exhausted sleep, there to dream haunting night visions in which—not only love— but all life, light, and color were completely shut out; in their place was only the endless grey of hopeless futility.

It was a typical afternoon well into the second month after Willan's departure, and Adlai was quite lost in her studies; when of a sudden there was a noise that made her jump and her heart give a leap. For from farther down the hall, a familiar voice could be heard shouting, promptly followed by the excited barking of hound dogs. There was the scurrying sound of servants' footsteps, along with the frantic voice of the headmistress hurriedly calling out rushed orders. Slowly Adlai rose from her chair, closing her book with deliberate precision and care as she slowly straightened up. Her heart was racing and her whole body was already shaking violently, as she attempted in vain to compose her expression while smoothing her hair away with trembling fingers. Taking in a deep breath, she swallowed hard, squaring her shoulders as she turned and left the study.

Servants were hurriedly pushing past her, yet she scarce seemed to notice. Willan was back again—in a way that was so familiar, yet at the same time strangely surreal. Slowly she moved forward as if in a dream, each step belabored. She had been waiting for this for what had seemed like forever; but now that it was here, she almost wished that it hadn't come at all.

And then, next thing she knew, there he was—just as she had remembered him. Tall, stately, and oh, so handsome!

"It's so good to have you back to Dombrey, my Lord!" Ardath exclaimed, throwing her arms about his neck and embracing him affectionately as a mother would her returned son. Adlai swallowed hard. He had not yet noticed her; perhaps it wasn't too late, and she ought instead to hurriedly return back to her studies. It wasn't as if he actually needed to see her; indeed, he might not wish to see her at all.

"Adelheide! No, wait! Do come here!"

Adlai felt her heart flutter wildly in her chest before she even turned around. All at once she was being spun around and hoisted off of her feet high into the air. Willan's bright blue eyes and smile were shining up at her as he whirled her about, his joy-filled laughter echoing through the corridor. She caught her breath as Willan set her down again, a shy blush stealing across her face. She had hardly dared hope that he would miss her, much less that he would be so ecstatically thrilled to see her again. Whatever did it all mean?

"Oh, it is *so* good to be home again!" Willan exclaimed aloud. "And especially when I tell you all the news!"

Adlai cast a confused glance towards the headmistress, who likewise appeared equally baffled and astonished.

"Why, whatever has happened, my Lord?" Mistress begged perplexedly.

"It's over! It's *over*! The war, all of it! At last, we can be free now to live in peace in our own lands, with no more fear of the Shadow!"

"What!?" Adlai and Ardath gasped in unison.

"Vanquished! Completely and utterly vanquished! And his armies set to route back to the Shadowlands from which they've sprung! Oh, is this not a day for great rejoicing?!"

Willan caught up a stunned Adlai by the waist, and began twirling her about the floor once more, and dazed, dizzy, and practically giddy from laughter and excitement, she fell in after him… *Could it possibly be true? Were all fears at last behind them?*

"Oh, after all these years! At last my father will be able to return and take up his place here, where he belongs!"

Adlai's thoughts were flying about wildly, a breathless, excited blur of so many different emotions and feelings. She wanted to laugh, to cry, to scream from sheer happiness and relief!…Perhaps now that he was no longer duty-bound, he might at last feel free to consider other things…? He seemed so light-hearted and carefree now, just as she remembered him afore.

Looking up at him, she felt uncertain what to make of it all…No, there was no mistaking it: there it was again in his eyes, the same happy, warm, tender look she had seen there so often in the past. It was plain that whatever ills had passed between them were long gone; her faithful, loyal, dutiful friend had returned to her at last. Jubilantly, Willan suddenly pressed her close to his breast and squeezed her tight, and Adlai gave herself up to it with a happy, contented sigh…She could stay right here, just like this, for forever…

"Craving your pardon, Milord," the headmistress' voice cut abruptly through the momentary silence, "But Lady Adelheide must return to resume her studies."

"Cancel them! Cancel them all!"

Willan's voice was ecstatic, and he was still looking intently into Adlai's eyes with a certain shining warmth, almost as if he were seeing her for the very first time.

"Why, if you say so, my Lord!" Ardath stammered in reply. For an instant Adlai inwardly mirthed at her obvious look of aghast surprise at Willan's brash candor and open attentions towards her.

"I shall inform her tutors at once!"

Ardath's voice was unusually shrill and high-pitched, almost to the point of a squeak. There was no mistaking the look of visible discomfort and unaccustomed awkwardness, as she scurried past them like a startled shrew and swept out the hall. Adlai suppressed the wild urge to giggle out loud at this strange sight: the old witch fleeing before her like a frightened spider, completely drained of poison and deprived of all her powers to torment. It seemed as if the dawn of spring had suddenly burst upon her soul after an eternity of winter's nights. Never before had she ever felt so happy, while blushing with pleasure she gazed back up into his enraptured face.

"Everything is going to change now!" He burst, his voice swelling with uncontainable joy. "And we are *all* going to be very, very happy!"

His eyes ran down quickly over her grey, colorless garb, and suddenly she felt herself flinch with slight embarrassment. She wasn't dressed in anything remotely flattering or lovely—did he still think she was beautiful?

"You're not going to wear these anymore!" Willan declared in authorative, matter-of-factness. "I made some purchases while on my return journey home, from a merchant specializing in rich silks and fine cloths, and I've brought you back near an entire wardrobe!"

At that moment two of the servants approached, both sweating and staggering under the weight of a heavy chest. Without a moments' hesitation Willan instantly flung open the lid. Adlai let out a gasp. Inside were all manner of the richest and costliest gowns she had ever laid eye upon, as Willan held them up for her to see. Reaching underneath the fabrics, he suddenly produced several small ornamented boxes. She let out a dazzled cry of surprise: stunningly beautiful jewelry of the finest craftsmanship met her amazed eye—all manner of gold and silver, bracelets and necklaces dripping with the most breath-taking jewels imaginable. She could scarce believe her own eyes, as with trembling fingers she reached out to touch them. Never before had she owned anything so lovely before in all her life—nor in such sudden abundance…Was it possible that dreams really did come true, and that at last Willan had finally grown into the Savior-Prince she had always felt he would be?

"Those are mine?" She gasped.

"All of it! Every last piece!"

She tried to blink back the tears threatening to spill over, but it was too late. Every tortured, agonized moment of her former life was now finally worth it, just for this—to at long last be prized, treasured, and loved.

"I don't know what to say! Only you shouldn't have!" She cried as she threw her arms around his neck.

"*Yes*, I should—and should have done ages ago," he answered firmly.

"I don't even have words!"

"Then you approve?"

"Approve?! Of course I approve!—My only fear is that you have emptied your purse on my account!"

"It is *my* pleasure and will that you should be treated like the lady that you are," Willan spoke reassuringly in a tender voice, "So let's have no more talk concerning my purse."

He brushed a few loose strands of hair from her eyes, running a finger affectionately down the bridge of her nose.

For several moments she hesitated before him, still not sure whether or not to believe her own eyes. Whatever had happened, which had so utterly transformed him? She had waited so long, that it almost seemed too good to be true. She had all but given up hope, all but banished her yearning desires into oblivion. But now, here it was: visible, tangible proof that he still did—that he always had—cared for and loved her.

"Adlai, there is one other thing which I would speak with you about," Willan pressed in a quieter, more discreet voice. Gently taking both her hands in his, he gazed so intently into her eyes that for a moment she felt she couldn't breathe.

"There is something which I have longed for all my life; and now, at long last, I've finally found my heart's desire. Please—I hope that you won't think me at all rash in doing this so soon—"

Adlai let out a little scream of wild joy and excitement. "Oh, Willan!"

She flung herself about his neck again.

"Oh, I knew you'd feel as much!" Willan cried jubilantly. "We've always been so close, you and I, such kindred spirits."

Seizing her by the hand, he hurriedly led the way back through the milling gaggle of servants.

"In fact, you've been so much like a sister to me, that I knew I could count on you—not only to approve my choice, but to aid me in welcoming our new guest."

Adlai's smile instantly vanished. Her heart felt as if it had instantly sunk like a cold, hard brick of ice in her breast, as she suddenly let go of his hand. *Was she actually hearing what she thought she was hearing?...After all of this, it couldn't—it just couldn't be possible...could it?*

Willan seemed completely oblivious to her dumbfounded response. With breezy, confident step he quickly sailed past her through the foray of heavily laden servants issuing their way through the open hall. Then slowly, through the haze of scurrying bodies, at last she saw it—a small retinue of young ladies waiting in attendance, all of whom discreetly bowed their heads in reverence and parted, as Willan strode straight into their midst. Another personage slowly stepped forward from among the retinue of female attendants—the tall, regal figure of a graceful young woman, her feminine form partially hidden beneath a light and airy cloak of pale blue silk which enveloped her like a canopy. Her delicate hand was extended propitiously with a slight bestowing air for Willan's taking, as he pressed it with eager fervor to his lips, then turned back towards Adlai.

"Adelheide," he said, straightening his shoulders ceremoniously as he drew himself up to full height, a broad, pleased smile flooding the whole of his satisfied expression, "I wish to present Lady Afwin of Gavriel, Princess of the courts of the Southern Kingdom of Sundor—my Bride."

CHAPTER 25—HEART-ACHE

The words were still hanging in the air, echoing like a resounding gong in her hearing, yet somehow she couldn't make them register. She felt dumb of understanding as she grasped to comprehend the full meaning of his words, yet it was as if he were speaking in some strange, foreign dialect. She could feel her lips opening and closing, attempting to formulate some response to this sudden, abrupt announcement. Her tongue seemed turned to lead as she stared—still uncomprehending—at the spectacle before her. Her eyes wandered blindly from his exhilarated face to that of the serene maiden waiting upon his arm.

The young woman gave Adlai a gracious acknowledging tilt of her head in token of a bow, then slowly loosened the hood of her traveling cloak. It fell away over proud, delicate shoulders, a profuse abundance of sunshine-gold spilling down in cascading tresses over her perfectly formed bosom. She had large, tranquil eyes, almost the exact same hue of sky-blue as Willan's, and there was a certain undisturbed calm in the sweetly peaceful smile that graced her mouth. Her smooth ivory skin seemed made of alabaster; her high brow, slender nose, gently sloping cheekbones—all the way to her delicate cherry-red lips—were perfectly fashioned. In fact, her perfectly proportioned features seemed more like the molding of sculptor; she had all the regal appearance and ethereal beauty of a goddess, rather than of mortal flesh and blood. Her every movement was carried with such an easy yet stately grace… Indeed, Adlai could scarce imagine that such a celestial creature could have ever (at any time in her life), been capable of doing anything remotely clumsy or awkward...She was flawless perfection, in every way. And Adlai was now acutely aware of how substantially lacking her own powers of beauty, grace, and allurement were in paled comparison... Standing there in Afwin's presence, everything about her which had, afore, been painfully awkward and out of place, was now all the more unbearably so, to the point that she nearly would have liked to have fled away to conceal her misery. She didn't think that she would ever feel pretty again. Everything in her seemed to wilt, until all that was left was dull, plain, common, and uninteresting. Afwin's flowing garments fit her form perfectly, and had all the rich touch of elegance and royalty. With shamed embarrassment Adlai again was made acutely aware that she was still clad in the same dull grey frock she had worn for weeks now.

Her heart sank with an agonizing pang into her chest: never, not in a thousand years, could she have ever hoped to win Willan's heart against so effortlessly lovely a competitor—one so benignly unaware of the fact that she had just innocently stolen away the long-coveted prize of another, and for which the other had painstakingly toiled so long to earn. And if Afwin's unparalleled beauty was not enough to thoroughly convince Adlai once and for all that every hope to which she had hitherto clung was now utterly lost, the giddy look of complete, enraptured bliss in Willan's eyes and smile said it all: he was helplessly smitten, besotted past all hope of return. Never before had she seen him like this. Willan, though of a light-hearted disposition, was at the same time always of a dutifully serious and sober nature; his conscientious behavior and the lordliness of his manner made it evident that he was ever self-aware of the great responsibilities unto which he had been born. In previous months before his journey, the kingdom's state of affairs had seemed to age and drain him, sapping away much of his vigor and strength. When off to himself there had often been a droop in his brow, a weariness in his eye, and a heaviness in the way that he carried himself...Yet here was none of that now: in place of the serious-minded future sovereign, experienced and enwisened beyond his years, here instead was a carefree youth; in place of ceremony and practiced precision, now he was rapidly stumbling through his words amidst happy nervous laughter.

Adlai was only catching snatches of what he was saying, as he recounted the whole of how, upon arrival at the capitol of the Southern Kingdom, he had met the lovely Princess—one and only daughter of King Menasis. Indeed, if it had been someone else, Adlai would have found the shyness of his sheepish grin and hasty awkwardness vastly amusing—if only it had not been Willan...*her* Willan. She was now witnessing the change in him which she had only ever dreamt of seeing...only it was not for her, but for someone else.

She was hardly able to hear anything that he was saying now; it was as if she had found herself suddenly in some sort of strange dream—a nightmarish, hellish dream—in which the characters were all vaguely familiar, yet strangers at the same time. It had all had the surreal feeling of one caught in the unsure reality between waking and sleeping.

"I thought I had wandered into a dream!" Willan exclaimed, his face alight with buoyant feeling. "And the only guilt I feel in taking her as my wife, is that now the courts of the South shall be forever robbed of the brightest light that ever illuminated their palaces!"

Almost before Adlai knew what was happening, Ardath was suddenly pushing past her. With a joyful cry she ecstatically flung her arms about the young woman in a greeting.

"We are pleased and honored to welcome you, my Lady!" She cried, turning back with tear-filled eyes and trembling chin towards Willan. "At last this house shall have a *true* Lady to preside over it!"

At this, she cast a slight side-long glance towards Adlai.

"And to think that his Lordship should so surprise and take us unawares! Oh, we are so ill-prepared to welcome your Graces!"

"There, there, now, Heromena!" Willan was laughing. "I'm certain that all is in impeccable order under your care, as always!"

Adlai stared at Ardath: was she *truly* so sincerely overjoyed to be receiving the new Lady of the House, or was her jubilation merely the result of being overcome with relief that Adlai, *herself*, had not turned out to be Willan's new bride-to-be?

They were all embracing and laughing together, as the headmistress dabbed at her eyes with a handkerchief amidst gay smiles and happy tears. They all fit together—even Ardath. In many ways they almost had the appearance of a small family at last reunited: mother, son, and new daughter…and Adlai had never felt so alone, unneeded, and out of place. Willan might as well have been a thousand miles away on the other side of the earth. In some ways she felt like an uninvited stranger or eavesdropping spy making (by her very presence) an unwarranted intrusion on their happiness. This was *their* celebration… not hers. Not one tiny shred of it belonged to her.

"Adlai?"

She started. All eyes now turned to her now. Willan was still smiling, but there was the tiniest hint of awkward concern and perplexity in his eyes. Adlai swallowed, fighting hard to force down the enormous lump which had suddenly swollen to a painful size in her throat. Burning tears were rushing to her eyes, hard as she tried to blink them back. No matter what, she could not—she *must* not—allow Willan to know that she had still entertained the ridiculous notion of his possibly being in-love with her. He must never know that, even up until just a few short moments before, she had actually anticipated that *she* was the one whom he had intended to wed and make his wife.

"I'm very happy for you both," she returned quickly, in as warm and sincere-sounding a tone of voice as she could muster.

Inwardly she prayed that they might not see how her lips trembled behind her forced smile. For several seconds she fidgeted helplessly, straining like a bobbing fish upon a hook. All laughter and merriment had died away, as the eyes of all now looked uncomfortably in her direction…It was too late, at this point, to hide anything anymore.

"Your Grace must be exhausted after your journey, and no doubt must wish to retire?"

Ardath's voice broke the dreadful silence. The headmistress was staring in her direction, yet the expression in her eyes was one which she could not read: was it concern, even pity?

"By your leave, Milord," Ardath continued hurriedly in a cheery tone, "I shall hasten at once and see to it that Lady Afwin's chambers are in readiness."

With that, she gave Willan an affectionate, motherly kiss upon his cheek, then turned to leave. Yet as she swept past the girl, their eyes met for a brief instant. Whatever she had seen in the old woman's eyes was gone now: in its place was the unmistakable look of cold triumph. A cool smile played smugly on her face, while with an undisturbed air the headmistress straightened her shoulders and raised her head higher. Adlai swallowed hard again, choking down her tears. She might have known that the headmistress could never have passed by the opportunity for gloating exaltation, however brief…And she wanted for the girl to be made to feel it.

Ardath's footsteps faded away down the hall. Afwin's calm eyes were now surveying Adlai with discreet yet slightly more curious attention than before, and Willan seemed suddenly to have run out of things to say, as he sheepishly fumbled over himself. His smile had already begun to take on a painfully strained and crooked bent, while the usually cool pallor of his face was growing visibly redder by the moment.

"I think I shall go help the servants with the preparations!"

Adlai half surprised herself at the sudden bluntness with which the words blurted from her mouth, especially since she was not in the least inclined towards helping prepare *anything*, for anyone. Yet it was the best cover and only reason she could contrive for excusing herself so abruptly, without further explanation. She just needed to get away as quickly as possible. With a forced smile and hasty nod of her head to Afwin, she hurriedly departed, avoiding Willan's glances as she went. She did her best to ignore the mortifying sensation that their eyes were still following her down the hall as she made her hurried retreat. It was all she could do not to break into a run so that she might the more quickly flee the scene of her humiliating disgrace.

The bustling hubbub of activity faded away as she exited along a side corridor. Her own reflection caught her eye as she passed a nearby window. Slowly, she hesitated before it: a freckle-faced adolescent girl with unruly hair stared back at her—dull eyes, pug nose, large teeth, and vacant expression... *However could she have been foolish enough to believe that perfect, flawless Prince Willan—could ever have fallen in-love with that?* It was true that she had seen herself a thousand times in her sixteen years... But never before had she felt such despairing pain and miserable, bitter disappointment at what she found there.

"You're a fool!" She whispered hoarsely. Swallowing hard, she choked down the unbearable lump burning in her throat and pushed on past.

Her face was burning with intense heat, and a throbbing pain was shooting through her head, as if her brain would suddenly explode. Tears were swimming over her eyes in a flood. Blindly she pushed open the small back door leading to the gardens.

Head pounding, she stood in the chilly silence for several moments, her eyes wandering in a daze upon her surroundings. *What had just happened? Everything here looked the same as it had just hours before, and yet at the same time—suddenly, and without warning—everything that was familiar had come to an abrupt end... Nothing would ever be the same again.*

The last of the leaves had fallen long ago; there were nothing but bare limbs left to cloak the boughs of the trees. But for the arched stone walkways, there was little other reminder that this place had once been green and alive, or that flowers had ever once bloomed here. Winter had stolen it all away. There was nothing left, but the lonely sound of the wind echoing into desolate silence. Everything was cold and dead.

Adlai found herself standing at the garden's center, facing the pool. She glanced down. The ring Willan had given her was still on her finger. Her mind was reeling in blurred, torrid confusion. However was it possible for any one soul to feel such awful, wrenching pain?... Could even Death remove its sting? Or would it follow her beyond the grave, and haunt her in the here-after?

She wanted to disappear, to never be seen or heard from
again. She had no one left to turn to and pour out her heart.
Loneliness was her new companion now, wrapping itself about her
like a suffocating blanket, enfolding her in its limp, cold embrace.
A cold wet wind whipped against her trembling frame, but she
hardly stirred... She was already cold and lifeless on the inside.

Adlai stopped short. She had come to the southern edge of
the garden, and its encircling stone wall now loomed before her.
She wasn't certain why she had wandered here, except perhaps that
the south side was the furthest away from the house; and as there
was hardly a window facing this end, it was quite remote and she
was sure to be obscured from view... If only there was a way to
slip beyond these walls...to simply disappear into silence, forever.

A sudden creaking made her jerk. It had come from her
left. Her eyes ran over the corner section of the wall, along the
foundation. Where had the noise come from? A large pile of dead
tree branches, amidst a mound of mulch, clippings, and wet leaves
had not yet been hauled away to be burned. Empty barrels and
crates were stacked high against the wall. A tingling went through
her... It was probably just the wind... But perhaps she ought to
return to the house...

Creak!

There it was again! So close, that it made her jump this
time. It was accompanied by a soft rustling. A shaggy head of
hair—with long pointed ears—could just be seen disappearing
beyond the burn-pile... Gunar. Whatever might he be about, and
where had he gone? Adlai circled cautiously about the pile,
standing on tip-toe so as to see over the top of the wreckage, but to
no avail. With a grimace, she hoisted up her long skirts and
clambered up upon the nearest barrel. Balancing herself
precariously, she strained her eyes in the direction of his
disappearance, but to her shock there was nothing. *Surely he could
not have simply vanished into thin air?!*

All at once she espied it—a pair of cellar doors set against
the house at its base. Perhaps they led to the store-rooms? She
frowned to herself, once again glancing down at the rubbish and
rickety kindling which still stood as a barrier between herself and

the doors. Cautiously she climbed onto the pile of crates. They were far from steady, and she teetered uncertainly a number of times as she clambered from one to the next. At last she dropped panting before the cellar entrance. The doors were set with a pair of iron rings for handles, and the planking seemed partially decayed, though she barely noticed as she rested her weight against them to catch her breath.

All at once there was a creaking, followed by the sound of dry rot splintering. The rotted boarding beneath her instantly gave way, and with a startled squeal she fell through. The wind was knocked out of her as she hit belly first. With a groan she turned and lay dazed on her side, then at last staggered shakily to her feet. A few shafts of day-light filtered through the dilapidated wooden doors overhead, dimly lighting upon the dank stone floor beneath her. The stone stair leading back up to the overhead doors lay crumbled away to nothing. Adlai strained, but try as she might, there was no going back by the way she had come. Dejectedly she sank to her knees, rolling onto her side as she curled into a huddled ball like a small kitten and let out a shaky sigh. No one would ever think to look for her here, and she wasn't certain if that fact alarmed or relieved her. All her reasons for existence were gone now, stolen away in a single, deft swoop of cruel Fate. Everything and everyone was against her. Nothing was as it seemed; she could be certain of no one… *Who was Gunar, and why was he here?*…He seemed to be always watching…*waiting…But waiting for what?*…Whatever his intent for her, she had the uncanny feeling that once she had fulfilled her purpose, those sharp claws and deadly fangs would at last tear open her heart…He had saved her from the Creatures of the night, it was true. But sooner or later, his inherent nature—the darker, malevolent nature of the Beast—would win out…And she might well once again be in very grave danger of becoming the prey… Perhaps she already was.

A sudden grunt echoed behind her. The hair on the back of her neck began to bristle with sweat …She already knew who was waiting in the darkness behind her, as she turned to face him. Gunar's frame stood etched against the black void yawning out behind him, his one eye glinting in the dark like a flickering flame, and his outspread wings scraping against the low vault of arched ceiling above. Adlai rose up slowly, squaring her shoulders and keeping her eyes fixed warily upon him as he approached... She must not show him her fear. His heavy paws barely made a noise in the hushed stillness as they soundlessly padded the floor beneath...In every way he had the practiced stealth of an experienced predator. The steam of his breath filled the air before her face like a vapory cloud, as slowly he rose up to his full height...He was even taller than she had last remembered.

"I—I don't know what you want with me," she faltered, "But I know that your coming here has marked the beginning of darker days. Whatever it is that you want, I—I think you should know that—I won't be part of your game."

Gunar answered not a sound in reply. She trembled, waiting for a response as she watched his eyes glint in the dim light, yet his expression did not so much as flicker. Swallowing hard, she opened her mouth to speak again:

"If you're going to kill me, then just—just do it."

He let out another grunt, yet she couldn't tell if it was one of assent, or of agitation, or even fury.

"You are not afraid to die, then?"

His calloused question echoed harshly with a low growl, and she could feel chills now peeling down her spine.

"No—no, I'm not," She trembled.

There was silence. At last he lowered his face so that it was completely level with her own:

"Do you want to die?"

His question hung in the air, in a way that almost seemed to taunt her—like a cat toying with a mouse before striking. She stiffened and closed her eyes, preparing for the inevitable as she slowly tried to clear her mind of all fears and emotions...This was it. In the next few moments, she was going to die. For some reason, she was almost feeling strangely relaxed with it. She was going to be at peace. She was at last going to be free from all her inner pain and torment...A tranquil, euphoric calm washed over her ...All she had to do now was to yield...

"Yes," she breathed, in a voice so small that she could scarce hear herself.

"You are quite sure?"

Something about his persistent questioning sent a disquieted fluttering through her stilled thoughts. *Why was he doing this? Why didn't he simply finish her?!* Then suddenly, another thought flashed through her mind. It was that of the Muses' prophecy. It was true that they had spoken of the foreshadowings of darker days—but they had also predicted hope... Here in the midst of all this heartache, was it possible that there was still hope? It had been prophesied that she was destined for royalty, privilege—possibly even for happiness. She had a *purpose*—a destiny to fulfill. And if she gave up now—if she died—then she would never see anything which *might* have been...All limpid feelings of placid, mindless serenity connected with death were suddenly gone: in their place was suddenly the instinctive *need* to live, the will to survive, to fight—or to run.

Adlai's eyes flew open...Gunar was gone.

CHAPTER 26—THROUGH ANOTHER'S EYES

For several moments she stood staring into the empty space where Gunar had been just moments before. What did it all mean? Had it happened at all, or had her lonely thoughts conjured up this latest encounter out of a sheer need to escape from life—or perhaps to find again a reason to live?...Whatever had happened, Gunar was no longer here. Instead, a long, wide tunnel with a vaulted ceiling stretched out before her into darkness. Where did it lead to? One thing was sure: wherever it went, it was her only way out. Taking one last look back towards the light, she took a deep breath, and slowly began inching her way forward into the darkness.

It felt as if she had been moving forever at a pace slow enough to exasperate a snail, when her hand suddenly struck upon something—it was the gnarled roots of a tree, through which a tiny sliver of light peaked through. She must be nearing the surface. All at once there was a creaking noise. The roots seemed to come alive; with a groan they began to untangle themselves and unwind. Within moments they were stretching outward, fanning into a great arched doorway. Rays of light spilled through the gaps in the roots, emanating from the wide opening. Hesitantly she entered, then let out a low gasp of amazement. Luminous light was everywhere, shining through a long corridor created by the arched, whitened boughs of row upon row of trees. A rumbling sound behind her made her glance back: the roots were once more returning to their place; the doorway had disappeared.

In amazed awe she wandered on, until at last she came to the edge of it: a great forest loomed beyond. Faint moonlight was spilling down through the quiet wood, and a gentle breath of fresh air brushed her face like a caressing whisper. Limbs of trees loomed over her, their branches swaying gently in the tranquil light of the stars above. Adlai stopped and looked all about her. She was standing on the hilly summit of a quiet mountain top, a serene valley just beneath, through which a river ran. The mountains to the north spread out, on and on; she could see now that there were even more mountain ranges than she had ever before known. What lay beyond all of that, she wondered? Would she ever get the chance to discover what else there was of the world?

"It's beautiful, isn't it?"

A familiar voice startled her. It was Gunar.

"Have—have you been waiting here all this time?"

"Aye, I have," he replied, leaping down quickly from the massive boulder rock where he had crouched, and striding over to where she stood. She trembled a little.

"So—you really were down there with me, weren't you?"

His eyes were filled with a somber expression, but he made no reply.

"Why did you do that?"

"Do what?"

"Lead me into a trap—the castle cellar?"

Gunar was silent a moment.

"So that you would learn to forget what lies behind, and remember that for which you have been destined."

"Why did you let me believe that you would really kill me?"

"Meeting with Death causes one to see and remember that which is of the greatest importance in life—I wanted you to remember all the reasons for which you are still needed—alive."

"And after that? What then?" She asked in a slightly bolder tone. "Are you intending to kill me?"

Gunar silently surveyed her for several seconds.

"I only take the lives of those whom I have been ordered to take. There are many good whose lives are cut short, yet few notice; and many evil, whose lives have been prolonged—for a purpose. *Everything* has a purpose—," he said in a low voice, drawing up very close to her, "Down to the very last second that your body breathes its last…Never forget that."

"Everything has a *purpose?*" Adlai snorted. "What you just described doesn't sound like purpose—it sounds cold and cruel!"

"The hearts of men must be tried…and this can only be through sifting," he answered quietly. "Pain and suffering…does carry a purpose."

"Oh?! And what might that be?" Adlai suddenly snapped. "I don't know who you are, or who you work for, but you need to stop this—do you hear?! We are not just pawns to be used in your sordid game!"

All of the hate and frustrated anger she had been keeping bottled up inside suddenly felt ready to boil over. She was sick and tired of being toyed with, wearied to death of the endless fear and worrying over what evil might lie waiting, lurking in the future. And she was more than disgusted with all this talk of higher, omnipotent powers. Whoever and whatever they were, they seemed without heart or natural feeling—utterly removed and detached from the pain and suffering of the lesser beings under them.

"What is mankind to you?" She demanded through barred teeth, returning his gaze evenly as she squared her shoulders. "Just test subjects for you to study and observe, use and abuse to your own purpose, as you see fit? Are we nothing more than a laboratory experiment, or objects for your own amusement?!" Her eyes narrowed: "You tell the one who sent you that I've had enough!"

Gunar stared at her for a moment in a way that was both calm and serene, his posture relaxed and unaffected.

"I can't explain to you now all the reasons why you have had to suffer," he said softly, "But one thing I can promise: everything which you have had to endure until now—*all* of it—is, and has, been worked out for your greater good, and for a higher purpose. They may not of *themselves* be good, but they are all being worked *for* the good…Just believe."

Adlai hesitated, eyeing him suspiciously. She wasn't sure what to say to all this, and was too confused to reply.

"As to the rest of what you said regarding your death—" he turned his face away now as he continued, "On the day when you pass from this life into the next, you will see me again. I will indeed lead you into the after-life… But not in the manner in which you suppose."

Adlai stared at him quizzically. He was speaking in riddles again. Was he mocking her? The reassuring tone of his voice sounded as though he sincerely meant to comfort and put her at ease through his morbid promise.

"All will be revealed to you in due time," he continued, "And on that day you will fully understand all. But until then—" he turned back to her. "Until then you must be content to simply *trust*."

She looked at him quizzically. His statement seemed both incredulous and ridiculous, as though he took her for a simple-minded fool. He could read thoughts, and he was a master

manipulator at mind-games. Somehow, he was trying to lure her—
she was not about to take the bait. Folding her arms stubbornly
across her chest, she raised her eyes defiantly:

"Why ever should I trust you?" She demanded coolly.

"Because my past faithful service to you requires it," he
answered evenly.

Her mouth slowly closed. It was true; as strange and
bizarre as his manner and statements appeared, he had never
actually harmed her—in fact, he had saved her more than once.
Gunar was continuing:

"I know the thoughts and plans that I have for you—and
know this: they are *not* to harm you, but to give you a future…and
a hope."

He took a step closer and held out his hand:

"Trust me."

Adlai looked down at his outstretched palm, then looked
back uncertainly into his gaze—there was a gentle, almost tender
expression in the one distinguishable eye.

"Trust me," he whispered again. "Please…*trust me.*"

He was so close to her now that she could feel the warmth
of his breath on her cheek. Something about the plea seemed to
tug at her, almost to pull and draw her in. There wasn't a hint of
guile or trickery, in either his tone or his expression, and for an
instant as she looked into his eyes, a startling new sensation came
to her…He could read and understand her thoughts, but for a
moment it seemed as if she actually knew and could feel *his*. It
suddenly seemed as if she were seeing herself—watching herself—
from somewhere outside her own body…through his eyes. And
what she saw so startled her, that she almost could not bring
herself to believe it. The tender, trembling vulnerability of a
helpless kitten, mixed with the raw courage and invincible strength
of a great lion. The sharp perception and keen foresight of an
eagle, combined with the gentle harmlessness of a dove; the
trusting innocence of a lamb, and the untamed spirit of wild horse.
The simplicity of a child, and the complex beauty of a grown
woman. There was no awkwardness, no flaws, no faults at all—

only pure, matchless, and exquisite loveliness…in the exact same way that Lady Winter had shone her.

And then it was as if she were traveling with him through her own mind—every fear, every worry; every personal affection and tender care; every foolish, petty notion; every conceited, selfish motive, and childish, petulant whim—*everything* lay out in the open. Never before had she seen herself so plainly… He truly could, and had, seen it *all*. Sudden guilty shame washed over her: she might as well have been stripped naked. At this she blushed so heavily with embarrassment that she instantly jerked away. But to her surprise he held her fast. In discomfited dismay she realized with shock that he had been holding her hand over his breast the entire time. Embarrassed, she tugged away.

"Wait!" Gunar whispered, pulling her hand gently back. "Wait—there is more."

Adlai swallowed hard as he again pressed her palm against his bare skin. She could feel herself starting to tremble all over. It felt peculiarly intimate.

"Ssshhh," he soothed, "Your heart's beating wildly. I'm not going to hurt you…Just listen."

His fingers tightened ever so slightly over her own, until her hand was enveloped within his grip. She gulped and stared. Scars traveled over his chest close to where her fingers lay, and under her touch she could feel the soft, quiet rhythm of a heart-beat. Another blush came stealing over her cheek, and a sudden shyness filled her, as again she looked up into his face…There it was once more: she could see herself from somewhere behind his eyes… And even more, she could sense feelings—feelings that she knew were not her own… Pity… tenderness… and passion. To her shocked surprise she now realized how greatly she had misunderstood him. She had always afore mistook his placid, immovable nature for lack of any sort of feeling or personal attachment—now she realized that nothing could have been further from the truth. Here, wrapped up in this private part of him which he had allowed only her to see, here she sensed the deepest, most alive feelings she had ever known… In some ways, she almost wondered if they might even run deeper than her own. And here at the center of his being—something about her had aroused intense, strong emotion... He was captivated by her... But why?

She had tried so hard for so long to try to please another, to be worthy of Willan's love, only to be discounted, over-looked, and dismissed... She had grown so used to seeing herself through how she imagined Willan saw her, that she no longer even knew what she looked like. Yet here, in Gunar's eyes, she was starting to see it—all of it. For the first time, all that she was, all that her entire being encompassed, was being desired. He—Gunar—wanted her—all of her. Whether he could not see any of her fatal flaws and ugly faults, or he had simply and deliberately chosen not to acknowledge them, she did not know... All that she knew was that through his eyes, there now stood nothing other than a beautiful, perfect soul... A Princess. Through his eyes, she could see none of the guilty blemishes which seemed so constantly to mark her—only one who was completely and utterly adored.

She was quivering all over as he slowly released her hand. Was it actually possible that what he felt for her was love? Had the Beast fallen in-love with the Lamb?

"Do you—do you truly feel that way?" She asked tremblingly.

A low, purring rumble emanated from his chest, and a painful smile twisted itself across his scarred face. Slowly, softly, he turned her hand over in his. She found herself surprised at how small her own now appeared, enveloped within the size of his hand. Tenderly, he interlaced his fingers with hers. For a fleeting instant she found herself wondering how it was that such infinite power and might could be captured by one so vulnerable and owning of so much weakness. Of life's many paradoxes, this was sure to out-rank all others.

Her gaze wandered once more to the branded scar covering his left breast. All at once she noticed something—it was not a single tree, but *two*—one overlapping the other, their trunks and roots intertwined.

"What trees are these?"

"The first is Isadore, the Tree of Life—one of two trees planted by the Ancients in the heart of Avaelon."

"Avaelon?"

"Yes—that mystic realm in which Immortals and Man once both walked free."

"And the other?"

Gunar swallowed, his jaw slowly clenched. His smoldering eye darkened, and he turned away.

"Eigdrasill, the World Tree."

Adlai stared at him perplexed. Every time she thought she was coming closer to discovering who he was, another mystery loomed beyond. Gunar seemed to have already dismissed it from his thoughts, however; he was gently tracing the lines of her hand with the rough tip of one finger, taking great care not to scratch her with his claws.

"No matter what," (there was a tone of earnestness in his voice), "No matter what happens, or what I do, I need you to remember this moment."

Her lips parted to speak, yet she could find no words. If only she understood him better, if only she knew everything, and he wasn't so strange to her. Gunar didn't seem to require a response, however, as he turned back to face the forested wood behind them.

"Come," he said abruptly.

Bewildered, Adlai followed after. The forest all about had a peaceful calm, as the stars twinkled down from their place in the heavens above. Woodland creatures were settling into their burrows, and the little birds in their nests; and in a small far off clearing, she espied a mother deer grazing quietly with her fawn. Snowflakes started to descend, their fragile forms falling delicately upon the frosty ground. Soon everything was coated in a thin, glistening coverlet of pure white. Yet strangely, Adlai noticed that she did not feel cold anymore as she continued trailing on without a word after her silent guide.

Suddenly, in the distance, she caught glimpse of a wondrous sight that nearly took her breath away. It was a shimmering light atop a tall pine tree, freshly laden with the new-fallen snow. Beneath it, a dazzling party of strange beings had gathered round about, gaily dancing and twirling in fluid, graceful movements. Little lights atop silvery staffs circled the outer edges of the glen, and in their dim light Adlai caught sight of the faces of the bearers…It was a company of Woodland Spirits and Winter Nymphs, their soft voices raised in gentle symphony together. Forest creatures and animals were gathered round beneath the tree, assisting the Spirits in wrapping garlands of holly and nuts, pine-cones and wreaths about the tall pine, while all about were twined brightly colored ribbons and streamers. Birds of every sort—snowy owls, doves and pigeons, blue birds and robin redbreasts all sat perched in its branches. Glistening snowflakes glittered from its boughs, while icicles dripping from the branches glistered like a thousand crystals. The Woodland Spirits appeared as effervescent vapors, with frosty garments clothing their translucent forms as they frolicked about with hardly a care. The Winter Nymphs were clad in deep shades of pine, leafy green, and cranberry red, while the Elves who silently watched from the outskirts were all dressed in stately robes of scarlet, lavender and purple, and deepest blue rivaling the hues of the starry night sky above.

"It's the marking of the Winter Solstice—they are making ready to welcome in Winter's Eve, before the New Year," Gunar whispered in a hushed tone.

"Oh, it's beautiful!" Adlai breathed.

"Careful, do not let them hear or see you," Gunar warned in a whisper, crouching down beside her. "They do not suffer themselves to be seen by mortals."

Adlai looked back at him suddenly. So it was true! The stories Dr. Hindley had told her were not merely folk-lore, after all!

"You know about it?" She inquired wonderingly.

Gunar was silent and did not return her gaze. After a moment he opened his mouth to speak.

"The Spirits of the Earth were once much the same as the Muses and Nymphs, and liked to think of themselves as being infinitely wiser than mankind. There was a time when they, too, could travel back and forth from this world into theirs."

"Whose?" Adlai prodded. "Whose world?"

"That of the Guardians and Keepers of Old Earth. Being Spirit, they were not bound to the confines of this world…until…until the day they joined man in his folly."

"But isn't it true that some of the Nymphai joined them in their revolt?"

"A few, yes—but most were too wise and knowing to be lured by dark deceptions… The Spirits, on the other hand… They mindlessly followed one after the other, like blind sheep—and their short-sidedness was their undoing. Since that day, their entire race has been bound to the earth and her domain; never more can they leave it, but like the mortal race must dwell as sojourners here, and must serve and care for the earth until they return to it— ashes to ashes, and dust to dust. Unlike man, however, they have no souls—they are Spirit—and Spirits were never meant to end, but to live on forever into eternity. But since they joined with man in his rebellion, they have also been brought under the Curse, they must also partake in tasting of Earth's death… And once a Spirit dies, naught remains. When they pass from life they return and become once again a part of the Earth. In this way their life is allowed to live on. They have never forgotten their shame and disgrace, and how they allowed themselves to be deceived by a race they deem inferior to themselves."

Gunar's words continued to echo in her ears. She had never before thought of what it would be like to be without a soul. And though (in intellectual theory) she had always supposed she believed in the concept of souls continuing on into an after-life, the truth was that she had never thought too seriously about it. But now of a sudden, she found herself incredibly grateful. What must it be like, she wondered, to die—and simply cease to exist—almost as though one had never been? Could any fate be worse or more futile than that, she wondered? Never before had she been aware of how her belief in the after-life (however loosely she may have clung to it) had actually provided a sense of peace and comfort, even in the darkest moments. How awful to take one's last and final breath, knowing that it *truly* would be your very last—either for this life, or any other? To simply vanish into nothingness? …It seemed so tragically unfair…and so hopeless. Inwardly she vowed that she would never take her immortal soul for granted again.

"Each race is given different strengths and abilities," Gunar continued. "If it comforts you at all, the earth spirits are not at all like humans in their emotions. They have forgotten and no longer understand the depths of love, any more than they are capable of feeling any sort of physical or emotional pain. In truth, their fickle character is much like the uncertain, ever-changing nature of Earth itself. In so many ways they are lesser beings than man himself, since they do not so much really *live*, as they do simply *exist*. They mindlessly follow their whims out of instinct, without thought or much of conscious choice, for they have chosen not to raise their thoughts any higher. That, in and of itself, would spell out the annihilation of their souls, were they in possession of such. That is why they aren't human. The essence of humanity—what makes him a living soul—is his choice to live, to struggle, to love, and yes—to feel pain… Or to choose to deaden himself to both, and lose both his humanity and his soul to damnation…To whom much is given, much is required."

Barely a leaf rustled as Gunar turned silently away back into the brush. Adlai gazed back a moment longer, then reluctantly followed behind. They were going deeper into the wood now. Shivering, she noticed that it was growing colder and darker than before, even though the snow had disappeared. The trees here were thinner and fewer in number, and she was becoming uncomfortably aware that nothing else seemed to be moving or stirring throughout the wood, save the two of them. All sound had completely died away; the only noise that could be heard was that of a low, moaning wind stirring the tree tops. Gunar had slowed his pace now, and seemed to be moving more cautiously than before; he seemed to be keenly alert and intently focused, as with a wary eye he watched the surrounding wood. His long pointed ears stood attentively on either side of his head, and his long tail hung stiffly erect, so as not to brush the ground. Stealthily he padded ahead with nary a sound. At last he halted and stood motionless.

"What is it?" Adlai whispered.

"We're almost there," Gunar answered back in a hushed tone. "Keep close."

His hand closed firmly over her own, and gratefully, she accepted it. There was something comforting about his presence in this eerily silent and desolate place. Suddenly he stopped short. Just a little distance ahead, she could see a stream gurgling. No grass grew on either side of it, and the waters touching the surrounding shore were dark in color, while a misty vapor rose from its surface.

"We must follow the stream, up the river, back to its place of origin—to the Source of All Life."

CHAPTER 27—THE SOURCE OF LIFE

Gunar was leading up hill. Adlai held his hand fast as she struggled after up the rocky ravine through which the stream flowed. Glancing over her shoulder at the rivulet, she suddenly froze: she was almost sure that she could distinctly see the blackened forms of long shapes floating soundlessly in the current.

"Gunar, what is this place?" She shuddered hoarsely, clinging more tightly to his hand.

"This place was cursed long ago," Gunar replied in a hushed voice as he helped her find her footing. "Whatever you do, do *not* look directly into the water—look only to me."

Adlai nodded, averting her gaze and trying to keep her eyes only on her feet as they continued on. At last they reached the brink of the hill, and Gunar halted again.

"Over there," he murmured.

He was pointing to something a short distance away from them. They were standing upon the edge of a great lake. An island rose up above the middle of the lake, hanging suspended in mid-air, from which a great white tree rose upwards to meet the heavens. The tree's circumference filled the whole of the island, its gnarled roots trailing all the way down to the dark lake below. Above ground, its trunk was sectioned into twisting colonnades that stretched out into an arbored pavilion, widespread branches reaching up like spires to touch the starry sky above. Tranquil falls of water spilled silently over the edges of the floating island, pouring into the basin below. Shafts of blue light emanated from the alcove, swirling energetically in the stilly night like aurora borealis. The beauty and loveliness of the place seemed a perplexing contradiction to the deathly still waters below, over which not so much as a breeze stirred its untouched surface.

"What you see before you is a remaining remnant of Avaelon. Long ago it was torn away and thrown to this far corner of the world…" Gunar paused, a far off look in his eye. "We go to see the Lady of the Lake," he resumed at last in a hushed voice. "Be on your guard: there, you will be tested. Remember, look not either to your right, nor your left—only look straight ahead. And whatever you do, do not—under *any* circumstance—drink the water!"

Adlai shuddered at his words. The waters before her looked so putrid and diseased, that the mere thought of drinking from it made her feel nauseated. Gunar paused, and his grip on her hand tightened.

"Heidi, do you trust me?"

The question startled her. Up until that moment (at least for the last couple of hours) she had felt that she did, but hadn't given much thought to it. But now, here it was with its piercing directness… and she wasn't sure how to answer.

"I—I think so," she faltered. "Yes, I believe I do."

Gunar was again staring at her with that penetrating gaze, his fiery eye seeming to burn away all false fronts, until it cut through to the very core of her being. She flinched slightly, turning her eyes uncomfortably away from his.

"I only ask because where we are going—it is *expedient* that you trust me, and that you do exactly as I tell you. I can only guide you to safety if you follow my Eye."

Adlai nodded meekly.

"Why must we go there?" She queried.

"Some lessons can be taught. Others must be shown."

She swallowed. Something inside her was dreadfully afraid, and everything inside her wanted to shrink back and pull away to safety, far from this fearful place. She took a deep breath:

"How will we get there?"

"Hold on!"

Quick as a flash, he snatched her up, wings unfurled as he made a flying leap over the precipiced brink. In a mere matter of moments they were soaring far above the lake, the floating island rapidly approaching in the distance. And then next thing she knew, they were already alighting upon the edge. With a gasp she dropped from his arms upon the floor, pausing to catch her breath.

"Remember what I said!" Gunar warned. There was a harsh note of severity in his tone. Shakily, she nodded.

All was still and deathly quiet now. In silence they entered through the twisting archways of the great alcove. The sweet smell of spring water filled the air like a delicious perfume. A great pool of water lay at the center, its murky depths unfathomable and seeming to stretch on into endless depths inside its encompassing chalice of earth and roots. Narrow, bridged pathways led the way to the pool's center from every sector of the pavilion. There, a great fountain loomed high above; chutes jutted out from it in every direction, pouring out into the pool below. Over this, a silver sphere of interchangeable rings spun round and round while suspended in mid-air. Each ring rotated within another, turning independently on its own axis, and at the very center of all these, a glowing orb of pale blue light emanated forth, shedding incandescent light upon the gushing fountain beneath. And below the widespread fountain, a stone statue stood mounted upon a dais, a thin, twisted band of gold set as a coronet upon her head. Her face was turned away, as if staring into the fount's wide stone foundation. Perplexed, Adlai wrinkled her brow: had she seen these things before?... It was very reminiscent of the stone statue and ringed sphere from the Manor garden.

"Gunar," she asked, pointing towards the great sphere, "What is that?"

"That," he replied, "Is the symbol of all the Worlds combined—physical, mystical, and spiritual. It is also the symbol of Time—past, present, and future. When all become rightly aligned together, the Last Battle will take place—and the Days of Man will be at an End."

Adlai shuddered slightly and turned away. All along the perimeters of the place, thin sheets of dark water like mirrored panels cascaded down. She hesitated before one. The timid reflection of a fragile teenage girl stared tremulously back at her with frightened eyes. It was her own reflection. Adlai shook herself and abruptly turned away, trembling. Was she really such a pathetic, scared little creature? Slowly, she paused before another panel: the face was much the same, but this time the expression was marked by impudent scorn, while a mocking smile stood out from beneath contemptuous eyes. Swallowing hard, she hurried on. She wasn't sure what it meant, but it was probably best that she not look into any more of the waters' mirrors. She was nearing another one, and deliberately she quickened her step... Something about these mirrors frightened her... What might she happen upon this time, if she dared look? ... Whatever she did, she must not look again... A gusty wind whipped round her as she passed, sending an icy chill racing up her spine. Inadvertently, she halted and unwillingly turned towards the silently cascading panel of water. She could already feel that something was already watching her, waiting... Whatever reflection now waited in the mirror, she was now dreadfully afraid.

A horrified gasp escaped her lips. It was indeed her own face, though seemingly older now. Steely, soulless eyes stared coldly back into her own, a malevolent smile creeping triumphantly across her lips.

"You poor, sad creature!"

Adlai started. *Was her reflection actually speaking to her?*

"Too cringing and frightened to ever rise up and embrace the powerful woman you were meant to become!" A heartless voice mocked from somewhere inside her own head. "A woman who knows no fear or pain…Instead you settle for being nothing more than a trembling weakling, frightened by its own shadow… You look to everyone else to save you, but you won't lift a finger to save yourself! You sicken me!"

"Leave me alone!" Adlai begged, covering her ears in a futile effort to make the voice ringing through her mind disappear.

"You can't escape me!" The reflection leered, "You'll *never* be able to escape me, because deep down in the darkest recesses of your soul, you *want* this!"

Tears stung her eyes now. It was true. She had felt a darkness lurking deep inside her soul, a darkness lusting for power—the kind of power that could set her free and make her invincible. She was tired of being dominated by everything and everyone, including her own feelings. She thirsted for an unconquerable strength and unswerving confidence that would forever make her impregnable to all doubts and insecurities, the kind that would render her fearless in the face of terror… But most of all, she hungered for the kind of power that could steel her heart from all hurt or vulnerability… But to attain such required a price she had not yet been willing to pay, and she had been holding back … Was it possible to lose all feeling and emotional attachment, without at the same time losing the very essence of her humanity—her soul?... It was true that she feared the woman in the mirror, feared the darkness of which she was capable…but she was also equally afraid of what she might become on her own without her: alone, invisible, and helpless—forever a captive to the shackles of her own limitations, inabilities, fears and pain.

"I am everywhere you go," the voice hissed, "I am with you all the time—I *am* you!"

A deafening roar suddenly tore through her eardrums, instantly silencing the sound. Adlai quaked violently at it, turning shakily about in the direction from which it had sprung: it was Gunar.

"I told you," he warned grimly, "Keep your eyes fixed *only* on me!"

A bridge now lay before them, leading to the fountain at the center of the garden. He was already padding his way across.

"Keep close!" He called back.

She swallowed hard and somberly fell in after, a mixed feeling of guilt and relief over his intervention. Nothing about this place felt right, and more and more she was having the unnerving sense that they were not alone. There was an inhuman Presence here, forbidding and threatening, yet luring and beckoning all at the same time. And in addition to her mounting dread and apprehension, she was suddenly also feeling very tired. Up till now, all of her senses had been tense and alert. But now she felt overcome by weariness, exhausted by the cares and toils of the previous day. It seemed they had been travelling for hours on end, and that without rest, food or libation... She was beginning to feel very thirsty... If only she could have a drink to refresh herself after their journey... Again her nose tingled at the sweet aroma of spring water. *Surely the tantalizing fragrance was not coming from those morose, black waters?... But where, then, was it coming from?*

Adlai shook herself, remembering what Gunar had said. She had to stay focused.

"Gunar," she whispered, as they neared the center where the statue stood, "Who is that?"

"Look—there's an inscription engraved there, at the base," he pointed. "Read it.""It says—'Guard your heart above all else, for it is the Wellspring and Source of All Life'." She squinted. "And there's something else written below it...'Remember Edrea'." She looked up perplexed. "Edrea? Who was that?"

"A Sorceress. Legend says that she was once a Dryad Nymph, who fell deeply in love with a mortal man. But he spurned and left her for another. In her inconsolable anguish, Edrea chose to languish here, growing ever hardened by her grief. Her constantly flowing tears formed the stream and pool which you now see before you, and into them she poured all her bitterness, despondency, malice and hate. Her heart turned to stone, and with it, the rest of her—body and soul. But her *spirit*—her spirit lived on. In her black hatred, she vowed vengeance upon the Sons of Men, invoking a curse upon all who should drink of this spring. None of them who come hence, e'er return again. It is said that the very air here is a poisonous vapor, causing men to hallucinate. Deluded by false visions of all they desire, they fall prey to her curse; forsaking all, they abandon the lives they were intended to live for the pursuit of their elusive fancies. Here they languish, bound captive to the futile imaginings of their own foolish hearts, 'til at last they perish and pass into Shadow. It is from their spirits that she gains her ever growing power, feeding upon the life-source of those seduced by her spell."

Adlai shuddered.

"Why did you bring me to such a place?" She asked tremulously.

"Because I wanted you to see with your own eyes the danger of holding on, when you must learn to let go and forget…As long as you hold onto the Past, you cannot live in the Present—any more than you can move on into the Future. Let Yesterday go; embrace and live in the fullness of Today, or you will never see Tomorrow. You cannot move forward, if you are ever looking back. You cannot rise to Champion Victory, while at the same time choosing to remain a Victim to Defeat."

Adlai looked down at the ground with embarrassment. She had always taken it for granted that she *was* a victim—she had never before thought of it as a personal choice of any sort. Yet now as she stared upon Edrea's stony countenance, it was plainly clear. Choosing to hold on to Willan would produce nothing but despair, and a life lived in insignificance and futility. …There was no *purpose* in such a life…But perhaps…perhaps if she learned to let go, she might actually be able to discover and live out her destiny after all, even if Willan played no part in it.

"Gunar," she called his attention suddenly, "Look at the direction of her gaze—I do believe there's something there!"

Adlai was already following after the statue's empty stare at the fount's marbled base.

"That part of the molding looks different than the rest. And there appears to be something engraved there." She squinted.

"I can't quite make it out."

"It is in the Ancient Tongue. Few know it anymore."

Adlai slowly straightened, looking up at him with a suspicious curiosity.

"But *you* do," she prodded.

He made no reply.

"How old are you, exactly?"

Gunar stared at her in silence for a moment.

"I have seen days without end… But that is not important now."

"Well then, what does this say?"

"It reads, 'Ask, and it will be given to you; seek, and you will find; knock, and the door will be opened to you'."

"Is it a riddle?"

"No. It is a phrase from a text of Ancient manuscript."

"Then what do we do?"

"We do as it says."

"But how?"

Again he made no reply, but placed his hand firmly on the center plate of the molding and pushed. All at once there was a great scraping and screeching; the marbled stone grated over the floor with a groan as it slowly moved from its place, opening up like panels to reveal an inner chamber within the fountain's base. Adlai gaped as she followed after him; together, they entered the chamber in silence. The walls closed again behind them. All at once there was a quaking, as the floor stones began to move beneath their feet.

"What's happening?" She cried out in a panic. Gunar grabbed hold of her hand and held her steady.

"We go down into the very heart!"

The stones fell into place, one after another, like a stack of tiles, until they formed a spiral staircase, rotating down into the depths. Gunar's face faded away in the black darkness before her fearful eyes as they descended, though she could still feel his hand firmly grasping her own.

"It's alright, I'm still here." The gentle sound of his voice was soft and soothing. "I haven't brought you this far to leave you here…Nor will I leave you…Ever."

With that he pressed her hand more tightly. Adlai swallowed down her nervous apprehension, trying to still her shaking, sweaty hands.

"You said that phrase was a fragment from a piece of Ancient manuscript?" She asked, trying to distract her thoughts.

"Aye, it is."

"And what does it mean?"

"It means that with faith, *anything* is possible. But the key word is possible, *not* easy."

Adlai smiled, because even in the dark she could feel him smiling at her. How did he always manage to remain so calm?

"The trouble with many," he continued, "Is that they seek after things for which they were never meant…And unfortunately, they find them…along with many other troubles and woes. Just because a door lies facing you, does not mean that it is wise to unlock and open it."

His tone grew sober again.

"So how does one know what to ask for, and what not to? Or what doors to leave alone?"

"First, by trusting the Powers Above… He already holds your best interests at heart. He much desires for you to ask…But even more, he also desires for you to trust his infinite wisdom, when he deems it necessary to guide you in a direction other than as you had prayed. Many ask, but few know when to let go and simply trust."

"And second?"

"Many ask, pray, and seek to open doors to things which their wayward hearts desire, and which they already know in their conscience to be wrong. But rather than accepting this truth, they stubbornly seek to bend the Divine Will to their sway."

"You say that they know in their conscience, but not in the heart?"

"The heart is deceitful above all things—there has never been any evil invented, for which man's heart has not found a justifiable excuse. But the conscience—the conscience can never be led astray…it can only be deadened…And once dead, the final destruction of that soul is made complete."

Adlai shuddered.

"How does one avoid such a fate?"

"There is no such thing as Fate—there is the Divine Destiny intended for a man, and then there is the destiny he himself chooses. And no man turns to darkness overnight…It is always one tiny step at a time, one compromise at a time. Such steps become life's staircase. Beware the uncertain grey areas of life, where moral principles become obscured in the shadows— never entertain any desire of which your conscience is in doubt, no matter how beneficial or advantageous it may seem."

All at once the moving stair stopped short with a jolt. A light suddenly flickered in the gloom; then one by one, torches simultaneously lit themselves all around them. They were standing in a room encased and walled by glass, through which she could see the black waters of the pool moving fluidly all about them in eery silence. She swallowed… They were completely surrounded by water on all sides.

Here and there inside this inner chamber of stone and glass, leafy vines hung like partitions over various sections of the walls, and entwined themselves around pillars. At the center of the room stood a raised gold basin and lever upon a granite step. And behind it and facing them, a stone statue stood with open hands, inviting and beckoning towards the basin. A tremor passed through Adlai.

"Gunar," she trembled, "Is that not the same statue?"

His hand again tightened on her own.

"I told you, her spirit is everywhere here. Pay her no mind—heed only me, and she can do you no harm."

She shivered. There was a discreet smile upon the statue's carved lips, and her sculpted eyes now seemed trained on Adlai's face. Again the girl's nose almost wriggled with the tantalizing aroma of fresh water.

"Look!" Gunar called to her. "Here is a doorway!"

He was busily pulling away vines draped over one portion of the wall. Adlai tore her gaze away from the filled water basin to look at him.

"I see nothing," she answered, confused.

Gunar looked at her with a grin.

"Ye of little faith, have you been with me so long, and yet still know so very little?"

"But there's nothing there!" She protested.

"Heidi, that is because I *am* the Door."

And to her surprise, he suddenly began to stretch out before her, flattening into the wall like a stained-glass mural, his great wings forming an arch above his head. Behind him tranquil visions of a wide open countryside of scattered vineyards and orchards, peaceful rivers and streams came into view. The branded scar on his chest suddenly burned bright like hot coals along the rough outline of the entwined trees emblazoned across; from there, the fiery trail licked its way down through the wreath of twisted roots covering his breast, winding round and round until it ended at the grisled scar over his heart. A warm smile again filled his face, and his ember eye glowed like a light illuminating the darkness.

"Hide yourself in the shadow of my wings, and I shall keep you as the apple of my Eye. I will show you great and wondrous things which you do not know!"

His voice was soft, yet booming at the same time; authorative, but gentle. And suddenly she was in even greater awe of him than she had ever been before. *Who was he?!* Who was this strange Creature, who at times seemed as much a Princely Lord, as an untamed Beast? In one sense he commanded her unquestioning trust and allegiance; and yet at the same time, he called and pled to her in the tender manner of one captivated by desire for her love. And now, after so many unanswered questions, he was inviting her to enter into his secret world of wonder. What things might he now reveal, she wondered excitedly?

Her feet were already moving towards him, when again the smell of water wafted through the air with its intoxicating scent. Inadvertently she hesitated before the basin. It was now being held in the repositioned hands of the statue. Adlai licked her dry lips.

She was so thirsty, that it was almost more than she could stand… She could no longer remember a time when she had not been filled with this unquenchable, insatiable thirst… Had there ever before been a time when she had been satisfied?

"Heidi, don't yield to it!"

Gunar's tone was harsh and commanding.

"I'm so thirsty!" She murmured weakly, unable to drag her mesmerized eyes away from the gold water basin. "I don't think I can go on without a drink!"

"Whoever drinks of this water will thirst again!" He cried out. "You will die thirsty! *Resist it!*"

"Just a small drink—just a sip, that's all I need!" She answered feebly, stretching out her trembling fingers to touch the golden brim. She was shaking and sweating all over, her flesh burning as though with a fever. There was a magnetic energy about the place, and it all seemed to be pulling inwards towards the basin.

"I know you're thirsty! But Heidi, you're almost there! Just a few more steps, and you'll have all you'll ever need!"

The sound of his voice echoed and re-echoed faintly in her mind. The room was starting to reel. Dimly, she thought she caught a glimpse of him staring at her with those piercing eyes. But something about him didn't feel right anymore, and a strange suspicion was now growing inside her distracted thoughts.

"You're lying!" She accused loudly, stumbling forward. "You don't care if I die of thirst!"

Her fingers stroked the edge of basin longingly, as she slowly reached for the lever.

"Heidi, don't! It's a trap!"

These last words fell on her ears as no more than the lull of a distant wind. All other thoughts were far out of reach; all that remained was her consuming thirst.

"Just a drink," she murmured.

Dipping the lever, she lifted it to her lips. A surge of flavor gushed through her pallet. It had all the sweetness of new wine, and more; never had she tasted anything so good… It was so wonderfully intoxicating; it utterly satiated all of her senses. She couldn't get enough…Before she knew it she was gulping straight from the basin, her face, hair, and arm sleeves soaking wet. At last she rose and let go a satisfied sigh. Slowly, the lever dropped from her hand. It sank to the bottom of the bowl, where it struck like a gong. Instantly a rumbling vibration reverberated in a wide arc across the room. Adlai's knees buckled, and she collapsed. Everything was becoming hazy, and the room was spinning as though she were drunk.

All at once she could hear the familiar sound of Willan's voice calling her name, as his face came into view. A happy, ecstatic smile lit up his face as her gaze met his.

"I thought I'd lost you!" He cried, tears filling his eyes. Tenderly he stroked her hair, pulling her close to himself. "I've been such a fool—I could never love anyone the way I do you."

And then he was kissing her—soft at first—then hard and passionate. A dreamy sigh escaped as she drooped in his tightening embrace, his lips which were now drinking in her own. She was starting to feel limp and listless, and the air about her had grown heavy and stagnant. He was still kissing her, as though he never intended to stop.

"Willan!" She gasped, twisting her face away, "Willan—I can't breathe!"

She tried to pull away, but his arms only grew stronger around her, as his lips closed more forcibly over her mouth. Suddenly his hands moved roughly to her throat, tightening into a choke-hold. Hard, steely fingers squeezed against her wind-pipe, a stony thumb shoved painfully into her throat's cavity. She sputtered, choking and gasping, as her eyelids fluttered open. The hazy image of his face was now changing shape, shifting, metamorphosizing… It was no longer Willan's face anymore…It was the Stone Statue.

Edrea's features were rapidly gaining color. Her dark eyes lit coldly upon the horror-struck girl for only an instant, as a triumphant, malevolent smile flooded her face. Then without another sound Edrea fell upon her, sucking the very life from her lips. She could feel her spirit ebbing away, as if her soul was already departing from her body…

She was only dimly conscious as Edrea suddenly let her drop from her morbid embrace. Her mouth was sour now, the bitter after-taste of ash and gall on her tongue; her stomach had turned to acid and was burning with fiery pain, the pit of her gut settling like stony lead... In fact, all of her felt like lead—her head, her chest, her arms and legs, all the way down to her fingers and toes. She could no longer move or turn; her joints were stiff, and there was a paralyzed numbness in her face and all throughout her body... Her blood had gone cold... Out of the corner of one eye she caught glimpse of her reflection in the glass wall around her, and her heart froze: the lifeless face staring back at her was stone.

Things were moving around her...it was water. The protecting wall of glass was melting away before her eyes. Like a curtain it was drawing back, and a flood of water was now gushing into the room. Stone faces and bodies were everywhere, entangled in the roots surrounding the bottom of the pool. The great Tree itself seemed to be coming to life, yawning and stretching its way out with creaks and groans. Of a sudden she realized she was being hoisted through the torrents of water. The roots were entwining and fastening themselves around her, pulling her into the depths of its underwater jungle.

All at once Gunar's face was pressed to her own...was he kissing her? A finger twitched, then her arm jerked, as air again filled her lungs. Immediately she was flailing and kicking against her bonds. Faster than the swish of a knife Gunar's claws deftly sliced through the roots coiled fast about her. Next moment he was tugging her through the water. With a gasp they broke through to the surface.

CHAPTER 28—IN MY DREAMS

Adlai jerked upright with a scream, her eyelids flying open. It was dark. She blinked: she was sitting up in the middle of her bed, back in her own chamber—what wild trick of the imagination was this? What could possibly be going on?

The aging household physician had apparently been dozing in a nearby chair, for he awoke with a start and hurried to her side to readjust a hot compress resting on her forehead.

"There, there, now!" He soothed.

Presently there was a slight scuffle from outside; a light flickered under the landing, and the door hesitantly opened. It was the chamberlain, still in his dressing gown, his night cap set haphazardly on his graying head. Pushing the brim of it away from his bleary eyes, he shakily lifted the candlelight higher and peered anxiously at her.

"Begging your Lady's pardon, but has something disturbed you? Are you quite alright?"

"I—I don't know," She stammered out.

What was happening to her?! Was it all just a dream? And if it had all been just a dream, then where had it begun? Had *any* of the events of yesterday happened at all?

"Is Lord Willan returned?" She asked.

The old steward gave her a look of startled surprise.

"Why, yes, your Ladyship," he answered confusedly, moving closer to her bedside and lifting the candle higher.

"Is everything alright, Milady? Shall I fetch him for you?"

"Yes—yes, if you could please fetch him at once!"

The Chamberlain nodded quickly to both her and the apothecary, and left without another word. Wearily Adlai sank back on her pillow and let out a heavy sigh, shakily brushing away a patch of stringy wet hair, as she feverishly pulled the blankets up closer around her. She was cold and hot all at once. Her fingers ran nimbly over a tight swollen lump on her temple.

There was the sound of voices outside; the door abruptly opened, and Willan himself was striding quickly across the room to her bed. It felt as if it had been ages since she had seen him last, and the mere sight of his face—so tender and anxious now with concern—all but brought tears to her eyes. Dropping down to one knee, he grasped her hand in his, and with the other began to gently stroke her hair away from her eyes.

"It's alright!" He whispered reassuringly in his old familiar way, a compassionate smile on his face as he looked worriedly into her eyes. "It's alright, everything's going to be alright now!"

"Willan, what happened?"

Willan's lips parted to speak, but before he could answer a new voice interrupted.

"Willan, is she quite alright?"

Adlai started at the unwelcome intrusion: Afwin's silhouette was etched against the open doorway for a brief moment, before softly making her way across the room. Willan smiled warmly up at her, reaching up to clasp the small delicate hand nestled on his shoulder. Adlai swallowed hard, sinking back slowly into her pillow... *So it was really true, after all*... Pulling the blankets up tighter about her, she turned her face to the wall, unwilling that either of them should espy the tears now filling her eyes.

"Is she any better?"

Afwin's quiet voice was filled with genuine concern, and Adlai half winced. In some ways Ardath's prating and contempt were easier to bear than this: in the headmistress' case, she had the one consolation of at least being able to hate her back... But how could one in good conscience hate another, for no greater crime than simply being more greatly loved and favored by Nature? She envied Afwin, but there was nothing in Afwin's character to blame or despise... And this made her own inner heart-break the more bitter-sweet. There was an exquisite loveliness about such pain: she knew she could never wish Willan any heart-ache of his own, and with Afwin standing faithfully at his side, the surety of his future happiness was now secure...There was nothing for her to do but suffer in silence, with the small comfort that even if her own heart bled away to nothing, at least it was for his sake. If only the cost of his greatest happiness had not had to come at the price of her deepest pain…

"What happened?" Adlai mumbled in a muffled voice from inside the bedclothes.

"The new gardener—what's his name? He found you fallen through an old entrance to the wine cellars. You hit your head very hard, and have lain feverish for well over two days now…Whatever were you about, clambering around some burn-pile wreckage?"

His voice was still gentle and concerned, but once again there was the usual tone of reproof, so that Adlai was now beginning to despise herself. Why was it that she was never able to gain his attention otherwise, save by the constancy of her own fool-hardy, renegade behaviors? She couldn't seem to keep out of trouble long enough to ever make him notice her other better qualities. She was furious at herself now for wasting all those years, chasing one idle pursuit after another. If only she had known that it would one day cause her the loss of the one person whose heart she yearned for more than anything else in the world. If only she had borne with Ardath, yielded herself in humble submission, and had exhibited the same quiet virtues Afwin possessed—Willan might have esteemed and loved her as much… But now it was too late. And there was nothing more bitter than regret.

To add to her humiliation, Adlai was certain that her own secret, forbidden desires had not escaped the notice of the docile Princess; indeed, it seemed as if nothing escaped the quiet notice of Afwin's soft, luminous eyes. Her sober gaze had a penetrating effect, as if experience had taught her well how to read the intents and motives of others. And Adlai had the uncanny sense that she was now keenly aware of her own feeble, awkward attempts to mask the wounded hurt and disappointment of her bruised heart.

Willan leaned forward to kiss Adlai's face, and she stiffened under his touch, wincing as she tried to steel herself from the flooding torrent of emotions. She would never again be able to fling her arms around his neck and hold him close, as she had done in the past. Those days were over now. She had to learn to manage her grief alone.

"I think she'll be alright now," the physician interrupted. "Best now to let her rest."

After the others quietly left, her mind drifted away into restless dreaming. Sunny visions of Willan flitted before her, like fire-flies against the shadowy backdrop of a warm summer's eve. Yet he was always somewhere off in the distance far ahead of her, out of touch and out of reach, unable to hear her, though she kept calling his name. On and on she followed hard after, but each time she got close, his form vanished away like a mist, only to reappear in the distance, even further away than before. She was crying, stumbling and struggling up over the brow of a hill as she wandered on. The grass was tall and green here, like a shrouding blanket waiting to shelter and hide her. A warm, gentle breeze blew over as in the month of June, and stars twinkled above in the lavender sky of early night. Wearily she sank down amidst the tossing sea of grass, curling up like a small child in her cocoon of cool, fresh scented green.

Suddenly the overhead skies became black, as dark, billowing clouds rolled in, unfurling their anger and fury; a clap of thunder rent the air, as jagged streaks of lightening flashed across threatening skies. Rain poured down in torrents upon her, and the dark forest around became filled with all manner of frightful, terrifying sounds. Swirling darkness closed in, drowning out her sobs in the noise of the tempest. All at once a strong hand closed upon her shoulder, and another clapped tightly over her mouth. In vain she struggled, twisting about in blind terror as she strained to see the face of her attacker.

"Peace—be still! It's alright!"

A voice called out against the din. Adlai halted inadvertently. The skies were clearing, and a soft light was already breaking through. What was that sound? ...To her surprise, she realized that it wasn't a new sound at all, but rather the *absence* of sound... The darkness and chaos were nowhere to be seen, heard, or felt—it was simply gone without a trace. All was hushed into peaceful silence. There was no further sound, other than the gentle rustling made by the wind, the soft singing of a nearby cricket, and a still, quiet purring—which, although faintest of all, was still somehow the most distinctive sound she now heard. A warm breath was beating down gently upon the bare-skinned nape of her neck, as she turned to see a familiar face.

"Peace," Gunar purred softly again in her ear, "Be still."

There was a quiet rumbling that emanated from deep in his chest, like the low contented grunt of a lion at leisure. With a single word he had silenced the storm. But even more, he had silenced the raging sea at her core… He had spoken peace to the storm in her heart.

"The one you're looking for isn't here," he whispered softly. The blunt tips of his claws combed gently through her tangled hair, and his hand brushed across her cheek. For a moment she stared at him, lips quivering as she searched for words to say, yet found none. Suddenly she flung her arms about his neck and buried her face against his throat, her tears falling like rain against his warm skin.

"There, there, now," he breathed in husky voice. "Beauty will yet rise from the ashes… All things are made beautiful…*in their time*."

There was something in the tone of his words, something which comforted her where there had been no comfort to be found before. As he breathed once more upon her face, she suddenly felt deliciously warm and peaceful all over… The Beast's breath was no longer hot, foul, and rank, as she remembered from afore. Instead it was invigorating to her senses… It was heavenly… so much so, that for a fleeting instant she almost thought she could kiss him. Slowly he pulled her to himself, wrapping his arms tightly about her like a sheltering fortress. Once again a low, contented rumble sounded from his chest. His strange animal noises—so seemingly beastly, inhuman, and frightening from before—were now the sound of comfort; they were the calm, relaxing sounds which signified safety. It was the sound of strength, might, and protection…And underlying all of this was the subtle, yet unmistakable note of bold, relentless ferocity, like that of the great king of beasts when carefully guarding his young… A slow realization was dawning on her now: there was an almost reverent awe, even a worshipful esteem with which she now regarded him—and to her surprise, she realized now that something deep inside her had always felt that way…But even more surprising was this new emotion: she felt shyly self-conscious as her cheek lay pressed against his breast, the rhythm of his heartbeat drumming in her ear. Never before had she felt so small and helplessly weak, in a way that was so mysteriously wonderful. She was aware that her own heart was fluttering wildly in her bosom, like the quivering wings of a dove taking flight into skies of freedom after years of captivity… It was enraptured ecstasy…

"I must be dreaming right now," she sighed happily. "Is this really happening?"

"You are dreaming, but it is really happening," he replied.

"But how is that possible?"

"I know your thoughts, so I can reach you and talk to you—even in your dreams."

Adlai snuggled more closely to him, burying her face further into his chest.

"I can hear your heart," she murmured. "It's singing."

Gunar's head was turned so that the blighted half of his face looked away, but she could see that a smile now crossed his lips. And once again she found herself struck by his appearance: his features, though ruddy and rugged, were remarkably striking— what had he once looked like? Were it not for his present scars, his more animalistic traits and wild appearance, she felt that she would, at one time, have been deeply flattered to have been the lady of his favor. Surely many women had desired him once… What a face and form he must have cut, before the Curse had taken away his humanity.

"Gunar," she began falteringly, "What happened to you?"

A low, sad sound—almost like the despondent whine of dog, rose up together with another rumble in his chest. He sighed deeply, as his long ears drooped and his massive wings slumped upon his shoulders. Adlai felt a twinge of pain for the hurt her question had awakened. More and more she was coming to care deeply for him... Beast or not, he had chosen to be *her* Beast... And every step of the way, he had always been there and fought to protect her—body, soul, and heart.

"I—I'm sorry, I didn't mean it like that," she started to apologize.

"It's alright," Gunar answered softly, but his face remained turned away.

She bit her lip, and her brow furrowed a little... *Did she dare risk going on?*

"I—I just meant—you were a man once, weren't you?"

"Yes—and no."

Adlai stared perplexedly at him. What was he saying?

"So—you *haven't* always been this way, then?"

"No."

Adlai sighed in confusion and slumped slowly backwards on her elbow. Thoughts—and questions—were once more flooding through her head. *Who and what was he?... And who or what had he been?*

"I chose to become this way," he continued without looking back at her. "I chose this form, and this body."

Adlai started. *Was he saying what she thought he was saying?—That he had actually chosen Evil? Why?!* Just when she was beginning to feel that she could wholly trust him, doubts and suspicions were coming back again. And despite all the moments she enjoyed in his company, they seemed to always return to the same place: she, orbiting in lost circles about him, futilely attempting to gain answers, and he stubbornly and deliberately refusing to allow her to come any closer. For someone who wanted her implicit trust, he hardly reciprocated as much in return. More than ever she could barely contain the swarm of frustrated questions threatening to unleash themselves, and it required all the resolve and self-control she could muster to resist the compelling urge to demand straight-forward answers from him. She took a deep breath:

"Did you choose that too?"

Gunar turned back slowly to meet her gaze, her eyes wandering over the jagged scars running across his face. The question hung tremulously in the air for a moment.

"Yes," he replied quietly, without so much as a tremor in the calm frankness of his voice, "I did."

"But *why?*"

"Because it pleased the will of the One who sent me—I told you before, I do nothing of my own accord, apart from his will."

Adlai felt a sudden surge of furious indignation. He was so—so beyond anything she had ever met or dreamt possible—in forcible strength, swiftness of speed, and powers of mind. Why, then, did he choose to live like a slave? Were she herself capable of such feats, she would never bow her knee again in submission to another... The very notion was scornful. Was he truly so weak, as to be incapable of acting independently apart from this Being to which he so often referred? What domineering authority was it which held him so mercilessly bound to its own unswerving will? And how could he knowingly subject Gunar to so much pain and suffering? She felt a sudden contemptuous spite rise up inside her: if Gunar truly wanted her, then he would have to fight—not just for her, but for himself as well. Because whoever it was to whom his loyalties were bound, *she* was never going to yield. Perhaps there was more at work here than she had before thought possible... Maybe it wasn't just up to the Beast to save her...maybe she needed to save the Beast.

"It's not what you think." Gunar's voice interrupted her thoughts. "No one takes my life—or my power to choose—from me. Rather, I *choose* to lay it down, and to submit myself to the authority of One whose will and purpose are higher than my own. I am one with him—in heart, in mind, in purpose—we are inseparable."

"So—in other words—you're some sort of unified force?"

"Force—no. A force has no feeling or emotion, no individuality or personality. No, we are distinctly separate from one another, and yet one and the same. This body I now inhabit was prepared for me, and this form was chosen so that a higher purpose might be accomplished."

"But what you're saying doesn't make any sense!" She burst out. "How could such a thing be possible?!"

"For *you*, and for anyone else here in *this* world, it's not possible—so I do not expect for you to understand or comprehend what I am now telling you."

"Wait—" Adlai held her hand up in protest—"Are you telling me that you're from another world, and that you're actually nothing more than a spirit inhabiting the body of someone—or something—else? How am I supposed to know who and what you *really* are?!"

Gunar shook his head with a laugh. There was a patient, unconcerned smile across his face, so that for a moment she was again disarmed by his seeming undisturbedness over her wrathful, wary suspicions.

"So easily mistrustful!" He laughed. "In answer to the latter, you don't know—you must *choose* whether or not you are willing to trust me. The choice is yours alone to make. In reply to the former question, the answer is No. This *is* my own body, or rather, the body and form that I chose. I am equally spirit *and* flesh." Gunar thoughtfully plucked a few long grass stalks, as if still searching for words. "I am...power... masked inside weakness."

Adlai fell silent for a moment.

"Weakness? But—why?"

Gunar tossed the grass stalk away from him, then looked back at her with a soft smile.

"So that you would not feel so alone."

Her mouth opened to speak, but no words came out. And for reasons she could not understand, she suddenly wanted to cry. There was an expression of pity and compassion in his eyes, and she could feel his gaze going straight down into the depths of her soul, to the loneliness and helplessness buried at her core. But here was a pity that she was unused to receiving: it was not the condescending pity of one who was somehow advantageously above her, but rather of one coming alongside her... one who *related* to her. This was not the sympathy of one who was either superior, or inferior to her, in any way. Instead, it was that of an equal—and try as she might, she could not refuse its humble, unpretentious and unassuming gesture—she could only receive it. Her whole life she had despised the weakness of her position, inwardly holding herself in contempt that she had no power to rise above the humble dependency of her lowly circumstances, and was continually thrust upon the mercy of others. Embittered and wounded pride had sunk itself like a double-edged blade inside her heart, and there had been nothing to do but swallow it. The knife had remained buried with no one to remove it….But now…now it was as if Gunar through the simplicity of pure compassion, was drawing the knife up from the depths where it had lain dormant for so many years…And it hurt…It felt as if every insult, every act of contempt and derision, every snubbed hurt, every oversight was suddenly being pushed to the surface—and the pain was more than she could stand. Suddenly she was dissolving into angry tears.

"I didn't ask for this! I never wanted to be a burden!"

Her words broke out haltingly in almost indecipherable sentences through the torrent of broken sobs.

"I *hate* myself for being so worthless!" She burst out. "I hate myself for never being good enough! For being so—so *weak*! Why do others only ever see a problem—a broken object that requires fixing?"

Adlai wrapped her arms tightly about her knees and buried her face in her skirts, her fingers digging into her shoulders until the knuckles whitened. She wanted to hide from the pain of her inner shame, wanted to hide herself from everyone—including him—but it was too late. The damn had already broken. There was no concealing the desolation she felt.

"Why can I never make myself into what they all want?!"

For a moment she hesitated, raising her tear-streaked face to look up into Gunar's quiet eyes. To her surprise, she saw pain written in his expression. It was as if all the raw hurt of her painful nakedness was being reflected back to her.

"Why does no one ever want me, and why do they always leave me?!... I'm always, *always* alone!"

Something wet dripped down her forehead and ran down the side of her face… Gunar was silently crying too. She could feel his tears trickling down through her hair and running down the back of her neck. Why did he feel so much for her pain? No one else had ever cried for her, much less with her. Pain had always been a very private, very personal and lonely experience. Yet here he was, not only witnessing and acknowledging her pain, but joining and sharing in it too. If it were possible for all her hurt to have been poured into a single crucible, then Gunar had just drunk the whole bitter draught himself… Why did he care so much?

"Heidi, there's something I want you to have—something to reassure you of my constancy."

As he spoke, he tore off the insignia sewn onto the corner hem of his cloak.

"This is the symbol of my family's crest—keep it with you always."

He pressed it into her hand, as she looked up at him in surprise. For all his gifts and power, there really were very few personal articles which he owned. It humbled her that even in his impoverished, meager state, he still wanted to give to her—and not just anything, but something of personal value from his previous life—perhaps all that was left to remind of family, and of a life that was once free…

"No, Gunar, I can't! The emblem of your kin?"

But Gunar only closed her hand over it.

"This is all you have left of your people now, isn't it?"

He answered nothing.

Adlai fingered the seal, turning it over in her hands. There it was again: the white rose, the great tree, and the Griffin… *What was it all meant to symbolize?*

"I've seen this Griffin before," she commented.

"I know."

"And the tree? It's the same one marked over your breast, isn't it?"

Silence.

"And the white rose? I do believe I've seen that before too, though I've always believed it to be the symbol of the white citadel of Ruoyn Attilyn."

"It's a flower from Isadore, the Tree of Life."

"Two Trees," she murmured, touching the outline on his chest. "Gunar, what do they mean to you? Why won't you tell me about them?"

He looked at her for a moment.

"Someday you will hear the story, but right now is not that time... Just rest."

Gently, he folded his arms about her, and they now seemed the most wonderful place in the world. Even from earliest childhood memories, Adlai had not the vaguest recollection of having ever been truly held, except for the occasional embrace from Willan. And even those had an empty feeling about them...But here in the arms of the Beast was the deepest, truest sense of belonging she had ever known... She wasn't alone anymore.

CHAPTER 29—TO HAVE LOVED AND LOST

Adlai awoke with a start. Brilliant sunshine was streaming in through her window, and a lark was chirping gaily to himself as he hopped about on her window sill. Sighing contentedly, she closed her eyes again and rolled over sleepily in bed... She had been having such a lovely dream... If only she could remember what it had been... Whatever it was, a lingering, warm sense of peace remained.

Of a sudden something crumpled against her cheek. Resting on the pillow beside her head lay two white roses. Slowly she picked up the long stemmed blossoms. What did it mean, and who were they from? The glass-paned window stood ajar, and a slight breeze was stirring the curtains… If Gunar's signature mark of the white roses wasn't enough to assure her that it hadn't all been a dream, there beside them lay the seal crest.

A part of her felt deliciously cozy at the thought. But another part of her felt strangely embarrassed. It was all too sudden. She was still grieving her loss. And no matter how caring or how wonderful he might be, he was still a Beast—no amount of dreaming or wishing was going to change that, anymore than it would make a way for them to have any possible future together… Even if she could forsake all and follow him, he was under the Curse and control of another. Until and unless that was broken, it was utterly impossible.

With a sigh she dropped the roses and seal on her bedside table and looked about. No breakfast trays had been brought, and there was no indication that supper had been provided either. She couldn't remember when she'd last eaten, and she was now famished. Irritation flared in her face: she was used to being ignored and overlooked, but this was different—now she was being replaced and forgotten. Everyone else could fuss all they wanted over the Princess, but was it too much to ask that she still be allowed to carry on with life? How could Willan allow this? …It wasn't fair, and it wasn't right.

All at once something caught her eye: she had failed to notice the trunks and chests which had already been delivered to her room, but here they were. Scrambling from the bed, she excitedly threw open the lid of the nearest one. Slowly, carefully, she lifted up one beautiful gown after another in astonishment; each one was made of the richest, costliest, and most beautiful materials she had ever touched, from deep shades of aqua sea-greens and emerald blues, to the palest, rose-bud pink; all were lavishly detailed with gem-stones and pearls and an extravagant abundance of lace. She let out a gasp of delight. There were dark velvets and miniver furs; embroidered boots, jeweled belts, and elegant coats suited to great ladies of court. Then at last she spied something in the far bottom; slowly, she lifted it up into the light. It was *perfect*—and just what she was looking for. It was a luxurious floor length gown made of the finest crimson and scarlet fabrics, and magnificent enough to have been made for a queen. It was in every way regal, yet daring and audacious at the same time.

Quickly she made her way over to a standing looking glass, draping it across her form as she peered at her reflection. Already the intense color made her eyes appear brighter, and her hair to shine with a fiercer fire. A satisfied smile played over her face: just because Lord Willan had found a new lady, didn't mean that she had to remain condemned to stand in the shadows.

Tugging the dark fabric over her head, it slipped effortlessly down over her bared shoulders as the heavy skirts fell to the floor with a great swish. There was yards and yards of it, and the back of it trailed out behind her over the floor as she practiced sweeping back and forth before the mirror… The curvature of her bare shoulders peeked out above puffy sleeves that seemed to swallow her whole with their extravagance, and the plunging jeweled neckline revealed slightly more of her feminine form than had ever before been displayed. A sly smile crossed her lips. Here at last were a few new charms which everyone at Dombrey were about to encounter from Lady Adelheide!

A short while later she was hurrying down the long pillared corridor towards the mess hall, her amber waves falling in freshly plaited curls over her back and shoulders from where it was piled at the back of her head in lady-like fashion. Her pale white bosom was trembling slightly beneath the abundance of crimson silk and satin. She had never worn anything so elaborate in all her life, and was fast finding that it took a little getting used to. It felt as if she were swathed in yards of fabric from head to foot, so that she had to walk much more slowly and deliberately than as she was accustomed. She was peculiarly self-conscious of how her feminine figure was set off to advantage by the tight-fitted bodice and low, plunging neckline of her gown. There was no trace of the teenage girl from the day before; it seemed as if just moments had passed in her sudden evolution from girlhood, to a fully-fledged woman of alluring sensual charm and winsome grace. And with every advancing step she was feeling bolder and stronger. It was as if something had unlocked her from the shy, uncertain child plagued with self-doubt, to a woman of prowess—or was it merely that she was now on the prowl? Willan had never seen her like *this* before… Was there yet a chance that she might catch his eye?

One of the roses was tucked inside her jeweled neckline, its snow-white petals off-set by the rich burgundy of her gown and the rosy blush of her skin. In her hand she nervously clutched the long stem of the remaining rose. A tinge of guilt bit at her. Willan's gifts were meant innocently for her to enjoy, not to use as bait… And what of Gunar? It seemed so brazen to take his gift with hardly a thought, and use it to decorate herself for another. Either way, she felt guilty of using them both—and of hurting them both, whether she wanted to or not—Gunar, because he loved her; and Willan, because he loved another—and she was seeking to encroach on his affections. The thought of seeking to lure him away suddenly made her feel vile and dirty. After all of Ardath's scathing accusations—was she actually about to prove her right in her surmises? Did she truly care nothing for the hurt her actions might cause others, if only her own personal happiness were secured? What sort of scandal and national offense might it incur, if she actually succeeded in winning him back from Afwin?...Either way, she felt frightened—afraid of what might become of her if she didn't succeed, and afraid of what the consequences might be for them all if she did… All the respect she held for Prince Willan—how much of it would she lose, if she were to cause him to break his solemn pledge to another woman?

And what about Gunar? She suddenly felt a surge of resentment. Why should she have to reason thus with herself, as if she needed to explain herself to anyone? Whatever had happened the other night was now in the past—Gunar had consoled her, and in weakness she had allowed herself to be drawn to him. But today was a different day. He would be a fool if he expected for her to grow to be in-love with him… And she would be a greater fool, if she ever again entertained the notion of falling for the Beast.

...And Afwin?... It was nothing personal. She had unwittingly taken what another wanted, and it was only natural that she should give it one last fighting chance to get him back. If Afwin loved him half as much as she did, then she herself would have done no less. One woman's gain was the other's loss. One of them had to be the loser, and the frank truth was that she stood a good deal more to lose than the Princess... She had never meant or wanted to hurt anyone, the lots had simply fallen this way. And someone's heart would have to become collateral damage... The harsh reality of the situation was that there was nothing the least bit fair about Love... There never had been, and there never would be. Adlai dismissed her fractious scruples and reasoning with an exasperated sigh, and re-doubled her step.

All in the mess hall was in uproar. Servants were bustling and scurrying about faster than she had ever seen before, hurrying through with steaming platters heaped with all manner of roasted meats and vegetables, as well as puddings, cakes, and fruits garnished with all manner of elaborate confectionary trimmings. In the center of the great hall a frazzled Ardath was delivering frenzied orders to the cooks and directing the servants, when she instantly stopped short at the sight of Adlai. Her eye at once became cold and steely, as her gaze slowly trained up and down Adlai's figure with critical deliberation. For an instant Adlai flinched and looked away, but then with fresh determined boldness raised her unshrinking gaze to meet that of the older woman's. Their eyes locked. The corner of the headmistress' brow arched in a half enraged, half quizzical manner, as if daring the girl to defy her. Adlai raised her chin a little higher and stared her back coolly in the eye. Instantly the older woman's expression flickered and gave way; her face blanched and her mouth fell open incredulously. For a second she appeared as if she were ill. Slowly she swallowed and squared her jaw in her usual tight-lipped manner. There was a trace of fear in her eye, as if she recognized that her grip of power was crumbling. Without a word she turned away and went on ordering the servants.

Adlai could feel herself trembling nervously all over. She was giddy and elated all at the same time. The war with Ardath was not yet over, but for the first time in her life she felt as if she had won a battle. The tyranny of the witch had been challenged; perhaps it would not be long now before her downfall. Heaving a breathless sigh, with a lighter heart she turned and swept out of the dining hall.

"Excuse me," Adlai stopped one of the servants, "Where is Lord Willan?"

"He's out on the open terrace overlooking the courtyard, together with Lady Afwin, Milady."

The paunchy older man gave a quick bow of his head and hurried on. Adlai gave her hair a nervous flip; squaring her shoulders, she drew herself up to full height and headed towards the front of the Manor. She had hoped she might find Willan alone, and was more and more coming to resent the interference of Afwin's continued presence. It felt so stilted, so unnatural, to try to converse with Willan while in the presence of his new lady. She had known that things were about to change between them, ever since the awkwardness of Willan's departure. But this was more than a change... They had years and years of history together... *She* was the one who knew him best... Surely there must be something of their past relationship which the Princess could not completely eclipse. Well, if he had forgotten, she was now bound and determined to make him remember all which they had once shared.

Adlai reached the large door to the terrace and slowly pushed it open. It was a wide, open balcony overlooking all that lay before the Manor house; from here one could see all the sprawling moors and mountains which lay beyond. It was largely spacious enough for an entire company to gather, and far off at its edge Willan stood leaning upon the ivy-covered baluster. Afwin was holding tenderly to his arm, and the two of them seemed so sweetly contented and engrossed in one another's company, as if the whole of the outside world had utterly ceased to exist to them.

Adlai swallowed hard. The bitter pain of jealousy stung. Seeing them together in this way hurt more than she had remembered. It was too much to hope... Her stinging conscience told her that she needed to let him go... But couldn't she still hold onto some part of him, no matter how small a part it might be?...*Nothing* between them should have to change *that* much...

Willan looked up suddenly in Adlai's direction as she approached. A sudden look of shocked surprise flooded his face, yet what it meant she could not distinguish. She thought she caught a glimpse of startled surprise and admiration, but she couldn't be sure. In some ways it seemed as if he were seeing her, the real her, perhaps for the first time in his life... But whether or not it was for the good, she couldn't tell. But of one thing she was certain by the look in his eye: she was no longer, nor ever would be again, the young teenage girl she knew he remembered. She was a woman now—and there was no doubt by his countenance that he saw this. But there was something else in his eye which indicated an uneasy discomfort about something in her transformation. Already he was turning discreetly away, as if there were something in her appearance or character with which he had unwillingly found fault. But what was it? Surely he could not object to the dress, since he had bought it for her himself? ...Or was it that underneath it all, he saw into her motives?

"You—you look well, Adelheide," Willan smiled rather awkwardly at her. "We're glad you're feeling better," he added, wrapping an arm tightly about Afwin's waist. "We were all quite concerned about you, weren't we, my Love?"

Willan beamed warmly down at Afwin, softly brushing her ear with a kiss as he did. A discreet blush passed over the Princess' face, and she smiled graciously at the other young woman in her usual calm, quiet manner. Adlai suddenly felt as if she could stand it no more.

"Yes," she answered dryly, clearing her throat, "I noticed that when I awoke this morning. It would seem that the servants are all so busy now, that my meals are now being overlooked."

Willan suddenly looked more awkward than she had ever seen him before, laughing nervously as he tried with difficulty to avoid her gaze. The serene steadiness of Afwin's tranquil demeanor changed only slightly, as with a gracious bow of her head she interjected:

"I think I shall see what my ladies-in-waiting are about," she said quietly.

Willan's arm loosened, though the reluctant look on his face indicated that he would have rathered not. He reached out to clasp her hand for an instant, as with another courteous nod of her head the Princess quietly left. Adlai did not raise her eyes to meet his until the sound of Afwin's soft footsteps faded into the background. She was trembling all over. Half of her felt ready to burst into a torrent of angry, hurt accusations; the other half of her now wished desperately that she'd never come at all or said anything.

"I'm sorry for the oversight, Adlai," Willan was nervously licking his lips and trying hard to force a smile. "I promise it shan't happen again."

He smiled again, in that exaggerated manner which always indicated when he was under strain.

"Adlai, I know this probably isn't the right moment to ask this, but everything's been happening so quickly—"

"Yes! Yes it has!" She interrupted a little too eagerly with a shaky laugh.

Willan nodded, and they both laughed nervously.

"You see—what I mean, that is—what I've been wanting to ask you—"

Adlai held her breath, and slowly stepped closer...

"My mother's ring," he managed at last. "I asked you to keep it safe for me—until my return."

Adlai swallowed, staring hard at him. He had made it seem like a gift—as if it would be hers to have and cherish forever... *Could he possibly be asking what she thought?"*

"I know Father would have intended for it to be given to my wife, as it belonged to his."

"Of course," Adlai heard herself stammer.

Slowly she slid it from her finger, and numbly dropped it into his hand.

"Thank you! This means everything to me," Willan smiled gratefully. "Oh, and not to worry Adlai—I promise soon to replace it with some other pretty trinket."

A pretty trinket? Was that really all he thought it was to her?

Adlai's lips parted to speak, but no words came out. Everything about seemed uncommonly quiet and hushed into awkward silence. Willan scratched his head and fidgeted somewhat in a manner she had never seen him do before. *Why was he suddenly looking at her as if she had become a total stranger to him?!* Hot tears were springing to her eyes, much as she strained to keep them from showing.

"Things—things really *are* going to change between us...Aren't they?" Her voice faltered.

Willan lowered his eyes, as if unable to meet hers.

"No—" he started with a laugh, then stopped short as he uncomfortably cleared his throat: "And yes."

This last word hung in the air like a heavy, toxic vapor. Willan bowed his head in silence for second, as if pondering what to say next in addition to this statement. Adlai waited in breathless silence as at last he straightened himself up fully and looked her directly in the eye:

"Adlai, we're not children anymore. And the day will soon come when I shall be required to rule the kingdom in my father's stead. And even though I won't be free to keep you company in the old way, now you have someone who can be a better guide and companion to you: Afwin loves you already, I can tell."

He paused to give her a reassuring smile, as he took her by the shoulders.

"Why, in no time at all I'm sure you'll both be the best of friends. And even though I know Lady Ardath has *perhaps* not guided you in the *gentlest* of ways, yet now you shall have another fine lady to better assist you—why, she'll be like the sister you've always needed!"

Willan gave her a pat on the shoulder, as he leaned in to give her a quick kiss on the forehead. Adlai could feel her eyes welling up to the brink.

"I never wanted for a sister," she breathed back in a tiny whisper. "All I ever wanted was you."

Willan's jaw dropped in stunned, mute silence. Adlai wait for several agonizing moments, the torture growing with every passing second. At last he let out a deep sigh.

"Adlai, I can no more be to you what you want, any more than you can now be of what I have need. Your day shall come soon. In time you will come to see that I was right, and that it was all for the best, when you give your heart to another."

She felt as if she couldn't move, paralyzed by these last words. It was as if he had handed her a death-sentence… She would never truly live again.

Willan turned to move away. A tear trickled over, and ran down the side of her face. She shut her eyes tight as his cold shadow passed over her shoulder.

"Willan!" She cried out suddenly. He stopped and slowly turned back to face her.

"In all the years we've spent together, did you ever once— even for a brief moment—ever see me the way that you see her?"

A pained look filled his eye, almost sorrowful and guilt-ridden in its expression.

"No," he answered in a strained voice, "Not the way that I see *her*."

With that last word, he left.

It was as if she couldn't breathe, her heart fluttering like a maimed bird inside her chest. Listlessly she slumped against the baluster molding. It seemed as if she had just been run through with a dagger. Dimly, she noticed that the palm of her hand was sticky and slippery. A little stream of blood was already trickling between her white knuckles, running down the thorned stem she still clutched tightly. For an instant she stared vacantly at the blossom, then slowly crushed it inside her fist. The soft white petals were now bruised and torn, their perfection marred with bloody stains. A mild wind stirred and carried off some of the broken petals, soundlessly whisking the tattered bloom from her outstretched hand.

The thudding of hoof beats echoed distantly in her ear. A dark, bare-headed rider on horse-back was approaching in the courtyard below: a startlingly handsome face was staring back at her with soft, velvet eyes like a starry midnight sky. He was completely clean-shaven, the well-defined features of his face set like chiseled marble. This was boldly contrasted by thick black eyelashes and wavy curls, his coal-black hair waving in the wind. A thick leather brigandine covered the breadth of his chest, while a slate-colored cloak streamed out behind him like a ship's sail; it was fastened with thick cords to the pauldrons at his shoulders by clasped brooches. The corner hem of his cloak was embroidered with an insignia, and Adlai dimly saw that it was a replica of a great white tree with wide-spread branches.

The rider glided fluidly along with every motion of his blue roan's gait, as if he had been born on a saddle. He did not appear many years older than Willan, yet his bearing strongly indicated that he was infinitely more experienced. Leather bracers covered his forearms, and what was left to be seen of them was tanned and weathered, suggesting that he had spent most of his life in the wilds of the frontier. Willan was trained in the arts of horsemanship and warfare, but the truth was that he'd spent far more time cooped up in his study; he had never known actual combat (beyond that which his trainers had provided), nor had he ever actively fought in a war. Contrariwise, this man bore all the look of a highly skilled and experienced warrior, his keen quick eyes absorbing every detail and movement about him at a single glance. Unlike Willan (who had rarely spent a cold night away from the comforts and ease of manor life), the rider seemed more the nomadic kind who had roamed far along lonely roads and untraveled wilderness, than to have spent much time within castles and townships.

The mangled, bloodied rose sailed softly down with the wind; a gale of petals fluttered on the breeze past the rider as he drew up near the front of the Manor. For an instant he eyed the place where the rose lay fallen upon the dismal cobble stones, a few remaining petals still clinging to the leafy stem in battered beauty. Immediately his eyes darted up to the place where she stood, his dark eyes now searching her own, a pensive question written in his gaze.

Adlai swallowed hard with a start. She didn't know this stranger, and already she had indiscreetly aroused both his notice and his curiosity to her inner turmoil. A moved look of compassion flickered across his countenance, as if he had just read the tragic script seared in bloody ink across her heart. The nakedness of her private pain was plainly reflected in his eyes, and the image they mirrored back to her was the portrait of a forlorn, desolate young woman, whose heart-ache had just been laid bare for all the world to see. Sharply she drew back, shrinking away behind the embarrassed feelings of humiliation washing over her. Without waiting another instant she turned and fled from the balcony.

She barely heeded the startled cries of indignant irritation from disrupted servants, as she pushed through the clamoring bustle in the halls and fled out one of the side doors. Out through the courtyard she rushed, and ran until she reached the stable where Storm was kept. Without bothering to saddle him she threw herself onto his back.

Suddenly from nowhere, Gunar was there by her side, his hand resting firmly on her arm.

"It's going to be alright!" He urged gently. "Please, don't do this! Come away with me someplace where we can talk alone."

Burning hot tears were streaming down her cheeks as she turned to face him:

"I'm sorry—I can't this time."

"Heidi, you don't understand—" his tone more earnest this time, "There's something I must speak with you about—"

Adlai interrupted him with a shake of her head:

"I'm sorry."

Without waiting another moment for a response, she grabbed hold of a large tuft of Storm's mane and dug her heels in his side. With a whinny Storm charged through the open doorway. Within seconds horse and mistress were dashing past the manor, hooves clattering noisily on the cobblestones. She caught glimpse of the dark stranger just dismounting his horse as she raced past, and their eyes met for mere instant. Then suddenly without warning he leapt back into the saddle, whipping the head of his horse about with severe yank on the reins:

"Yah!"

A frenzied feeling of giddy terror rushed through her: she'd had humiliation enough that day already. It was awful enough that Willan now knew her long kept secret of pining desire; she hardly wanted the entire castle to know of it, much less a newcomer, and total stranger at that. *Whatever would she say? How would she explain?* For once she wanted desperately to be alone, and she was frantic not to be caught. Whoever this stranger was, she could not—she must not—allow him to know any more about her.

They were flying through the streets and towards the town gate, and Adlai leaned in close towards Storm's head, his ebony mane and tail flying like long, black streamers in the wind. In a matter of minutes she and Storm were outside the township, hooves kicking up dirt as they plunged out upon the open moor. Tightly she clung to Storm's mane as they sped onwards; they were racing at a terrifying speed, and she hoped at this pace that they had already succeeded in losing the stranger in black. Everything was flying past, as she turned to cast a quick glance over her shoulder—just to be sure. A blur of black appeared somewhere in the corner of her eye, along with the heavy echo of hoof-beats in hot pursuit.

Adlai froze in terror. The stranger was shouting something at her now, calling her to slow Storm's gallop. She strained her eyes ahead: a canyon was fast approaching. The gulf was too wide—they'd never make it to the other side. Suddenly her whole body felt like dead weight, her limbs the sloppy consistency of porridge. Her tongue felt like dry cotton clinging to the roof of her mouth, and she felt light-headed and numb all over. Everything seemed to be spinning, and to her dismay she realized she was swaying from side to side, her shaky hold on Storm's mane growing weaker, until at last her trembling fingers completely fell away. They were almost to the brink of canyon…The horseman's cries became more frantic, and he urged his mount to press in harder. He was so close now that she could almost hear the heavy breathing of his steed, and felt the weight of its body brush past her. Then everything grew dark, and before she knew it she was falling helplessly from Storm's back.

Instantly she was seized about the waist and heaved upwards, her body thrown with a jolt against a saddle horn. It felt like a kick to the gut, and she could no longer breathe. Tiny lights spun before her eyes, as everything went dark…

CHAPTER 30—TALL, DARK, AND HANDSOME

Adlai coughed and sputtered. The mouth of a leather pouch was being pressed to her, and water was seeping through her lips and running down the side of her face. Choking and gasping, she turned shakily, eyelids fluttering as she squinted in the bright sunlight. The stranger was bending over her. Those startlingly beautiful eyes, like lipid black pools, were staring back into her own, in an expression of grave pity and concern. Stiffly she pulled herself up on sore elbows, rubbing her skinned arms as she uncomfortably avoided his questioning gaze.

The sight of the gulf nearby made her stop short. Storm was not far off; his head bobbed about nervously as he let out a snort, then wearily lowered his muzzle, his muddy hooves shakily pawing the ground. Adlai hoisted herself with difficulty to her feet, but her knees instantly buckled beneath her.

"Easy, easy!"

The stranger caught her by the arm. Adlai dodged his concerned stare and pretended to examine her dress for any sign of damage. She had felt almost beautiful less than an hour before—even enticing. Now she only felt dumb and stupid. She wasn't even properly attired for riding, and she'd given no thought to where it was she wanted to go.

"But for a little dirt and mud, your dress doesn't seem to have suffered much harm," the stranger reassured. "I'm sorry if I caused you any hurt—I only meant to reach you in time."

Adlai nodded awkwardly, still refusing to look into his face.

"Thank you," she fumbled. "I—I'm fine now," she lied, even though her legs still felt like churned butter. "I'm quite alright," she repeated forcibly, trying to muster her most convincing tone of voice.

"Here—I'll help you."

"No, thank you, I can assure you that I've no need!"

The stranger did not seem to inclined to accept this, for he refused to relinquish his steady grip on her arm.

"Just the same, allow me to assist you," he persisted quietly.

At so close a proximity, she was now realizing with discomfort that even if she could avoid looking into his face, it was now impossible to ignore other things—such as how tall, well-built, and muscular he was, along with how small and childish she felt in comparison. Biting her lower lip, she twisted her jaw a little as she tried, unsuccessfully, to think up a believable excuse by which to explain her rash and ridiculous behavior… To add to the humiliation, she was now becoming acutely aware of how greatly he had jeopardized his own safety in order to protect hers.

"I—I often come riding out here," she stammered. "It—it was nothing—I was perfectly alright—but thank you just the same for your kind service."

She gave a curt nod of her head, and somewhat indiscreetly shook off his hold on her arm. Giving a tight-lipped smile and a quick half curtsy, without another word she turned bluntly on her heel.

"You really shouldn't be riding just yet—give it just a few more minutes," the stranger responded firmly. Adlai let out a disgruntled sigh.

"I am most grateful for the service you have rendered me, good Sir, but I can assure you *most solemnly* that I am well capable of making my own way back to Dombrey, unaccompanied."

"You fainted not more than two minutes ago," he returned dryly.

His tone was flat and direct, if not somewhat resonant, and surprisingly commanding, even though he had barely raised it. To her chagrin, she found herself reluctantly compelled to obey.

"You should be examined by a physician once we return— just to be sure."

"Oh, no, no!" Adlai started in protest. *Whatever would Willan think of her? And what might Heromena of Ardath do about it?* She was feeling far less bold and self-assured than she had a short while before. Ardath's authority over her had not yet been resigned... Perhaps she had picked too premature a time to challenge the headmistress.

"That is to say," she feigned with a casual shrug as she cleared her throat, "I wouldn't want to trouble anyone. They're all so very busy, you know—what with the Princess and wedding preparations and all, so I—I—"

Her voice broke off inadvertently, her lips opening and closing as she racked her brain for something to say. The stranger surveyed her in silence, although there was no mistaking the hint of quizzical skepticism in his eye. Adlai's mock confidence gave way to hopeless misery.

"You—you won't say anything about it to anyone, will you?" She queried anxiously.

For several moments he continued to study her in silence, though whatever his thoughts, she could not read. At last he turned away with something of a chuckle.

"Well, I suppose there's no real need for that, now, is there?"

She looked up quickly in relief. To her surprise, she realized that it was the first time she had actually looked him full in the face since their meeting, and she was at once overcome with awe at how beautiful and manly he was in appearance. There was a laughing twinkle in his dark eyes, and a disarming, easy smile that shone above the dimpled cleft in his chin. It was nearly impossible not to smile back.

"Thank you, Sir Knight," she smiled with awkward shyness and a quick bow of her head.

"All the same—" the stranger interrupted, "I must insist 'tis not in your best interest to ride alone the rest of the way—I'll tie your horse behind mine."

Adlai stiffened. Handsome as he was, the embarrassing circumstance of their meeting still had her itching to be out of his sight. But what excuse was she to give, when he was so insistent—and that, almost deliberately so? Her heart was beginning to pound nervously at the thought of the long, silent ride back to the castle.

The rider seemed disinterested in waiting for her response. Already he had produced a rope from his saddle bags and was quickly striding past her. In a matter of moments he had already fashioned a make-shift bridle and fitted it firmly over Storm's ears and muzzle, then briskly led him back to where his own horse awaited. Storm whinnied skittishly, his ears lying flat against his skull, as he eyed the rider nervously with big round eyes. The stranger finished tethering the other end of the rope to his saddle horn, then patted Storm's muzzle as his turned back to Adlai with a smile.

"Ready now?"

Adlai bit her lip and gave a forced smile. Next moment the stranger was lifting her up into the wide saddle, and in another instant had leapt up behind her.

"Could I trouble you to pass me the reins?"

He was so close that she could feel the warmth of his breath blowing softly on her ear. One arm he circled about her waist to clutch the saddle horn, while the other hand was extended in waiting. Adlai swallowed again; deftly snatching up the reins, she dropped them into his outstretched hand and turned away.

"Thank you."

The ride back to the Manor was a long and silent one. For herself, she could think of nothing to say, and the stranger for his part offered no comment to her silence. She found her thoughts once again returning to what sort of explanation she could offer on her return.

Whatever the rider's thoughts, he kept them to himself, yet she sensed keenly that he was thinking of her the entire time. His arms were wrapped so tightly about her, that she could feel his heart pounding against her back. She could feel his breath like a caressing wind upon the bare nape of her neck, trailing down over her trembling breast. And even though he was not exactly embracing her, she couldn't help but feel that such closeness was deliberate. For try as she might to inch away or even shift slightly in her seat, he responded only by drawing his arms the more closely about her, as he nudged his horse to move faster. Willan was the only man who had ever been so familiar with her, and she trembled now at being so pressed against a strange man's body, and having his skin touch hers. Had they met upon different circumstances, there was a chance she might have been flattered— maybe even blushed with pleasure at being so audaciously rescued by a warrior so strong and handsome in appearance. But her present embarrassment alienated all such thoughts of romantic inclinations far from her mind. There was sure to be talk at the Manor when they returned together, and the thought of being publicly exposed to harsh reprimands in front of him made her feel nothing but dread.

Adlai roused herself. They had already arrived at the castle courtyard. The rider slid from his horse, then turned to offer her his hand to dismount. Hesitantly she accepted it. Servants were already hurrying from the house. Suddenly she felt a hand on her shoulder. It was Gunar. He was again heavily cloaked, so that hardly any of him was visible. His hood lifted slightly, but he wasn't looking at her—instead he was intently watching the newcomer. At sight of him the Stranger stopped short, his eyes locked in Gunar's silent stare.

"Bellwether!" He breathed.

The black crow perched on Gunar's shoulder squawked loudly. His hood raised higher now, as he briefly looked the other man full in the face. For an instant his one ember eye blazed hot, yet he answered nothing. Confused, Adlai turned perplexedly from one face to the other. *However did they know each other?! And why had the stranger called him by a different name? What did he know of Gunar?*

The discomfit of the momentary silence was interrupted by Willan's arrival.

"Ah, our newest guest has at last arrived!" He exclaimed, clapping the newcomer about the shoulder in warm welcome.

"Lady Adelheide," Willan announced, "I wish to present: Lord Tristan Marcus Justis Cornelius, son of Traejen, of the House of Rhoer OgDaen."

The Stranger bowed low in respect, slowly raising his gaze to meet her eyes.

"Welcome, my Lord," Adlai curtsied, hardly daring return a glance to his deepened stare.

She could already feel herself trembling again under his gaze. *What was it about him that affected and disconcerted her so?* Willan was handsome, to be sure… but now he almost seemed slightly common-place compared with Tristan's darkly handsome looks. She shook herself, agitated. She was still deeply in-love with Willan, she was sure of that. After all, she had loved him for as far back as she could remember. But so much was happening—and it was happening all at once, in a catastrophic tidal wave of conflicting emotions. Was it any wonder that she was having all these vulnerably confusing emotions—first regarding Gunar, and now with this strange newcomer?

They had just reached the platformed rise at the top of the staircase before the great arched doors, when Lady Ardath unceremoniously swooped out upon them. To Adlai's relief she scarcely seemed to notice her, as hurriedly she began rapping out instructions to the servants for the new guest's accommodations. Suddenly she stopped short. Her visage paled dramatically, as, startled, she stared transfixedly into Tristan's face.

"It's you!" She whispered hoarsely, in a voice so low that it was all but inaudible to all others present, save Adlai. "You haven't aged a day!"

Tristan seemed as much startled and confounded at this strange admonition, as the flummoxed headmistress addressing him. He turned away with an awkward smile, as he let out a stilted laugh. Baffled and mystified, Adlai surveyed them both in bewilderment, trying to decide what to make of the puzzling paradox. This man had barely been on the castle premises a few minutes, and already he had attracted the disquieted attentions of two persons—two individuals who had, mysteriously, been able to identify him, though he had never set foot there before... *What did it all mean?!* Should she be frightened—or relieved—that both Gunar and Ardath seemed alarmed and unsettled by his presence? If he was not a friend of Ardath, then that was hardly cause for concern—but Gunar? What was *his* role in all of this? ...Again the sensation of prickling mistrust was tingling through her. Discreetly, she cast an eye back over her shoulder. Gunar was still standing there, watching.

"Begging pardon, Milord," Ardath hastily recovered herself. "I mistook you for another. Please, this way."

She ushered with her hand towards the vestibule, then stiffly swept past Adlai without so much as a glance. But there was no mistaking the angry tears burning in her reddened, glassy eyes.

CHAPTER 31—BELLWETHER

Adlai barely touched her plate at supper that evening. Instead she sat toying with her food, a tangled mess of thoughts, musings, and suspicions twisting in her head, until her stomach was as much a muddle as her distracted mind.

"Adelheide, are you not well?"

Afwin's tranquil voice softly cut in through her brooding contemplations. Adlai started. The Princess was gazing concernedly at her, a sympathetic look of worry in her usually serene expression.

"Yes, I'm fine," she mumbled back in response.

"Ho now, Adlai!" Willan called out in robust spirits, "You must eat! I swear, you've become naught but skin and bones in my absence!"

Hot anger flushed in her face now. How dare he pretend to care, after everything else? She had no need for his token gestures anymore.

"Pray excuse me," she uttered huskily, as she rose from the table. "I'm weary and must retire."

Ignoring the questioning looks and exchanged glances of others, she curtly bowed her head, and retreated from the mess hall. She had barely ducked out through the doorway, when she heard Willan's voice calling behind her.

"Adlai, please," he begged apologetically, "I'm sorry. I know that things are about to change, but you must know that you are still loved and cared for, by everyone here."

She blinked. Was he really fool enough to believe his own words?

"You're blind," she retorted hoarsely. "And besides, I'm not a child anymore—I've no more need for your concern, much less for your patronizing."

Willan stared dumbfoundedly at her for several moments. With a nod, she hurriedly fled.

Out in the stall Storm was quietly munching dried corn and oats. Quietly he nuzzled her with his muzzle while she stroked his mane. All at once the creaking of the stable door broke the silence. Adlai whirled about. Gunar slowly emerged from the shadows. Quickly she attempted to wipe away her tears, though she knew there was nothing to hide the redness of her eyes. Why did he always have to intrude during those moments when she felt the most exposed and vulnerable?

Gunar moved in closer, laying a hand softly on her cheek.

"It wasn't you, Heidi," he whispered tenderly. "It just wasn't meant to be."

His words did not remove her heart-ache, yet for some reason she suddenly felt a slight sense of relief. It was as if a glimmer of truth had found its way to the darkened recesses of her confused soul... It was true. She wasn't meant for Willan, she never had been... no matter how badly she may have wanted it... And it wasn't her fault.

"You're beautiful, Heidi," Gunar whispered again, "For so, *so* many reasons!" His fingers softly trailed her cheek as he reached out to stroke her hair. "Don't ever see yourself through any other man's eyes... only mine."

He pressed his lips to her forehead for an instant. In the dim moonlight, she saw a tear glisten in his eye.

"I know that you see me as little more than a Beast. But to this Beast, you are his one—and *only*—Beauty."

He cupped her face in his hands.

"I wish I had fingers like a man," he whispered, "Hands that could caress you without scratching you."

His hands slid over both her own. They were rough with calluses, and she realized for the first time with what deliberate care he always took to avoid tearing her skin with his sharp claws. Over the palms and backs of his hands ran all kinds of coarse, jagged scars. But they were beautiful manly hands as well, and all but swallowed up her own with their size.

"I wish I could really see myself as you do," She quivered, "But it's so hard...*so* hard...."

"I know," he sighed deeply again. "I know..."

And for the very first time in her life, she actually believed that it was true—someone else *did* know how she felt, in a way that was more than just empty words.

"Why do you care so much for me?" She asked.

Gunar took her hand and laid it over his left breast.

"Because this heart was meant for you."

His eyes quietly wandered through both of hers. For just an instant she felt a sense of total peace and belonging. But then it was gone. What was she thinking? She didn't belong in his world, any more than he belonged in hers. And it was ridiculous even to entertain the notion.

"Tell me," she asked, pulling herself away, "How is it that you know of this Stranger, so recently come into our midst?"

Gunar's face darkened, and he turned away.

"We fought together in the war. He chose one path, and I followed another."

"You dislike him?"

Gunar answered nothing.

"Why did he call you 'Bellwether'?" She asked more earnestly. "What is it that you're not telling me?"

"'Bellwether' is one of many names I earned during my time among men—a bellwether is a being discerning of future events... From there, you can guess how I came by it."

"And what of your prejudice?" Adlai probed. "Why do you so dislike Lord Tristan?"

Gunar searched her eyes a moment before speaking.

"Heidi, do you *trust* me?"

Her mouth opened to speak, but she couldn't seem to find the words. Although part of her earnestly wanted for her answer to be yes, she knew it would only be a half truth. That was as good as a lie...and it did no good to lie to one who could already read her thoughts. In reluctant shame she hung her head, unable to meet his gaze any more. Gunar's shoulders sank, as with a sigh he let out a dog-like whine.

"Then it does no good for me to speak."

She swallowed.

"I—I'm sorry. I just don't know what or who to believe anymore."

"If you will not believe my words, then will you not at least recall and believe my actions? My deeds speak for themselves."

Adlai couldn't even return his gaze.

"Heidi," he pled more earnestly, "My past faithfulness ought to demand your present trust."

"I wish I could," she whispered hoarsely, "Really and truly."

With that she turned to leave, then hesitated, and laid a hand on his cheek.

"Goodnight, Bellwether."

He pressed her hand tightly. The expression and color in his eyes was so soft now, that even their appearance seemed more human than ever before.

"Goodnight, Ieuna," he whispered back. "Be careful whom you trust."

Adlai turned again to leave, but then stopped.

"I know that you have already read my mind, and know everything that has happened—including how I came by that name."

Gunar surveyed her in silence for a moment.

"Aye," he replied, "I have."

"Well, I was wondering—that is to say, do you know something about my past—or my future—which you're not telling?"

He hesitated.

"I told you: I can only reveal that which I have been given permission to reveal."

Adlai felt a gnawing twinge of bitter disappointment.

"That's about as much as I expected from you—I don't know why I even bother."

"But," he interjected, "I *can* promise that if you stay close, that I will be able to protect you from harm."

She eyed him a moment.

"So you've said before. But words just aren't enough for me anymore."

"You know that I've never made an empty promise. When has a single word of mine ever fallen to the ground?"

Adlai swallowed and lowered her eyes.

"Goodnight, Warrior King from the Hillside."

"Goodnight."

There was a dejected look in his eyes as she turned away.

The Manor grounds were now hushed in silence. All lay in slumbering sleep as Adlai softly reentered the great House, and stealthily crept through the shadowed halls.

Suddenly she caught the indistinct sounds of muffled voices coming from the direction of the solar. The light of a candle spilled through the crack of the partially open door. The voices grew louder as she neared, one hot with bitter anger: Lady Ardath. *Whatever could it be about?* Cautiously she stole forward on soundless steps, and peered through the opening: Ardath's back was to the door, and before her stood Tristan.

"After all these years, you think you can suddenly reappear and show your face?!"

The headmistress' voice broke forth in a vehement torrent of rage.

"Athaliah, I told you—I am here on business."

The headmistress was shaking with anger, and from the strain in her voice, it sounded as though she was crying as well.

"But of course," Ardath spat bitterly, "I should have known you'd never have the heart to come for any other reason."

"Let's try to avoid making this a personal matter," Tristan answered bluntly. Even in the dim light his face was visibly strained and tense.

"*Personal*?!" Ardath leered as she let out a raucous laugh. "You abandoned me—and her! You hid your eyes from your own flesh! And now you come crawling back for *my* help?!"

"Athaliah," Tristan's voice was both pleading and authoritative. "I am here to serve on behalf of your Lordship's ally, King Menasis... And yes," he added with a resigned sigh, "It is true that I have also come seeking a favor—I need her help."

"She won't see you," Ardath returned coldly, "Not after what you've done."

Tristan took her hands earnestly in his and searched the old woman's face.

"Don't you want to know why I've been away so long, what it is that I've been about all these many years?"

Ardath stood rigidly.

"I gave up wondering countless decades ago," she retorted hotly.

"Please," Tristan entreated. "Just speak with her for me."

"She cannot be found," Ardath said coldly. "Not unless she chooses to be found."

"She will."

"I've tried many times—you honestly believe you will fare better than I?"

"I have my reasons."

"And how can you be so sure?" Ardath sneered.

"Because it's her nature."

The old woman glowered at him for several seconds, a look of bitter resentment mixed with a fleeting glimpse of something else—was it a dim flicker of hope? Ardath's lips tightened again in a white line.

"I will see if she will communicate with me."

Tristan breathed a relieved smile.

"Thank you."

Ardath hardly acknowledged him, but stiffly turned to leave. Adlai started. *Where could she hide?!* A tall column adjacent a nearby corridor was a sprint away... The harsh sound of the headmistress' footsteps were briskly approaching...

CHAPTER 32—CONFESSIONS

Adlai's heart continued to thud in her chest for several moments after Ardath's shadow disappeared down the corridor. At last the sound of her footsteps faded away to nothing. Heaving a sigh of relief, she slumped against the column, a flurry of new questions now racing through her brain. *However had the formidable Heromena of Ardath come to know this man, and how were their lives connected? Why was it that everyone who had previously been acquainted with him had all, mysteriously, been known under different names?! And who was it that they'd been talking about?*

Suddenly her thoughts were interrupted as she was seized by the wrist with a yank. Before she knew what was happening, she was being jerked out from her hiding place. With a startled gasp she toppled into Tristan's arms.

The young Lord appeared as much shocked as herself.

"Lady Adelheide! I crave your pardon! I mistook you for—"

He did not quite complete his sentence, as though still searching for something to say in explanation.

"Pray forgive me," he managed at last. "These are uncertain times."

Adlai gulped.

"Are you going to let me go?"

Tristan slowly loosened his grip and Adlai wriggled free, but his gaze still lingered on her.

"What did you mean?" Adlai inquired, stiltedly attempting to avoid his penetrating stare. "I thought that the war was over—wherefore have you cause for fear?"

Tristan breathed a troubled sigh, a dark brooding look in his eye.

"All is not as it seems."

Her eyes widened.

"What do you mean?"

"The Shadow has vanished—and that is *all* we know. But how, where, and *why*, we know not."

"But Willan seemed so certain that it was over! How can you be sure?"

"I was there. I was there that day on the battlefield, when our enemies where vanquished."

"And you saw it? Then why question it?"

"You cannot simply 'vanquish' Erebus!" Tristan burst in agitation.

Adlai flinched. His eyes were almost wild.

"I was there—I was there the moment that the armies of Earth subdued him. The Black Heart is not mere flesh that can be slain—he cannot die!"

Adlai felt herself suddenly go hot and cold at once.

"What are you saying?" She quivered.

"I am saying that I have reason to believe that he eluded us—and that we have all been deceived. This is all part of a darker, deeper, much more elaborate scheme than any of us could have ever imagined."

Adlai was already trembling all over.

"Is that why you've come?"

Tristan's lips pursed grimly in a firm line.

"Hmmmm." He heaved a weary sigh. "My sources have led me here. Outwardly, I am here on King Menasis' bestead, but in truth I am here on a mission of far greater import. I have reason to believe that the Shadow has somehow changed form, and has slipped in across the borders of the free lands."

It was all more than she could take in, and she suddenly felt lightheaded. Her knees buckled, and before she knew it Tristan was catching her up in his arms. Her head lulled onto his shoulder. Silently, he carried her into the solar and set her gently on a chair.

"Here, drink this," he urged, as he poured her a glass of wine.

Adlai accepted the goblet with trembling fingers.

"His Lordship is right—you must eat more, so that your constitution and spirits can grow stronger."

She nodded shakily in between sips, but her mind was spinning with racing thoughts, and a subtle suspicion was growing in her mind.

"Why did you call her by another name?" She asked warily. "How come you to know Heromena of Ardath?"

"Athaliah?" Tristan sighed. "I knew her long ago—long before 'ere she came to these parts. Who she was then, along with what she has become—are two entirely different matters."

"She seems greatly to resent you."

Tristan sighed again.

"And for that, I suppose she has probable cause. I failed her. I cannot expect her to forget and overlook that… But I had to answer to a higher calling." He hesitated. "She is greatly altered from how I recall—and not just in years. A darkness has entered her soul, and has all but quenched the light. I remember a tender, trusting young woman—not this."

Adlai's eyebrows shot up.

"You knew her when she was *young*? How old *are* you?!"

Tristan cleared his throat uncomfortably and managed a smile.

"Adlai, I know little to nothing of you. *But*—" he hesitated, "For some strange reason I cannot know…I feel that perhaps I can trust you. If I take you into my confidence, will you most solemnly swear to not reveal my secret?"

Adlai stared at him in confusion and aroused curiosity. Before she had only seen his strengths. But now, now he seemed so openly vulnerable, tired, and strained, as though he were carrying the weight of the world on his shoulders. And something about that made him instantly relatable. She well knew what it was to carry hidden burdens, fears and terrors, the like of which others knew nothing. And she had been forced to carry it all alone. Willan hardly ever let her into his own private world—if anything, he had shut her out. And Gunar? For all of his seeming tenderness and protective care, he seemed ever cautiously determined to keep her from coming too close. It was obvious that he greatly desired her trust, and yet he himself trusted her as much or as little as he would a stranger…perhaps even an enemy. He had secrets which he would not—probably ever—reveal to her. What sort of confidence and friendship was that, one in which the trust was so obviously slanted and one-sided?... No, it was plain that he was hiding something. And yet here was this man whom she had known barely a day, and already she was starting to feel a kindred spirit to him. They both had secrets, they both knew what it was to push on alone, bowed under the yoke of invisible oppression. And he was willing to risk possible endangerment by allowing her into his private world.

"Yes," she breathed, "I do."

Tristan beamed, and for the first time since she had laid eyes on him, the restive heaviness which seemed to preoccupy him lightened, and his face and shoulders relaxed. He took in a deep breath:

"I am not what I appear." He paused, as if measuring the full weight of each word before venturing further. "My strength and life-span are greater than that of a mere man…You might say…"

His voice trailed off, as though he was uncertain whether to continue or not.

"And Ardath?" Adlai prompted, changing the subject, "Was she once a lover of yours?"

Tristan's face clouded momentarily in confusion, then suddenly broke into quiet laughter.

"No, no!" He laughed. "I've never transgressed a woman in that way. No, Athaliah—*Ardath*—is my distantly related kinswoman. She is not of pure blood as I am, however, so she has aged more progressively, even though she is younger than I."

Adlai's eyes again widened.

"How old are you?"

A small smile touched his lips.

"Too old to look upon a young girl, and think of her in the way a man does a woman."

His eyes were lingering upon her again, a hindered glimpse of longing stealing through their gaze. She felt her heart suddenly flutter wildly in her chest. He was so close to her in the stillness of the darkened room, that she could almost feel his breath brush her quivering breast. Tristan hastily straightened himself and cleared his throat.

"Well how old is she, then?" Adlai managed, trying to think of something else to say while vainly attempting to hide her excited trembling.

"You have only ever known her as Heromena of Ardath, I presume? And for how long has she served in the King's House?"

"I assume since before I was born," she answered confusedly.

"And before?" Tristan pressed.

"I hardly know—I have always thought her to be a distant and more humble relation to the King—perhaps one born of misfortune, and thrust upon his kindness."

"If that be so, than she is *very* distantly related, indeed, considering she dandled your Sovereign upon her knees!"

Adlai stared at him incredulously. She had always suspected Ardath of being something other than a mere mortal.

"Tristan," she asked cautiously, "What is she? And why would you have anything to do with someone like her?"

"You mean because of the darkness she exudes?" Tristan interjected. "Adlai," he remonstrated gently, "I am not unaware of such things. Part of my returning is that I seek to restore her, to draw her back into the light. I know not what ills or malice you may have suffered at her hands... But I sense that her inner demons have wounded and afflicted you as well. We all need to be pulled back from the ledge sometimes... I only hope that I am not too late...If you could have only seen her, as I once knew her to be—"

He stopped short, emotions suddenly flooding his face, so that he turned away. Adlai hardly knew what to think of what he was telling her. Was there actually hope for someone like Ardath? Was it possible for her hateful soul to ever be freed from the poison of its own bitterness? She wasn't sure whether she herself was willing to give the old woman the chance for redemption. Still, there was something moving about Tristan's conviction.

"How come you to be acquainted with Gunar?"

Tristan peered at her perplexedly for a moment.

"Ah, is that the name he now assumes?" He laughed. "Here is another soul I once knew under a different name—and different circumstances... Back then, he was called Caen—Caen MiCael. 'Bellwether' was simply a nick-name given in jest. No other had shrewder eyes, his arm when wielding a sword, nor his strategic skill in planning battle."

"So, his identities begin to multiply," she mused contemplatively to herself... "*Caen*... But how many others does he have...?"

She roused herself from her broodings. Tristan was still standing there.

"So what happened between the two of you? What happened to him?"

Tristan's face sobered in a grave, almost saddened expression.

"He was a good man, an excellent soldier, and an exemplary warrior—one of the finest, and the bravest. During the thick of the battle, he pressed in hardest. He smote the Black Heart, weakening him. In an instant, the ravaging armies of the Enemy turned to dust before our eyes. But the Spirit of the Shadow cannot be overcome by mere human strength alone. It fled, deceiving and luring him into pursuit. I begged him to wait and not pursue alone, but he wouldn't listen. I tried to go after him…We were separated. When I found him again, he was as you see him now. And worse, the Shadow had vanished without a trace."

Adlai exhaled slowly, shaking her head.

"But what exactly *is* he now? Whatever happened to him?"

Tristan shook his head somberly.

"I've never seen any mortal man bitten by the Curse, and go on to survive as he has. I've never seen a man endure such excruciating torment either—it was terrible to behold. Others succumb to the Beast… But Bellwether…He was stronger of heart than others. I believe the reason his transformation has not *yet* been made complete, lies solely in the sheer force of his will to not be dominated by it… And he is *still* fighting it."

Adlai paled.

"You mean that he could still change?"

Tristan nodded sadly.

"I'm afraid yes, if he for an instant allows the instinct and nature of the Beast to over-rule his will to overcome it." He sighed. "It must take *all* the forced concentration of his will to fight it, every second of every single moment that he breathes."

Adlai smothered the rising lump in her throat, trying hard to stifle her tears.

"I had no idea—how dreadful!"

"Yes—it is dreadful. Every emotion and conscious thought of his must be subdued, in order for him to prevail against it."

Suddenly it all made sense. That was why he was always so seemingly detached—he *had* to, in order to keep from allowing his emotions to be become aroused and turn into the thing he hated most. And Tristan's explanation also explained much of what he had hereto been keeping secret from her…and perhaps for darker reasons… *How could she have allowed herself to be so blind?!*

"What is this Curse that has bound him?" She queried.

"They say that it is a Curse which Men brought on themselves. Four millennia ago, on that cursed day when Earth's inhabitants allied themselves against their Immortal keepers, they bound themselves by a sacred, solemn Oath, solidified by the shedding and mingling of blood. No force on earth can undo its binding power… This is the price men paid for wanting to become Gods." Tristan let out a scornful, embittered laugh. "Paradise was forever lost, and their souls remain forever bound. Their seared consciences are dead; they heed no other voice, save that of their Master—the Black Heart himself, the Ancient Evil of the Deep."

Adlai shuddered.

"What will happen to Gunar now?"

Tristan sighed deeply and closed his eyes, as though steeling himself against some dark and terrible thought.

"I do not know. Those I have seen with the strength and will to fight it, were all dead within a day… How he has managed for so long, is utterly beyond me… I can only pray that he finds the will to survive, for however long he is forced to endure…I pity him… Death would be an infinite kindness, compared to the fate with which he now contends."

"He is dying, then?" Adlai faltered.

"I'm not sure. He is strong—the strongest I've ever known. And it is such power for which the Shadow seeks, to continue his personal evolution… Perhaps that is why it personally sought him out and lured him…"

Adlai sat in stark silence, her ears ringing with the echo of Tristan's words… Gunar had spoken of being led and directed by his Master… Could it really be what she now thought? Had an emissary of the Shadow found its way into their midst?

"A Vessel," she murmured. Her thoughts were reeling. "Tristan," she asked in a tremulous voice, "Why do you think he is here?"

He pursed his lips grimly.

"*That* is precisely what I am trying to find out."

"What should we do?"

"We shall watch and wait. It is best that we study him, learn. Hopefully in so doing, we shall not only avoid great disaster before it strikes, but also I hope to find a way to restore him again, if there be any way possible."

Adlai was growing to admire Tristan more and more with each passing moment. He had so much courage in the face of danger, so much faith and compassion—even for the undeserving.

"You care for him," she murmured with a smile.

He heaved a weighty sigh.

"He was once my friend. I hope to save him, before it's too late…"

He studied her for a moment, an expression in his countenance which she could not read, yet found herself shyly warming under. At last he cleared his throat and turned away.

"It's late—you really oughtn't to be here with me at this late hour, my Lady."

"Yes—quite," she laughed nervously. She didn't really want to leave, but could think of no excuse to stay longer. Everything about him was beginning to fascinate her. Reluctantly she rose to leave.

"Adlai!" He seized her quickly by the hand. "If you ever have need of a friend, you have one in me—I'm here for you."

A blush flooded her cheeks at his words. With a gulping nod she turned to leave, but hesitated at the door.

"I'm glad you've come to us, Lord Tristan."

He nodded soberly in response. Yet there was no disguising the sparkle that instantly lit in his eyes, even though hardly a smile touched his lips. With another nod, she closed the door behind her and left.

The Manor was very dark now as she softly made her way through corridors and on upstairs. Not a sound stirred. Then all at once she caught sight of a faint, flickering light disappearing down a narrow hall to her left. Peering in the darkness, she wrinkled her brow perplexedly. Whoever could be up at this hour? For an instant she bit her lip, then cautiously followed after at a discreet distance.

It was a narrow passageway. She had never really ventured this way before, as she had always assumed that it led to some other main serving room in the castle—such as the kitchen, perhaps, or the wine cellar, or the servants' quarters. The passage had just taken another bend, when she suddenly stopped short with a gasp and quickly pulled herself back into the shadows. Ardath's familiar form was etched before a darkened doorway, holding up a jangling ring of keys. Gingerly she inserted one of them into the rusted keyhole of a musty door lock… Adlai drew in a sharp, apprehensive breath. With a creak the small arched door opened, and the headmistress entered.

For a moment she hesitated, unsure whether to follow or not. Everything in her was tugging at her in fear to turn back, yet still she felt overcome by the drawn urge to follow. Something about all this was strange—stranger than usual. And after Ardath's peculiar behavior that day, Adlai had a keen inkling that more than a few answers lay behind that door. If she was ever to learn the truth, she had no choice but to follow after. With a deep breath, she crept forward.

CHAPTER 33—THE SCOURGE

Adlai practically jumped out of her skin as the old door abruptly fell back into its frame with a harsh creaking noise. A narrow stone staircase descended down before her. Heart pounding, she cautiously crept forward. Down, down, down it went, until she was certain that it must be leading straight into the very bowels of the castle. Then all at once the passage came to an end: an enormous chamber opened up before her. The narrow stair continued on along the wall, the exposed side of it making a sheer drop like the edge of a cliff over the chamber below. As she inched her way along the wall stones, she could make out Ardath's form far below, lighting candelabras stationed in a circle. At their center upon a mounted dais stood a great round table, its surface as smooth and transparent as mirrored glass. Ardath finished lighting the last of the candles, then slowly ascended the steps leading up the platform. The stilly silence of the drafty chamber began to echo with the sound of whispering voices emanating throughout the room; the voices grew louder until they reached a hissing noise as she approached and at last stood before it. Slowly she extended her hand over its top. The crystal clear reflection immediately turned to black, and its smooth surface began to move like the tossing of a sea.

All at once the fiery image of a great Griffin appeared, its shrill shriek tearing the air. Ardath shook visibly and stumbled back with a cry of alarm, as though frightened half out of her wits. For several moments the angry black sea surged about restively. The floor began to tremble, and the walls and ceiling quaked. Dirt and broken rock rained down, toppling into the waves below.

Then suddenly everything became as still and silent as before. A deathly silence hung like a hush in the air. Ardath's entire frame was still shaking; trembling, she again approached. Unsheathing a dagger from her girdle, she deftly sliced through the flesh of her open palm. Blood dripped down over the mirror, and the old woman laid her hand upon the surface where it pooled. The top began to swirl like a cauldron of darkened storm clouds, and again the room began to fill with the sound of whispers— thicker, louder, and increasingly menacing this time. Raising the blood-stained dagger into the air, she began to chant incantations in strange sounding words. *Was she chanting in the forgotten tongue of the Olde World?* Her voice grew louder and more commanding, her steely tone resonating with authorative severity. At once the rim of the table burst into flames. Ardath let out a pained gasp, her body going into rigid convulsions. A clash of thunder ripped, as forked streaks of lightening split through the air all around the candle-lit circumference. Slowly she began rising off the floor, her body levitating high above the table. Then suddenly she began to spin wildly, as though some exterior force were whipping her about. A large shadowy shape began to circle in the air above her. For an instant it hovered… Then in the next moment it swooped down upon her with a great rush. Ardath let out a piercing scream.

Adlai did not wait for more. She was already madly dashing back up the stairs and along the passageway as fast as she could. It felt as if invisible hands were reaching out to grasp her and pull her back, as though the malevolent presence of that place were trying to suck her back into its depths. She did not stop running until she was safely back inside her own room. Cold sweat was prickling along her spine, soaking the back of her dress and running down her forehead into her eyes. Something had happened in that room—yet what exactly, she did not know. But she now had the unsettling sense that whatever entity had been awakened, it was now personally aware of *her*, as well. A nauseating feeling was growing in the pit of her stomach. She felt as if she had been the unwilling participant in the pagan ritual, as if she had unwittingly invited it in… She could feel something clinging to her, as if something was trying to crawl into her thoughts and slither into her soul…and it wasn't letting go. Adlai quivered and grimaced distastefully, as if she had just tasted something foul. Then with a shudder she ran and flung herself into bed, pulling the bedclothes tightly over her face… Gradually the heavy thudding of her heart ebbed away, and her eyes closed into a troubled sleep…

Her eyes popped open. There was nothing beneath or around her; instead, she seemed to be suspended, floating… Everywhere she was surrounded by water. A dark, shadowy form was just pulling away from her face. Adlai flailed, as a terrified scream bubbled from her lips. Faster than a shaft of light, the form darted away and hid inside the craggy crevice of a rocky formation nearby. *It was Edrea… It had to be Edrea.*

"Ieuna, it's alright!" A familiar voice called to her.

Adlai stopped short. A waif-like form slowly emerged.

"Jhonreia…?" She gasped in astonishment.

The Mermaid hung her head and hesitantly drew closer. Something was wrong… Her form was bent, almost listless. And as she came into the watery light, Adlai noticed that her bright color was gone, and her face was haggard and ashen. Her eyes protruded from gaunt features, and crumbling scales were falling from her body.

"Princess?" Adlai gasped. "Whatever has become of you?!"

"A deadly Curse has come upon our domain," the Sea Princess answered in a voice that sounded as though it had aged by half a century. "The Kingdoms of the Sea lie sick and diseased."

"What happened?" Adlai asked quickly.

"Come," Jhonreia replied, taking the girl softly by the hand, "I will show you."

They swam on together through stilly waters. And everywhere they went, an unnatural, deathly silence filled the expanse. There was no current, and there were no schools of fish to be seen anywhere. The only sighting Adlai made was of an occasional lone sea creature, just as it flitted to hiding behind crevices and rocks. The abandoned carcasses of water fowl lay decomposing on the ocean's floor. There were no brightly colored sea flowers or plants to be seen anywhere; instead, a thick, slimy paste covered everything like mold, its toxic particles floating thick through the water.

"How did this happen?" Adlai begged, astounded. The Princess gazed at her sorrowfully; a tear glistened in her eye, but she answered nothing.

All at once they stopped. The caves and undersea ravines had ended; there was nothing but an endless field of crumbled ruins before them. Statues littered the ocean floor for as far as the eye could sea—lifeless bodies of all different species and ages: here, in this valley of death, was the final destiny of the Merfolk… She was standing on the edge of a mass Tomb.

A sudden sound made Adlai start: a small Merchild was whimpering helplessly, his sickly body barely stirring as he lay stiffly cradled in the shriveled arms of a Merwoman's decaying corpse. His eyes stared helplessly at her for a breathless moment that seemed to stand still in time. Then gradually he became quiet, and his eyes unseeing. A tiny, quivering light arose from his breast and slowly ascended upward through the sea.

Adlai broke down into sobs, as Jhonreia quietly laid a hand on her shoulder.

"His soul is going the way of our people to its final resting place. He is no longer in any pain," she comforted.

"What must be done?" Adlai pled.

The Mermaid eyed her sadly, a painfully grieved expression on her face.

"*She* must be stopped."

"*Who?*" Adlai begged in bewilderment. "*Who* must be stopped?!"

Jhonreia pointed silently. Adlai followed the direction of her gaze out across the ocean. At the outskirts of the silent graveyard rose an undersea mountain, atop which a great fortress was built. It was constructed entirely of the bones and skeletal remains of every sea creature in existence, both great and small. A low boom rose up from the depths of the earth beneath, and a glowing light like an ember emanated from behind the peaks of its towers. Veins of fire ran down the mountain's side, darting all over the cracked surface of the ocean floor. Adlai trembled.

"What is that?"

"The House of the Sorceress of the High Seas," Jhonreia replied somberly. "These lands were once the glorious kingdom of the Merfolk. The Great City of Herculantis was once situated peacefully upon the slopes of that mountain, which you see before you. But a great Evil awakened the slumbering giant beneath the earth. The mountain began to rumble and shake; then suddenly the volcano sprang to life—and in single moment, the Great City of the MerPeople was gone—swept away and turned to crumbling ash beneath the raging sea of fire."

Jhonreia discreetly wiped a tear from her eye as she paused in her narrative, though her proud brow remained resolutely staunch and unmoving. An ache rose in Adlai's chest, and she was moved to pity at sight of the noble Princess, still so strong despite being reduced to so helpless and humbled a state.

"We were once tens of thousands," the Mermaid continued, "But now we are no more than seven hundred, taking shelter amongst the hidden caves of the deep. The poisonous gases have caused much sickness and death among those still living, and our numbers are falling daily."

"And your father?" Adlai asked anxiously.

"My father Anteaon fought bravely to save his people—" the Princess' voice faltered for an instant. "But he fell—" her voice broke off.

"The Great Sea Serpent of the Deep," she managed at last. "T'was by it the mountain erupted, and by help of its power that she conquered. It is she who drinks up the life of my people."

The ground beneath them trembled and grew hot again, and they both fell silent. All at once Adlai grabbed the Mermaid's hand.

"Something's wrong!"

She pointed anxiously at the ocean floor. Thin veins of fire were again rippling over its surface.

"They're not flowing away from the mountain—they're running back towards it!"

For a brief moment they both stared: it was as if the streams of lava were teeming with life. A deep groan arose from the depths. Then everything began shaking violently. The ground split open and rocks separated, as lifeless bodies strewn above toppled down into its depths. The volcano's mouth lit up brighter than before, and a hissing roar sounded forth.

At this Jhonreia clutched her hand so tight that it made Adlai wince. Her face had become ghostly white.

"It's coming!" She breathed. "Leviathan—that Ancient Serpent of Olde, risen from the lowest regions of Hell!"

All at once a fiery rain of lava erupted from the mountain top. A wide path of it wound its way in and out, coiling and recoiling its way around the blackened slopes all the way to the bottom. Suddenly it rose upright like a cobra, its glassy sides peeling molten red like fire. Two scorching red eyes flicked in the darkness, as liquid flame gushed forth from its jaws. In an instant it slapped the valley with its tail. The whole ocean floor quaked violently. Both girl and Sea Nymph were knocked to the floor. In terror they clung to each other, unwilling spectators to the ghastly sight before them.

"She knows we're here," Jhonreia breathed tremulously.

Adlai followed her gaze. A single form could now be seen gliding swiftly like an eel through the darkened depths to meet them. The heated waters grew cold and turned the temperature of ice as she approached. Multiple black arms snaked out beneath her, their tentacles churning the mud beneath till it rose in billowing clouds, grinding to powder the barnacled crustaceans and remains of the Mer People. Tangled hair thick as seaweed streamed through the water over her head, lashing about her bared arms. In one hand a glowing trident was brandished, streaks of lightening shooting up from its fork. The creature's face was distorted by bony protrusions like a crab's shell, crusting into horns around the edges of her face.

Adlai let go a fearful gasp as the Sorceress drew up sharply before them, circling round about her like a shark. At last her mouth opened in a leering smile. A long tongue slid out from behind her fangs, slithering like a snake along the features of the girl's face. Adlai recoiled in revulsion.

"So, you've at last brought the mortal child here? You must be truly desperate!"

The Sorceress let out a jeering laugh.

"And what good did you possibly think she could do? No might compares to mine!"

Adlai was trembling so hard now that she shook.

"Ah, poor Lamb!" The Sea Witch mocked. "Strayed too far from your shepherd now, have you?" Her face suddenly turned to steel: "You're weak and pathetic! And you're nothing but a bitter disappointment. Go crawl back to your feeble, wasted life— you're of no use here."

She spun round to glide away. Adlai was still greatly frightened, but something in the taunt of her words pricked and burned her.

"You know nothing at all about me!"

Her voice rose barely above a whisper, but at the sound of it the Sorceress stopped short and whirled around.

"Oh? Don't I?"

A malicious smile twisted across her face.

"I know every fear that keeps you lying awake at night. I know every ounce of self-contempt and inner-loathing you fight to conceal. I know every willful, indulgent, self-centered act you've ever committed. But most of all, I know that you hate yourself for being everything that you are, and for your inability to become all which you are *not*."

Adlai stared befuddled, unsure how to answer all these painful revelations of herself. Here in the presence of Evil, with every inner weakness so effortlessly exposed, she felt even more naked and vulnerable than before.

"How do you know that?" She asked hoarsely.

The Sorceress leered again.

"Because it was by your weaknesses that I found my own strength." Again a cruel, ruthless smile curled across her lips. "I *am* your Future."

With a raucous laugh she lunged for the girl. Adlai let out a scream, as she was torn from Jhonreia's arms.

"She can send Anteaon your regards!" The Witch called back over her shoulder. With that she flung the girl under one arm, and leapt atop the head of the Sea Serpent. In an instant the ground churned to mud so thick, that everything disappeared from view. With a sickening lunge the Great Serpent darted and slithered swiftly back across the valley floor.

Adlai sat bolt upright in bed, her own screams still ringing in her ears. Had it all been a dream?... It had seemed so real. So real in fact, that she was still trembling with the last image of those fiery eyes of the Serpent. And yet here she was, blinking in the early morning light. Recollections of the night before—and of Ardath—came flooding back. And hard as she tried to brush away the feeling, she still had the uncanny, unsettling sense that whatever it was which she had witnessed in the lower chamber—

that wasn't the end of it. *Whatever was she to do?* She felt so desperately helpless and alone. *Who could she turn to? Whom could she trust?* Memories of her conversation with Tristan came slipping back to her now. *She could go to him—he would understand.* He was probably the only person in all the world now who would.

CHAPTER 34—DANGEROUS GAMES

The mess hall was milling with servants as Adlai breathlessly burst through the door. Everyone was so busy, though, that scarcely anyone seemed to notice her. Tristan was sipping a mug of ale in silence, a far off look in his eye, as if practically oblivious to everyone else present. Hesitantly she approached, trying as she might to stave off the strange trembling which had come over her. Of a sudden he seemed aware of her presence, for he quickly turned in her direction. A warm smile broke across his face at the sight of her, like sunshine on a frosty winter's day. Adlai felt her heartbeat quicken beneath his gaze.

"Milord," she addressed him with a reticent curtsy.

He reached out and quickly grasped her hand.

"Please, we're friends—there's no need for formalities here. I am simply…Tristan."

Suddenly it seemed she could scarcely breathe, as all other thoughts flew out of mind on a gale of flaming sensations. She had felt this way before, with Willan…But just as quickly, her happy thoughts vanished. *Yes, she had felt that way before—and her feelings had misled and betrayed her… She wasn't ready for that to happen again…She would never be ready for that to happen again. This was business, not a romantic interlude. She required his help, not his affections.*

"Might I trouble you to speak with you in private?"

Tristan's eyes locked briefly on her own, before giving her a quick nod of understanding.

"Of course, right away," he replied, rising swiftly to his feet.

They both turned to go, when they stopped short. Ardath was approaching. Adlai blinked. Was it her imagination, or did the headmistress actually appear several years younger now since she had seen her last? Ardath's skirts rustled softly as she moved in calculated silence. Every step was marked by unhurried deliberation, her eyes trained unwaveringly upon the young girl like a predatory beast stalking its prey. A chill ran through Adlai... *She was too late.*

"Lady Adelheide, as the highest ranking Lady of the House of DuReiyne, it is your duty to assist in waiting upon the Princess. Until now, you have grossly neglected your responsibilities to his Lordship, in welcoming his Lady to the household and familiarizing her with her new home."

Adlai could feel her blood growing hot. Stiffly she bowed, trying to hide the flare of unbridled anger rising in her face, as she lowered her eyes to the floor in feigned submission. She had all but been treated as a common servant—been ignored, shunned, abandoned, and abused. Ardath had done everything in her power to break her spirit and turn her into a timid, mousy creature, too afraid of her own incompetency to ever attempt to lead in any way. She had never been prepared to act the part of hostessing Lady of the House, and now she was being accused of rude neglect and ill-breeding? *Whose fault was that? What right did Ardath have to suddenly impose on and thrust her into such a position?... Did she suspect that Adlai knew something, and was she trying to stop her from telling Tristan?*

"Milord," Ardath acknowledged Tristan with a curt nod, forcibly taking hold of the girl's arm as she did. Then almost before she knew it, Adlai was being swept out the hall, leaving behind the young Lord to stare after their departure with reluctant silence.

"You are of age—it is time you acted the part," Milady continued condescendingly. "There is to be no more running off, no more gallivanting about the countryside—and *no* more skulking about the castle!"

Adlai gave a gasp as Ardath gave her a sudden sharp twist on her arm, spinning her about to face her. Her eyes narrowed coldly.

"Is that clearly understood?"

Her steely tone was smooth as the slithering of an asp's forked tongue. It was as if the girl was an insect which she could just as easily crush under her shoe without remorse. A twinge of fear slid down her spine at these last words. *Did Ardath know that she had followed her last night?*

The next few hours were wholly tiresome. Afwin's apartments were a hubbub of women's voices. All were laughing and conversing gaily together, but Adlai wanted none of it. How strange, that here in her own house she should feel more a stranger than their newcomer guests? It was a ridiculous joke that she should pretend to play the part of hostess to Afwin and her retinue. This was the Princess' new home now; *she* was the new Lady of the House. And Adlai herself was little more than a guest in it.

Wearily, she turned back to others. Many of the ladies were excitedly quipping about the handsome young Lord Tristan Marcus Justis Cornelius, newly arrived to the castle. Afwin was quietly sitting at her needlework, and appeared content to give little more to the conversation than a token gesture in the form of a nod or smile. Occasionally her eye was filled with a far off dreamy look, and at the occasional mention of Willan's name a warm blush would steal across her cheek. And every now and then she would cast a discreet glance towards Adlai. Adlai had wished for so long that she could find some reason to dislike her, for causes other than that she had been her unwitting supplanter. But she could not. And more and more she found herself feeling empathy for Afwin, if only for a fleeting moment. For all of her beauty, pedigree, and wealth, and all the admiring attention showered upon her, she still seemed alone and slightly out of place. And though they were worlds apart, yet in that lonely, empty space was the one tangible bridge linking them together.

Silently Afwin laid aside her needlework, and softly motioned for Adlai. Reluctantly she obeyed, and took up a seat beside her.

"We have not had the chance to become much better acquainted," the Princess said warmly. "And I should very much like the friendship of my Lord's kinswoman, if you would so permit me."

Adlai was humbled by the Princess' meek gesture of kindness and acceptance. Were it not for the awkwardness stemming from her lingering feelings for Willan, she felt sure that she would have otherwise been more than happy to have had Afwin as a friend—perhaps even as a sister.

"You look much as I feel," the Princess sighed with a small laugh. She lifted her eyes only briefly to cast a sober glance upon the other girl. "I was often alone."

Adlai looked up quickly.

"You, Milady?"

Afwin smiled.

"My mother died when I was very young. My father's court knew more of men and warriors, than of female company."

A twinge of a smile crossed Adlai's lips at this. They were perhaps more alike than she had supposed.

"Meeting my Lord Willan was the first time I ever felt my heart had found its resting place…Yet for all of the love we are blessed to share, my heart still carries a small emptiness. I have gained a husband, but I have lost my home with my father and all that was once familiar… I know not when I may see them again."

In spite of herself, Adlai felt a growing admiration for Afwin. She was a royal Princess, yet she possessed none of the haughty arrogance or fine airs which Adlai had often supposed accompanied nobility. Instead, she was genuinely sincere and compassionate, unpretentious and open—almost vulnerably so.

Afwin took her gently by the hand.

"You must dislike me," she said apologetically in a sympathetic voice.

"Milady?"

"I've seen the look in your eyes when he enters the room—you must've loved him very much...It must pain you—now that I am taking him away."

Adlai's lips quivered. She searched for words as she attempted to choke down the hard lump rising in her throat. Embarrassed, she turned away so that the Princess would not see her eyes redden with tears.

"It's alright," Afwin laid a tender hand reassuringly on her arm. "I understand."

Adlai gulped back her tears and tried hard to smile in reply. Despite the pain, she felt strangely relieved by the Princess' gesture, even if she wasn't yet ready to accept her as a friend and bring her into her confidence... That might be awhile in coming.

The rest of the day passed at a tedious pace. She did not again get a chance to speak with Tristan. Every time she so much as glanced in his direction at supper, she could feel Ardath's eyes boring through her. Her penetrating gaze never seemed to leave, and Adlai was growing more and more alarmed by this rekindled obsession. Somehow, she knew—she *knew*... and Adlai had to get help from someone—soon.

That night she lay tossing in her bed, unable to sleep. Whatever was she to do?... All at once a yawning noise echoed from the chimney. It grew louder as it descended. Trembling, she turned towards the fireplace. A single log lay cold on the hearth. Then all at once, the spark of a flame appeared amidst the charred embers. It glowed brighter and brighter, a thin whiff of smoke trailing upwards, until it framed a tall shadow. A silhouette—the ghostly form of a woman—stood upon the darkened hearth. Cold, dark eyes stared straight into the girl's horrified features, as a malevolent smile twisted across her face. Adlai cowered in terror, hardly able to drag her eyes away. *She had been right to believe that she had unwittingly invited in the presence of Evil.*

"What do you want?" She gasped.

The apparition's smile grew broader:
"*You.*"

The sound of heartless laughter echoed through the room. Then suddenly the bed hangings and posts burst into raging flames. The entire chamber was on fire. There was a screeching, splintering noise overhead; then all at once the overhanging curtains came crashing down. They barely brushed her, as Adlai quickly rolled and leapt from the bed. Coughing and choking, she dashed for the door and jerked at the handle. To her surprise it wouldn't open—it was locked from without. She began beating on the door.

"Fire! Fire! Help! Someone, please! I'm trapped in here!"

She gave the door one final kick, then desperately looked about for some means by which to break down the door. Through the smoke she could see a tall candle stand. Snatching it up and mustering all her strength, she charged and rammed the door. Again and again she fell upon it, but to no avail. At last she staggered back, and it fell from her sweating hands with a clatter. Scorching flames and billowing smoke were everywhere. *How and where could she possibly make her escape?* The only other opening to the outside was the window. It was the only way. Carefully she began inching her way towards it.

A sudden noise from the ceiling made her look up with a start: an overhead beam was crashing down amidst a rain of fiery rubble. Adlai let out a terrified scream and ducked, narrowly missing it. Dashing to the window she threw it open and peered out. There was a tree a short distance away—if she was lucky, there was a slim chance she could reach it in a flying leap. Adlai swallowed hard. If she missed, she would likely be falling to her death. She glanced back at the raging furnace behind her—there was no other escape route. If she tarried, she was as good as dead—a broken body was better than being burned alive. Backing up several steps, she took in a deep breath—then made a run for it and jumped.

For an instant she was hurtling through the air towards the tree, her flailing arms straining to reach the sturdiest limb that was nearest…She missed. Instead her fingers managed to grasp a slender branch. For half a second she hung swaying back and forth precariously, the branch bending dangerously under her weight.

Adlai twisted about to face the house. Lights could be seen appearing through the windows, and shouts accompanied with the sound of running footsteps.

"*I'm out here!*" She shrieked. "*Help!*"

A splintering noise filled her ear. The branch was breaking.

"*Help me!*" She screamed.

Desperately she reached for another branch. The cracking noise was growing louder... Then all at once there was a snap—and she was falling, the sound of her own screams ringing in her ears. Excruciating pain shot up through her leg as her foot struck—then she hit the ground hard. For several moments she lay dazed, the wind knocked from her lungs. With a painful groan she rolled over. She hurt everywhere—the left side of her face had been grazed, and she could feel a knot swelling on her temple. Her ribs were badly bruised from the force of impact, while her right hand was sprained. And the splitting pain in her extremity indicated that she had at least fractured her leg...But she was alive.

Dimly, she was aware that the shouts were becoming louder. Slumping on the ground, she gazed up numbly at the blazing inferno inside her bedchamber window... Adlai squinted through the haze... *Was it her imagination, or did she glimpse Gunar's face for an instant peering down at her amidst the flames?* Everything was becoming blurry. She was just losing consciousness as the image of Tristan's face entered her view.

Adlai moaned faintly. Hands were hoisting her up and carrying her back into the house. The halls were filled with bodies and faces. Her head was spinning, and her body felt listless. Through her delirium she thought she caught sight of a familiar face—Lady Ardath. She was standing silently in the partially open doorway of her bedchamber, still clothed but with her hair undone, a lit candle in her hand. And just behind her Adlai thought she caught glimpse of something else—a black circle scrawled upon the floor, surrounded by lit candles. At its center a small pigeon lay lifeless, feet bound... its neck had been throttled. The flickering flame lit upon her features for just a moment. There was no mistaking the ominous look of black hatred in her eyes.

Adlai glanced up: Tristan was supporting her head, a grave look of deepest worry on his face.

"Please," Adlai rasped hoarsely, grasping hold of his hand. "Don't leave me alone!"

Tristan nodded quickly but said nothing. There was fear in his eyes.

A door was thrown open, and next moment she was being lowered onto a bed. Willan's voice could be heard calling loudly for the physician and ordering for the room to be cleared. At last the only one left with her was Tristan.

"Tristan?"

Her fingers fumbled for his hand.

"I'm here!" He reassured her, touching her head.

"She tried to kill me!" She croaked through puffy lips.

Tristan stood stone-still and silent, and she felt a tremor pass through his hand.

"Please, you can't leave me alone!" She begged. "I'm frightened!"

"There's no need to be afraid!" He whispered. "I'm here, and I'm not going to leave your side!"

He pressed his lips to her forehead. Adlai burst into sobs. Next moment the whole story was pouring out—everything she had witnessed in the Lower Chamber, and all concerning Lady Ardath. Tristan listened attentively in rapt attention, his face growing more pensive and distraught with every new detail.

"I'm so sorry to have brought this to you, it's all my fault!" He cried.

He heaved a guilt-laden sigh, clutching her hand tightly as he shook his head in distress.

"Adelheide, you must never take such a risk upon yourself again, do you understand?"

She nodded weakly.

"But what are we to do?"

Tristan seemed to think hard for a moment, a dark look of foreboding on his face.

"I must learn what she is about," he answered gravely. "And for that, I must ask your silence on this whole matter—at least for now. Tell no one what has transpired—there is far more at work here than we yet know, and I must get to the bottom of this, before a greater evil is unleashed upon us."

Adlai's eyes were suddenly swimming with tears.

"I can't stand it anymore!" She wept. "I'm ready to go mad from it all!"

Tristan clutched her hand more tightly in his, pressing it to his lips.

"I promise—no more evil shall befall you! You have my word."

She shook her head miserably.

"There's nothing you can do now—it's only a matter of time," she replied hopelessly. "She wants my life—and she will take it."

"Then she shall have to take mine as well!" Tristan burst loudly. His eyes were blazing fierce, and he gripped her shoulders firmly. "I swear to you—my body shall lie cold, 'ere I ever allow her to touch you again!"

He crushed her to himself, gently rocking her as he kissed her hair. Adlai closed her swollen eyes. The pain in her heart regarding Willan had been slowly dissipating ever since his arrival. Her Prince had failed her. But here in his place was a man perhaps more worthy of all the trust and affection she had already given…In so many ways, he was becoming her Savior. Her eyes closed. She could rest now.

CHAPTER 35—WITCHCRAFT

True to his word, Tristan hardly left her side for a moment over the following days, whether waking or sleeping. And during those brief moments when he had to excuse himself, he always made certain that she was attended by at least one of the servants in his absence.

On the eve of the fifth day Tristan announced that he had a surprise for her.

"I think you've had enough of four walls, don't you? Some fresh air ought to do you some good."

He smiled as her face brightened. Presently, there was a knock at the door, and the steward appeared.

"Begging your pardon, Milord, but his Lordship wishes to speak with you."

Tristan turned with an apologetic look.

"I won't be long, I promise," he said with a bow of his head.

Adlai tried to stifle her growing apprehension as he vanished from sight behind the closed door. The serving woman had not yet reappeared, and she was now completely alone for the first time in days.... Was it safe now?

Suddenly there was a rustling behind one of the draperies.

"Who's there?" She whispered tremulously.

A tall shadow emerged.

"Gunar! It's just you," she managed in relief, relaxing again upon her pillows.

"I wanted to come to you sooner."

"Then why didn't you?"

"My company hasn't been desired of late."

Adlai shifted uncomfortably. All at once she noticed something: Gunar had multiple fresh and distinct burn marks— over his eye, across his cheek bone, and over the backs of his hands. And even though his cloak concealed much of his body, she thought she caught a glimpse of blisters across his chest and stomach. *Whatever had he been about?*

"I've brought you something—it should help."

From under his cloak he produced a carefully carved crutch.

"You went to all this work—for me?" She asked, admiring it.

"T'was no trouble."

Suddenly the door opened and Tristan reappeared. He stopped short at the sight of Gunar.

"Bellwether!" He said, recovering himself. "I'm rather surprised to find you here. A gentleman shouldn't come alone into a lady's personal apartment."

Gunar raised his eyes evenly to look Tristan full in the face.

"No, a *gentleman* should not," he growled.

Tristan's fingers moved indiscreetly to his sword. Gunar seemed to disregard him and turned back instead to Adlai.

"Whenever you need me, you have only to call—I will always answer."

"Thank you for your services, but I believe we have everything well in hand," Tristan interrupted.

"I wasn't addressing you," he answered dryly, "Nor are your behests any concern of mine."

"Gunar!" Adlai cried in shocked surprise. "He's only trying to help! There's no cause for rudeness!"

"Is he?"

Gunar's boring gaze was fixed penetratingly on the young warrior. But after several moments he turned away.

"I shan't impose on you longer. Milady," he excused himself with a bow of his head, and turned to leave. He paused before Tristan.

"Not a hair of her head is to fall to ground," he uttered in a low growl. "Is that understood?"

And with that, he was gone. Tristan let out a sigh of relief.

"Pray forgive his behavior," Adlai apologized.

"He's very watchful of you," Tristan noted. "And no—it's I who am sorry. I failed him when he needed me most—I can't blame him for hating me, nor thinking me incapable of properly protecting you."

"Whatever happened, I'm sure you tried your best," she answered reassuringly.

Tristan answered with a saddened, wry smile:

"If only my best had been enough."

His shoulders sank with a heavy sigh. Suddenly he looked exhausted and worn, as if he had been carrying a heavy burden for a many a long year.

"Shall we be going?" He asked with a tired smile.

She nodded with a ready grin, clutching her new crutch as Tristan wrapped her up warmly. In a short while they were atop the battlement walls.

"I thought you could use some fresh scenery," he said, gently setting her down on the parapet.

"It's beautiful!" She breathed. "To think I've lived here all my life, but never seen the country from this view point!"

Tiny lines crinkled around a broad grin on his face, in a disarming way that only added to all his rugged charm. His dark brown eyes twinkled with pleasure.

"This is the first time I've seen you look alive, since the moment I first beheld you…I am *truly* happy for that."

Their eyes locked for a moment, Adlai found herself lost and speechless under his gaze. Uncertainly, she turned away. It frightened her to feel this way—to be so suddenly…and strongly… attracted to this man. All at once she caught sight of Gunar far below. He was staring up at her in silence, watching… She swallowed. *Why did she suddenly feel as if she were acting faithlessly towards him?*

She shook herself. Gunar had imposed his feelings on her—she was not responsible for how he felt, if indeed the feelings he had expressed actually *were* true, and not a deception. Besides, she wasn't giving her heart away to anyone—all she wanted was to be happy. To just be able to enjoy a single, unfettered moment, in which she was not being made afraid, nor made to feel pain, shame, or guilt… No one, not even Gunar, should begrudge her that right. If he truly cared about her at all, he should be glad for her happiness, not seek to imprison her.

Adlai looked away, turning her gaze back towards the setting sun. A dark cloud had slowly appeared on the skyline, swiftly making its way towards them. It was quickly gaining speed, until at last she saw that it was a great flock of black birds.

"Tristan, look—" she pointed.

He squinted.

"They're flying low, against the wind, and in the wrong direction," he mused in a low voice.

The party of fowl quickly descended, circling in wide formation over the castle spires, their shrill cries echoing back and forth to one another as they wound round and round like a circling army. Adlai's blood went cold. Everything else seemed to stand hushed and stilled in their wake…Then suddenly, they swept down upon them without warning.

"Look out!" Tristan yelled, shoving her aside.

She collapsed against the stone parapet as the bodies of fowls rained down thick as hail about her. Their shrieks pierced her ears; claws were scratching and tearing at her, beaks falling like relentless daggers on her flesh, pecking, boring, and gouging. Adlai let out a scream of terror, vainly attempting to shield her face and head from the vicious assault. Tristan threw himself over her, shielding her with his body.

"*Go on! Get out of here!*" He shouted loudly, beating the birds away.

They sailed away just as quickly as they had come, and again began circling the castle. Their circle tightened until it enclosed upon the Bastion tower, situated afar up at the end of the curtain wall, upon the overhanging cliff of Dombrey Manor. Through the loophole of the narrow window opening, Adlai caught glimpse of someone standing in the shadows—Lady Heromena of Ardath. The birds continued circling and screaming for several moments; at last their cries faded, and they flew away in the opposite direction by which they had come. Adlai let out a horrified gasp and turned to look at Tristan. He too was staring at the Bastion. But Ardath was no longer to be seen. Several soldiers had already come running to the walls.

"Take me away from here!" Adlai shuddered to him.

"Yes, yes, at once," he answered quickly. He hastily lifted her in his arms and carried her back, but the whole way she could feel his heart pounding in his chest.

The doors of the great hall banged about on their hinges, as Tristan kicked them wide open. There was no longer a look of fear in his eyes—only anger, as with long strides he proceeded forth. All present fell silent at his entrance, until the only sound left was that of his heavy boots as he made his way to the center.

"Lord Tristan—Adelheide!"

Willan cried in alarm, quickly making his way forward. His face grew instantly pale at the sight of the scratches on Adlai's face, and bloody gouges on her arms.

"Whatever happened?!"

Tristan's visage was kindled, his eyes hot and blazing.

"We have a great Evil dwelling in our midst!" His voice rang out with authority. "We have been rendered impotent by use of Witchcraft! We must be purged of this Darkness, 'else it will destroy us all!"

Gasps and shuddering cries, mingled with shocked whispers and murmurs sounded back and forth from every end of the hall.

"Who has done this?!" Willan demanded. His expression was equally incensed. Tristan lowered his eyes for a moment, the hint of a burdened look of guilt and regret in his face.

"A trusted member of your House, Milord," he answered, clearing his throat.

"Is anything wrong, Milord?" A voice suddenly interrupted.

All eyes started in the direction of the intrusion: Lady Ardath.

Adlai almost rubbed her eyes, just to be sure they were not playing tricks on her: no, there was no mistaking it—the headmistress looked even younger than before. Slowly Ardath made her way forward with deliberating steps, her eyes staring unwaveringly upon the young Lord. Tristan took in a deep breath, his eyes darkening grimly and his jaw firmly set:

"Lady Heromena of Ardath, I charge you with witchcraft, treason, and conspiracy to murder!"

Questioning whispers and muttering voices quickly ran through the harrowed assembly. But Ardath held her ground, continuing to stare evenly into the face of her accuser.

"You dare enter this house as a guest, and accuse me of such crimes?" She demanded with a dry laugh. "Lord Tristan, I'm beginning to think the torments of war have deranged your scarred mind."

"I know of what I speak, and Lady Adelheide herself can bear witness of what I say!"

All eyes turned now to Adlai.

"*This* girl?!" Ardath mocked with a rhetorical laugh. "If that's your best witness, then you've a hopeless case, indeed! Lady Adelheide is well known for inventing delusions—why, even his Lordship knows this!"

She shot the girl a sly, triumphant smile. Adlai suddenly wanted to bury herself. Which was worse—the public humiliation and ill repute associated with all of her follies, or not having anyone present believe her, when she desperately needed it most?

Willan's face darkened at this last indiscreet mention of him by the headmistress. Ardath's taunting instantly went silent. Slowly the Prince stepped forward. For several moments he studied both women.

"Lady Adelheide," he asked, hoarsely clearing his throat, "Is this true?"

Adlai swallowed. *It was now or never.* She could already feel Ardath's steely gaze fixed upon her, daring her to speak. If she backed down now, no one would ever believe her again. And Ardath would be sure to leave no loose ends untied, the next time she tried to finish her off. Denial was as good a choice as suicide. Gathering all the resolve she could find, she took a deep breath:

"Yes," she replied trembling. Resolutely she looked Willan full in the face: "It is the truth."

Willan appeared momentarily lost, searching all three of their faces. He lingered last at Adlai. A desperate tear trickled down the side of her face, as she looked to him in silent plea. If he didn't believe her now, all would be lost. A flicker of belief crossed his eyes. At last he heaved a troubled sigh, and his shoulders slumped.

"Lady Heromena of Ardath," he began in a heavy voice, "You have been accused of the crime of witchcraft. You are hereby to be taken to the prison of the Keep, there to await trial."

Immediately guards moved forward and surrounded her. For a brief instant a note of fear fluttered across her arrogant, hardened demeanor. Her expression went numb in shocked surprise. Willan did not look into her face, as guards flanked her on either side and together they filed in silence from the hall. Suddenly Ardath halted, a pained, confused look on her whitened face.

"But—but I've served you," she pled with her young Master. "Everything I've ever done—it's all been for you!"

Willan turned away, as if unable to bear further the sight of her humiliation. Ardath's shaken gaze wandered from him to Tristan, then last of all to Adlai. For a brief and fleeting instant, Adlai felt an exhilarated moment of triumph as their eyes met… It was finally over—the prolonged tyranny; the hiding in the shadows, too afraid to be seen; the endless fear…*it* was over. She was no longer the headmistress' prisoner. Justice had been served. And now her tormentor was to partake of the same cup of suffering which she had forced her to drink for so many years… But why then did this not feel like freedom?

Ardath's eyes narrowed in virulent, black anger.

"It's you! This is all your doing!" She hissed at the girl, her countenance smoldering with hatred. "You're a Curse and a Plague to this House! You shall bring great Evil to us all!"

Her voice culminated in a shriek, as suddenly she tore past the guard and flung herself at Adlai. Tristan threw himself between them, barring the older woman's way. A maddened, deranged look filled Ardath's eyes, as she fought and clawed at his restraining arms. Adlai swallowed hard, trying to steady herself and quell her violent shaking. The headmistress looked more like a wild, savage beast than the once sophisticated, elevated head Lady of Dombrey. Willan's men-at-arms rushed forward to assist in restraining her. At last she gave up her struggle, turning her disbelieving eyes to Tristan.

"You would betray me for *her*?" She gaped in a hoarse voice. "You would turn your back on your own, for *her*?!"

Tristan was visibly shaken and distraught, and Adlai thought she saw traces of mist in his eyes. But everything in his posture refused to yield.

"I do as I must."

For another instant Ardath stared at him, incredulous. Then rage again filled her countenance.

"You think you have found your treasure," she laughed bitterly, "But she will be your undoing! She will be the undoing of all!" Her voice rang out loudly. Quickly she pressed in close to Tristan, so that scarcely anyone else could hear her: "*I have foreseen it!*"

"Be silent, Witch!" Tristan commanded. He motioned quickly to the Guard: "Take her away at once!"

CHAPTER 36—PRISONER OF THE TOWER

No one stayed long in the mess hall after Lady Ardath's disturbing departure. All moved about in dazed silence, as though the ominous threat of her warning could still be heard ringing against the walls.

Willan was visibly upset, and had promptly excused himself, a soothing Afwin on his arm. The Princess, despite her steady presence, also appeared slightly pale and shaken by the strange turn of events. Left alone as the others dispersed, Tristan turned back now to Adlai.

"Are you alright?" He whispered tenderly, gently brushing a piece of hair behind her ear. Adlai let go a whimpering sob and flung herself into his arms.

"There, there!" He consoled her, holding her close as he kissed her hair.

"I don't understand!" She wept. "Why does she hate me so?"

Tristan heaved a shaky sigh.

"Because you remind her of herself—of what it is that she should have been; of things she would like to forget…But her poisoned bitterness will not allow her."

Adlai drew a deep breath and pulled back.

"I want to speak with her."

Tristan viewed her uncertainly for a moment, quizzically shaking his head in worried concern.

"Lady Adelheide, I think it best not to go near her—for the sake of your heart, as much as your safety."

"I know—but I must. She knows something of me—something which I must know… I *have* to know why she said those things about me—what great Evil did she foresee?"

"Pay her no heed—they were the crazed pratings of a deranged old woman, who no longer sees."

Deep down, Adlai wanted to believe that to be true. But as desperately as she wanted to dismiss Ardath's ravings, yet there was still the troubling memory of the night vision she had received. What darkness awaited her future, such as would make her capable of bringing destruction to everyone and everything she had ever loved?

"Perhaps," she replied. "…But I am not so sure."

Tristan studied her for a moment.

"Milady," he pled earnestly, "Promise me that you will not seek her out—it's too dangerous!"

He clutched her hand tight, pressing it to his breast.

"Very well," Adlai complied reluctantly.

His face cleared in relief.

"Thank you… I wish to be able to sleep one night, without fear of harm befalling you."

He kissed the top of her head. And hard as she tried not to, she could feel herself melting under his tender touch.

"Thank you for not leaving my side," she breathed. "You are the first who has ever believed me. Without you, I would still be in peril."

He beamed. But a discreetly muffled sound made them both start. Gunar's stooped and heavily cloaked form was etched in the doorway. Tristan's smile disappeared.

"Do you want to see him?" He inquired in a low voice.

"It's alright," she answered, laying a reassuring hand on his arm, as she tried to disguise her discomfort, "You can go now."

"Milady?"

"I'll be quite safe, I can assure you."

"I shall leave you then, but only because you insist… But if you need me, only call for me and I shall come at once."

He sent a warning look in Gunar's direction at these words. With that he gave her a low bow, and strode away. Adlai now twisted about awkwardly to face Gunar.

"You have quite the talent for unexpected appearances," she said rather irritably.

The sheepish guilt she felt for her growing closeness with Tristan was confusing to her. She had done nothing wrong; why then did she feel as if she owed Gunar an explanation? Perhaps she had relied on him a little too heavily during her most difficult and trying moments, but she had meant nothing by it. And what was more, she hadn't actually *asked* for his help, protection—or really anything at all. If anything, he had imposed himself on her life and stubbornly insisted upon staying, whether she wanted him there or not. If he was foolish enough to hope for more than was realistically within reach, why should that be made her fault?

"Why are you angry with me?"

His simple, quiet question hung silently in the air. She gaped for a moment, hemming and hawing as she tried to find a logical answer. Suddenly she felt peevishly cruel. Why did it seem as if everything she did was somehow a source of constant pain to him, as if she were a small tyrant torturing a compliant minion... She was hurting him...And they both knew it... Why did he have to care for her so?... She was wearily almost beginning to wish that they had never met—then she would never have been caught in any of these exasperating and bewildering complications. She would have simply died that night. And that would have been the final end to her whole tiresome existence.

"Heidi, I'm not angry with you...You do know that, don't you?"

His question was gentle, tender... And for some reason it annoyed her.

"Why ever should I imagine you to be angry with me?" She retorted.

Gunar's soft expression didn't change.

"You know what is in my heart. You know I would stop at nothing to protect and keep you safe."

"Perhaps I don't *want* your protection anymore!" Adlai flared. "Did it ever occur to you that I might not feel the same way you do?! Why can't you just leave me alone?!"

She was breathing hard, and shaking and trembling all over. Gunar's staunch features didn't change; but slowly his unblighted eye appeared to grow misty. Then silently, a tiny tear glided down his cheek and melted into his beard. Adlai felt a pang go through her heart at his pain, and a guilt-ridden anguish filled her. She had done it again—acted impulsively, with no thought to how it might impact another... And she had deeply wounded him. In spite of her resentment, she could not hate him... And despite her attachment to him, she could not fully love him, even though he had a way of making her feel things she didn't fully understand. Her eyes were already stinging with tears and there was a hard lump swelling in her throat.

"Look, I don't want to hurt you," she begged, "I just need you to leave me alone for a while."

A heavy sigh rose shakily from his chest.

"It has never been my intention to force myself upon you. If you no longer wish for me to be near you, then I shall leave Dombrey."

Adlai's mouth dropped. She hadn't counted on him actually leaving... Previously she might have felt relieved, but now? It hurt to think of him suddenly gone... Though it seemed as if he had only arrived the other day, yet somehow it felt as if he had always been there. And the thought of him leaving made her feel as if a part of her life would be inexplicably missing. But she couldn't keep doing this to him. Holding onto him and not letting him go when he cared for her so would only further his hurt by dangling his heart.

"Perhaps that would be best," she replied shortly, though she was fighting back tears. Gunar stared at her silently for several moments.

"Is that truly what you desire?"

"For now, yes."

"Then I shall leave you."

He turned away.

"Bellwether!" She called hastily after him. "I want you to know that—that I truly value all of your kind services to me, these past few months."

"I regret nothing which I have done."

"Yes, I know," she smiled, stiffly blinking back her tears. "And I'm sorry that I have not been—that it could not be—as you would have liked."

Gunar took a step forward.

"But I will always be waiting," he whispered softly.

"I know that as well," her voice was moist. "That is why it's best that it end now, and that we part ways."

There was no mistaking the visible pain in his troubled eyes this time, no matter how scarred his visage was... And she hated herself for it. With a nod, he turned to leave.

"Gunar, wait!"

She hurriedly hobbled forward. His hood fell away from his head as she threw her arms about his neck and squeezed him close.

"I wouldn't be alive if it weren't for you—I will never forget you."

She drew back, wiping away her tears, as she gazed up at him for a moment. His eyes were filled with a bittersweet expression—one of pain, and yet shining with love. What was it about that face—so scarred, yet growing more dear, familiar, and beautiful with every passing day? Why did she feel so torn inside, as if half of her wanted to throw herself into his arms, and the other half wanted to run away?... He had a way of making her feel that she could trust him implicitly... Yet always after, the gnawing doubts, fears, and suspicions would come seeping in... She did not fully know him, and she was beginning to believe that she didn't truly know her own heart either, for that matter. If only she could make sense of it all... For a brief instant she caressed the marred half of his face. Then almost without meaning to, she leaned forward and kissed his scarred cheek. Gunar swallowed, not lifting his eyes.

"I'm sorry, I probably shouldn't have—I just want you to know that I *do* care about you," she whispered. "... But it could never work out between the two of us—we belong in different worlds."

Tears were streaming down his face.

"The only worlds separating us are those in your mind," he choked.

Adlai shook her head, biting back the river of tears threatening to spill over.

"I'm sorry, Please, let's just let it be. I don't mean you harm."

He lingered a moment in her gaze.

"I only go now because you wish it—I promised that I would never leave you, nor forsake you. But I will also never force my presence and my protection on you. But know this," he cupped her face in his hands: "I will *always* come back for you, the instant that you call for me. Even before you call, I will answer you."

She smiled, blinking through her tears.

"Where will you go?"

"Back to the hillside."

"Of course," she nodded.

For another moment they stared uncertainly at one another.

"If you'll excuse me," he broke the silence, "I shall leave at once."

He bowed awkwardly, then strode towards the door with his wide, wolfish gait.

"Only one last thing," he called back as he paused in the doorway. "Listen to your instincts—they stir inside you for a reason…If it's doubtful, don't do it—you already know of what I speak. Don't go back to doors which have been safely closed for your sake… Don't flirt with danger."

And with that, he was gone. Adlai lingered for several long moments after his footsteps had already faded away to silence, her thoughts still echoing with his warning. He had read her mind—he knew that she had been ruminating over whether or not to seek out answers from Ardath. And much as she knew she would probably be the wiser to heed his warning, yet it was always the forbidding in his warnings which seemed to incite in her a willfulness to act apart anyways.

It was still hard to get used to the fact that *she* was the one who was now free, and that it was the old woman locked away in the tower. Why was it, then, that she still felt in so many ways just as much a prisoner as she always had? She still felt bound to the pain, fear, and hatred of the past... Heromena of Ardath might indeed be gone, but the shadow of her presence lingered… Her memory was something which would never be forgotten, no matter how badly Adlai wanted to shut it out.

For several moments she waited in the hushed stillness of the silent hall. Suddenly she was overwhelmed by everything; before she knew it, she was shaking with convulsive sobs. This wasn't how she had anticipated it being. It was almost as if she had never left her cage. A surge of hatred welled up inside her. She wanted to be free, more than anything—and if it was the last thing she did, she was going to find a way to break Ardath's hold over her life, once and for all. She would show her that she was stronger and more powerful than any of the fears by which she had tortured her all her life… *But what should she do?*

Brushing her tears away, she deliberated over her earlier promise… She *had* promised—if not to Gunar, to Tristan… But with Ardath now locked away, was there really any danger left? … Perhaps facing the headmistress—now that she was contained— was the key to breaking free from the awful dread which still lingered in her consciousness. And besides, there were more compelling questions now—questions which needed answering… For everyone's sake. If she could only get the older woman to reveal what she had foreseen, then perhaps she could find a way to stop it… Perhaps she could avoid becoming the very thing which she feared.

The torches lit along the corridor cast long, ominous shadows across the darkened walls of the prison. Adlai felt her way along at a belabored, painstaking limp, leaning heavily on her carved crutch. She had never been to this part of the castle before, and now she wriggled her nose against the noxious odor. It was dank and putrid, and the continued rain outside caused a perpetual drip. There were no other prisoners to be seen, and only two guards standing at attention at the end of the passageway. She took a deep breath: that must be where Ardath was being kept. How strange it was that their places should so suddenly be exchanged—to think that now her jailor of so many long years should at last be made the prisoner, and she the interrogator. Yet even so, Adlai couldn't help but tremble against the shuddering fears of the past. *It was too soon to feel safe or relax her guard… Perhaps she should have never come…She should turn back now, before it was too late.*

"You reek of fear and petty weakness!" A familiar voice hissed.

Adlai stiffened.

"*I* am not the only one who is imprisoned here," Ardath's taunting continued, "You live every moment of your wretched existence in a prison of your mind!"

Adlai's face flushed hot with anger:

"All my life you have hated me—and I only want to know one thing: *Why?*"

The older woman slowly emerged from the shadows and drew up close in the flickering light. A hateful, leering smile filled her face.

"Because I knew what you were—what you would become! I foresaw this day, and all that would follow it!"

"How you come to be in your present condition is entirely of your own making, and has nothing to do with me!" Adlai retorted evenly, pulling away. "You're a Witch! ...And I'm nothing like you."

"Aren't you?" Ardath gaped in mock surprise. "You never feel the poison of hate stirring in your bowels, never feel the urge to act out your anger and exact revenge?"

Adlai swallowed uncomfortably, turning away so that the old woman couldn't see her face.

"We are not so very different, you and I—like me, you crave power—power that will enable you to rise above the torment of your fears—power which will cause your enemies to fear you... Power to bring about the fulfillment of all your deepest desires...It is the same hunger which drives all of us..."

Ardath clutched the bars and drew herself closer:

"You cannot deny that you have felt its presence in the dark veil of Night... You *feel* it tugging at you...*You have heard its call.*"

Adlai licked her dry lips. She was starting to feel feverish. "Silence, Witch!"

Ardath gave her a caustic grin.

"Strange that you should show so much contempt for that title, seeing as how you are well on your way to becoming a far greater one that I shall ever be!"

"I've heard enough!"

Adlai practically screamed. She was shaking and sweating all over. For several seconds both women stood staring at each other.

"It was a futile waste to come here," Adlai muttered, turning abruptly to leave.

"Been having night terrors of late, have you?" Ardath's voice called out behind her.

Adlai halted. Her blood was already turning cold at the words. A tremor went tingling all the way down to her trembling finger tips... *The Witch of the great High Seas... she had spoken that she was her Future.*

"How do you know of that?" She demanded hoarsely.

The older woman smiled coldly again.

"I know *many* things."

A wave of helpless desperation suddenly broke over her.

"Then help me!" She burst. "Show me what you know, and help me ensure that it never happens!"

Ardath eyed her in silence for a moment, then slowly inched forward.

"You want answers? You will find them in the place where he took you—at the Source of all Life."

Perplexed, Adlai wrinkled her brow. *Was she speaking to her in riddles now?* Ardath seemed to notice, and cast a wary eye in the direction of the guards.

"Remember Edrea!" She hissed.

Adlai's eyes widened in disbelief. Ardath let go a satisfied smile, nodding in answer to the girl's stunned silence:

"Ah, yes—you remember... You should...You're still there!"

A streak of terror vibrated through Adlai's being at these words.

"What are you talking about? I demand you answer at once!"

In vain she tried to sound as though she were in control, but inside she knew—they both knew—that she was anything but in control.

"We are heart, mind, soul, and flesh, are we not? It is possible to operate within one, while being absent from the other. Just as you may be present in your body, but in your thoughts be thousands of miles—or years—away."

"So...you are saying that she took a part of me?" Adlai breathed.

Ardath leered again, a knowing smile playing tellingly on her thin lips.

"Do you never feel frozen in time? You try to shake yourself free, but find you cannot? ...Your spirit lies in a prison, the shadows of your own thoughts... There you fester, and there you wait...But all the while, you are changing inside...evolving...into the very thing you fear."

Something inside Adlai suddenly snapped. Quick as flash she lunged through the bars and seized the Ardath by the arm.

"Tell me what to do!"

"You'll never find it again without me!" Ardath grinned. "The way is hidden to earthly eyes—only one with foresight can guide you."

Abruptly Adlai let her wrist drop and pulled away.

"I'm not letting you out of here. You're too dangerous."

"No more a danger to you now, than you already are to yourself!"

Adlai stared at her in bewilderment. The irony of it was, she was beginning to think this last part was true. She had always lived in fear of the headmistress. But now she was in fear of something greater—the brooding darkness already growing deep inside her.

"I don't need you," She answered dismissively. "He took me there before, he can do it again."

"Aye...But *will* he?"

The girl stared at her for a moment. A sardonic smile was twisting across the older woman's trenchant expression.

"Have you never wondered why he took you there to begin with, what his reasons were behind it, or even why he came at all?... Like myself, he also has the Gift—and was sent to stop you, just as I was!"

Adlai's heart stopped at this. She swallowed hard. *Had Gunar knowingly led her into a trap?*

"Lies!"

"Oh? And where was he the other eve when your bedchamber caught fire?"

Adlai stared at her several moments, her thoughts racing. How *had* he acquired those burn marks, anyway? Before she had thought herself delirious to have supposed she had seen him standing there. Why hadn't he shown himself, or sought to help her, for that matter?

"You doubt, yet you haven't the courage to answer your doubts. But an even more important question is: Why did he leave your spirit behind in Avaelon?"

The question lingered in the air, and Adlai was afraid to know its answer.

"Because a body without the spirit is dead!" Ardath's words broke out in a vengeful torrent. "You should have thanked me for seeking to speed you on your way—now your end will be prolonged in coming, the agony of it only intensified by acute and anguished suffering! You shall die with the blood of all whom you have ever loved upon your hands!"

Adlai squared her jaw and looked Ardath solidly in the eye.

"Then help me!" She whispered firmly. "Help me, and I shall put an end to this!"

Ardath studied her quizzically for a few seconds, a hint of suspicion in her eye.

"Are you absolutely certain that you are willing to do whatever it takes—*anything*—in order to bring all this to an end?" She inched her way closer to the girl's face, until their eyes locked through the iron bars. "Would you be willing even to give up your life here, and leave forever?"

Adlai swallowed hard. So many thoughts were swirling in her head. She had always felt such a prisoner here, always dreamed of the day when she could leave this place and be free— free, and never look back... But now that it was here... These weren't the circumstances under which she'd envisioned her departure, nor how she'd imagined it would feel.

Ardath saw her undecided hesitation, and a scornful look of barbed contempt again returned to her eye.

"Just as I thought," she sneered. "Even when other lives depend upon it, you will always look to your own first. You're a survivor—same as I—and in the end you will do whatever it takes to preserve yourself… As I said before, we are not so very different."

"Wait!"

The command came out so fast and so strong, that Adlai herself was almost taken aback—but it was too late to change her mind. And she was already seething inside over Ardath's accusing comparisons.

"I'll do it!" Her jaw was set and clenched.

Ardath smiled with satisfaction.

"Good."

She eyed the girl for another moment.

"There's something that I need—" she added, "And you must get it for me."

CHAPTER 37—ENEMY ALLIANCES

It was sometime later when Adlai was hastening with stilted difficulty back to the dungeon cell where the prisoner was waiting. In her hand was the locked box Ardath had instructed her to retrieve from her bedchamber… It was exactly as she had remembered from her childhood… *Whatever could possibly be inside?*

"I've done as you asked," Adlai breathed, casting a cautious glance back to the guards, standing facing each other at the far end of the hall opposite Ardath's cell. She slid the box through the bars and into Ardath's quick hands. Hastily the older woman drew a small key from a concealed pocket of her habit. A deft turn in the keyhole, and the lid opened. A gratified smile touched her mouth, but she snapped the lid shut again before Adlai could glimpse its contents.

"We should be going," she announced at once.

Adlai blinked, befuddled.

"I don't understand—however do you plan to leave this place?"

"*You* are going to lead us there," Ardath replied tritely.

"*Me?!*" The girl exclaimed in surprise. "However shall I accomplish *that*?"

"Like this!"

Quick as the flick of a serpent's tongue, Ardath seized hold of her wrist, a brandished dagger in hand. Deftly she sliced through Adlai's palm, then her own. Blood seeped between their fingers as she squeezed their hands together, the flat side of the blade pressed between their palms. The blade was black as onyx, and on its hilt were engraved strange runes. Adlai let out a gasp of pain.

"We are linked now, you and I."

"But we're still here?"

"Why ever would physical bodies be going to a spiritual realm?" Ardath retorted.

"We have to separate our spirits from our bodies, then?" Adlai asked confusedly.

Ardath answered with a dark smile.

"But how is that possible?"

"There are two instances in which a spirit can be separated from its physical vessel. The first is during sleep, when it is freed from its other conscious senses. Whatever do you think dreams are made of?"

"And the second?" Adlai prodded.

Ardath's smile grew darker than before.

"Near death, of course."

In an instant she seized Adlai by the jaw, squashing her face against the bars. Next moment it seemed the very air was being sucked from her lips. Adlai let out a horrified gasp, but could no more cry than she could breathe. She was losing consciousness. A final wisp of breath passed through her lips, and she was sinking to the floor.

Distantly, she heard the cries of the two guards, armor and swords clanking as they came pounding down the corridor. Across from her, Ardath's frame likewise lay crumpled in a motionless heap on the stone floor. But what was this? She felt suddenly light as air; it was as though she were floating, rising upwards. Looking back, she saw her unconscious body sprawled upon the floor, and others rushing forward to revive her. *Had she truly left her body?*

"We're running out of time," Ardath's harsh tone cut in.

A vapory shadow, with features resembling those of the headmistress floated in the air beside her.

"Am I dead?" Adlai gasped.

"No, not yet."

"Not *yet*?!"

Ardath did not bother with an explanation, but again seized hold of her wrist and tugged her downward. The keyhole of the locked box glowed bright and seemed to be rapidly growing in size, shooting up like a great arched doorway before her... Or were they shrinking? Another tug on her arm, and before she knew it, she was flying straight through it. Sharply turning tunnels and twisting passageways tangled the way all about as they shot through, but Ardath seemed to know where she was going. Familiar images like moving pictures lit up the way as they flew past.

"Where are we?"

"Inside your mind," Ardath called back.

"And where are we going?" Adlai cried again.

"Where we must! In matters of the heart, one must always go to the heart of the matter!"

With that, she suddenly dove head-long, as Adlai let out a scream. Everything was now streaking past them at hurtling speeds, so that Adlai feared they would collide. An aura of wavy bright light like a ball of aurora borealis appeared before them, and then they were sailing through. A poof of crystalline lights like a shimmering burst of stardust showered down all around, as Adlai stared in amazement. They were again standing at the garden center of Avaelon, the black fountain cascading silently down.

And before it stood the stone statue beside the basin. Adlai went cold.

"It's you! You were her all along!" She gasped.

Ardath let out a raucous, embittered laugh.

"Edrea? No—I am only the temporary vessel to her essence and powers."

"If you're not her, then who are you? How do you know of her?"

Ardath's eyes appeared to grow faintly misty, yet her mouth hardened in a firm line.

"One of her disciples… and someone who loved her very much… Before she was taken from me!"

The spirit's face darkened with anger, her eyes filled with hate as she glared down at Adlai. With a sudden twist she flitted away, alighting upon the ledge of the dais where the crowned statue stood motionless.

"Edrea, Great and Powerful, your humble servant has done all as you commanded. Lend me all your full power now, I pray, that I may do what is required."

A quiver of fear ran through Adlai at these words.

"You promised that you would help me undo the evil which is to come, not unleash more!" She exclaimed.

Ardath didn't answer. In her hand was once again the box Adlai had brought her, and she was unlocking it. An icy-cold wind whipped about, picking Adlai up like a feather and knocking her to the feet of the older spirit. Fearfully, she rose and peered inside the box: it was a beating human heart.

"Heart for heart, and life for life," Ardath whispered.

With that, she dropped it into the water basin. Instantly the organ became black and shriveled, swiftly decomposing into slimy sludge in the water. Trembling, Ardath lifted the bowl to her lips and drank. With a clatter it fell from her shaking hands, as she wiped the residue from her lips. A wildly elated look gleamed in her glassy-eyed stare.

"So this is what it feels like," she breathed aloud, "To have absolute power!"

Lifting the gold coronet from the statue's brow, she placed it upon her own forehead with trembling fingers.

"What have you done?" Adlai cried. "You promised that you'd help me put an end to all this!"

Ardath leered.

"I promised only that I would help put an end to all the evil *you* would cause."

Adlai held her breath.

"And the last requirement to be completed?" She asked trembling.

A sardonic smile filled the spirit's face:

"There's only one way to ensure that you never fulfill your dark destiny."

Horror flooded Adlai's face. Too late she tried to flee, but Ardath caught her.

"In what world would I ever help *you*?" She sneered.

Before she knew what was happening, they were hurling downwards through the winding staircase, back to the inner chamber at the heart of the island. And in the next moment she was being dashed to the floor. Stunned, she looked about in a daze. There was something running into her eyes…It was blood.

"Why am I bleeding?" She cried in a panic.

"Our spirits are being rejoined to our bodies for the last remaining rite," Ardath answered in a tone of indifference.

Adlai rubbed her eyes in the dim torch light and stared in disbelief. Ardath's voice sounded remarkably younger than before. All the wrinkles and signs of old age had completely disappeared from the older woman's face, leaving her appearance youthful enough that she could have passed for Adlai's own mother. Her hair was no longer silver, and there was a cold, unfeeling beauty to her features. With a wave of her hand, the curtain of vines behind the girl parted, revealing a great arched doorway that was heavily barricaded. Another wave from the Witch, and the air was filled with the shrill noise of stones grating, wheels grinding, locks turning, and bars sliding back into place. At last the door fell open with a groan. Sulfuric fumes and billows of smoke rose beyond the open doorway.

"Come, Precious," Ardath turned with a disdainful smile. "The re-writing of the Future awaits."

With that, Adlai found herself being swept and sucked towards the open door. Desperately she grasped the doorframe and clung to it with all her strength. Suddenly she caught sight of something she had altogether failed to notice before: a muraled door on the opposite wall. Idyllic countrysides in its foreground, and behind it a depiction of a winged creature... Beast. Friend or enemy, she had no way of knowing, but now he was the only possible chance she had left for salvation. *He had told her before that all she had to do was call... Was it possible that he could hear her even here?*

"Gunar—Bellwether, help me, please!"

The suctioning force behind her was growing stronger, tearing at her legs like a whirlwind. At last her fingers were ripped from their hold as she let out a shriek, and the door slammed shut. In moments she was racing through air and space on a raging wind. Ardath was moving steadily ahead of her through a sea of angry clouds. In the distance, the peak of an island volcano rose up above a restive ocean, its summit smoldering. Thundering noises rose from the ground, and the air all about was heavy and foul... *What was this place?*

"You should be familiar with this place—its haunted your dreams of late," Ardath called behind her. "It's a very gateway to Hell."

"Why are have you brought me here?" Adlai asked tremulously.

Ardath regarded her with a steely stare.

"As I said: a heart for a heart, and a life for a life."

"You failed to mention the part that included my death," Adlai gritted her teeth.

"And you failed to inquire as to all the particular details," Ardath rejoined. "You rushed to it, same as you rush to everything else. Death is one of the inevitable ironies of life. I'm simply saving you time in arriving at your final destination, along with further regret over your wasted and futile existence."

"This isn't what we agreed upon! You lied to me!" Adlai fought back.

"As I recall," the Witch returned coolly, "I asked if you would be willing to do *whatever* it took—*anything*—to undo your future, for the sake of saving everyone else. And as I again recall, you answered Yes... Consider this the ironic fulfillment of *both* our promises!"

CHAPTER 38—HEART OF THE MATTER

Adlai tugged in vain at the iron fetters on her wrists, chained to either side to the walls of a precipice. Sweat dripped in her eyes, and her wrists were becoming slippery with blood. All around the hot air was foul, thick, and stifling. Off to the side a great creviced opening marked the doorway leading back to the outside of the volcanic mountain. Far below her a gushing sea of lava churned on into hollowed out depths. Ardath stood before her at the cliff's edge, murmuring incantations in a strange tongue. Slowly she raised the knife in offering as her rhythmic chanting grew louder. The volcano answered with a thundering groan. The ground began to shake; rubble fell from the cavernous ceiling, and the flaming sea beneath seethed more restively than before. Then all at once there was an unexpected noise. Fearfully, Adlai peered down below. The tossing waves were ebbing away, as if a great drain had suddenly been pulled, and the volcano was now emptying its belly. A wild shriek rose from the depths, splitting the air as it echoed and re-echoed against the cavernous rocks. Something was stirring, writhing down in the heart of the volcano... Slowly it began twisting, coiling its way upwards...

Two fiery red eyes pierced the darkness, and a great scaly head emerged. It was just as she had dreamt: Leviathan, the great dread Serpent of the Seas. Rivers of lava gushed out from his fangs as it rose upright, head bobbing and swaying before its summoning mistress.

Adlai's harrowed gaze ran now to Ardath, who was turning back to her with a cold smile. Swiftly she advanced, and roughly began to loosen the cinched laces of Adlai's bodice.

"You said 'a life for a life'—what did you mean by that?" Adlai demanded, trying to distract the Witch as she stalled for time. *Gunar had always come to her rescue before... He had always saved her just in the nick of time... Please, oh, please, let this be one of those times!*

"Well?!" She insisted. "Of whose life did you speak?"

The Witch paused.

"Someone whose life you stole away."

"But I've never taken anyone's life!" Adlai argued franticly in bewilderment.

Ardath said nothing for a moment.

"The victim was from my past—not yours."

"That's absurd! You're mad!"

"Mad?!" Ardath shouted. "You've no idea what torment I've lived with all these years!"

"But I've never wronged you! I've never done *anything* to you!" Adlai pled.

"And now I'm ensuring that you never will," Ardath answered in a stony voice.

She gave another rough tug at the neckline of Adlai's dress. Suddenly the air was split by the loud shrieking call of a bird. The attention of both women jerked up with a start. Through the shadowed doorway a white dove fluttered. Adlai's face lit up at sight of it... *Hope...* Help could not be far behind. After a moment another larger fowl appeared, it's brightly colored plumage streaking away like a flaming sunset, and its eyes like tongues of fire: it was a Phoenix.

A quick wave of the Witch's hand, and a wall of flames instantly shot up from the rocky ground, barring the way in a semicircle around them. Quickly she snatched up the black dagger, poising the glint of its blade directly over Adlai's trembling breast.

"A heart for a heart," she uttered grimly.

Adlai stiffened and closed her eyes tight, every muscle tensed as she steeled herself for what was to come. But a sudden shriek startled them both, as the Phoenix burst through the wall of fire on ignited wings, swooping down upon Ardath as it deftly knocked the dagger far from her hand. Then just as swiftly it sailed away, back to the cave's entrance. Circling round about, it let out a shrill cry.

An earthquake rumbled all about, sending the Witch sprawling to the ground. Adlai blinked. A blaze was suddenly racing along the jagged outline of the doorway, lighting up runes carved into the arch. And on either side, the walls themselves seemed to be stirring. *Was it just her imagination, or was there something familiar about those strange, overhanging formations? Were the rocks themselves coming to life?!* From the oddly shaped stone, two giant forms were rapidly evolving, materializing out of the craggy back drop. With groans they twisted and stretched, wings shaking as they stiffly rose to their feet and stepped forward, armor clanking. Adlai let out a surprised gasp of relief: they were the same Watchmen Guardians of the Deep she had seen before.

Like the bellowing blare of a battle horn, they thundered out their challenge. Leviathan flared in fury; the sound of a death rattle drummed through the air as he reared like a cobra to strike, molten lava peeling from his scales. With a bloody war cry the winged Watchmen rushed forward to meet him, swinging their swords round their heads as they charged over the cliff's edge. The Serpent lunged and snapped, spewing lava from his jaws. Again and again he streaked back and forth like forked lightening, as the Watchmen whipped about in diving circles over his head, swords slicing through the air. A fiery spatter sprayed through the air, as a deft stroke flayed the monster's gullet. With a shriek he writhed and fell back, toppling downwards into the abyss from which he'd arisen.

Ardath let out a mournful wail at the sight of her ally's defeat. In a rage she turned now to face the Watchmen. Snatching up the dagger and lifting her arms above her head, she raised a savage cry. Rapidly she again began to chant in an unknown tongue, her incantations growing more vehement with every utterance, until it reached a piercing scream as she pointed the black dagger in the direction of the abyss. A streak of lightening flashed from the knife's tip and struck against the angry surge below, creating a whirlpool tunnel. Black, smoky darkness emanated from its depths. The black cloud quickly grew as it rose, until it consumed everything and choked out all light. A whirring noise as of an army of locusts ground the air, as a flood of bats swarmed past.

Adlai trembled violently, a tingling shiver racing down her spine... There was something more than unnatural about these new invaders. This was a darkness she could *feel*—a blinding blackness that penetrated to her very soul. For several moments they circled overhead; then without warning they rained like hailstones to the ground. Slowly they arose, and in a twinkling their black shapes transformed: no longer were they bats; instead, a fearsome black horde of demons now stood bowing before the Witch's raised dagger.

"Demons of Gehenna, Lake of Fire, I summon Thee! The flames of Hell must reclaim the heart of darkness! *Fight*! And spare not those who would rob Hades of its due!" She shrieked. "The powers of Hell know *no* mercy!"

In a twinkling the demon forces shot upwards to meet the Watchmen Giants, assailing them like a storm of hornets. Blood-curdling screeches echoed, while the stone warriors' wielded swords spun through the air. The Witch turned her attention now back to Adlai. With a broad, maleficent smile she advanced, dagger in hand.

"You are damned," she sneered, "So to the Damned you shall go!"

For a second the dagger glowed bright as fire, the runes on the hilt ignited. Adlai let out a scream, as the blade plunged through the air. But in a blink a flash of flaming color streaked past, deflecting the Witch's blow and throwing her on her face. The girl gasped in shocked surprise: the Phoenix lay in a smoldering heap, his bright feathers quivering; with a groan he lowered his magnificent head to the ground. A few paces away, Ardath moaned and collapsed on her side. With a cry of pain the dagger fell from her trembling fingers. Her hand was scorched, the imprint of the dagger handle seared into her palm like the brand from an iron. At the sound of the Witch's cry every head swung round in their direction. Aghast squeals and shrill shrieks flooded the cavern; in the flickering of an eyelash the demon horde pelted down upon the ledge. The ground trembled as they landed and rose upright with menacing growls. Adlai let out another startled gasp, as with a booming shout the Watchmen crashed down on either side of her chains, wings flapping while the rocks quaked beneath them. Slowly Ardath rose to her feet, a steely look of hatred in her eye. Hissing growls grew louder, as enemies glared and bared their teeth, the hellish fiends like a pack of wolves ready to fall on their prey.

"*Kill them!*" The Witch screamed.

In a wild surge they rushed forward, the Watchmen pounding out to meet them. Shouts, shrieks, and cries flew around. Then all at once a deafening roar issued from the rear. Instantly a look of terror covered the faces of the demons, and cringing they fell back like a wave. Then to her amazement, through the hushed crowd, the great White Griffin silently made his way. Adlai trembled at the sight of him. His power and magnificence was even more awe-inspiring than she remembered.

"You are free," he breathed.

Immediately the fetters about her wrists crumbled to powder and blew away on a breeze. With a relieved gasp Adlai fell to her knees. The pain from her broken ankle was gone, along with the swelling; again she felt just as whole and sound as she ever had—the only thing that remained was slash across her palm from the dagger's blade. Slowly she looked up into the Griffin's quiet eyes. They were just as she remembered—gentle, yet powerful, like fire burning away all before them, piercing straight to the soul. In his presence the air around was already lighter than before, a sweet scented breeze blowing away the putrid stench of the inferno below.

"You—you can't!" The Witch stammered in protest from behind him. "Hades has claims to her!"

The Griffin's head whipped about in her direction. An ear-splitting roar of fury bellowed from his jaws, like the wild scream of an eagle, but with the might of a lion. The force of it shook the foundation of the whole mountain, as if the great volcano itself bowed to his sovereignty. Shrieking in terror, the scrambling tumult of demons hurled back into the gulf from which they'd sprung. Defeated, Ardath sank to her knees in a faint.

"Go back to the Shadows, Witch!" The Griffin growled. "And tell your Master that no one plucks her out of My hand!"

With that he let out another roar, and Ardath crumpled to the ground. For a moment she writhed, her whole frame convulsing as if something were being shaken free. A wrenched gasp escaped her lips, and with it a wisp of smoke arose, twisting and stretching out above her until it reached full form, hovering like a shadow over Ardath's unconscious form.

"Go!" The Griffin thundered in command.

A ghostly shriek went up, as the phantom darted over the cliff's edge and was sucked up into darkness. Ardath let out a groan and feebly lifted her head. Her youth was gone; she looked again as much an old woman as she ever had.

"It is done," the Griffin spoke quietly, "You are free."

The old woman's eyes welled with tears, but the expression in them was one which Adlai couldn't read.

"It is time to return," the Griffin said. "Athaliah, leave the ghosts of the past to their own domain. Do not look back, and do not seek them again, or you shall utterly lose your soul."

With that he breathed upon her, and her image slowly melted away. Last to fade was her face, her eyes staring transfixed upon Adlai in frozen silence... Then there was nothing.

The Griffin turned now to the great motionless bird crumpled upon the rocks, feathers fluttering in the breeze.

"*Oh!*" Adlai cried mournfully, dropping to her knees as she tenderly stroked its head.

"Do not be afraid, Child," the Griffin consoled. "His feathers are iron—he's only stunned."

Sure enough, the Phoenix stirred, then slowly arose and flapped his wings. He was even more magnificent up close than she had supposed, his length spreading longer than a man's height.

"I've never seen anything so extraordinary!" She breathed in amazement.

"The Phoenix is indeed the most remarkable Creature," the Griffin agreed, "The more so, because there is only one of its kind. But never fear; he's stronger and more powerful than he appears. His days are without number, and even the gates of Hades are not enough to prevail against him."

"He cannot die, then?"

The Griffin shook his head.

"He will die, when the appointed time comes."

"How tragic," she murmured sadly, "That anything so pure and beautiful should ever have to end. Will another be born to take his place?"

"No," the Griffin answered quietly. "He is the first and the last."

There was something dreadful in those words… Something about them, which struck her to her very core.

"How much longer shall he have to live?" She queried softly.

"Much longer than you shall see, so fret not yourself," the Griffin answered comfortingly. "He will pass at the appointed time."

A far off look crossed his expression, and he stared off into the distance.

"When the cock crows upon a red Dawn, when Earth is stained with the blood of Innocence… When the Sacred Heart is exchanged for the Soul of Darkness, and the Curse is undone… When the debt to Hades is repaid, and Hell shall lose its victory… Then one shall burn so that another may be reborn… Ashes to ashes, and dust to dust… A life for a life."

While he was still speaking, the Phoenix stretched and took wing, soaring away majestically through the doorway.

"Come, Child," the Griffin continued, "It is time to go."

The Watchmen resumed their posts, and bowed low in obeisance as he passed through the gateway. Then slowly, they faded back into the rock from which they'd arisen. Adlai followed somberly, but hesitated under the arches. Slowly the Griffin turned back to her.

"What troubles you, Child?"

"He didn't come," She fumbled dejectedly. "Beast—he promised to always come for me, but he didn't… Not this time."

The Griffin eyed her in silence for a moment.

"No prayer ever goes unanswered. Many times, they are simply not answered in the ways expected… Rest in that knowledge, and trust that it is for your good. You have not the foresight to see all that is at work."

Nodding meekly, soberly she followed after. Suddenly everything about her was fading away, disappearing into a void so great that she felt as if she were but a speck of sand falling through its expanse. She was not certain if only mere seconds had passed, or an entire eternity; but the next thing she knew, her spirit was again hovering over a crowd of persons gathered about her unconscious form. Then it was as if her essence was suddenly being pulled down, sucked up inside a vacuum as she passed through the cold lips of her physical being, reentering her own body like a breath of air. In the next instant her eyes flickered open, and she was looking up into the faces of Willan, Tristan, the guards, and other members of the household staff, all bending anxiously over her. Their fearful expressions quickly turned to relief, as slowly she sat up in bewilderment and looked around.

On the other side of the prison bars, Ardath sat hunched in silence, with her back to her. If she was broken by defeat, her proud brow did not indicate it. Discreetly, she cast a sidelong glance at the girl. Their eyes locked for but a moment. A tear rolled soundlessly down the old woman's cheek, then without a word she turned away. Her right hand had been clutched to her breast, and now she opened it painfully. There was the seared brand over her palm. But with it Adlai glimpsed something else she hadn't seen before—runes and symbols, and the white mark of a great Tree… The same tree decorating the hem of Tristan's mantle... The same thunderstruck tree from her vision of a bloodied battlefield, and the same gnarled tree seared in grisly scars over Gunar's heart....*What did it all mean?*

CHAPTER 39—ENTWINED

"What happened back there?"

Tristan's voice cut through her thoughts. The others had just left after bringing her back to her temporary accommodations, and she had been lost in thought as she peered out the window. The charred remains of her former bedchamber could be plainly seen in the moonlight, a sobering reminder of all the harrowing events which had happened of late.

"Adlai, you promised!" Tristan's reprimand was angry, but he sounded shaken more than anything. "I should have never left you alone, had I known you'd go back on your word! Whatever possessed you to seek out an accused Witch?!"

Adlai stared at him blankly, as though she did not even see him. Her mind was swirling with too many confusing thoughts and questions. It seemed as if she had just come back from the dead... She felt numb, dazed, and senseless to everything else.

"Adlai, are you even listening to me?!"

Tristan had already strode over, and now he was giving her a rough shaking.

"You near frightened me to death! I—I thought—"

His voice had been strained, but now it cracked. There was the trace of tears standing out on his eyes.

"When you disappeared so suddenly, I didn't know what to do—"

He faltered again. Adlai's eyes flickered, and she suddenly snapped to attention.

"Wait! Did you say that *I* disappeared?"

"Yes! One moment you were lying there, and then suddenly you were gone—just like that! His Highness all but went stark raving mad trying to find out how to bring you back. But then the next instant, you reappeared. We all thought you were dead."

"So I really did leave," she murmured. "My body actually was taken and rejoined with my spirit."

Tristan furrowed his brow perplexedly as he stared at her with questioning eyes.

"Where did you go?"

Adlai hardly heard him.

"Back to the Source," she murmured distantly. "A life for a life... and a heart for a heart..."

"Adlai? You're not making any sense," he said more concernedly than before. "Are you alright?"

Adlai stirred.

"Ardath, what of her? Has she said anything?"

"She won't speak to anyone. She's been wandering about her cell like a deranged woman, talking to the walls and muttering strange things which no one understands. Adlai," he said stepping forward, "Are you *certain* you're well? Should I send for anyone? A doctor, or His Highness, perhaps?"

Her attention jerked back.

"Lord Willan—where is he?"

"Conferring with his counselors. The Witch is too dangerous here. They want to have her moved. But to do so requires exceptional caution, along with a heavy guard."

"Where will they take her?"

"They are searching for a Seer. Every entity has its own individuality. We must discover its source and persona, in order to know how to go about its expulsion. His Highness is set on this present course, in the hopes of restoring her and sparing her life... Otherwise he must sentence her to death by burning. But all of this requires diligent haste—word is already beginning to leak out to the village folk; and we do not want terror to spread."

"After all of this—he's still looking for a way to save her," Adlai murmured. "Hasn't she done enough harm already?"

Tristan swallowed and lowered his eyes to the floor.

"This is all my doing; it's all my fault."

"How can it be yours? Tristan," she shook her head vehemently, "Whatever your past connections to her—there's simply no way you're responsible for all of this!"

Tristan was shaking his head sorrowfully, his distraught countenance ridden with guilt.

"No, really! Tristan, hear me!"

She grasped both his arms.

"She chose her own path—none of this is your doing! You mustn't blame yourself for everything, Tristan! You've done so much to ensure my own safety—you've believed me, when no one else would. It's time you stopped carrying the burdens of others."

For an instant he stared earnestly into her eyes. Taking her hand, he pressed it to his lips.

"Lady Adelheide, you are the strongest, bravest woman I have ever yet met," he whispered. "No matter how others may slight or overlook you, never bow your head to them… You are, and will always be, a Queen in my eyes."

Adlai started at his words. *What was he saying?*

"Pray excuse me," he pardoned himself, "I must leave at once!"

"Wait! Where are you going?"

"To find someone who can help—a Necromancer."

"But they are forbidden!" Adlai exclaimed. "No, Tristan!"

"No, no," he quickly interjected, "Their sect is simply misunderstood. They do the same things as the Seers—if indeed there are any still in existence—they simply accomplish it in a slightly different way. They understand both Nature and the Spirit World, and they practice their craft in harmony with these to keep the balance. If what they do is for the greater good of mankind and our world, how can it be harmful? What difference is there between them and the Seers, save the manner in which they practice?"

"I don't know," Adlai shook her head confusedly. "I know little of such things."

Tristan took her hand in his.

"I will do whatever it takes to ensure your safety. I must atone for what I have done."

"How long will you be gone?"

"Where I must go is six days ride from here. I shall be back within a forte night."

With that he pressed his lips to her forehead. For a light giddy moment, Adlai felt as if she couldn't breathe. And then he was gone. He was barely gone from sight, and already she was wistfully longing for the moment when he would return.

Then all at once a sudden wave of panic engulfed her. Of everyone there at the Manor Castle, her personal safety was the one in greatest jeopardy. She had tried to put an end to it all—tried, and failed. Was there to be no solution? Every defeat was only increasing her growing desperation...

That night Adlai tossed and turned restlessly through wakeful hours. The cock was just beginning to crow as she rose wearily from her bed and paced to the window. All at once a blazing heat emanated from the center of her hand, burning through her flesh. Stifling a scream she staggered backwards with a gasp, and stared in disbelief into her open palm. The slice from Ardath's dagger was still fresh, but now it was glowing brighter than a flaming ember, and tiny red lines like veins were bleeding outward from it. Raised marks were fast appearing—strange runes and symbols... Adlai held her breath, inwardly praying against what she feared to see next: there it was—the outline of a great Tree etched into the palm of her hand. For several seconds she stared in stupefied horror. Slowly the recollection of Ardath's words came drifting back to her:

"We are joined together now, you and I..."

Adlai swallowed hard. She had no idea what it all portended, but one thing was clear—her fate was now somehow entwined with that of the Witch. And it was of paramount importance, now more than ever, that she find a way to revoke whatever sinister evil was at work. But how? Who could she turn to, now that Tristan was gone? To her dismay, she remembered that Gunar also had left… She had sent him away. That must have been why he hadn't come for her, even though she'd prayed for him to come. If he could hear her thoughts, surely he must have been able to hear her, even if she had been worlds away? Or had her rejection of him severed their connection?... No, he was simply done with her. And she couldn't entirely blame him. It was too much to ask him to come back.

But who else could she turn to? Who was left? Her mind raced. Willan had hardly ever listened to her before, and she was uncomfortably shy of the Princess, despite Afwin's gracious and kind manner. There was something disturbingly alarming about this new mark—something which filled her with deep dread and guilty shame… something about it which she wanted to hide and conceal from the world, as though she were pregnant with a deadly disease. Tristan had already told her that they were in danger of having hysteria break out among the townsfolk… Something more might be just the final straw to make the countryside go wild with crazed fear. No one could know about this. With all that had already befallen them, others might believe it to be an ill omen hailing in an even darker and more sinister evil. Even worse, it might be perceived as a Witch's Mark, and she herself supposed to be allied with the powers of Darkness… No, *no* one could be allowed to see it… She was truly isolated and alone in all of this, because she had brought this upon herself in seeking Ardath out. And as the older woman had bitingly pointed out, *she* was the one who was a danger to them all… *If only she knew what it all meant, and what she could do to stop it… But how?*

Suddenly a thought came to her—there was yet one there at the castle, one in whom she could confide—someone who was the wisest and most knowledgeable being she knew: Doctor Lucius Hindley.

Sweat was dripping into her eyes as, panting, she hurriedly reached the landing at the top of the tower stair leading to the old dwarf's apartments. Without hesitation she rapped earnestly on the door… No answer. Cautiously, she propped open the door and peered inside. Not so much as a sound greeted her ear, and the log on the hearth looked as though it had lain cold for well over a day. The Professor's affects lay scattered everywhere in much their usual manner, but there seemed to be some articles missing. Examining closer, she realized that most of his old maps were gone, along with his latest works which he had shared with her during her last visits. Wherever the old dwarf had gone, he appeared to have departed with great haste… *But why?*

With a sigh, Adlai cast another look about her. Suddenly she spied something: a piece of parchment lying open on the little table beside his worn armchair. It appeared to be a letter—and it was addressed to her:

My dear Child, pray forgive me for not apprising you beforehand of my sudden departure. A matter of great urgency has arisen; by the time you will have read this, I will already be embarked upon my mission. I journey now back to my home country in the mountains, to the Ancient City of EfraLoethe. Pray that I shall be able to return again with haste, and without hindrance… There is much at work, and I must find answers. Until we meet again, be on your guard—and may the All-Seeing Eye protect you.

Lucius

For several moments Adlai stood staring at the letter, unsure what to make of it, or what to do next. He was her last hope, and now he, along with the others, was gone. A lonely wind howling outside only magnified the deathly silence in the room. Her thoughts flew back to the prisoner in the dungeon. *For how long would she be safe?*

Something inside her snapped to attention: Dr. Hindley had relayed in his letter where he had intended to go; she could follow after and catch up. She had the advantage of youthful vitality on her side; *surely* she could manage to overtake an elderly dwarf? Her mind sped: she would be too conspicuous riding a stately horse like Storm; it was probably best to travel light and on foot. No fine clothes, nothing to draw attention to herself—nothing but the bare necessities.

The first light of day was already peeking faintly through the window. Down below next to the vegetable gardens, she could see a serving maid taking down the previous day's laundry from the wash lines... A thought sparked in her mind... Perhaps if she dressed as a young man...

Without delaying another moment, she snatched up what items were left in the Doctor's living quarters—a stale loaf of bread, some dried meats and fruits, along with some dishware and cutlery—and threw them into an empty satchel. She hesitated at the door, giving a last glance back to his work table. There was one map left, and it was lying spread open. Wherever Dr. Hindley was now, this map no doubt would help lead her there. Snatching it up, she stuffed it inside her bag and was gone.

Less than half an hour later, Adlai peeped out the servants' side entrance to the house. She couldn't risk drawing attention by leaving through the main doors of the vestibule. Swallowing, she gave a quick glance down to her clothing. Her drab, boyish attire was sure to help her blend in, and her thick hair was carefully tucked in under her hooded cloak. She felt vulnerable and naked in a man's breeches, and was unused to walking freely about without the rustling of skirts to hide the form of her legs. Willan's long dagger was tucked into a belt about her hips; the leather boots she had confiscated were roomy, if not rather loose. But still, all in all, she felt certain that she had managed convincingly enough to look the part of a youth. Taking a deep breath, she slung the satchel over her shoulder and closed the door behind her.

Casting a glance in the direction of the stables, she again thought of Storm. *Just a quick goodbye*, she thought. Skirting along the outer buildings, she quickly ducked inside his stall.

Storm was munching dry oats, but at the sight of her he immediately became stock still, his ears rising attentively as he stared warily at her in alarm.

"Storm?"

Adlai's brow wrinkled perplexedly with concern. *It was almost as if he didn't know her.* She took a step forward.

"It's okay, Boy," she whispered soothingly, raising a hand, "It's just me!"

Suddenly the seared mark on the palm of her hand burned hotter than ever. Without warning, Storm reared up and let out a deafening whiny. Adlai staggered back and tumbled in her fright. Just in time she scrambled out of the way, as instantly he bolted past her and flew out of the stalls.

"Storm!" She shouted desperately after him. "*Storm!*"

Her helpless pleas had no effect, however; already he was making straight for the gate. She could hear the voices of men yelling.

"Close the gate, quick! Grab the horse!"

Dodging behind one of the outer buildings, she saw Storm streaking through the open gateway, with servants running after, and men at arms waving and shouting. It would do no good to follow after; he would not come near her, and she had already risked waking too much notice. It was best to just disappear while she had the chance, and let the handlers retrieve him. Whatever it was that had spooked him, she sensed that her mission was more urgently expedient than ever. She desperately needed to find out what the mark portended, along with how to be rid of it— permanently.

It was too late to attempt an inconspicuous departure through the main gate. She would have to find an alternate exit. Making her way to the rear and being sure to stay out of sight, she made her way cautiously along the wall, searching for a place away from the notice of sentries along the battlements. At last she espied such a point. Thick vines and vegetation grew over the wall like a heavy curtain, making it easy to climb. Another quick glance over her shoulder to ensure no guard was looking, and she was up—deftly scaling hand over hand with careful stealth.

The skies overhead had already blackened under a billowing cloud cover now rolling in from the south, as a drizzling rain began to sweep in on sharp winds. In the distance echoed the clap of thunder, growing closer with every resounding boom. All at once a flash of lightening zigzagged above, striking the top of the wall directly above her head. For a instant sparks flew, as she jerked back to see if any of the soldiers on the wall had noticed.

"Over there!" She heard someone shout. Next moment an arrow whizzed by, striking into the rocks just beside her hand. Adlai froze in terror: her attempt at a discreet departure was now gone—and worse, she was being mistaken for a vagabond thief—or something more sinister. She couldn't risk getting caught without being forced to explain the truth and exposing her own dangerous secret—she *had* to escape!

Hand over hand she scrambled, grasping the spikes of the paling at the top as she hoisted herself up. Shouts could be heard coming from every sector, and men-at-arms were already pounding down along the battlements towards her. For a split second she hesitated precariously, struggling to maintain her balance as she peered down. There was only a narrow embankment against the wall—barely enough to land on. She'd be lucky if she didn't break anything. Another arrow whizzed past, grazing her cheek as it did. Taking in a deep breath, she whispered a prayer—and leaped.

A spike gouged her leg as she fell. Before she knew what was happening she was tumbling down the steep embankment, the shadowy shapes of the forest flying past as she careened down. After some two hundred feet she at last rolled to a stop. Breathlessly she picked herself up, snatching the fallen satchel before hurrying on with a limp.

Her right hand suddenly felt fiery hot. Tearing off her glove, she stared down fearfully: the branded mark was burning bright, sending searing pain shooting through the center of her palm. With a cry, she staggered to her knees.

Her head was reeling. It seemed as if the forest itself sensed a strange new presence, for everywhere she could hear the terrified calls of birds and wild shrieks of animals. What had

Ardath done to her, which had made the world about so savagely turn on her, as though she were the very vessel of Evil?

Blindly she spun about in all directions—she could no longer see; instead, images of fire were springing up everywhere, along with those of demons, the fiery serpent, the Griffin and the Phoenix. Memories of the image of Ardath appeared standing before her upon the ledge, a wall of shooting flames to her back. And then all at once her mind's eye lit up with the vision of the black dagger in her hand, the runes emblazoned in its hilt and blade blazing bright. At this the heat in her hand burned with redoubled fury, scorching through her flesh. With another excruciated scream, Adlai collapsed. She could hear voices hissing strange words all about her, their chanting incantations rising to a fever pitch, menacing and accusing in their tone. *Was she really allied with the Darkness now? Were Ardath's ominous predictions actually coming true, and was she doomed to follow the fate decreed for her?*

"I'm not a Witch," she murmured, "I'm not a Witch…"

Sight was fading from her eyes… Then it all went white.

She was not certain if minutes or only seconds had passed, as she opened her eyes and dizzily sat up. The mark was no longer burning. Slowly she replaced her glove and rose to her feet, glancing about in all directions. Through an opening in the thicket, she spotted the rise of building structures. She was standing upon the outer edge of the township, far below the castle. All she had to do now was make it through the village without being recognized, and she would be free.

In a short matter of time she was striding quickly through the village streets. The town was just beginning to stir as she passed by shop keepers opening up their businesses for the day. Keeping her eyes lowered to the ground, she tried to hide her trembling and imitate the easy ambling stride of a youth. Soon she was passing under the township gates.

Before her moors and farmland ran on for miles, eventually giving way to rolling hills. And beyond those, the wild, mountainous regions of the North rose starkly against the horizon, going on for as far as the eye could see… Somewhere in that vast no-man's land, the sleeping ruins of EfraLoethe, the Great City of the Dwarves, lay hidden beneath the snowy summits of Roiem, deep in the heart of the ancient realm of Glorin.

www.ingramcontent.com/pod-product-compliance
Lightning Source LLC
Chambersburg PA
CBHW060343260626
47160CB00006B/2191